The Secret Life of The Elephant Man

Milford Grove

The Secret Life of The Elephant Man is a work of fiction inspired by "The Elephant Man", Joseph Merrick, which employs dramatic license (imagined events and characters) for the purpose of entertainment. It is not based on any other work about The Elephant Man.

ISBN 13: 9781999654009

Contents

Author's Note

Thank you for choosing "The Secret Life of The Elephant Man."

I would like to thank the people who supported me and stood by me during the writing of the book, in particular my friends and family. I would not have succeeded without your help.

Prologue

Leicester Union Workhouse was a red brick institution of one and two-storey buildings located in the south-east of Leicester, a short walk from the Lunatic Asylum. A hexagonal perimeter wall surrounded the complex and its six working yards. The main building, where the destitute begged for admittance, resembled a vast, intimidating schoolhouse. Nine hundred paupers, the impotent poor, received charitable relief therein. Men, women and children were segregated and subdivided again by their age and social status. Each category of person carried their own degree of shame, able-bodied men without work, unmarried mothers in the same class as prostitutes. The men were destitute because other men were chosen above them and the women were destitute because they were no longer chosen by men.

There were many hopeless cases, the elderly and frail, the physically and mentally handicapped, the blind, the idiots and the imbeciles. The most hopeless of all was a hideously deformed, unemployed hawker who had been cast out by his father. His name was Joseph Merrick.

Joseph was twenty-one years of age and four years an inmate. Given his condition, it seemed prudent to house him within the Imbecile Ward, yet Joseph was not mentally defective and those who took his grotesque outer appearance for the character of his mind were astonished by his apparent intelligence. Joseph discharged himself twice a year and begged for work throughout Leicester, but none would employ him. Perhaps Joseph's biggest impediment was that he could not physically smile. Commerce depends upon vim and vitality and the thrusting confidence of youth, yet his face was a gigantic billboard of misery. There was every reason to believe that this forlorn and misshapen young man was destined for an unmarked pauper's grave.

It was a cold, calm February night, and in the small hours of the morning, the sky was as still as a pool of oil. Joseph sat upright in his dormitory bed with his knees pulled up to his chest and a pillow supporting his back against the iron bedframe. Joseph rested this way because the immense weight of his head made it impossible to lie normally. He had not changed into his nightshirt and still wore his drab brown-grey workhouse uniform. Joseph clambered out of bed, gathered up his bedsheet and walked between the two columns of sleeping paupers, careful not to drag his lame left leg. The inmates of the Imbecile Ward were strangely quiet tonight: no coughing, no murmuring, no tears, no voices, no nightmares, not even much snoring. They had honoured his secret intention with peace.

Joseph opened the dormitory door slowly to minimise its creak and entered the corridor. He crept past the door of the imbeciles' workyard and the door of the punishment cell to the door of the morgue, which, to his relief, was unlocked. The workhouse morgue was a whitewashed room not much larger than a police cell with a single wooden board bed and a rickety wooden stool. There was one window measuring two feet by two positioned six and a half feet above the floor. The moon emerged and a patina of pale green light illuminated a wall-mounted crucifix. Joseph dare not look the Saviour in the eye.

He placed the stool by the window and climbed on top. Joseph almost fell, but steadied himself against the wall with his right shoulder. The iron bracket of the window handle was embedded in the brick of the ledge, providing a sturdy fulcrum for a noose. Joseph tried to thread the bedsheet through the bracket, but the sheet was too thick for the purpose.

Joseph stepped down, placed the bedsheet under his left foot and tore a length of cloth, but fell back as the material gave way. The night porter must have been elsewhere in the complex as no one came to check on the noise. Joseph eventually succeeded in threading the strip of material through the bracket, but he could not tie the knot. The fingers of his left hand could have played the piano but the deformed fingers of his right had the dexterity of bloated sausages. Each time Joseph believed he had tied the knot, it slipped away from him.

Joseph considered simply lying back on his bed the way normal people sleep as his massive skull would surely snap his neck, but Joseph could not countenance dying like a bug on his back. Worse, he contemplated the nightmare of breaking his neck and not dying, condemning him to the limbo of paralysis. There were times when Joseph thought he scarcely resembled a man, but at least by the method of Judas, he could die like one. Joseph redoubled his efforts and finally threaded the ligature.

He imagined Reverend Summers paying final respects to his corpse whilst liberally marinating himself in guilt. "Could I have done more?" the reverend would ask himself. But if a man dies, his pastor does not forfeit board or lodging. Besides, thought Joseph, others will take my place and Summers will console himself that I am at peace and my soul is at rest. It is a great mercy when the sick deem it fit to die.

Joseph threaded the ligature over his head allowing extra room for the enormity of his skull, though the material snagged on his bony protrusions. The knot was inadequate and the sheet slipped from the bar. Joseph reached for the material, but lost his balance and stumbled onto his hands and knees. Every disappointment of Joseph's life came back to him, his father branding him a failure, the crowds tormenting him on his hawking round. A man who fails at his work fails his family and now Joseph could not even succeed in taking his own wretched life.

On his knees, in the position of prayer, it seemed appropriate to address the Lord. Joseph dredged his mind for a psalm but found only questions of self-pity.

"Why should I bear this pain, Lord? Why should I suffer?"

Joseph's questions met with silence, as his questions to God always did. That is why he took his questions to Revered Summers, but he already knew how his pastor would answer, because all a cripple can do is accept his lot, fear God and worship without question.

Joseph rose to his feet and approached the crucifix on the whitewashed wall. The cross was nine inches in length and six wide, dark brown in varnished wood. Jesus's head sagged to the right-hand side, his eyes were closed and he appeared to be sleeping. Joseph ran the tip of his non-deformed finger across Jesus's intricate beard. It was a lovely piece of workmanship, finely detailed, right down to the grooves of the Messiah's toes. The nails the Romans had driven into his feet and hands protruded through the flesh like hard little cysts.

If a soul was a lump of wood, religious instruction was the craftsman, whittling away throughout life. If a soul attained the form of Jesus or thereabouts, it would be displayed in heaven, whereas misshapes and offcuts were consigned to hell. Joseph did not know why the likes of Reverend Summers assumed the afflicted possessed beautiful souls, as if the severity of a man's disfigurement was proportionate to his human goodness. At this present time, Joseph's soul felt as deformed as his body and the word of God seemed like the crucifix, cold dead wood, an ornament of guilt by man.

Joseph slapped the wall with the flat of his good hand.

"Why should I bear this pain, *Lord*? Why should I suffer, *Lord*? Answer me tonight, damn you. Prove your worth!"

Joseph recalled the tribulations of Christ in the wilderness. Unlike Jesus, he was daring to test the Lord; he was also daring to curse the Lord. He had committed blasphemy and therefore deserved to die.

"You should strike me down at once," said Joseph, goading God like a child who fears the dark and enters the dark, only to find there is nothing to fear. For there was no divine retribution, no lightning bolt to the heart. There was only silence. Did God exist in the echo of a believer's voice and nowhere else, and if God would not answer him, would Satan?

Joseph crouched down on his knees in front of the cross and said, "Satan. For life as an able-bodied man I will give you my soul."

When a man rejects God the dead awake from their tombs and deafen him with screams of woe. Yet Joseph could not hear a single dissenting pauper among them. On the contrary, he imagined howls of approval, like a lunatic attacking a warder's face with a spike in full view of a holding cell, willed on by cries of insanity.

He continued, "Give me revenge on those who torment me, deny me, reduce me to vagabondage. Give me a woman. Give me love. Make me normal and I will give you my soul, a pauper's soul, for the quarter farthing it is worth."

Joseph's request was answered by the hiss of a serpent. There was now something else within the morgue, a creature, a demon, lurking behind him like a predator. This could not be his imagination. Joseph knew the beast was with him and had been waiting at the workhouse for years. The beast was in every corner of darkness, every cry of despair. The beast was tangible and was here in the morgue, hungry for another soul, thirsty for the blood of a deformed Christian invalid who until that moment had been pure.

Right now, Joseph would have swapped his twenty-one years of virtuous disabled life for twenty-one seconds as an able-bodied outlaw and the chance to die in a supernova of defiant gunfire. Joseph remembered his own mother, a good Christian who had worn worry and drudgery like her scrubwoman's uniform. She had not the will to remove it. Joseph could only remove his pauperage by shredding his skin and offering his inner being to Satan. His new body would be an amoral shell, but at least he would experience the pleasure of the world and finally know the exquisite touch of a woman.

Joseph felt a warm forked tongue wriggling on the back of his neck, tasting his skin. It was fitting that the beast was as repulsive as he. The creature opened its jaws like a giant Venus fly trap preparing to envelop Joseph's massive skull, or whichever part of his deformed and reviled body contained his soul. But what was a soul and what did it matter? The only thing that mattered above good and evil was not enduring a life of pain.

Joseph closed his eyes and waited.

At least one minute passed before Joseph found the courage to open his eyes. The moonlight exposed his paltry reality. He was still in the morgue on his malformed knees in the brown-grey uniform of a pauper. The only beast was a hideously deformed, unemployed hawker. The Saviour was dead on the cross. No one came, not God, not Satan, not even the porter. The failure of his life became obvious. He had put his faith in ephemeral promises, groundless hope, wish-making and imaginary beings.

For the first time in his life, Joseph realised, his only salvation was himself.

Chapter 1 – The Works of God

Tuesday, the 5th of August 1862 was for the burgeoning East Midlands town of Leicester another day of industry. Factory whistles sounded at daybreak, summoning thousands of worker bees to their hives, engineering works and ironworks, mills and factories, Stead & Simpson, Thomas Corah & Sons. Leicester was Britain's leader in hosiery, with shoe and boot production also escalating rapidly. Technological advances, such as the ingenious use of steam power at Crick's, drove manufacturing. Other hosiery producers followed Crick's lead and magnificent chimneys grew tall and proud, populating the blue sky of summer with clouds of steam. To an industrialist of romantic persuasion, those clouds were the dream of commercial destiny.

Those who enjoyed Leicester's wealth made their homes in leafy suburbia. New Walk was an oasis of cleanliness and serenity with a quiet central road flanked by sycamore trees. Wealthy families occupied palatial villa-style townhouses, employing live-in staff to cater for their needs. They also employed visiting domestic staff, like young washerwoman Mary Merrick.

Mary Merrick walked a mile from her marital home, a humble terrace on Lee Street, to the home of her employer, Mrs Carey. The young manservant Lister was quick to answer. He sneered at Mary's dowdy washerwoman outfit and let her in without saying 'Hello'. Mary wondered if there was ever a time when Lister would have flirted with her.

She collected the laundry bundle and went out to the rear courtyard, allocating herself an hour for the bed linen. Pounding away with the washing dolly was hard physical work and Mary sweated profusely. At times like this Mary thought about Mr Carey, his work and the fruits of his labours. Mary was unsure what

Mr Carey did for a living, but in financial terms it was at least one hundred times more important than clean bed linen.

Mary hung the linen to dry in the sun and set about her interior cleaning duties. She collected her soaps, rags and brushes, filled a tin bucket with cold water and tied her mousy brown hair into a ponytail. Mary started scrubbing the bottom step of the staircase and worked her way upwards. The soapy water stung her calloused hands and her bony knees went numb on the floor. The work of the washerwoman was tough and thankless, but preferable to fourteen hours at a loom. Mrs Carey was a decent sort and said that Mary could return to work after the baby was born.

It was not intended, at least not by her. They were still only courting, when, on a cold December evening, Joe proceeded with the act of love. Mary bore the fruits of Joe's persistence and now they were husband and wife. Mary hoped for a daughter, Joe for a son, but her only genuine concern was for the health of the child. Mary saw the District Medical Officer for the first time in her life and the doctor said that everything was normal.

It was fortunate that Joe had proposed marriage as the child would be legitimate and the little one, he or she, would not be tainted by the indelible stain of bastardy. Mary married in a cheap, bilious-coloured dress to hide her bulge, like a man hides a beer gut by untucking his shirt, as if the thin canopy of material could conceal sin from the Lord.

Mary was once a 'girl', briefly a 'spinster' and now a 'wife'. Soon she would be a 'mother' in addition to a 'washerwoman'. She would obey her husband, raise the children and work for the Careys. She would clean the stairs, clean the house and ensure that the bed linen was spotless. Mary's life was a series of obligations which would end with her death, although she did not know if she would be expected to clean the stairs leading to heaven.

Mary reached the second floor. At the bottom of the corridor was the room she was forbidden from entering, young Timothy Carey's. Mary heard fragments of gossip from the live-in staff. There was something wrong with Master Timothy and other children could not visit; he could not attend school and would likely remain a shut-in for the rest of his life. All Mrs Carey said when Mary started two years ago was she must never enter Timothy's room because of his fragile condition. Mary did not clean in the vicinity of the room and nobody objected. Joe said the boy was probably 'wrong in the head' or 'a misshapen one'. Mary knew the boy only by his sheets and his stains. She reached for her abdomen, stroked the outline of her baby and whispered a prayer for safe delivery of a healthy, normal child.

She was distracted by a crash from Timothy's room. It sounded like the child had fallen heavily or sprinted headfirst into a cupboard door. Mary felt sorry for idiots and imbeciles, but also feared them as she believed they were given to violent tantrums and possessed inhuman strength. She picked up her soaps and her bucket and made ready to leave, but then all was quiet.

What if Timothy is injured? thought Mary. What are the consequences of ignoring the boy? As the lowest-ranking member of household staff, she might be blamed, a convenient scapegoat when the parents were neglectful jailers. Why had God cursed the boy, when he loved him? Mary knew the answer was not for her. One must not question the Lord or one's employers, yet no decent person could ignore a child in pain.

Mary set down her bucket and approached Timothy's room. She heard Timothy's high-pitched voice and his strange words, his excited private language. Mary realised that Timothy was playing a game, inventing the sounds of imagined adventure, running around his room with imaginary playmates. Mary stood on a creaking board. Timothy detected a visitor and bounded for the door. The knob turned, but the door was locked. Timothy called out like an animal, kicking the door and pounding it with his fists.

The sudden, violent movement of her unborn child caused Mary terrible pain and she fell to the floor and stayed there. Her own agonies drowned out Timothy's howling and pounding and his endless cries for his mother. If God had an eye on her coupling with Joe and her pregnant belly, there might still be punishment yet.

Joseph 'Joe' Merrick loved his job as a brougham driver and considered himself the best in Leicester. There was no driver faster or smoother, with the same effortless command of horse, nor was there any with a smarter appearance, at least not in his opinion. Joe was very proud of his slate-grey woollen suit. He kept his brown hair short but maintained a fine pair of side whiskers. He was always on time and was five minutes early at the Leicester Navigation Company for his fare, Mr Millford. Joe toted Millford's travelling bags onto the brougham's roof and secured them with a length of cable, displaying his strong hands and the power of his shoulders. Millford, by contrast, was a small, serious man with a handlebar moustache. Joe estimated that Millford's Grosvenor overcoat cost more than he earned in a week.

Joe tipped his low top hat, grey with a black base, and smiled to show his good teeth. He had plenty to smile about, being trusted with an important client and reckoned that his stock with the commissioners of Hackney Carriages was rising. Milford did not smile back, owing to the stink of the raw sewage wafting across from the River Soar. Joe coaxed the horses, Betsy and Snowy, and eased the brougham forward. The horses set off in a military trot to signify 'I have a very important passenger'. Milford could have easily walked the mile and a half to the station, although as Joe's friend and colleague Barney often remarked, "Their lethargy is our livelihood."

A few minutes into the journey Joe noticed a drayman's cart moving erratically up ahead with the female passenger leant against a beer barrel in the back of the wagon. Joe recognised his wife, Mary, with her mousy brown hair and her plain but pretty face, stricken by the agonies of labour. The baby was on its way! Joe realised with regret that, as Mary had left work in the middle of her shift, she would not be paid for the day.

Joe continued to Leicester Campbell Street Station and was appalled by Millford's refusal to tip him. He did however pick up a better fare, a jolly merchant called Branning and his assistant. Joe took Branning to Corah & Sons in St Margaret's and the assistant tipped him a generous half-crown. Afterwards, Joe drove the brougham to the coachyard where he tethered and fed the horses. Joe's favourite part of the job was the ability to earn money continuously, beyond the confines of set working hours. In his opinion the man who signed up for a set daily wage was a fool and a slave, toiling in self-imposed mediocrity. Therefore, Joe was pleased to have completed his shift and more besides. After all, he told himself, the business of birth is no place for a man.

As a man without a son Joe believed there was something missing from his life. Proof he was a man, proof he was whole. He needed a son to stake a claim on things, not a daughter to give away. He did not even care about the consequences when he began his liaison with Mary. He was twenty-five and had waited long enough to marry. Joe fingered the half-crown in his pocket, further evidence things were going his way.

Joe called at the business premises of his younger brother, Charles. It was less than a year since Charles Merrick opened his tobacconist's, barber's and umbrella repair shop on Churchgate and he enjoyed good custom. His immaculate beard and mane of russet-brown hair were a testament to his barbering skill.

As Charles was wet-shaving a customer, Joe announced the imminent arrival. After handshakes from Charles and the customer, Charles offered Joe a complimentary cigar, but to his disappointment, not one of the good ones.

"Take two, it might be twins," said Charles.

"Might be triplets," said Joe, pocketing three cigars.

Joe entered Lee Street and walked towards his dwelling, which was located on a long terrace of identical houses. Women collected in their sun-dried washing and children played games in the street. Joe knew Lee Street was his temporary home and that one day he would occupy a mansion, like the house Mary cleaned on New Walk. If for some reason he failed in his quest, the family fortune would be secured by his son. No child held any interest for Joe, except for the possibility of his own and the boy he imagined was a champion of life, bigger, stronger, a better earner. The son must carry his father's honour throughout his life and one day his coffin. Joe had a feeling that both his son and his coffin would be solid, sturdy oak.

Joe entered his house expecting to find mother with child, but instead he found chaos. Mary was spreadeagled in his upholstered chair with Elsie Walker at her left side and Dorothy Robins at the right, holding Mary and mopping her feverish brow. Mary's legs were astride and between them knelt Bridie, the silver-haired old woman from next door who knew nursing. Bridie kept a hawkish vigil on events down below as Mary writhed in pain, oblivious to Joe. Joe did not like the way Elsie and Dorothy stared at him, as if he was responsible for her suffering, and he went to the scullery.

He opened a bottle of porter and had a drink. Then he opened another one. At least an hour passed.

Joe felt the same affection for Mary as an industrialist for a beloved conveyor belt. However, the value of the enterprise, 'marriage', would be determined by the end product: 'child'. Joe was getting seriously worried about the workings of the machine. Mary's cries of pain compelled him to go next door.

Old Bridie was still stationed between Mary's legs with Elsie and Dorothy by her side. Mary shrieked and strained, but nothing happened. Joe phrased a question as statement. "It should have come."

Bridie turned her worried old face to Joe, imploring him to be quiet.

Birth is the one time destiny depends on woman, so perhaps she was eking it out for as long as possible, to remain the centre of attention? Joe consoled himself with such thoughts to avoid the worst thought: what if there was something wrong with the baby?

Joe remembered all the wronglybuilts he had ever seen and stories of birth defects he had ever heard. Children with no arms, children with no legs, children born with enormous heads, hideous and misshapen, denied the mercy of death and condemned to life. Joe knew that the conception of his child was, technically speaking, a sin. If it was true and God existed, somebody had to pay. Was the agony of Mary's womb a lightning bolt of judgement to deform and disfigure his son? Or were the Lord and Reaper wrestling for possession of the babe?

"Sing hymns to counteract the pain!"

Nobody heard Joe, because Mary screamed as she gave the decisive push. Bridie drew the baby and held it in her arms, rubbing the infant with a towel. There was an absence of movement from the bundle and Joe thought the baby was dead. But then he heard the child's hiccupping breaths, the first cries of life. Bridie took the baby from the towel and held it upright. It had two arms, two legs. It was a boy, of all the proper proportions.

Joe had no time for religion, he left Mary to that. She sat on pews on a Sunday morning and blathered out the hymns. Her recent attendance had been sporadic, but she had been a churchgoer ever since she was a girl. It seemed that each dull, preachy Sunday had been a penny insurance and the policy had paid a handsome return.

Mary fondled the baby and kissed its head in delirium. Joe stepped in behind his wife. It was difficult to know where to touch her so he contented himself with patting her hair, which was saturated with sweat. Mary was close to fainting. Joe took the boy in both hands and raised him to the light. Despite Bridie's towelling, the child was still moist with blood. It mattered not, because in the child's face he saw the perfect reflection of himself. No matter how many more children he fathered, Joe knew this boy would be the best of them. His son would bear his name, Joseph Merrick.

Mary insisted on a middle name, preferring Carey for two reasons. Carey was the name of the long dead Baptist leader that she revered and coincidentally the name of Mary's employer. Mary registered the baby's name, took young Joseph to show Mrs Carey and said she was ready to return to work. Mrs Carey said her services were no longer required. Joe said he hoped Mrs Carey died of a fatal malady.

Mary soon found alternative domestic work in suburban Stoneygate. Baby Joseph continued his sterling progress, fed well at the breast and gained weight rapidly. The little fellow was a good sleeper, pleasing Joe no end. He eagerly anticipated fathering another son and watching the brothers roughhouse together, thus negating the remote possibility of either boy turning sissy.

Joe discussed such matters at length with Barney. Their favourite hostelry was The Lord Nelson on Humberstone Gate, because they served in pewter tankers. Joe drank porter, Barney mild. Barney was rotund, bearded and wore a stubby hat. Both of them leant against the bar, choosing to stand after long hours on the driver's box seat.

"Joseph will be six feet tall and as strong as an ox, a prizefighter, I'll tell you."

"Still in perfect health, I take it?" replied Barney, wishing Joe would change the subject.

"There was a do with his hand, swelling. The wife said we should fetch a doctor."

Barney rubbed his fingers together to signify 'money'. Joe nodded sagely.

"Meadowsweet, says I, and it cures the boy, without a penny spent on medicine."

They returned to their usual conversational topics, competition from horse-drawn trams and omnibuses, the annoyance of short, cheap fares. Although, as Barney maintained, in the modern era "Man should not work to walk."

Walk Joe did, back to Lee Street, stumbling in through the front door when he arrived home. Mary occupied the wooden rocking chair with Joseph asleep in her arms. She shushed Joe for his clumsiness, but Joseph did not stir. Mary reheated the stew pot in the scullery, then carried the baby to bed. Joe finished his meal and joined them. Mary was asleep in bed and Joseph was asleep in his cradle. A lone candle flickered. Joe could not resist touching his son. He picked Joseph out of his cot and held the baby, feeling the tender rise and fall of his son's sleeping breaths.

Joe recalled his own childhood in rural Leicestershire. His abiding memory was the drudgery of dirt, toiling in boggy fields by day, trudging back to the ramshackle family cottage by night. As Joe laboured, Leicester grew, chimneys rose, buildings towered; the promise of a new exciting world seemed to beckon him from the distance. Joe's father denounced this Babel with a raised shovel and dire warnings about 'townies'. For Joe the allure of modernity was irresistible, as it was for his brother Charles. With money in his pocket, a good woollen suit and a house, Joe felt he had travelled centuries in his own lifetime. One day he would go even further, open up his own shop, overtake Charles in commerce, move in next door to the Careys and laugh. As for the babe in his arms, something told Joe that this beautiful boy, his first and oldest son, had a special destiny and would rise above them all.

Joe placed Joseph back in the cradle and tucked him in. He kissed Joseph's head, smelt the beer fumes on his breath and blew them away, so as not to intoxicate the baby. Joseph's face was peaceful and innocent.

Sometime later in the small hours of the morning, Joseph's crying awoke Joe. He felt Mary leave the bed to attend to the baby. Joe tried to ignore it and go back to sleep. Mary's soothing words and Joseph's cries overlapped each other, until horror distorted the timbre of her voice. Joe scrambled out of bed and beheld the countenance of his son.

He could not have been more mistaken about the meadowsweet.

The private diary of Dr Henry Allenby, 18th September 1867

The professional life of a physician resembles the professional life of a judge. We encounter many indistinguishable cases. We prescribe a course of action in keeping with the established model. Our decisions are based on precedent. Seldom in his career will the doctor encounter a case so extraordinary as to obliterate precedent. Therefore I must commit today's events to paper.

The day began as any other at Knighton. I saw eight patients in the morning and was about to take luncheon, when my secretary, Miss Hubbins, entered the consultation room. Miss Hubbins said a young child had been brought in by his mother, a working woman. I asked if there was immediate danger to the child's life, and she said not. I instructed Miss Hubbins to refer the mother to her Friendly Society Doctor or Sick Club. Miss Hubbins hesitated. The sight of this child had clearly put her in distress and she was as pale as a spectral visitation. I decided to examine the child and told Miss Hubbins to send the boy's mother in first.

I estimated the poor woman was not yet thirty, but aging rapidly. She gave her name as Mary Merrick and recounted her tale of woe. When her son Joseph was a babe he was 'perfect as a pearl', yet now, at five years of age, he was terribly deformed. Mrs Merrick said that she had taken Joseph to many physicians and none could help.

If a child acquires any sort of blemish it is an agony to the mother. She sees the proverbial mountain in the place of a molehill because the child is perfect in her eye. But nothing could prepare me for the child she brought forth. The boy's face was entirely asymmetrical. The left side was virtually normal, but the right side was horribly deformed. The immensity of flesh reminded one of a gigantic ham hock. The left corner of his mouth sloped upwards and affixed his mouth into a grotesque, permanent smile. His cranium was a range of hillocks, convex bony protrusions.

I instructed him to undress. Clusters of abnormal bone growth were emerging on his back and his scapula. The skin of his backside was hardening like dried putty, giving his buttocks the appearance of rock. His feet and lower legs were mutating at a much slower rate. A small mercy.

The child's right hand was enormous. I have only witnessed swelling of such magnitude in severe allergic reactions. Yet when I touched his hand I felt not the retention of water but the accumulation of bone!

I adjusted his posture to ensure the boy was not slouching. He was not. His spine was curved and his torso crooked. He stood like an old walking stick. His genitals and his left arm were normal. Much of his lower trunk and the muscles of his stomach were also normal.

His mother instructed him not to fidget. "Yes, Mother," he replied politely. His voice astonished me as much as his body. I addressed him. "Can you count, young man?"

"Yes, sir."

"Please count to ten, young man."

He did so with ease. I implored him to count to twenty and asked him sums. Under different circumstances, this child may have been bright enough to ascend his class. However, it is incredibly unlikely he will live until adulthood.

I instructed him to dress and offered him one of the sugared sweets from the punnet I had purchased for my son.

"Thank you, sir," he said. I told him to wait outside. His mother showed him to the door and instructed him to behave.

I invited Mrs Merrick to sit. She stared at me with an abundance of hope as if I alone possessed the cure.

"Mrs Merrick, the closest condition to your son's is calcification. It appears he is growing bone upon bone. It gives me great regret to inform you there is nothing I can do."

Mrs Merrick's optimistic facade was the sum of self-delusion and she burst into tears. I tried to raise her sprits by pointing to advances in medicine science, how a myriad of cures emerge year by year.

Mrs Merrick replied somewhat curtly, "Know you of other physicians?"

"You are free to consult as many physicians as you wish. But the reality of this condition is that nature will take its course."

"Of all the boys, of all the children, why is he afflicted so?"

"Why does any child go blind, Mrs Merrick? Or deaf? Or lame? Or die during infancy? But this boy lives. Cherish him as he is, for the time he is yours."

Mrs Merrick nodded meekly. I merely confirmed the evident truth. Inhuman deformity has taken hold of the child with the ferocity of a forest fire. It is consuming all traces of a normal child and shows no sign of abating.

"Will our other children be the same?"

I questioned Mrs Merrick about her medical history. She possessed a strong constitution, as did her husband, and none of their families bore any trace of hereditary disease. I told her the balance of probability favoured healthy children. Mrs Merrick reacted as if she had already received a similar reply, but did not seem entirely convinced by my answer.

Mrs Merrick reached for her purse. I shook my head. She did not know how to react, being clearly unaccustomed to generosity of this kind. Then I envisioned her talking amongst her friends, of the kindly doctor who offers free treatment to the mothers of incurable defectives. Therefore, to my eternal shame, I accepted her meagre offer of payment.

Reverend James Summers was born and raised in Chipping Ongar. It was a picturesque town with rows of immaculate cottages and a busy market square, surrounded by fields of golden wheat and barley, and acres of meadow and pasture. Constable could not have painted a more romantic vision of rural Essex. There were three chapels in Chipping Ongar, two Anglican and one Baptist. Summers's father was the pastor of the latter and tended to the spiritual needs of a growing congregation.

Summers wanted to follow his father's vocation in a large town, as he believed Baptism was the perfect urban religion. There was no need to construct an elaborate venue of worship; a church was wherever believers congregated. His own chapel was a humble meeting house in Highfields, Leicester. The congregation worshipped in an assembly room the size of a saloon bar, with five columns of wooden benches serving as pews. Summers thought it was perfect. Leicester also provided a pilgrimage to the glories of the legendary Baptist, William Carey.

A bricklayer named Faulkner, who lived close to the chapel, had been killed falling from a scaffold. Summers counselled his grieving family, even though they had no religion, rallied the congregation and instigated an appeal for the Faulkners. Summers personally canvassed local merchants for donations. The appeal saved Faulkner's wife and children from the poorhouse. The curls of Summers's strawberry blonde hair were reminiscent of an angel. Summers would never be vain enough to invite a comparison, yet there were few in Leicester who were closer to God.

Increasing numbers of ordinary working folk attended chapel and sent their children to his Sunday school. They regarded Summers as a sensible man, not a zealot, who would instruct their children for this life as much as the next, a teacher who would help them to read, write and offer hope for a future beyond hard manual labour. Although it was rare to find a child older than twelve at his Sunday school. By that age the children were full-time workers themselves and had little use for education.

Most of the children were unremarkable, average in intellect, coarse of speech, some good-natured and others not. One boy did stand out and not for a pleasant reason. Summers remembered Joseph Merrick's first day at Sunday school. Half the class were in total shock, half were nonchalant, suggesting Joseph was known to them. Joseph wore long trousers, unusual for a boy. He must have been given the breeches to conceal his deformed legs. Summers had wondered if Joseph was also mentally disabled until he introduced himself in a sweet intelligent voice, tinged with a light lisp.

Joseph attended every Sunday school for ten weeks. He was the best young scholar Summers had encountered among the Leicester poor, raising his hand to every question and always with the correct answer. Summers spoke to Joseph occasionally, not wanting to display any obvious favouritism. During those conversations Summers discovered that Joseph's father was a coach driver, he schooled at Syston Street during the week and that his brother and sister were babes in arms. He also discovered Joseph's middle name was Carey, suggesting he was of good Baptist stock.

One afternoon after Sunday school when the children departed, Summers set about sweeping the floor. After several strokes of the brush he noticed Joseph Merrick and his mother had returned to chapel. His mother had hurriedly departed, leaving Joseph alone. Joseph was shy and shuffled his feet. Summers gestured for Joseph to join him. They sat together on the front pew, by the china urn that Summers used as his makeshift Baptistery.

"I take it there is something you wish to ask of me?"

"My mother asked me to ask you, if you could cure me, sir?"

Joseph's inappropriate question did not offend Summers. It spoke of his mother's desperation.

"Many mothers and many fathers of many infirm children seek my counsel. They believe I possess divine powers. Only Jesus can heal by miracle Joseph and I am not he."

"I wish to be normal, sir. Then I would not be bullied, or sad at heart. Nor would my mother."

"But Joseph, your condition is God's design."

Summers saw despair in young Joseph's eyes. The greatest challenge of his vocation was, like a physician, informing a sufferer they must bear affliction for life. Yet Summers felt his own faith like a mountain and wanted this child to stand with him at the summit.

"What if my body is the work of the Devil?"

"No, Joseph, no, no, no. There are many questions without an answer and no certainties in life. But through hope and faith and love and worship, we can free our souls from pain. Consider how you are blessed. You are a fine young man, a credit to your family and your mother loves you very much."

Summers held Joseph's good hand and began the Lord's prayer. He encouraged Joseph to join him. Their voices echoed around the empty chapel.

The sign above Uncle Charles's shop read 'Charles Merrick – Gentlemen's Hairdresser & Tobacconist'. Joe often remarked to his brother, somewhat bitterly, that the title of Gentlemen's Hairdresser rather than Barber made the enterprise sound pansy pink. Whenever he did, Charles replied with his standard put-down, "Well, Joe, when I was cutting hair, you were cutting corners." Joseph liked the way the remark always incensed his father.

A magnificent barber's chair was the centrepiece of the room, a throne of light-brown crafted oak, lovingly polished and carefully maintained with a crimson seat cushion and backrest. The material was worn and faded through popularity of use. Three wooden chairs were provided for waiting customers. Next to the chairs stood a small wooden rack of reading material containing an incongruous mix of books and journals, in addition to well-thumbed recent editions of the *Leicester Daily Tribune*.

The front of the shop smelt of shaving soap and hair oil, the rear smelt of dry, peaty tobacco. There was a colourful mosaic of tins: Ogden's Midnight Flake, Bell's Three Nuns, Shag, Navy Cut and Tom Tough. Charles also stocked an extensive array of other smoking paraphernalia such as tobacco pouches, cigars, cigarette papers, ornamental pipes and ashtrays. Charles devoted himself to hairdressing whilst Auntie Sarah took care of tobacco sales. The only time Charles stepped outside was to sweep dried horse manure from the pavement or take deliveries.

Old lettering advertising 'Umbrella Repairs' flaked on the shop window, but the only evidence of this discontinued part of the business was the backroom, which Joseph had christened 'The Umbrella Mausoleum'. A hundred old broken umbrellas lay on two tables, between mountains of tobacco supplies. Charles never expressly forbade Joseph from entering the shop by the front door, but gave him a key for the back and invited him to play with the umbrellas at any time. Joseph let himself into the back room at least once a week, listened to conversations taking place in the shop and read old newspapers and journals.

Easy inoffensive conversation came naturally to Uncle Charles. He had the gentle wit and conventional opinions of a man whose livelihood depended on being liked. Auntie Sarah was a naturally shy woman who gained confidence through marriage to a kind man. Tragically, none of their children had yet survived infancy. Joseph wondered if perhaps he was a temporary surrogate. In some ways he felt more part of this family than his own.

When his brother William and sister Marion were babies, Mary constantly examined the new arrivals, checking William's head, hands and feet. She panicked every time he cried and pulled away his swaddling clothes in a frenzy of desperation. When temporarily satisfied all was as it should be, Mary rushed over to young Marion to check her head, her hands and her feet. She no longer checked Joseph's body, however. She no longer touched him at all.

When Marion was six years of age and Joseph ten, she was taken ill. Her temperature rose, her limbs swelled. Mary screamed and clawed at her head. "It's happening again!" she cried. Joe marched Joseph out of the house and told him to wait with Uncle Charles. Auntie Sarah gave Joseph a blanket. Joseph slept in the umbrella room for three nights and said a thousand prayers for his sister. When Joseph arrived home Marion was smiling and well. Joe said it was 'something like measles', though his tone was grave. His true concern was for Mary.

Joseph watched the flesh fall away from his mother; not that she had much to give. Her worker's arms withered to bony chicken wings and her eyes retreated into the dark of their hollows. When Joseph asked her a question the answer took a minute to arrive and was barely a mumble, as if she was responding from a distant world.

Suddenly the Merrick house was a quiet place. Gone were the arguments about money his parents enjoyed so well. Mother took to her bed. Joseph took to the umbrella room at Uncle Charles's.

One evening, Joseph returned home from Uncle Charles's and walked the entire length of Lee Street without enduring a single taunt. When Joseph opened the front door, the silence was explained. Reverend Summers was waiting for him and extended his arms. Joseph knew he should cry and proceeded to cry as Summers cradled his massive head in his vestment.

Joseph's father forbade him from the austere burial at Welford Road Cemetery, declaring him too young to attend. He stayed at home with Barney's wife, Polly, who kept an eye on William and Marion. Joseph read the bible in a fitful way, skimming random sections, unable to concentrate on a single passage.

Joe took one day of leave following Mary's death and one half day for the funeral as an 'example to the younglings'. Marion had already assumed most of the domestic duties at Lee Street. Though she was barely eight years old, Marion was proficient with the laundry, clothing repairs and the stew pot.

A few days after the funeral, Barney came back with Joe after the pub. Joseph listened from the top of the stairs to his father's nostalgic reminiscence about his courtship with Mary. Joe recalled the October Pleasure Fair where he won a bottle of whiskey in a test of strength and how he and Mary drank the liquor and watched the stars.

Joe said, "She was an angel."

Barney said, "She was a princess."

"We were so happy together," lamented Joe.

The sentimental revisionism struck Joseph as strange.

Two weeks after his mother died, Joseph told his father that intended to visit her grave. He wore his Sunday-best suit jacket and the black necktie Joe borrowed from Uncle Charles, but had neglected to return. Joe helped him knot the necktie and pulled it as tight as a noose. Joseph visited a flower seller near The Corn Exchange and purchased a single red carnation. He hid the carnation inside his jacket in case anyone assumed the ugliest youth in Leicester was meeting a sweetheart.

The headstones of Welford Road Cemetery stood in odd lines, like enormous stone chess pieces on the shamrock-green grass. Joseph followed the co-ordinates his father had provided, away from the grand memorials, to the plots marked by cheap trinkets, to the tiny wooden cross engraved with 'Mary Merrick'. The cross was seven inches high and five inches wide. Uncle Charles had whittled the wood and attached the crosspiece. Joseph crouched on his swollen knees and produced the red carnation from his jacket. It had lost its shape and several petals on the walk to the cemetery. Joseph placed the flower on the small mound of the grave.

"Well, Mother," said Joseph, "I have come to say goodbye."

Joseph began his speech, peppered with phrases such as, "My great sorrow at your passing", "I know you are in heaven", "We will be together one day" – the lofty platitudes with which the living should address the dead.

The empty cemetery and impassive memorials seemed to mock Joseph's one-sided conversation and he could not finish his speech. He tried to picture his mother as an angel, serenely occupying a cloud in heaven, but could only imagine her fretting, pacing her cloud, impatiently waiting for Joe to join her and continue their arguments over small amounts of money. Worry and drudgery were the substance of her soul. As such, Joseph could not imagine her soul at rest.

Joseph knew he should believe his mother was at one with the Lord and that he was one step closer to the Lord as a consequence, but felt only dread before the immensity of death. And no matter how much he tried, Joseph could not escape the awful possibility that his birth had hastened her passing. Joseph hated the formality of this contrived conversation and the exalted status of the cemetery, which was nothing more than a storage field for mortified corpses. He did not go back there again.

Chapter 2 – Hawking

Leicester town centre had five main arteries of traffic running into the heart of a cobbled market square at the bottom of Haymarket. As Leicester's population had more than doubled in the 1860s, the heart became dangerously congested. Local merchants petitioned for a solution and in 1868 the town council commissioned the construction of Haymarket Clock Tower. The Clock Tower was forty feet high and eight feet square. Each side boasted a statue of one of Leicester's favourite sons, Gabriel Newton, Simon De Montfort, William Wigston and Thomas White. The Clock Tower regulated traffic as no vehicle could cut directly through the centre of the square. Haymarket was still chaos, but organised chaos and not without opportunity. A hawker by the Clock Tower could hope to present his wares to hundreds of customers per day. Hawking was regulated by the Commissioner of Hackney Carriages. Joe Merrick boasted that he used his considerable pull to obtain a licence for his sons.

Every morning at five o'clock Joe loaded the hawking trays at Merrick Haberdashery, the new shop and family home on Russell Square. The display room was ten feet in width and twelve in length. An oak tallboy crammed with merchandise stood against each of the side walls, with a glass display counter positioned at the rear. The display counter was reserved for the most expensive items, an array of hats and watches for both men and women. Marion stayed at the shop and kept the counter, a pretty young salesgirl in her white chemise.

Joseph's tray was an old wooden box, eighteen inches long, two feet wide and six inches deep. Joe packed in items from the shelves, balls of wool, needles, threads, buttons, collar stiffeners and tins of shoe polish along with the matches and cigarette papers he purchased on the cheap from Uncle Charles. Joe helped

Joseph on with the tray, which was secured to his shoulders by two leather belts. Joseph winced at the weight. Joe then pulled a woollen mitten, the size of an oven glove, over Joseph's hugely deformed right hand.

Joe attended to William's tray, which was loaded with lighter but higher value items including a selection of watches. Father exhaled with pride at the sight of his youngest son, who was fourteen years of age but looked eighteen, by virtue of his height. William's cherubic face and sandy hair certainly added to his sales appeal, especially with older women who saw in him an idealised son or future lover.

Joe nicknamed William 'The Talking Till' and treated him to a good second-hand suit, which formerly belonged to a young town clerk. Joseph, by contrast, wore a hand-me-down, his father's threadbare old slate grey suit. Joe now wore a khaki waistcoat over a white shirt with the sleeves rolled up. The look said 'dynamic shopkeeper' even when the takings did not. He produced a cigar from his top pocket, one of the cheap ones he regularly scrounged off Uncle Charles and tapped it against Joseph's forehead.

"How many shillings of merchandise must you sell each day?"

"Ten shillings, Pa," answered Joseph, guessing where this line of questioning was leading.

"And how often have you struck the target?"

Joseph remained quiet.

"How old are you, Joseph?"

"Seventeen."

Joe placed his hand on William's shoulder.

"Your brother is fourteen. But this boy, this man, is a veritable talking till! Ten shillings are his morning's work."

Joe gestured to Marion. "Your sister performs wonders on the counter here. But I do not think you could sell me a bottle of porter if I were dying of thirst."

William laughed. Joe continued, "Remind us why you were dismissed from your previous employ."

When Joseph was thirteen, his father had secured him a full-time position at the cigar factory on Lower Hill Street, hand-rolling cigars for ten hours a day, six days a week. Joseph found the work difficult enough with his deformed right hand, but further mutation made the task impossible. Joseph was fired at the age of fifteen and Joe had never forgiven him.

Joseph held up his enormous right hand to answer his father's question, but Joe shook his head and tapped Joseph on the chest to signify an absence of heart. Not for the first time, Joseph wished he was Charles Merrick's son.

"You have been given a second opportunity to prove yourself, yet you continue to disappoint. The eldest must provide the most."

"But Pa ..."

"There will be no excuses, no more! Excuses are the province of the poorhouse."

Joe's evocation of the workhouse was chilling. William kept his smile. He was a good son, a great hawker and physically gifted. Misfortune was something that happened to other people.

Joe implored William, "Recite your hawking rhyme!"

William was eager to comply.

"The teaser resides at the front of the tray, for that is where enticements lay,

Lead on thread and sell on string, once they've bought that they'll buy anything.

Housewives are best cos they're easily sold, because you are young and they are old.

Smile as you walk, get known around, then you can sell on a watch for a pound."

Joe laughed heartily and slapped his thighs. "This young fellow is a talking till!"

William and Joseph left the shop and went their separate ways. William had a roving brief, to explore the busy thoroughfares of Leicester and call door-to-door on his easy-touch housewives. Joseph walked the half mile to Haymarket. It was early October and day had not yet broken. Joseph paced in a slow circular motion around the Clock Tower, taking deep breaths in an attempt to combat his anxious nausea.

First light broke at six o'clock and the good people of Leicester flooded into the Haymarket like a tidal wave. Joseph bobbed about the front of the Clock Tower as flotsam, simultaneously attempting to keep his feet, hold his nerve and sell. 'Haberdashery' was a mouthful, especially for one with a lisp, so Joseph focussed his sales pitch on specific items: "Needle and thread, miss?", "Matches and papers, sir?" After his regrettable failure as a factory worker Joseph was determined to prove himself at hawking.

The day started well. A motherly woman of forty purchased a sewing kit for ninepence. Several working men bought matches, yielding a shilling. Joseph's customers paid little attention to the deformity of the vendor. Early morning was his favourite time. Passers-by were still clouded by sleep or too busy going places to really ogle his deformities. Afternoons were a different story. Men tried to knock off his hat, children kicked his shins and ran, women asked their questions of inane cruelty.

"Were you cursed?"

"Is your mother like you are?"

"Do you not know you're a wrong'un?"

It was impossible for Joseph to hide completely as the Clock Tower was accessible from all sides. His usual trick was to circle around the Clock Tower, away from the cause of trouble, until they lost interest. This approach defused many situations, including several occasions when large mobs got worked up about him. Whenever Joseph circled the Clock Tower the stone sons of Leicester seemed to peer at him from every side.

During the mid-afternoon lull, a fat man in a good suit approached Joseph. He shushed Joseph's attempts at sales talk and purchased his entire stock of boot polish, matches and cigarette papers, along with two shoe horns and three men's dressing kits. When combined with his morning sales, Joseph had ten shillings! It was a hawker's dream. Joseph limped back to Russell Square as fast as he could, eager to share his success with his father and collect more stock.

Back at Merrick Haberdashery, Marion was at the display counter showing a well-to-do female customer a new hat. Joe hovered by the woman's shoulder, practically salivating with avarice. Joe noticed Joseph at the window and tried to wave him away. Joseph entered the shop, but Joe pushed him back through the door and on to the street, as if shooing a stray cat. Joseph heard Joe address the customer in his most obsequious voice. “Just one of our apprentices, ma’am” Joseph walked back to the Clock Tower and positioned himself for the evening rush, hoping for a few more sales of the remaining items, and, at last, the praise of his father at supper.

Before long the Haymarket was crowded with workers, many recent migrants from the villages of rural Leicestershire. It was easy to spot the newly arrived men of the country, with their broad shoulders, full cheeks and healthy complexions. Given a year or two of machine work their sturdy physiques faded or deflated to flab and their faces assumed a grey pallor. Joseph watched as they shuffled back home, to their cramped houses of many children. Whatever natural advantage those children inherited was soon negated by the poverty of diet, squalor of living conditions and the acrid air of industry. The man of the field begot the son of the slum, next in line at the machine.

If the best features of country life were bred out of the city man, arguably the worst remained: his small-mindedness, his fearful parochialism, a suspicion of outsiders. It was the mindset of an urban majority who lived in large towns and never ventured beyond the few familiar streets of their psychic village.

Someone broke Joseph’s observational trance by slapping him across the back of the head. The assailant knocked off his cap and tins fell from his tray as he stumbled, but Joseph managed to keep his feet. Joseph turned to face his attacker, a muscular worker in overalls, with the sun-bleached blond hair of a farmhand cum recent factory worker. The man was flanked by two work colleagues, smaller men, rodent men, each holding the rank of ‘Bully’s mate’.

The bully picked up Joseph’s cap and put it on his head. He danced around Joseph, gurning his face and making sounds to impersonate an imbecile. Joseph hoped the bully would stop and lose interest, but around he danced, as if Joseph was a human maypole. Pedestrians stopped to watch the ad hoc street entertainment. Their laughter burnt him.

The bully stopped and handed Joseph his hat. As Joseph reached out to accept it, the bully pulled him into a vicelike headlock. All of his hawking wares crashed to the floor and children dived in to steal them. The precious coins fell from his pocket and children clawed each other for the money. Onlookers were in hysterics. Joseph bit the bully, sinking his teeth deep into his forearm.

The strawberry-blond yokel lowed like a cow.

The bully released his grip and his two friends restrained him with great difficulty, fearful of the consequence of his murderous rage. Joseph shouldered his way through the nearest line of onlookers, but the crowd pursued him along Eastgates. A man speared Joseph's ribs with an umbrella, a woman swung her purse in his face. They punched him, they kicked him. The spirit of the witch-hunt and tormenting village idiots remained.

Joseph took to bed and did not rise the next morning. He got up in the afternoon and, though his body was stiff and sore, he was relieved not to have broken a bone. He slept a few more hours until the aroma of the evening meal sent him downstairs. Joe and William were already seated at the table. Marion placed the stew pot in the centre.

"Guess who sold a watch for a pound?" said Joe to William. "You did, didn't you?"

William nodded.

Joe glared at Joseph. There was thunder in his cheeks. "And guess whose hawking licence was revoked for fighting?"

Joe picked up a piece of bread from the centreplate and pointed it at Joseph. "You will get not one crust here till you earn one."

"We can all support Joseph, together," said Marion.

Father ignored her and rose from his chair.

"Every chance you have squandered. This enterprise, this family, struggles because of you."

Joseph was on the verge of tears, but did his best to hold them.

"I do not blame you for this condition of my body, so why do you blame me?"

"You killed your mother."

Joseph tried to get at his father, but the table acted as a barrier and his movements were inhibited by disability. William held Joseph by the shoulders and Marion positioned herself between father and son. Joe stood behind the table enjoying his verbal victory.

"You're a great man, Father. How I respect you."

"Get out."

"A generous soul, a compassionate fellow. Not one trace of malice or bitterness."

"Get out!"

"I am crippled, but so are you, by cheapness and greed. You cannot keep pace with your brother."

Father was at breaking point and Joseph did not care.

"When Uncle Charles was cutting hair, you were cutting corners!"

Joseph expected a lunge forward, a physical attack. Instead Joe spoke remorsefully, like a drunk in sobriety. "You cursed my life from the day you were born."

Joseph collected his Sunday-best suit jacket and his bible, wrapped them in a bundle and left the shop. Russell Square was extremely dark and the street lights were as faint as miners' lamps. Joseph felt a hand on his shoulder. Marion pressed an apple and a piece of bread into Joseph's bundle and embraced him. The warmth of her body contrasted with the coldness of his father and Joseph cried. Marion wiped her own tears, released her grip and rushed back inside the shop, so as not to displease her father by siding with his disowned son.

Joseph walked to Uncle Charles's shop and let himself in the back door to the umbrella room. Charles shot down the stairs in his nightshirt, with a fire poker in hand, ready to fight a burglar. Charles said, "It's you boy!" He found Joseph a blanket, a book of matches and some kindling. Joseph started a small fire in the hearth and wrapped himself in the blanket. He sat on a chair cushion, propped his back against a table leg and wolfed down the bread and apple Marion had given him.

The sound of a passing horse and cart woke Joseph. It was morning, the fire was ash and a tin mug of lukewarm tea had been left by his side. Joseph heard Charles and his customer traverse the usual conversational terrain: all those new buildings, the price of things, town gossip, family. Joseph heard his name mentioned.

"His condition," said the customer, "it is terrible, is it not?"

"Joseph is a very hard worker, a young man of good character." Charles raised his voice, as if sensing Joseph was listening.

"Then why not apprentice him yourself, Charles?"

"Are you ready for the hot towel, Mr Robinson?" replied the cheery barber.

Joseph wrapped the blanket tight around himself and finished the last of his tea.

Around noon, Charles brought Joseph a thickly cut cheese sandwich and another mug of tea. Joseph thanked his uncle profusely and told him about the argument with Joe. Charles said he was welcome to stay until he got back on his feet. Then Charles said Auntie Sarah was expecting again. She had been ordered to rest in bed for the duration.

Joseph stayed three more days, until the pains of the beating left him. Charles brought Joseph a sandwich twice daily and several cups of tea. To his enormous credit, Charles was patient and friendly. The only sign Charles might be under pressure from Sarah were the good-natured but persistent questions he put to Joseph regarding his immediate work prospects.

On the third morning, after another sandwich and mug of tea, Joseph gathered his bundle. He found a pencil and wrote a thank you note on an empty tobacco carton. Joseph wedged the note under an old umbrella and quietly exited the rear of the shop whilst Charles was busy with another man's hair.

Joseph walked to Leicester Union Workhouse on Sparkenhoe Street. The main building of the workhouse complex was a leviathan of modern architecture, two storeys high and sixty yards wide, as solid and imposing as a judge. The front door was the mouth of a meat grinder, feeding the gristle of scrounging paupers into the blood-red brick. A central block of turrets peered down like the rising head of a cobra. Circles in the turrets performed the function of interrogating eyes, boring into the supplicant and extracting the truth of their pitiful failure. The frontage of the workhouse made Joseph feel small and ready to serve, dirty and shameful for his wretched destitution. He was a stranger, a boy, preparing to knock on the door of mighty city walls and request food and shelter for free. It was a miracle any man dared enter at all.

Joseph went for a walk instead, circling the workhouse via Highfield Street, Titchbourne Street and College Street, feeling the gravitational pull of his destiny, like a small piece of driftwood dragged towards the centre of a whirlpool. He reviewed his other choices. He could go to Reverend Summers and ask for a bowl of soup. But then there would be the awkward questions regarding his scarce attendance at chapel. And, when his faith was stronger, Joseph shared Summers's quiet frustration with those casual Christians, who only reach for the Lord when they are drowning.

Joseph stopped in an alleyway on College Street and placed his hands together to pray. He asked God to forgive his lacklustre attendance of chapel and his failed efforts at work. Joseph asked God what he should do and waited for an answer. No message arrived, no words, no sound. Yet he could not believe the Lord had forsaken him.

What if the silence of God's voice was not evidence of his absence, but the confirmation of his presence? If a man is to receive his judgement based on his worldly actions, then surely 'free will' is the test of man, for his decisions are the sum of God's teaching. Joseph considered his options. He could go to the West Bridge line and lay his head on the tracks. He could throw himself into the River Soar. Or he could throw himself on the mercy of the Leicester Union Workhouse. To live in disgrace or die in dishonour, which would please the Lord?

Joseph passed the front gates of the Workhouse and entered the grounds. A blood-red wall of shame received him.

Chapter 3 – The Workhouse

The observational operating theatre at the London Hospital was, in the estimation of Dr Gilbert Greystone, a superior facility. The operating table was the centrepiece of a spacious amphitheatre, with standing room for up to fifty pupils. Light shone from behind the audience, through a giant greenhouse window, measuring ten feet by ten, at a pleasing angle of forty-five degrees. Additional illumination was provided by lamplight if needed. The lamp was suspended four feet above the operating table on a low-hanging steel chandelier. The theatre was an artist's studio, a shining study in white. As for the present artist in residence, Gilbert was firmly convinced that no pupil surgeon could fail to be inspired by his work.

Gilbert expected to operate before a full auditorium, but some oaf had scheduled a lecture for the same time. It had come down to a choice, observe Dr Gilbert Greystone or listen to Dr Frederick Treves. As Treves's lecture was more likely the shorter, and would provide an early escape for libations, apathy prevailed. Just three students sauntered into the operating theatre, already stinking of booze from luncheon.

Two lowly porters brought in a stretcher and hoisted the patient onto the slab, O'Malley, a fifty-year-old Irish scrubwoman with the brow of an imbecile, already dazed from a minor sedative. Gilbert privately considered The London Hospital a cesspool full of human flotsam who drifted in from the East End's river of filth. Gilbert disdained any form of conversation with patients or their families, as it would be necessary to simplify procedural explanations to the level of baby talk. To describe himself as an expert of all things 'down below' would have been to disgustingly denigrate his profession.

Gilbert ordered the pupil acting as dresser, a nonentity by the name of Whitney, to dispense the chloroform. As Whitney proceeded, Gilbert recalled his most recent surgical triumphs.

Sir Phillip Grainger was taken ill whilst visiting almshouses for the East End poor and rushed to the London Hospital. Gilbert was called to attend and discovered that Sir Phillip had been battling on with a severe stricture of the urethra. Gilbert's older colleague, Jarvis, thought a risky external incision would be necessary. But, thanks to Gilbert's skill and dexterity with the urethral sounds, danger was averted without recourse to extreme measures. Sir Phillip also praised Gilbert's 'hand of velvet' with the catheter. Gilbert received an open invitation to the Graingers' manor in Berkshire along with a bottle of twenty-four-year-old Scotch. Gilbert did not drink alcohol, but considered the gift to be indicative of the finest taste and foremost breeding.

The wife of Gilbert's former teacher, Professor Bridgegate, required the urgent removal of a diseased ovary. Bridgegate had long retired, being old and unsteady of hand, but specifically sought Gilbert to perform the surgery and save the life of his beloved spouse. Due to the presence of a large tumour, fatal haemorrhage was an immediate risk, but Gilbert, through sheer surgical excellence, prevailed. Gilbert considered Mrs Bridgegate an equal partner in the dance. Her general health was outstanding owing to a great deal of exercise out of doors, a first-class diet and the abjuration of over-indulgence.

The Bridgegates conveyed their gratitude via a delicious fruit basket and a charming garniture of antique porcelain. The operation brought Gilbert much professional kudos and he subsequently published an extremely well-received paper on the subject, remarkable achievements for a man of but thirty and four.

Procedures on quality people were a rarity for Gilbert. Women like O'Malley were his daily meat, another heifer in the line of bestial East Londoners. Yet Gilbert applied to The London Hospital specifically to engage in prolific work, to develop techniques for saving decent lives, whilst musing upon methods to reduce the proliferation of dross.

Back in theatre, O'Malley had fallen unconscious. Gilbert instructed Whitney to dispense the antiseptic via Lister's carbolic applicator. Whitney raised the smock and Gilbert recoiled at O'Malley's bloated, distended abdomen and network of varicose veins.

He classified this body as a testament to indiscriminate breeding, gallons of gin and the poverty of a wretched lifestyle. O'Malley's ovary was also diseased, yet there could be no further comparison with delightful Mrs Bridgegate.

Gilbert beheld the shimmering steel of his surgical equipment, the silver claws of his cervical dilator, the keen retractable blade of his bistoury cache and of course, his trusty scalpel. Gilbert poised above Whitney, eager for his assistant to complete the carbolic preparation. With his scalpel in hand and a look of hunger, Gilbert resembled a ravenous diner presented with a shoulder of lamb.

The procedure passed by in something of a blur, but by the end of it, Gilbert's surgical apron would not have looked out of place on a Smithfield butcher. Gilbert saw now his three brattish pupils, pale-faced and sober, struggling to down hold their liquid lunch. Gilbert snapped Whitney out of his trance, instructing him to sterilise his surgical instruments.

Afterwards, he returned home to Thurrock Terrace, Bayswater, retired to his study and completed a brief report about the patient's demise, building on the theme of inoperable, before limbering down with light stretching exercises and a gentle rotation of the Indian clubs. Gilbert watched himself exercise in a mirror on the mahogany bookshelf, proud of his lithe torso and muscular forearms, the tight skin on his clean-shaven face and the lustre of his short, light chestnut hair.

Gilbert washed in a basin of ice cold water, vigorously applied a coarse towel to his body and parted his hair neatly to the right-hand side. His manservant, Andrews, brought a freshly laundered evening suit to the bedchamber. As Gilbert changed into his cool linen shirt he shared the elation of Chionis of Sparta after his triumphant Olympiad, blood still high but clean and refreshed. The higher man is a speeding arrow propelled by the force of will.

Gilbert walked briskly and purposefully along the north and east boundaries of Hyde Park, one mile to Mayfair, where his Taygetus Eugenics Society hired rooms at Dr Vale's club. Gilbert ignored the subservient greetings of the doorman and entered the function room to the rear. Vale addressed the twenty men in attendance, mainly fellow medical professionals. Vale was an orthopaedic surgeon at St Thomas's Hospital and obsessed with criminal anthropology. He was short and tubby with receding black hair and he cultivated those few remaining strands like a miser. Gilbert had first met Vale at a major eugenics conference, where Vale had attached himself to Gilbert like a young boarder besotted with his house captain. It was Vale's doe-eyed worship that encouraged him to form his own eugenics society, named after Mount Taygetus in Greece, where Spartan mothers reportedly cast their defective offspring from the summit.

When Vale saw Gilbert ghost into the room, he interrupted his talk on the cranial abnormalities of offenders with a rather fey wave. Gilbert acknowledged Vale with the nod of a hero as to a distant admirer. Vale concluded his lecture to polite applause.

"It is my great pleasure to introduce the founder of our society: surgeon, leader, friend, Dr Gilbert Greystone."

Gilbert strode to the front. There was real spice in the crisp applause and the twenty sounded like a hundred. Gilbert positioned himself to speak and looked into the devoted, eager eyes of his audience. He saw two distinguished guests, surgeons and knights of the realm. Gilbert knew that only a born leader could command the respect of much older men.

"An explorer ventures to the Serengeti and enters the plains in search of lions, expecting a mighty roar. He hears only whimpers; every lion is lame. When he rolls a ball of wool to this pathetic pride, they shuffle off on crippled legs in fear. Suddenly, our intrepid fellow is struck on the head by a falling eagle. Its wings are too weak to fly! Darwinian Natural Selection applies to every species on the planet, every species bar one, ours."

"Hear, hear!" said the well-bred members in unison.

"Modern society preserves the runt of the litter, against logic, against nature. Humanitarians call this 'freedom', humanitarians call this 'progress'. 'All are born as equal,' they cry. So then let us ask them, if two drooling imbeciles copulate in the gutter, what is the destiny of the child? Prison, the workhouse, or professor of mathematics at Merton College?"

Vale laughed hysterically, on the verge of an aneurism. Gilbert was lauded by applause.

"How do we protect the organism from infection, the better part, the higher part? We apply the basic principles of antiseptic surgery. We sterilise. We have this solution at our immediate disposal, but cannot act, because the humanitarian has infected the law!"

"Change is at hand, gentlemen. Men like us, questions in Parliament, the irrefutable logic of eugenics. Mark this, we will have our cure. And when we do, man shall beget soarers and roarers and thus ensure the survival of the fittest!"

The society rose to their feet, affording Gilbert an impassioned standing ovation. Nevertheless, his glory was tinged with sadness. It was all very well preaching to the choir, but the only way to drive progress was through great numbers of new converts, men of influence, to evangelise eugenics and take bold, practical action where necessary. It was time to spread the gospel to that Babylon of broken defectives, the workhouse.

Six months after his committal to Leicester Union Workhouse, Uncle Charles sent Joseph a few shillings, enabling him to sign out and search for work. Joseph collected his possessions from the Paupers' Clothes Store and tramped the streets all day, at first going about things systematically, calling on employers who engaged large numbers of menial workers. Some declined by polite refusal, others by outright threats. Everywhere crowds followed Joseph. "Where's your shoe polish?" shouted one man, who recognised Joseph from his hawking round.

Joseph used his money to purchase a bowl of soup and one night's accommodation at a communal lodging house in St Margaret's. He resumed his search for work the next morning, desperately trying any shop or commercial premises on Humberstone Gate. A smartly dressed old man with a pipe approached Joseph and said he was a regular customer of Charles Merrick. The old man added with nonchalant offensiveness, "Have you considered becoming a freak, young fellow? I have paid to see odd bods who were nowhere near as deformed as you. When the fair is here next, present yourself. You might find fame among dwarves and giants."

Joseph said, "I would rather die."

The old man said, "You might have to."

Back at the workhouse, Joseph was interviewed by the Receiving Officer, who determined he was deserving of re-admittance. Joseph handed over his clothes and took the obligatory entrance bath in a tub of ice-cold, dirty water. They handed him a uniform. It was a grey shade of brown, or a brown shade of grey, depending on the light. It was a fitting colour for a second-status human being, a pauper, a failure. It smelt of another man's sweat.

Joseph discharged himself from the workhouse whenever Uncle Charles sent money. There was no change in his employment prospects. Shop windows, however, confirmed new developments within Joseph's body. He was still mutating. The right-hand side of Joseph's skull had ballooned as if he were a two-headed creature. There were now three protrusions on his forehead, each resembling a gigantic bannister knob.

The back of Joseph's head was one colossal mass of bone and weighed like a hod of bricks. His body resembled an unfinished sculpture, with large areas of stone still waiting to be chipped away. No matter how Joseph tried to correct his posture, he was nothing less than crooked and ungainly. He was twenty-one years of age, but felt more like fifty. He could have been fifty, or fifteen. His deformities defied any classification of human age.

If a pauper was physically or mentally impaired they received an appropriate classification, Idiot or Imbecile, Deaf or Blind. On paper Joseph was a normal inmate, though latterly he found himself housed within the Imbecile Ward. Joseph slept and worked with the 'hopeless cases'. His daily task work consisted of oakum picking, shredding old rope with a rusty hook; these shreddings were then sold on to shipbuilders. He was occasionally set the task of breaking small stones with a hammer for builders' aggregate. The larger stones were given to the stronger, able-bodied men.

Joseph became friendly with a man of thirty named Timothy Carey, who was classified as an Imbecile. Timothy liked it that Joseph's middle name was the same as his surname. Carey was very small, with translucent skin, a result of spending his life as a shut-in at the family residence in New Walk, Leicester. Carey longed for a life outside, and had broken free of his room and the clutches of his mother who showed him no love and treated him like a silly child. After a fruitless search for employment, Carey admitted himself to Leicester Union Workhouse. Carey believed he would one day find work, get married and live a life like other people. Joseph wondered why Carey did not request money from his family, assuming they possessed wealth in abundance. Carey said he wanted to stand as a man on his own. If moral courage equated to wealth, thought Joseph, Carey need not work a day in his life.

One morning after breakfast, pease pudding and one pint of tea, the paupers were set to work. Women washed clothing and linen, mended uniforms and scrubbed floors. Able-bodied men broke stones, whitewashed walls, tended animals and saw to repairs and carpentry. Joseph picked oakum along with the other defectives in their workyard. For some reason Carey was absent. A porter arrived, called for Joseph and he was taken to the Master's parlour.

Mr Harrison's wood-panelled office was located on the second floor of the main building. Harrison sat at his desk, scrutinising the weighty tome of the workhouse admissions book. The Master was a large man with a heavy build, barrel chest and a full, thick beard. Harrison reminded Joseph of the famous cricketer, Grace, yet his office was a homage to rugby football, with pendants, team photographs, trophies and mounted kit jerseys. Harrison was formerly the headmaster of a prestigious public boys' school. Joseph felt intimidated, like a pupil who does not know if he is in line for praise, a pep talk or punishment.

"You have been here some three years, nearly four. You discharge yourself periodically. In the last year you have discharged yourself not once." Harrison looked up from the ledger. Joseph swallowed and prepared for punishment.

"I am going to ask a question of the utmost seriousness. The provision of relief depends upon your answer. Merrick, do you want to work?"

The answer seemed so obvious, Joseph thought the question might be a trick.

"Yes, sir."

"Splendid!" bellowed Harrison. He slapped the table with the palms of his hands and sprang to his feet.

"Roar it then. Roar it like a lion! 'I am ready for work!'"

Joseph took a deep breath and announced unconvincingly, "I am ready for work." Because of his swollen mouth and lisp, Joseph spat on the 'r' of 'ready'.

"Just this very morning a man named Carey stood where you are and exclaimed, "I am ready for work." He is gone, Merrick, discharged himself, wants to take up the cudgels. I do not expect we will see him again. What of your quest for work?"

"My condition, sir. It prevents me."

Harrison sighed. "When you are here you are constantly employed. If you can walk you can work. If you can't walk, sit and work. You have one good arm and two useable legs, a damn sight more than many who have served their Queen. If one faculty is diminished, emphasise the exceptional development of another. If a young fellow cannot walk or even whistle he is of no use as an errand boy, but if his sense of smell is akin to a bloodhound, that young fellow is a prince of the gasworks."

"I am truly grateful for your words of advice, sir. It is just my standing here. I am not an imbecile, sir. I was not recorded as such on my admittance."

"We can't have you associating with the rank and file fellows. That is not the point."

Harrison walked over to a team photograph of various well-bred boys in their rugby uniforms. A younger, carefree version of Harrison towered above them like a proud father.

"Westerbridge, January, 1875, snowed a blizzard. There was a howling northern wind, whipped you like a cat o' nine tails. Only a lunatic would have ventured outside. Naturally, I summoned the boys for rugger. Some boys ran back shivering to the fire, some boys ran back crying to matron! The snow turned to hail, the wind turned to ice. After three hours of arctic scrummaging, four warriors remained. I lined them up and I said to them, "The last boy in for supper shall be named as captain!" They stood there like guardsmen, unblinking! Lars Smith, Calvert, Lovell, brave Bill Hoskins ..."

A tremor affected Harrison's eye. His bottom lip quivered under his beard. He cleared his throat and walked back to his desk.

"Your present destination is the morgue here. No hope for this world, little for the next. Life is not a measure of acumen, but a question of character. Do you understand?"

Harrison shut the admissions book. Joseph nodded, suddenly nauseous. If he opened his mouth to speak, he feared he would bring up his meagre breakfast.

Private Memorandum

Dr Vale,

You propose the creation of a layman's guide to eugenics. The argument you present is that, to expand the membership of our Taygetus Eugenics Society, we must appeal to men of great influence with inferior minds. What an irony. What a tragedy. Nevertheless, I grudgingly concede and convey the following notes.

Sincerely, Greystone

An Introduction to Eugenics

At Taygetus Eugenics Society our goal is to ensure that the best human specimens proliferate. A question we are often asked then is why do we focus our attention upon the worst examples?

Let us take the example of the finest youth, with his chiselled muscularity and equal strength of intellect. He stands before Mount Taygetus and takes a deep, purposeful breath, yet his feet are ridden with worms! The youth must urgently attend to the lowliest parasite; only then can he ascend to the hitherto uncharted heights of his physical and mental being. In other words, unless the best of humanity rids itself of the worst, we will not advance a step.

Mentally defective delinquents are the lowest substratum of humanity and are defined within three main categories: feeble-minded, idiots and imbeciles. We will illustrate these definitions with case studies from the London poor.

Feeble-Minded

The subject is Johnson, 25 years of age, the son of feeble-minded parents. He is illiterate, with subnormal intelligence, though capable of basic conversations. Asymmetrical head, vacant eyes, jug ears. Genitals normal.

Sporadic gainful employment. Habitual petty criminal, resides in fourpenny dosshouses. Jailed for his part in a housebreaking gang, 3 years hard labour. His gullibility made him a malleable accomplice.

In terms of mental deficiency, the feeble-minded are the highest of the lowest. Typical offences: assault, drunkenness, theft, accessory. The feeble-minded should not be confused with morons. Owing to their complete absence of intellect, the feeble-minded are pawns to the will of morons.

Even if a feeble-minded defective lives a lawful life, let us not underestimate his detrimental effect on the race. Johnson's brother is 28 years of age and also feeble-minded. No previous convictions. Wife dullard. Five children to date, two surviving, both mental defectives. Family are poorhouse 'in and outs'.

The Imbecile

The imbecile possesses the subnormal intelligence of the feeble-minded, yet lacks the moral faculty. 'Imbecile' is the all encompassing classification; 'Moral Imbecile' is also acceptable.

The imbecile may appear to be an amiable buffoon, harmless on the surface. This is a perilous postulation, akin to assuming it is safe to touch a jellyfish because the outer appearance is soft. On the contrary, the imbecile is the most dangerous type of defective. The inability to apply moral judgement dispenses of man's inner watchman, his basic decency. The 'Should I?' cognition of moral dilemma is as far from the imbecile as the planet Jupiter.

Gregory, imbecile, 30 years of age, common labourer. Dismissed from his most recent employ for dereliction of duty. Even if he is set the simplest task, lugging crates, he becomes restless, throwing his load to the floor and disobeying reasonable work instructions. Verbally, he communicates in short broken sentences, "You me friend", displaying the linguistic capacity of a savage after ten lessons of English from a well-meaning missionary.

His cranial malformations are pronounced. Facial features display atavism, in other words, a regression to primitive humanity. Rheumy constitution. Genitals underdeveloped, though reproductive function unimpaired. Gormless expression, massive forehead.

His life has taken a triangular trajectory between prison, workhouse and slum. When not incarcerated he takes up with a low woman, also an imbecile. Six bastards between them; two idiots, four imbeciles. The female imbecile is predisposed to drunkenness and prostitution. Gregory's own mother sold her body for gin.

The imbecile commands our attention as a mainstay of penal institutions and workhouses. He is not the most impaired, but he is the most damaging of all defectives. The infamous Bean clan of East Lothian are perhaps the most heinous example.

The Idiot

The idiot is not to be confused with the catatonic. The catatonic is a veritable human mannequin, dead when alive, unmoving and entirely unresponsive to external stimuli. The idiot may at times resemble the catatonic; he is virtually brain dead, but is at least partly reactive and responds to authoritative verbal commands as cattle respond to the stick.

The idiot's mental capacity is the last flicker of a waning candle. Mercifully, the flicker is fainter in his loins, which are entirely undeveloped. Physically, idiots resemble stunted dwarves and grow to the size of large children. It is worth noting here that, remarkably, two idiots kept in the same building can and do reproduce. The offspring arrives with the unexpectedness of a hidden potato crop. As you would expect, the progeny defies description.

Smith, aged 24, is a prime example. Unable to work and shunted away, he was eventually left to the street and arrested for vagabondage. The District Medical Officer could not diagnose insanity, nor could he declare that Smith was knowingly capable of crime. Therefore Smith was taken to the workhouse, where he will inevitably end his days. Unemployable mental defectives are a terrible drain on us all.

Conclusion

The solution in all cases is sterilisation, in the following order, owing to birth and crime rates:

1. Imbeciles
2. Feeble-Minded
3. Idiots

Sterilisation is the process by which men and women are rendered infertile via surgical intervention. The procedure for the female is relatively straightforward and there are several techniques at the disposal of surgeons. Morbidity is as low as 5% and diminishing with ongoing medical advances.

Sterilisation of the male is accomplished by vasoligation. In layman's terms this surgery is the equivalent of re-engineering a complicated pipe network. Vasoligation is still in the experimental stage. The procedure has been employed as a last resort in terminal prostate conditions.

In men there remains the option of removing the threat altogether, although in adult males, the procedure confines the patient to an invalid carriage. The eunuchs of history were emasculated before puberty and worked with the brain, not the body. In defective delinquents the intellect is nil. Vasoligation, therefore, is the perfect solution, preventing further breeding, but also ensuring the subject is capable of basic industrial labour. Vasoligation also renders the subject impotent, an unintended benefit.

Quite insanely, British Law does not allow for the sterilisation of defective males or females or further experimentation on these deficient types. But as Britain laments the vast sums squandered on defectives, the dawn of eugenics draws near, breaking high above the mountain, as our youth ascends to the summit!

Other types for future consideration:

Lunatics

As a result of their insane behaviour, lunatics are usually quickly identified and incarcerated. They are safely detained and not of urgent attention.

Epileptics

The epileptic is consumptive in appearance with hollow cheeks, pallid skin, a malnourished body, and the suspicious, furtive eyes of a pickpocket. The epileptic, like the lunatic, is easily identifiable and in most cases spends life as a shut-in or is permanently incarcerated. The epileptic is unlikely to breed prolifically, as the physical strain of sexual activity triggers convulsions.

Other Races

Vulgar colour prejudice has no place in eugenics. In terms of intellect, the ancient Greek of olive skin is yet to be surpassed. In the present day, the Japanese enjoys arguably the world's finest national culture complemented by his formidable Samurai ethic. Problems occur, however, when a savage race is set loose within a civilised race, not unlike the frenzy of a fox in a chicken coop. The lower classes engage in wanton sexual relations, purity gives way to miscegenation and inevitable birth defects occur. If the creator intended to mix fish with fowl, pheasants would spawn in rivers and salmon would nest in trees. Society must regulate marriage in the first instance and sterilise lower races in the second. For further instruction see *The Problem Of And Solution To Negro Overbreeding* by St John Greystone (1857).

Criminals

Sterilising every criminal is an undertaking of impossibly vast scope, akin to a single trawler netting every fish in the sea. However, one could argue the current penal system models a feckless fisherman. As he casts defective specimens into the sea to breed again, the delinquent is set free, having allegedly paid his debt to society.

Vale: Circulate this communiqué to every Workhouse Master in London and surrounding boroughs.

James Summers's Sunday was as hectic as ever: morning worship at Highfields, followed by a myriad of ad hoc discussions with parishioners. Summers delegated Sunday school teaching to his team of diligent volunteers, enabling him to deliver divine worship at Leicester Union Workhouse. Summers held the position of Workhouse Chaplain in addition to his other responsibilities. When interviewed for the position, Summers expected to field a range of denominational questions, assuming the Master, Harrison, would prefer an Anglican. However, after confirming that Summers was willing to work without payment, Harrison offered him the job.

Summers conducted divine worship in the cavernous dining hall. A central walkway divided two vast columns of tables and benches and the aroma of institutional cooking prevailed. Summers addressed hundreds of paupers attempting to make services broadly ecumenical to include all, regardless of creed. Summers injected as much enthusiasm as possible; nevertheless, there was an unspoken chasm of pain. Families, who would have worshipped side by side in the outside world, were separated and segregated. Perhaps a husband and wife caught a fleeting glimpse of each other, or their children, across the dining hall. Summers found it virtually impossible to reconcile worship with an institution that punished families for communicating, but he also knew the Lord was a beacon of light.

After worship Summers visited the paupers' quarters, providing as much pastoral counsel as time allowed. When Bonnie Edwards was deserted by her husband, a housepainter, she had no choice but to admit herself and her three young children. Summers counselled Bonnie during the darkest times and arranged a special visit from her children to the women's quarters. Shortly after, Bonnie found work at a hosiery factory and discharged the family. Mother and children now lived happily together on Sussex Street.

Others were less fortunate.

Summers had made the acquaintance of Harold Parsons, a hardworking bobbin turner from Bell Lane. Parsons wound up in the poorhouse along with his wife and children after an industrial injury to his hand. Despairing of ever finding work and blaming himself for his family's pauperage, Parsons hung himself with his bedsheet. Parson's wife was so deranged with grief that she had to be manacled to a restraining chair. Mrs Parsons was now a permanent inmate of the lunatic asylum and her four young children were effectively orphans.

When Summers looked into the eyes of his congregation he wanted to see love and hope, not fear and defeat. He was especially concerned about Joseph Merrick. When Summers visited Joseph in the imbecile ward, Joseph explained that he had exhausted all avenues of work and the goodwill of his Uncle Charles. It was not the first time they had discussed such matters, although on this occasion Summers sensed an awful despondent finality, not unlike his last conversation with poor Harold Parsons.

Searching his mind for practical solutions, Summers remembered his friend Pastor Drummond from the North-East of England. Over the last year Drummond had founded a small, non-conformist theological college at a disused farm near Bamburgh. There were now a dozen students and Drummond had established a smallholding. Students worked the land by morning and studied by afternoon. Pastor Drummond was a progressive thinker, well to the left of conventional theology. In his last letter Drummond said he was able to accept one student as a scholar.

Summers told Joseph to write to Drummond, provide testimony and state which books of the bible were his favourite and why. Summers requisitioned the writing materials for Joseph.

The next week Joseph returned with an outstanding essay drawing parallels between Job and his trials of unemployment. The essay also included an extremely mature debate on Ecclesiastes and the issue of free will. Even if Joseph was unsuccessful, the exercise had raised his spirits and affirmed his faith. Summers posted the letter and Drummond replied almost immediately, stating that Joseph's brilliant essay, along with Summers's character reference, had virtually guaranteed him the scholarship!

Joseph shared the good news with Summers as they sat on his bed in the dormitory.

"Your struggle has been rewarded, Joseph. See how the Lord listens?"

"Pastor Drummond is keen I provide details of my condition."

"Be honest and explicit, so it is not a shock when he welcomes you."

"You have kept my spirits in the darkest times. I cannot deny my faith was tested, at times to breaking point. At times, Reverend ... at times, my faith has broken."

"Joseph. The term 'test of faith' is a curious one. I once had a great argument with my brother to this end. I have come to believe that when people speak of a test of faith, they actually refer to a change in fortune. Many believe they deserve good fortune because they follow the word of the Lord. They forget the worldly fate of Jesus, the crucifixion. Why then should any man expect greater favour than the son of God?

"If faith guarantees good fortune, religion is nothing more than catchpenny insurance for modern atheists. The good are not always rewarded on this earth, Joseph, and heaven is for believers only. Therefore, if suffering on this earth means an eternity with the Lord, we must embrace suffering. If ever your faith was broken, it has been remade. I only wish I had put this as elegantly to my brother when his faith was tested."

Summers was one of the new breed of Baptists who would only baptise adult believers. Due to fate and misfortune, Joseph had missed his turn. Had they been in chapel, Summers would have invited Joseph to the baptistery and asked if he acknowledged Jesus Christ as his Lord and saviour. On the affirmative Summers would have helped Joseph lean to the urn and immersed his head. But they were presently far from chapel, in the workhouse Imbecile Ward and six beds down a so-called mental defective named Richardson was waiting for counsel.

A handshake sufficed and Joseph thanked Summers for his help once again. Summers wondered how the water would have settled between the unusual bulges and ridges on Joseph's forehead. Summers remembered once telling Joseph his body was the work of the Lord. The Lord had finally blessed his work. It was a thing of beauty.

Dr Gilbert Greystone and Dr Horatio Vale travelled all over London canvassing workhouse masters who might be amenable to their cause. These get-togethers followed the same pattern: a meeting with the master under the pretext of 'free advice to improve the health of inmates', a tour of the institution, drinks and good-humoured mutual respect. When Gilbert and Vale introduced the topic of eugenics many masters expressed a disdain for defectives, often hatred. Then came the proposal. Would they, the master, be willing to provide a defective for sterilisation? A diseased uterus or defective bladder would provide an audit trail of deniability. If any malpractice was alleged, they could all point to official records, which would record nothing more sinister than the altruistic locum work of two generous surgeons. Master after master withered away like snails, retreating into shells of moral cowardice. They all lived in fear of the Metropolitan Asylums Board.

As persuasion had failed, outright bribery remained an option. Gilbert was reluctant to enter into the world of grubby envelopes. Even if he had the will to bribe, the coffers of Taygetus Eugenics Society were all but empty. Members had wealth, but were reluctant to part with it. When it came to improving the race, they preferred hot air and platitudes to affirmative action and risk. In no way would they countenance Gilbert's bold clandestine action. Yet Gilbert was convinced that without practical action eugenics was nothing more than high-sounding humbug.

Only one master leapt at the chance of clandestine sterilisation, a man who Vale nicknamed Dogface. Dogface had also requested to sit in during the procedure on the chosen candidate, a male idiot. In the build-up to the operation Gilbert reread his father's tome, *The Problem Of And Solution To Negro Overbreeding*. St John Greystone's theories on vasoligation were almost thirty years old, but aeons ahead of their time. Bad news arrived the day before the scheduled procedure: Dogface had been arrested for embezzlement and subsequently sentenced to seven years. A damned shame. Gilbert and Vale were now taking leave from their respective hospitals and boarding trains to the provinces for one last effort to convince a master.

They disembarked from the locomotive at Leicester Campbell Street Station and hailed a brougham for the workhouse. Gilbert and Vale could have walked the half mile, but Gilbert said arriving by carriage afforded them the correct status. Vale read a copy of the *Leicester Daily Tribune* and summarised a sub-headline.

"Carey, a so called 'unfortunate', dies neglected in the gutter. An imbecile, I'll wager."

"The reaper would lessen our burden," said Gilbert.

Vale folded up his newspaper. "Whilst we have this moment, to address the funding issue, should not our members with significant means make an appropriate contribution? A man with your means, for example. Or at least seriously consider it?"

Vale bookended his rambling question with a simpering smile. Gilbert replied, "When my father died I was not of age. My mother was tasked as executor. With the estate I stood to inherit, I could have bought every workhouse master in London and several mansions besides. Then Mother died. It transpired the estate was worth twenty-nine pounds, six shillings and fourpence."

Gilbert laughed and shook his head.

"Mother's family were morons, bleeding hearts, Quakers. She'd been got at, Vale, unbeknown to me. Whilst I was boarding at Rutley she was funnelling money to the family. They sent the fortune to America."

"But why?"

"So free slaves could build new lives, in new settlements and embrace free enterprise in their wondrous 'free country'. My rightful inheritance paid for schools no child attended, libraries of books unread, and hospitals for venereal disease. All humanitarians are cut from the same cloth. Their charity is the timber of Tay Bridge!"

Vale buried his head in his newspaper and made a mental note never to mention money to Greystone again.

The Master Harrison greeted Gilbert and Vale and introduced his wife, the matron. She was a quiet, circumspect woman who bowed her head in deference to husband. Matron excused herself whilst Harrison gave Gilbert and Vale the grand tour of the institution. Gilbert thought no man who so effortlessly dominated his wife could be all bad.

Harrison showed Gilbert and Vale through to the able-bodied male and female quarters, then out to the workyards. Unskilled men were employed in rock-breaking, the skilled men in joinery. The women washed bedclothes in buckets and turned the mangle. Despite efforts made towards cleanliness, the reek of unwashed bodies was pungent and intense. Harrison was extremely proud and positively evangelistic about the children's educational facilities. His industrial training rooms employed boys in shoemaking, carpentry and metalwork. Across the corridor girls learned to sew, iron clothes, cook and nurse children.

It was an ordinary workhouse, ordinary to good. The inmates went about the same kind of tasks with the same results. Some left, others died. The main difference was physical oddity. Gilbert thought at least half of the 'normal' paupers were obviously feeble-minded, with hardly a well-formed head in the bunch.

Harrison had used to be the headmaster of Westerbridge, the boarding school Vale's nephews attended, and had developed a reputation for his rigorous character-building initiatives. Vale's description of these measures impressed Gilbert and, when Vale revealed Harrison was now a workhouse master, Gilbert was keen to meet him. Harrison seemed motivated by moral imperatives rather than avarice, imperatives designed to produce an elite. But would Harrison have the stomach for the boldest solution of all?

Harrison led Gilbert and Vale past the infirmary, the morgue and the punishment cell and opened a heavy wooden door leading out to the imbeciles' workyard. He invited Gilbert and Vale to step through.

Gilbert saw many idiots: a pair of twins with the classic full moon foreheads and Chinese eyes. There was a textbook imbecile with a bulging, baking-potato brow and cannonball upper back. A demented old man tried to say 'Hello', but a tough overseer called for silence. The imbeciles picked oakum somewhat tokenistically and Gilbert noticed no truly fascinating specimens until, by the back wall, he spotted the most revolting creature.

It was male, with a head of inhuman proportions, as if the recipient of a grievous beating. Gilbert thought back to the gnarled and calcified knuckles of a prize-fighter he had dissected as a medical student. The creature's face was lopsided, with the right protruding more than the left, and the sloping mouth of a stroke victim. The lips puckered into a negro mouth, but this man was white and Gilbert noted no further evidence of miscegenation. The right hand was a monstrous appendage, transmuted to a claw.

Gilbert could not determine if this creature was an idiot or imbecile. Something about him defied categorisation. Alarmingly, his left hand was entirely normal and from the speed of his work, the man's co-ordination was normal, even good. Vale's hands were trembling. He must have been kicking himself for not bringing the callipers.

As the man went about his repetitive, menial work, Gilbert remarked to Vale, "Here we have history in the making."

"Our boys and girls receive the finest industrial education, acquiring skill and know-how, yet no amount of technical training can replace the construction of character. If only it were possible to form a poorhouse rugby football cup. The game should be compulsory for boys of the lower orders, or any youth for that matter ..."

Harrison paced around his master's parlour, addressing most of his remarks to the Aladdin's cave of sporting memorabilia. Gilbert played with his glass of water. Vale nodded along with Harrison and gulped his brandy. Gilbert waited patiently for his moment to interject.

"I must say, sir, today has been of enormous benefit and interest. Your industrial programme is first class. Although your imbecile ward commands our undivided attention."

"You confuse me, sir," replied Harrison. "You said your intention was to improve the health of my men. My good men."

"Mr Harrison," said Gilbert, "together we can advance the health of our race."

Gilbert and Vale left their seats and launched into their well-practised double act, a dramatisation of Gilbert's eugenics guide. Knowing administrators like Harrison were misers of the public treasury; Gilbert and Vale also deployed an arms chest of statistics, quantifying the fiscal drain of defectives. Vale placed a copy of their eugenics pamphlet in Harrison's hand. Harrison flicked through the pages and addressed Gilbert.

"Sterilisation? Is this not retroactive? Closing the gate after the horse has bolted?"

"On the contrary, sir, it is proactive. An end to defective foals."

Harrison nodded in agreement, but added, "I can hardly take this proposal to the Guardians Board."

"Mr Harrison. My colleague Dr Vale and I have met dozens of workhouse masters. Every single one of those men agrees with the principle of eugenics. But they lack the courage for practical action ... My colleague Dr Vale has a nephew at Westerbridge."

"'Vale'? I'm afraid I do not recognise the name. I departed Westerbridge seven years ago."

"They remember you, sir," said Gilbert, examining a team photograph. "How can they forget the way you transformed puny boys into virile young men? Officers and gentlemen, the vanguard of Britain."

Harrison's chest puffed out with pride, until Gilbert added, "How can they forget the boy Hoskins, who froze to death during rugger?"

Harrison sank into his chair, disoriented by memories of death and disgrace. He spoke weakly.

"What was I to do, have them pick daisies? It was my duty to hone them as men, as leaders of men."

"And so you did, sir, by weeding out the weak. That is why we have come to you, Mr Harrison. You are a bold man, brave, fearless. They made you a pariah for doing your duty. But one day, when eugenics is enshrined in law, there will be a statue of you."

"Of marble," added Vale.

"Of gold," said Gilbert.

"A statue, within your own *lifetime*!"

"In fifteen years time the Imbecile Ward will be empty! You'll go down in history as the man who stopped the rot!"

Harrison's head was like a tennis ball between them. Gilbert anticipated a question about legality.

"The procedure can be easily categorised as another medical matter."

"An imbecile lacks the wherewithal to make accusations," added Vale. "And if he did, what of them?"

Gilbert leant close to Harrison with the soft, syrupy demeanour of a tailor assuring a client he looked like a lord.

"Just give us one man, sir. Your worst man. The dregs of the Imbecile Ward."

James Summers occupied the ground floor of a townhouse in Stoneygates. He earned an average salary, but a small annuity enabled him to afford good lodgings. Every Sunday evening, Summers observed the same routine. He retired to his rooms around seven, boiled water on the cooking range and prepared a bath. After he had bathed and dressed, Summers retired to the cushioned chair in the sitting room and allowed himself the indulgence of a glass of port, whilst studying his bible. Yet Summers was denied his peace this Sunday, because he could not stop worrying about Joseph Merrick.

That afternoon, Summers had approached Joseph in the Imbecile Ward, expecting to hear more good news about his impending departure. Instead, Joseph handed him a letter from Pastor Drummond which read: 'Dear Joseph, I must regretfully inform you of tragic events at our college. A fire destroyed the main barn and killed several of the animals. Unfortunately, due to the strain on our treasury ,we are unable to offer a scholarship at this time ...'

Had Joseph's full disclosure of his deformities proved too much? Was Drummond a liar? The story of the fire seemed too fantastic not to be true.

Summers had offered counsel to Joseph at low points in his life, but today was unquestionably the lowest. It seemed as if this fine young Baptist had descended into an unreachable abyss.

"The world is full of criminals, thieves and murderers who act with impunity. They possess fine physiques and robust good health. They also enjoy good fortune. I thought I was supposed to be better than them?"

Summers wanted to console Joseph with appropriate remarks and attempted to visualise his bible and the word of the Lord as it appeared on the page. This technique enabled Summers to recite flawlessly from memory. But today the words withered and fell from the page, like dead birds in a solar eclipse. Summers resorted to a stock response. "Together we will find strength in prayer."

"But will my prayers find the Lord? Will they ever?"

"Joseph, you have been dealt a terrible injustice. I do not have words to compensate. All I can do is implore you, whatever happens, please do not move away from the Lord."

"On the contrary, I am close to him, Reverend. Far closer than I would want to be." Joseph added bleakly, "My body is a yew tree. It has killed all life around it."

Joseph's dire circumstances brought to mind fateful events from Reverend Summers's youth.

When the chaplain of the workhouse in Ongar was taken ill, Summers's father volunteered his services immediately. Reverend Alexander Summers had the ability to create an instant rapport with anyone, high and low, from the destitute tramps of the casual ward to the workhouse officers and guardians. The reverend also made an extra effort to visit sick paupers in the infirmary. Young James Summers followed his father from bedside to bedside and prayed with the ailing poor, the terminally ill and even the consumptives of the infectious ward. The work invigorated his father, until he developed a chronic cough. His father refused to see a doctor, until his coughing of blood could not be ignored.

His father insisted on working for as long as he was physically able, although his health broke within the year. Summers's elder brother Luke returned home from his university studies in Canterbury. The two brothers prayed by the side of their father's bed along with their distraught mother. After a long, traumatic coughing fit, their father died the next day.

As James Summers was already training in his father's vocation, he expected to field a volley of unanswered questions from his family. He did not have to wait long. The Sunday after the funeral, Luke and mother did not dress for chapel. They waited for Summers in the drawing room. Mother sat by the window. Luke stood by her side, holding her hand. Mother delivered a teary, vitriolic monologue, condemning the injustice, searching for answers. "Why has God let a good man die?"

Summers tried to respond as his father to these common questions of doubt, but sounded like a bad actor despoiling a good script. Luke interrupted him.

"Next you will tell us this is a *test of faith*."

Luke's manner infuriated Summers, aggravating the pain of his own immense grief. He picked up his father's bible, held it to Luke's face and said, "This is not a lucky rabbit's foot." Mother restrained the two brothers from coming to blows. James Summers left for theological college, Luke returned to Canterbury. Their mother died inside a year. Luke insisted on a secular remembrance service. They never spoke again.

Man deserved nothing more than his judgement, but surely a fine young man like Joseph Merrick deserved at least one moment of happiness on earth? And if his prayers were not answered by God, would he not be at risk of satanic temptation? If suffering brings man close to God, does it not bring him close to the Devil?

Summers's vision changed. The empty bible of fallen words ran dark with blood. He did not know the hour, but outside his window there was not a star in the sky, as if the creator's work was submerged by the darkness of evil. Summers fumbled in the locked drawer of his desk and located his small sum of savings. He found an envelope and placed the money inside. He wrote Joseph's name, the address of the workhouse and attached a stamp, a penny lilac. The posting box was a five-minute walk.

The night was colder than one could seasonally expect and a painful chill penetrated Summers's vestment. The wind seemed alive with sinister spirits and whispered voices. Summers tried to ignore the sounds, but when he heard the hiss of a serpent, he ran to the posting box and thrust the letter home.

As he walked home, Summers assured himself there was nothing to fear, that he had misheard the wind or his mind was playing tricks. He was struck by the absurdity of a spiritual man turning to logic for comfort. It was a night where prayer had given way to pragmatism. Summers now accepted the salvation of Joseph's physical life could only be achieved through practical means. If his small gift helped Joseph to preserve his body, it might also preserve his soul.

When Summers returned home and sat back in his chair he realised his vestment was drenched with sweat. His throat was bone dry and his lungs ached. He coughed violently and painfully, as if bringing up a collection of dusty old knives. He pitched forward and reached for his handkerchief. The taste of wine was replaced by the salt of blood. Summers's image of the bible returned to him; black, white and clear, yet the only words in his mind were an idiom, 'Like father, like son', and the tears stung his eyes with joy.

A porter summoned Joseph from the imbeciles' workyard and escorted him to a waiting room near the main dining hall, to meet a visitor. By the letter of workhouse regulations the porter should have accompanied Joseph into the waiting room, but he was content to remain outside.

The visitor was a little older than Joseph's father, aged about fifty. He was short and stout, with a pair of prominent sideburns reaching to the bottom of his cheek, a bowler hat and a red and grey chequered suit. He was clean-shaven, apart from the sideburns and his overall appearance was smart, but seedy. The man eyed Joseph like a sculptor surveying a work in progress, assessing the merit of what is already there, as well as the creative possibilities. The man offered his hand, the fingers stained with tobacco. Joseph offered his left hand and shook the man's right in an overhand grip.

"Sam Thomas," the man said, in a voice of many cigars. "It is a minor miracle your note found me. I thought it was a hoax. As I behold you in the flesh ... may I call you Joseph?"

"Yes, sir."

"It is Sam."

Joseph detected rough compassion in the voice.

"Would you be willing to remove your tunic?"

Joseph unfastened the buttons of his grey-brown top coat with his nimble left hand. He felt no embarrassment. Sam's request brought to mind a visit to a doctor's office when he was a child. The top coat snagged on his bulging right forearm. Sam helped him off with the garment and then his undershirt. Joseph came free of his clothing with his back to Sam. He remained still, waiting instruction.

"Turn again, very slowly."

The waiting room was the size of a prison cell with whitewashed walls and a single high window, just like the morgue. Joseph recalled his ridiculous attempt at suicide, after his last meeting with Summers, when his deformed right hand prevented him from tying the ligature. He fell to his knees, cursed God and offered his soul to Satan like a tin of shoe polish from his hawking tray. Joseph believed his prayer was successful, but his imagination played tricks in the moonlight. It was the zenith of his hunger and despair, his desperation for a change in fortune.

As Joseph completed his turn Sam struck a match and lit a cigar, a blatant infraction of workhouse regulations. But to get this far past the gate Sam must have already bribed the receiving officer, the porter, or both. Joseph started to unfasten his trousers.

Sam said, "That will not be necessary."

Joseph wondered if Sam was impressed, but strangely enough, he did not care. It was the calm of a new understanding. When Joseph lost his hawking licence and any hope of respectable employment, his deformity was a secondary consideration. His most disgusting feature was not an absence of beauty, but an absence of work. Had he earned well, he would always have a place at the table. For Joe Merrick and society at large, the tragedy was not what he was, but what he could have been. Someone useful.

Joseph was excluded from humanity, but also spared its hypocrisy, the mirage of gainful employment and the delusion of hope. He was free from God, free from his family and temporarily free from shame. Suicide absolves life of its failings. He who refuses death demands more of existence.

An envelope of money had arrived after his suicide attempt. The address was not written in a hand Joseph recognised, but could only have come from Uncle Charles. The generous sum seemed like a severance payment. Joseph purchased writing materials and a stamp, his letter found its intended destination and now Sam Thomas, a freak show proprietor, was ready to deliver his verdict.

"A human curiosity is seen for minutes. The punter assumes they work for minutes. But the human curiosity must be seen again, and again, thousands of times. And then there is travel, constant travel. You sleep beneath the stars in summer. You earn well, but you pay a price. To leave the workhouse is easy. To leave society is hard. There are good crowds and bad crowds. The bad crowds leave you trembling. They will curse you, every blasphemy."

"I thought you might be the answer to my prayers."

Sam laughed spontaneously and smiled. "A life on the road as a Freak of Nature, what say you, young man?"

Joseph replied with clarity and conviction, "I am ready for work."

The next morning Joseph collected his father's old suit from the paupers' clothes store and handed back his uniform. Just as he was about to sign out, Harrison swooped and bizarrely told Joseph there was 'No great hurry' and he could 'Stay a while', acting like a desperate hotelier. Joseph signed the line, confirmed his freedom and bade goodbye to Harrison, using language that would have made a navvy blush.

Two large wooden wagons, not unlike gypsy caravans, waited by the front gate. Each wagon was emblazoned with ornate swirling patterns, in yellow, red and green and drawn by two well-kept horses. Sam climbed down from one wagon; a tough but friendly-looking man sat atop the other.

"No luggage then?" quipped Sam.

Sam helped Joseph ascend the wooden steps of his wagon. Joseph reached the top step without losing his balance, but was startled by the sudden arrival of a carriage speeding into the workhouse complex. The horses of Sam's wagon lurched forward and Joseph was about to fall, but someone grabbed him from within the wagon and pulled him inside.

Joseph landed on a soft mound of flesh, the body of an enormous woman. He slid off her breasts and her belly and sat by her side. Joseph felt her breath on top of his head as she peered down to inspect him. As they were sitting it was difficult to estimate her height, but she was definitely a giantess. Her dark brown ponytail was as long as a man's arm.

The coach bounced forward and the journey began. Joseph beheld his other new comrades. Sitting opposite was a man with a crooked body and another man with a skin disease. A non-deformed man, a younger, showier version of Sam, sat to the left of Joseph. The other curiosities eyed him like a fish in a tank, following the introduction of a more colourful specimen. The showy man greeted Joseph with a cheeky smile and little more than a raised eyebrow at the extent of his deformities.

The crooked man was slightly built with dark, receding hair. He held his left shoulder higher than the right.

"Young man, can you guess my act?"

He turned his body ninety degrees to reveal a large, protruding hunchback.

"Let me give you a hunch."

Groans greeted the punchline, suggesting it was often delivered. Though for Joseph, the hunchback was like a man with a grazed knee, boastfully revealing his wound to a man with a severed leg. The showy man began the proper introductions.

"Hunchie, Scaley Boy, Big Mavis. Sam you know, Harry drives the other wagon, and I am Mr Charlie McCallion."

With his disreputable bootlace moustache, low top hat and brown and gold chequered suit, Charlie came across as a good-natured petty criminal, with the low glamour of a card sharp or the seller of a get-rich-quick scheme.

"You must be Joseph Merrick?" said Charlie.

Joseph nodded and noticed that Scaley Boy was staring at him aggressively.

In his suit jacket, open-necked shirt and flat cap, Scaley Boy was dressed like a regular man in his Sunday best. Yet a curious skin disease gave his flesh a pale reptilian quality. Scaley Boy's teeth were chipped and sharp. Joseph wondered if this was home dentistry to complement his act or the consequence of belligerent brawls.

"Mary, Mother of God," said Scaley. "You are one ugly bastard."

The others waited for a response from Joseph.

"That is why I am here."

After a short delay, the troupe broke into laughter, all except Scaley, who continued to glare and seethe.

Charlie uncorked a dark bottle and passed it to Joseph. Joseph took a deep swig, his first taste of alcohol since the daily bottle of porter his father had allowed him at home. He expected ale or port wine, but instead swallowed hard liquor. Joseph suppressed his reflex to gag, as he could see the others were watching him. Mavis gave Joseph a gentle nudge with her elbow because she wanted the bottle.

Joseph watched through a crack in the boards as the wagon travelled through Knighton, Oadby and Great Glen, the small towns and villages surrounding Leicester. He was already in uncharted territory, the furthest he had ever travelled from home, amongst new companions and engaged in mysterious work. Joseph re-examined this troupe of curious vagabonds. Hunchback and Mavis had nodded off. Scaley entered a stupor. Charlie passed the bottle back to Joseph and the euphoria of alcohol warmed his body.

Charlie said to him, "From this moment forth, you are legend."

Dr Vale addressed the Taygetus Eugenics Society at the club in Mayfair. He positioned a pair of callipers above a simian skull proving, beyond doubt, that criminal and primate shared 'cranial kinship'. Vale droned on; ten was the hour. Gilbert fought the onset of sleep. It was a far slimmer crowd, six regulars, plus a new attendee, stout and inscrutable with a scrubbing brush moustache and receding combed-over hair. The man concentrated on Vale's speech, affecting an expression of serious, but blank contemplation. Gilbert ignored him and turned his mind to recent events.

Even after the Leicester debacle, Vale remained convinced that a suitable subject would be found. Every upbeat remark from the little man reminded Gilbert of failure and Vale began to grate in the manner of an evangelical Christian. In response, Gilbert became a regular absentee of Taygetus Eugenics Society meetings under the flimsiest pretext. Gilbert's apathy spread through the group. Members drifted away, some to other eugenics societies. It was ironic that the pursuit of purity was riven by factioneering, yet Gilbert believed that each and every subgroup of eugenics comprised a united body of apathy.

To Gilbert, eugenics was a set of blocked intestines, where the fuel of greatness had been solidified by inaction. The immovable waste product was human destiny, which was becoming more toxic and unappealing by the day. The only movement from anyone who counted was a form of decorous, intellectual ballet dancing. Without some sort of total purge, Gilbert was certain that nothing would change.

"Dr Gilbert Greystone?" said Vale, inviting Gilbert to speak. Gilbert considered refusing, but stepped to the front.

"Several days ago, as I rode in a carriage, I noticed a creature emerge from the gutter, a gigantic rat with the incisor teeth of a walrus. They were stained with blood, the offal of an abattoir, or a kill."

Gilbert's tone was weary, but his visceral storytelling had the men in suspense.

"The rat encroached onto the street and the driver did not spare the horses. I heard the crack of the whip, the splinter of bone and a screech of maimed agony. The rodent's cry pierced the night."

"I watched from the window behind. The wretched creature drew forward on its front legs, dragging its hindquarters. Would it live, would it die? One thing was certain. It would not breed. It could not breed. The vermin had been neutered. I behold everything we have worked for and I wonder ... is our vehicle fit for purpose?"

There was a pause of seconds. Delegates were unsure how to interpret Gilbert's ambiguous speech. The stout newcomer led a round of applause.

Gilbert suddenly realised that his involvement with this rather mediocre society was over. His life at its best was a singular journey, guided by purity of purpose. The involvement with others and therefore reliance on others had diluted his purity, sent him off course, made him less of a man because they were *lesser men*. He must free himself of these people, of Vale, and strike at his yet-to-be-determined moment in history, with a single diamond dagger of will.

Gilbert shook hands with the men as they filtered out, enthused because this was the last time they would meet. The new man waited until last. He approached Gilbert and Vale, pumped their hands and gave his name as Dunham.

"What is your line, Mr Dunham?" asked Vale.

"That is quite a story, sir!"

Gilbert braced himself for another self-aggrandising success yarn.

"My father owned a cannery, Dunham and Co. He died when I was young man and I assumed overall control. My workforce, what a sight! Drunkards, wronglybuilts and weaklings. They were hardly fit to draw breath, let alone complete a day's labour. I once knowingly employed a sane epileptic. After two hours of running messages he bit through his tongue with convulsions. I sold up for the sake of my sanity and invested in architecture. The craftsman is a superior worker and the property his tithe. I turned each penny of my inheritance into a purse of gold."

Dunham, Reginald H.B. Dunham. Many of the magnificent new buildings in the city were constructed by his company.

"I am delighted to make your acquaintance, Mr Dunham," said Gilbert. "Surely 'Sir Reginald' in a matter of time?"

Dunham brushed aside the compliment, determined to finish his monologue.

"I attempted to share my good fortune, Dr Greystone. I thought back to the wrecks of the canning factory and how their lives might be improved. I purchased food parcels for the poorest boroughs, I built sports halls and almshouses. I performed these acts anonymously and sought not one word of thanks. My task was hopeless. If one man rose above the miasma of his surroundings, one hundred more drank themselves to death or contracted syphilis. I came to the inevitable conclusion that those who have the most deserve the most. We are ordained through birth."

Dunham's squandering of wealth on wastrels should have been a source of derision. Instead it reminded Gilbert of his mother's deceit. Gilbert felt a close affinity for Dunham, particularly as his folly had led him to eugenics.

"I am no reader, sir, but when your pamphlet was passed to me, I devoured your words like a banquet. I saw the employees of my cannery in your concise definitions of deficiency. The feeble-minded, idiots and imbeciles, slack-mouthed, drooling, with not the slightest inclination to work. And malformed children sired by the score! I have now a choice: philanthropy or affirmative action. What would it take to sterilise a few of them?"

Gilbert experienced the pleasure rush of a salesman when a client has convinced himself.

"Well, sir, we have asked this question of many workhouse masters. The law can be easily bypassed. The masters themselves are the barrier."

"They lack your strong moral conviction, sir," added Vale. "They require inducements."

"Informal inducements," said Gilbert.

Dunham rolled his eyes, reached into his pocket, pulled out a cheque book and an ornate silver pen. He dashed off a cheque with a well-practised flourish and handed it to Gilbert.

"I wish to become a patron. Is that agreeable?"

The sum was £1000 for the Taygetus Eugenics Society. Gilbert endeavoured to keep his voice steady.

"Sir, with the God-given gift of your patronage, we shall set about purging the race."

Chapter 4 – Beauty

When young Jonas Powell dreamed of joining the infantry, it was not combat he longed for as such, but army discipline. The licentiousness of the average civilian worker disgusted him. When Powell's father was not at work in the shipyards of Selby, he did not draw a sober breath. Soldiers were well known for their drunken carousing, but Powell did not imagine himself as any ordinary private. He aspired to the most spartan conditions and elite regiments, the Coldstream Guards or the Grenadiers.

Aged sixteen, Powell travelled to Leeds and volunteered for service. He astonished the recruitment sergeant by swallowing the Queen's shilling with water, not beer. Powell expected his medical examination to be a formality, only to be informed by the examining physician that the hip he fractured as a child had not properly healed and his right leg was classified lame. Powell returned to Selby, to the shipyards and the slovenly civilian life he despised. He brooded on his options, even considering making passage to America, until in 1844, the North-Eastern Railway company subsumed the Leeds to Selby line. Powell answered a recruitment poster and his stern manner impressed.

In the draconian rules and unbendable regulations of the North-Eastern Railway, Powell found discipline at last. He was pedantic, machine-minded and beloved by management. Over the next thirty years they promoted him through the ranks to station master.

Powell saved his money and did not marry until he was thirty-five. His escalating salary allowed him to move his wife and children to the Chapeltown district of Leeds. Chapeltown was already home to an affluent middle class, but the construction of new houses and suburbanisation allowed entry for the aspirant lower middle. Powell purchased a spacious stone terrace on Francis Street, with a small front garden. It was a slightly crooked property, sandwiched between two more symmetrical terraces, like the irregular piece of bread in a sliced loaf. Powell was also a marginal status inferior to his neighbours, both merchants, with whom he had nothing in common. Powell did not care; he did not care for much. He thought all that mattered were the operational procedures of North-Eastern Railway. His daughter's predicament was the test of everything.

Every night after the evening meal, Jonas Powell and his wife retired to the front room. Mother occupied an easy chair and set about her needlework. What she lacked in skill, she made up for in industry and the walls held more than two dozen of her framed patterns. She swallowed a tablet in between threads, one of her little pills from the sanitary chemist on shopping parade to help with her nerves.

There was no talking. Jonas Powell occupied a wooden chair and scraped the blade of his cut-throat razor up and down a sharpening strop. He went about his task with serious application as if preparing the blade was an extension of his scared station master's duties. His midnight-blue uniform jacket hung in the corner of the room like a ceremonial robe and his braided peaked cap rested on the altar of the mantelpiece next to his bible, the company rule book, 167 yellowed pages and subsections, meticulously read and committed to heart.

Mother flinched and jabbed the needle into her thumb. The young men were back from work. Sidney Powell stood by his father, who he closely resembled, being tall and raw-boned with a craggy pugilistic face. The younger brother, Archie, trailed behind Sidney, smiling weakly. Archie was a pudgy child-man, with a nervous simper. Both brothers wore their midnight-blue uniforms, father having eased their passage into the company. Father continued scraping the razor. Mother sucked blood from her thumb. Her embroidery motif read, 'There's no place like home'.

Upstairs, Alice Powell stayed alone in her bedroom. She stared out of the window across the rear yard to the backs of the terraces on Cowper Street. Alice took a piece of bread from her pocket and nibbled at a corner. She had taken to eating meals in her room, bits and pieces smuggled from the pantry when the others were at work or when mother was shopping. This would have been unthinkable before, as Father demanded all meals must be taken at the table. But then, a lot had changed.

It was dusk and light grew dim. Alice left the window and examined the contents of her room, the unemptied chamber pot, the soiled bedsheets, unwashed for so long they had given up their stink and a single cupboard containing the garments from her former life.

When she left school aged twelve, Alice was advised by a teacher to apply for employment as a trainee clerk because, in progressive Britain, such work was now available to bright young women. Alice found a clerical position at the Town Hall 'dotting i's' and 'crossing t's'. Everyone told her it was a good job, but Alice hated the tedium of the work. She believed she had no other option but to persevere, until a life-changing transformation occurred in her body. Although she was always pretty, Alice blossomed into a beautiful young woman.

Alice learned of this transformation not from her reflection in the mirror, but from the reaction of men. They held doors open, tipped their hats, jousted with their elbows to sit near to her on the tram. They stared at her, awestruck, as if she possessed the answer to their every question. When they eventually plucked up the courage to speak to her, they blushed and stammered over their words and wrung their hands, as if her beauty had enfeebled them.

There was a corresponding change among her girlfriends. Some of them dropped Alice altogether; perhaps they hated her apparent lack of effort. Alice did not use colour or powder as she was naturally beautiful, with a pristine complexion, an intelligent face and sparking, light blue eyes. Her hair was long, black as ebony, tightly and densely curled. It spoke of her inner vivacity. Alice possessed a near flawless physique, with her breast of curved marble, buttocks of ripe peach, an achingly slim waist and beautiful, shapely legs. She would have surely excelled at any athletic discipline had she the slightest inclination for sport.

Briggate in Leeds town centre was renowned as the best shopping street in Yorkshire and home to The Thornton Arcade, a glass-roofed cathedral of retail. One Saturday, for a dare, Alice sauntered into the most exclusive ladies' boutique 'Pour Femme' and asked for a full-time position. The proprietor, Mrs Marber, a former ballerina who had married an industrialist, offered her a job on the spot. Alice left the dull world of clerking forever.

The boutique was a finishing school of sorts, with Mrs Marber tutoring Alice on etiquette, how one should address a customer as 'Madame' not 'love' and so on. Much to the delight of Mrs Marber, Alice sold huge quantities of merchandise, double the amount of any other assistant. Alice could not account for her success as she did not consider herself a gifted saleswoman. Mrs Marber remarked somewhat cryptically that "The customer buys the vendor." Alice earned more than her older brothers at the railway and on her best week of commission earned as much as her father.

Alice bought fine clothes with which to display her delectable physique, preferring the pencil dress to the crinoline or the bustle. She was one of the few women to possess a corseted figure without recourse to torturously tight lacing. Men followed her wherever she went and Alice sometimes wore her most figure-revealing pencil dress to cause a commotion on Chapeltown Road. Her motivation was not vanity, but fascination. She genuinely wanted to understand why it was happening. Alice was not obsessed with the other sex, as many of her friends seemed to be. She kissed a few boys from curiosity, but the only men who really interested Alice were those who showed no interest in her.

Alice opened the cupboard in her bedroom, picked out a black shawl and wrapped it around the lower part of her face, beneath her eyes. This enabled her to brave the long mirror on the inside door. She raised the grubby night dress she had worn all day, every day for a week, hoisting it high, holding the hem beneath her eyeline. Alice's body was still beautiful; it would elicit the longing of man, or the envy of woman. Her clothes would still complement her body, but any attempt to dress well would be doomed by the condition of her face.

By staying in her room and becoming invisible, Alice hoped she would be forgotten, because then they would leave her alone. There would be no more children singing songs or throwing things at the house. No more ironic wolf whistles or marriage proposals shouted in laughter. People thought the Powells were odd. It was a view shared by Alice herself. But now some strange illness, curse or pure bad luck had transformed the daughter into the oddest of them all.

Alice, distracted by a noise, lowered her nightdress. She recognised the distinctive footsteps of the menfolk, the three of them ascending the stairs in single file formation. Their rapid approach had the tempo of a military quick march. Instinct told Alice to fear and she darted beneath the bedsheets like a frightened animal. The door opened and Alice sensed the men encircling the bed. She kept the bedsheets over her head and the shawl tight around her face. Father called 'Alice' in a tone of voice he might use to instruct her to fetch him his newspaper. Alice remained motionless. Father was in no mood for games.

He pulled the top sheet from her grip and reached for the shawl. Alice rolled out of bed on the other side as her brothers moved in. Sidney got there first. Alice raked his face with her nails and he pushed her against the wall. Sidney balled his right hand into a fist and swung for her jaw, but Alice ducked Sidney's punch and his knuckles smashed into the wall, blasting a crater in the plaster work. Archie grabbed hold of Alice from behind and trussed her arms. He was strong and his grip was unbreakable. Sidney aimed his fist at her defenceless face and Alice winced in anticipation of the hammer blow. Father shouted, "No!" Sidney lowered his quivering fist and grinned as if great sport was imminent.

Father gestured for Archie to guide Alice to her knees. Sidney also got in behind her and yanked back her hair to expose her throat. Father crouched down in front of her and extended the blade of a razor. Alice thought Father was going to slice her gullet, but instead he tore the shawl from her face and exposed the hated beard. It was two inches in length and unkempt from lack of washing. Archie whispered, "Sorry." Father began his haphazard barbery, hacking at the hair with the razor and ripping it free. He scraped on and on. Alice was blinded by tears.

After the shaving, it took Alice several days before she was able to examine her face in the mirror. It was not a pretty sight. Her cheeks were rare as underdone beef and father had cut her several times with the razor. The scars were the width of penny coin slots, covered with dark red scabs and itching like angry insect bites. Several clusters of facial hair remained. Alice could not tell if this was new hair or if Father had simply missed some. She knew from experience that any previous attempt to remove the whiskers simply resulted in faster, thicker growth. Sure enough, within a week, Alice had the beard of a rugged outdoorsman.

She no longer left her bedroom at all, although some concessions were made to her basic needs. Mother placed food and drink outside the room once a day, meaning it was no longer necessary to pilfer from the pantry, or descend the stairs. Whenever Alice left her chamber pot outside the room it was emptied and returned. A washing bowl and towel were placed outside the door from time to time.

Alice slept through days and nights. When awake and with no reading material, she distracted herself by watching the backs of the houses on Cowper Street, observing the neighbours and their commonplace lives. Wives and mothers pegging out the washing, children playing after school, fathers and husbands returning home from work, the ritual of the evening meal, bedtime. Alice discovered that it was simultaneously possible to observe human society, whilst being totally excluded from that society. It was simultaneously possible to long for inclusion, yet also resent the herd.

Alice believed that her former beauty had estranged her from own family. She had been a butterfly perched on the surface of their dull, solid, railway world, tragically disabled by disfigurement at the moment of flight. It was as if her beard was revenge for daring to be different and it was obvious that Sidney, at least, took great pleasure in her punishment. Yet if beauty threatened to elevate Alice above her family, disfigurement had brought her crashing back to earth. Afflicted with the beard, she was an immobile invalid, whose limbs could be positioned this way or that, a burden but not a threat. She was safely controlled, safely contained, a shut-in who could be smothered by malignant love if necessary. Alice supposed that Mother still loved her because she prepared the meals and emptied the buckets of waste. But then, Mother was the type of woman who would love a caged bird, not for its beauty or potential for flight, but because it was a captive like her.

She was still only twenty-one years of age, yet despite all the misfortune of her life, Alice could not accept that this squalid reality was her destiny. The people outside were no more forgiving than her father and brothers, but the world was a bigger place to hide.

Alice pulled off her dirty nightdress and threw on an old sky-blue bustle as if dressing for an urgent appointment. She located the overnight bag she had purchased for fourteen shillings but never used, packed a pencil dress, two shawls and some undergarments. She also packed her two most impractical but expensive Artistic Dresses, hoping to sell them back to Mrs Marber at Pour Femme and use the money for food and lodging. Alice tied her greasy black hair in a ponytail and wrapped a shawl around her face. She about was to open the bedroom door when she heard the stampeding approach of her father and her brothers.

Father burst in, flanked by Sidney and Archie. They all wore shirt sleeves, in readiness for restraining her. Archie applied a bearhug from behind and forced Alice to her knees, just like last time. Sidney grabbed her ponytail and yanked her head back. Father tore Alice's shawl and muffler away, exposing the beard. Alice croaked, "I can't breathe," and Sidney released her ponytail reluctantly, at Father's instruction.

Father took the razor from his pocket and extended the blade. Alice kept her head still to make it easy for him. But as Father prepared his left hand to take hold of her beard, Alice lunged forward and sank her teeth into his index finger.

He cried in pain and dropped the razor, whilst attempting to prise Alice's mouth open with the fingers of his free hand. Alice shook her head like a ratting dog. Archie released Alice, assuming she would release Father. Though once free, Alice rolled like a crocodile, with her father's finger in her mouth. He fell with and rolled with her, emitting a frightened, high-pitched squeal.

Sidney booted Alice on the left elbow and the sharp pain caused her to relinquish her bite. Father scrambled to his feet with his finger chewed to pieces and ran from the room, wailing in agony. Sidney dived on Alice, pinned her shoulders with his knees and wrapped his strong, wiry hands around her throat, crushing his thumbs into her windpipe. Alice thought her eyes were going to explode. "Oh well," she told herself, "I'm going to die."

Archie attached himself to Sidney's back like a blubbery octopus and pulled him away. Sidney reached behind him, grabbed Archie's arm and threw him over his shoulder. The floor nearly gave way beneath him. Archie got his arms up to protect his face as Sidney rained punches into his soft, doughy forearms.

Alice heaved for breath and regained her senses. She picked up the razor from the floor and rose to her feet a second before Sidney rose to his. She swung the shimmering blade of the razor, catching Sidney by surprise, slicing through the skin of his cheekbone, downwards, diagonally, towards his top lip. Sidney's cheek hung from his face like the sleeve of a vagrant's jacket. He pressed the flesh back in place on reflex, as if catching a fastened towel that had slipped from his waist. Blood arrived a moment later and when it flowed it gushed, oozing through Sidney's fingers in a crimson river, down his shirt, onto the floor boards. Sidney's legs crumpled and he smacked his head against the wardrobe on the way down to unconscious oblivion.

She hurdled over Archie, who was crying and writhing on the floor like a child in a futile tantrum, and followed the trail of her father's blood downstairs to the front door. The door was open and a scrum of twittering neighbours blocked the front gate. Mother watched Alice from her chair in the living room. The room was a gallery of her tapestries. Trite slogans and lopsided flowers, framed in glass. 'There's no place like home', 'A penny saved is a penny earned', 'A stitch in time saves nine'. Mother held her latest offering to Alice. Her smile was empty and her eyes were glazed from the pills. The legend read: Every daughter is her Mother's rose.

Alice seized the frame and flung it to the floor, picked up a wooden stool and smashed the work to pieces, as if beating a snake to death. She held the stool by a single leg and swung it at the wall, destroying a line of tapestry displays. Mother ducked and cowered by the sideboard and begged her to stop. Alice pirouetted for extra momentum and flung the stool through the front window, showering the neighbours with shattered glass. She sprinted through the back door, heading north, up Cross Francis Street, past Cowper Street into the expanse of fields between Chapeltown and Newton. It was dark and the grass was wet with dew. She had never run so fast in her life. She thought she was floating. She thought she could outrun them all.

She was felled by a rugby tackle around the legs. Men pressed in to restrain her, neighbours. Alice kicked and screamed. She clawed at them and bit them. Father's flesh was still imbedded in her teeth. She was becoming a lunatic. She was becoming an animal.

Chapter 5 – The Freaks of Nature

Lincoln's Easter Pleasure Fair certainly lived up to its name. More than fifty attractions pitched up in a field on the outskirts of town with coconut shies, shooting galleries and gingerbread stalls alongside chestnut wagons, drinking booths and waxworks. Steam roundabouts were the major new attraction, exciting carousels of spinning mechanical horses revolving to the command of pipe organs. Fortune tellers did a roaring trade and snake oil merchants peddled their wares, like Dr Longstaff with his Cure-All Pills and Cretan Bull virility tonic. Scantily clad young women paraded, strolling seductively around the showground, attracting attention, leading crowds to the fighting booth. Sam Thomas, however, thought parading was a bunk and put his faith in his barker, Charlie McCallion.

Charlie placed a grenadelike firecracker on the ground in front of him, put a match to the taper and covered his ears. The report drew the attention of a sizeable crowd. They were greeted by the sight of Charlie, with his brown and gold chequered suit and disreputable bootlace moustache, standing in front of the novelty booth.

Flimsy wooden boards had been pieced together for a superficially impressive frontage, eight feet high and fourteen feet wide. The boards were covered with ornate, swirling patterns, like multi-coloured shooting stars in mysterious green, sluttish red and seductive yellow. The colour scheme was not too dissimilar to the other lurid attractions, but the sign above promised the most salacious spectacle of all: The Freaks of Nature. Charlie commenced his dooring routine announcing the arrival of "... The most remarkable human wonders on earth. Beast men, oddities, defects of birth. You all will be amazed, I wager. When presented with the Freaks of Nature!"

A dozen punters lined up, an even mix of men and women. The men wore their Sunday suits and bowler hats. The women wore their boater hats, best shawls and dresses. There were courting couples and newlyweds, workers up for fun; one couple brought two children, a boy and a girl.

"A good, clean show, for intelligent families," Charlie assured them.

The punters entered the booth from the left-hand side. Admittance was one penny for adults, a ha'penny for children. Harry was the money-taker. He was tall, powerfully built, and clean-shaven with a new bowler hat, courtesy of a rude and rowdy punter in Boston, who challenged him to fight and lost. Harry was tough, but his boyish face lent him a pleasing aspect. In contrast to Sam and Charlie, Harry rarely said a word.

They followed Charlie through the ornate wooden facade into the tented area behind, which was dimly lit by lamplight and partitioned into curtained areas. There was a damp but not unpleasant smell from the straw on the ground. The tent appeared to have a hermetic seal, its own singular atmosphere of tense anticipation, emanating from the promise of human defilement.

Each curtain was embroidered with the name of the curiosity. Charlie stood by the first curtain for 'The Hunchback'. The punters stopped giggling and waited in silence for his first announcement.

"There once was a fellow known as Peter, drove a wagon. Whistled like a bird, he did. Liked to look at maidens, did our Peter, when his eyes should have been on the road. Suddenly, a gypsy boy steps in front of his wagon. That boy was crushed to pulp!"

Charlie punched the palm of his hand and the echo of his flesh sent a shiver through the crowd. Charlie put his arms in a cradle and acted out the story.

"He held the boy to his wailing mother. She threw down her bundle and cursed poor Peter. "May you be stricken by bodily torment, like my poor broken boy!" And, folks, she was good to her word. Because from that moment forth, he became The Hunchback!"

Charlie pulled back the curtain and revealed Hunchie, with a riding crop and horse's rein in hand. Hunchie wore a white smock over his trousers and turned slowly to reveal the outline of his canon ball hump. Charlie stepped in behind Hunchie, paused to draw out the tension, then lifted the smock. Hunchie was indeed a genuine hunchback with a pronounced curvature of the spine. His deformity was far more severe than the average birth defect, but as Hunchie had good skin, the paying punters were deprived of any interesting warts, boils or skin diseases.

"Pity poor Hunchback, twisted by a gypsy curse."

Hunchie rarely said more and didn't need to. Sam regarded him as a solid opening turn, professional, without vanity and happy with a short routine. Charlie dropped Hunchie's curtain and darted to the 'Bride For Goliath' partition. His fast, all-in-one movement regained the attention of the crowd.

"From twisted man to titanic woman! Twenty pounds when she was born, six foot tall by the age of twelve. And by the time she reached full womanhood, this Cumbrian giantess ..." Charlie took a deep breath, "stood seven feet eight inches and weighed more than forty-five stones!"

Charlie's outrageous lie created laughter, but as Mavis was six foot three and more than twenty stones, she would not disappoint.

"Married a standard size fellow, she did and though the exact details of their wedding night must remain sacrosanct, the precious secret of husband and wife, by morning he was dead, every bone in his body broken. Too dangerous to lie with man, her only hope is betrothal to a giant. Behold Big Mavis, a bride for Goliath!"

Mavis sat on a stool and stared into a hand-held vanity mirror whilst brushing her long brown hair. She was enormous, twice the size of a normal woman, and the crowd whispered amongst themselves, a good sign. Suddenly, Mavis rose from her stool to her full soaring height, dwarfing all in attendance, including the men, and revealed the full horror of her wedding dress.

When it was first tailored, the dress was white as virgin snow. It was now the grey of sleet and Mavis's huge frame strained at the seams which threatened to burst at any moment. In the outside world this would have been an unspeakable travesty; in the novelty booth it was perfect harmony. Unsettling, disturbing, wrong, the ideal costume for a bizarre bride.

"One day my prince will come," said Mavis. She crossed her arms, pumped up the meat of her biceps and added, "He'd best be the size of an omnibus!"

There was chattering among the punters, some nervous laughter. As Charlie dropped the curtain he heard the pop of a cork. Mavis loved her whiskey and seized every opportunity.

"From the highest bride to the lowest beast, the slithering pit of the jungle!" Charlie directed attention to Scaley Boy's curtain.

"Brave Lord Barnaby set sail for New Guinea, to explore exotic, untamed lands. Three days into the deepest, dangerous jungle he came upon a slaughtered tribe! These poor souls met death not by man, but by monster! Men and women, eaten to the bone, by fangs, yes, giant fangs! Yet amongst the pit of bodies and skeletons he found one living creature. Stand well back for Scaley Boy!"

Scaley lay face down on a grey woollen blanket, in a pair of thigh-length khaki trousers, with the bottoms scissored into triangles of teeth. His props were three rabbit pelts, caked in chickens' blood, and a cow's thigh bone obtained from an abattoir in Ipswich. Scaley flicked his arms to his sides, flung back his head and hissed like a serpent. The nearest punters jumped back. Scaley writhed on the floor, exposing his back and contorting his body with some dexterity. His pale, reptilian skin disease covered his entire body. Scaley also shaved his head to complement his act.

A distant note from a penny whistle entered the tent. Scaley froze, then swayed his head from side to side, mesmerised by a soothing tune, not unlike the flute of a lullaby. The punters looked around, attempting to ascertain the source of the music. It was Hunchie behind his curtain, with a blanket over his head to muffle the sound. They would never know.

"Music makes him as tranquil as a lamb," said Charlie.

Scaley swayed his head, sank down to the floor and curled up to rest. Charlie gestured to the final curtain in the far right-hand corner of the tent.

"You have enjoyed the whores desserts," announced Charlie, always mispronouncing hors d'oeuvres. "The bowl of soup before the meat and potatoes. If you are infirm of constitution, please God do not proceed. The mere sight of the next fellow has induced heart failure."

It was likely to be a silly anti-climax, but the punters wanted to prolong the fun and trusted Charlie enough to follow him. The final exhibit occupied its own special enclave. The curtain was larger than the others and more elaborately designed, with an ornate silver legend on a royal blue fabric, advertising 'The Elephant Man'.

"A pretty young wifey walks home from the fair. She's expecting a youngling, her head is full of dreams. Little did she reckon upon a nightmare. An elephant breaks free, stampeding straight for her, hooves of thunder, tusks of ivory, teeth of a giant devil. 'Watch out, missus, for the love of God!' Only just escapes with her life. As for the youngling? He was born, and he grew and he grew and he grew. Treasured by his mother, but tarnished by the beast. I give you, The Elephant Man!"

Charlie pulled away the curtain and there stood Joseph Merrick, naked but for a sort of toga. Not one of the punters could undersell their shock. Their eyes darted between his hills of deformity, his bulging face, his colossal skull, his massively oversized hand, his tree-trunk calves and hooflike feet, the curious circle of bone around his right shoulder. Joseph began a slow 360 degree rotation, displaying the weathered sandstone of his back. Apart from the knotted flesh of his buttocks and his non-deformed private parts, Joseph's full body was on show.

Seeing Joseph for the first time was a sensory overload, the equivalent of a half bottle of whisky downed in one. Men swayed, disoriented, as if disembarking from the merry-go-round. Women were on the verge of tears. The two children in attendance hid behind the curtains of their mother's dress. The atmosphere was one of unease, even dread. Nature had brought forth a creature like no other and the onlookers did not know what to do with themselves.

The revelation of Joseph's body was rarely accompanied by mockery, partly due to the toga. He no longer wore the garments of modern man, or the uniform of a worker, which meant 'they' could not mock his ludicrous incursion into 'their' human society. Joseph was as timeless as a face of rock, as unworldly as a fragment of meteor.

"My friends, do not be alarmed. You are safe with me and cannot be harmed. I come not to scare, but to share a story of how a boy born an elephant became a man ... My name is Joseph Merrick."

Joseph had given this crowd the most awe-inspiring sight in the history of the British freak show and now he was giving them more. Men, women and children were agog.

"My friend speaks the truth. My mother was frightened by an elephant. But she recovered, in time for my birth. And there I arrived, perfect as a pearl, with not a blemish upon my skin. But the elephant had slept and awakened. Mother could only watch as my body ..." Joseph intentionally let his voice falter at this point, as Sam had coached him.

"Not a doctor could help. We turned to our faith. Despite all, they were happy times.

"But then, Mother, God rest her, was taken by an angel. I was bereft and poor. Four years I spent in the workhouse. Long hard years. I immersed myself in the bible, I prayed for salvation. Then, praise be, I received this invitation, to travel the land and tell my tale. I am happy and free from pain. I am sure Mother is watching from heaven. Indeed, the day she left the earth, I was handed an envelope containing her poem."

The poem was Sam's suggestion, but the words were Joseph's. He knew the text by heart.

"I was frightened by an elephant and now you look like one.
How will you cope and build a life, now that I am gone?
By sticking to your bible, respect the golden rule.
Be kind of heart, and good to all and be nobody's fool.
The Elephant he changed my life and yours that fateful day.
But I would not change my little boy in any other way.
By the time you read this simple verse, I will have surely died.
But despite your crippled arms and legs, son, you are my pride."

Joseph bowed his enormous head a fraction to signify the end. The punters, for their coarse manners, broke into polite applause. Charlie replaced the curtain. Harry entered from the front of the booth, holding a jute sack. Charlie said all collected monies would be put towards Joseph's 'medical care and medicines'. Coins flew in. Most of the nobbings would be pocketed by Sam with the rest split between the troupe to be squandered on strong drink and hard tobacco.

Charlie opened the door to the right of the booth and gestured 'this way out' to the punters. Some raced away like giddy children in search of their friends, to bring them to the must-see attraction. Others staggered off in search of the drinking booth, in need of a stiff one.

Sam positioned himself at the front of the booth, dooring. "Look here!" he exclaimed. "Satisfaction guaranteed!" Within seconds a new line had formed outside the 'Freaks of Nature'. Charlie took over from Sam and his patter and enticed more punters forward.

Inside the tent Joseph sat with a towel draped across his shoulders, like a prizefighter in between rounds. He ate a piece of bread and a Cox apple, making the most of the five minutes before he showed again. He was startled by a hand on his shoulder. Sam had slipped into the booth. He beamed at Joseph with tobacco-ridden teeth and said, "Let's send them home happy."

Sam had respect for the paying punter. He believed they should be well fleeced, but well entertained and should always go home with something, a small piece of swag or an indelible memory. If the punter left with nothing, the resentment of one town would be harvested in the next. No punter who paid to see The Elephant Man would ever feel cheated.

"It is a curious thing," said Joseph, "to have done well."

Sam replied, "When I was a boy, I watched James Burke batter Bendingo, seventy-six rounds to a draw. I thought no other man could withstand such punishment. Then I met you. The punishment kindled a fire. It's grown with every crowd, every town, every penny of your pay. Every fighter wants to be remembered in history. They also want to be rich. That is the prize for the pain."

Charlie led a new crowd into the tent as Sam slipped out of the booth. Joseph finished his towelling. It was time for the next round.

Joseph showed more than thirty times that day. The crowds were boisterous but well-behaved. Only one drunken lout acted up. A subtle rabbit punch from Harry subdued him.

When the light faded and crowds dispersed, Joseph changed back into his everyday clothes, a functional black trouser and suit jacket combination that Sam had purchased from another showman. Joseph had taken great pleasure in cutting up his father's old suit and the fragments of material were now employed as general purpose cleaning rags.

The troupe gathered together in the tent. Harry broke open a crate of ale and handed out the bevvies. Sam laid out bread and meat from paper wrappers with extra for Mavis. They all tucked in, laughing, swapping stories of the day. Hunchie played his penny whistle and even though Joseph and Charlie had been talking all day, the ale soothed their throats and they joined in the singing: *Scarborough Fair*, *The Drunken Sailor*, *The Wild Rover*, *Early One Morning*, *John Barleycorn*, *The Maid of Amsterdam*.

After a good few drinks, Scaley reached into his bundle and produced a small rag doll and a lady's hat pin. Scaley said the doll was a hexed voodoo doll and if anyone displeased him, he willed their face onto the effigy. The victim would suffer a variety of agonies such as 'dysentery, syphilis, cancer of the rectum, the choice is mine'. Sam asked if Scaley had anyone in mind. Scaley stared at Joseph and said, "Disrespectful usurpers."

Mavis said, "You're a little pansy who plays with dollies. You are not a Scaley boy, you are a Scaley girl."

Scaley jabbed the pin into the doll repeatedly, muttering, "All of you. This is all of you." Accidentally skewering his hand, he yelped in pain, causing much laughter. It was the banter of the ignorant and the damned, but it passed the time.

The troupe camped behind the tent, where the horses also grazed. Charlie, Hunchie, Scaley and Joseph slept in one wagon, Sam and Harry in the other. Mavis slept in a separate tent pitched beside. Joseph did not need much room as he sat upright to sleep, with a blanket wrapped around him and a rolled-up overcoat for a pillow. Even with the others snoring beside him, Joseph always slept like a baby.

Next morning, after washing in the communal water bucket, Sam said it was pulling-down time. Most of the other showmen had already departed and the field was covered with yellow grass imprints of their wagons, rides and stalls. Empty brown food papers drifted here and there in the breeze.

Mavis remained inside her tent. She had a terrible temper in the mornings and Sam usually let her rise of her own accord, preferring to be a few minutes behind schedule than awaken the wrath of a giantess. Sam volunteered Hunchie to hurry her along. Hunchie tentatively prised open the flap of Mavis's tent.

Sam said, "Give her a nudge."

Hunchie reluctantly patted Mavis, but withdrew his hand as if something had bitten him. Joseph was close by. He reached into the tent with his good hand and touched Mavis's calf. Her flesh was ice cold and mortified.

Hunchie removed his cap and held it to his sternum.

Chapter 6 – Eye of the Storm

The troupe arrived in good time for Cambridge Midsummer Fair. Pitches were first come, first served at the rural showground and Sam Thomas's 'Freaks of Nature' secured a potentially lucrative central position. Sam had been in the business for years, but was still considered an outsider, a flattie, by many of the showmen and the families who were born to this way of life. Sam was extremely circumspect about his early days in the business. Rumour had it that he was once a travelling comedian, with humour as dry as gunpowder.

Harry's muscular presence deterred any protests about the chosen pitch, which on this occasion occupied the ground next to Brady's Ghost Show.

Harry provided the muscle in more ways than one. Harry was the gaff lad, a wizard with carpentry and building-up. He could erect the wooden frontage of the booth in just a couple of hours. Charlie helped Harry stake out the tent to the rear. Scaley, Hunchie and Joseph helped set up inside. When the booth was finished, the men passed a bottle between them in the midday sun, grateful for the hardships of a showman's life, for avoiding the confinement of a factory on this fine summer's day. Hunchie complained about Sam conveniently disappearing off to the railway station and leaving them to the heavy work, but everyone knew the importance of his mission.

"What of this new acquisition?" asked Scaley. "This belle?"

"Sam said only that he knew a man, who knew a man, who knew an *exotic maiden*."

Charlie's tone of voice evoked sex on a faraway desert island and for a moment Joseph was lost in magic.

Scaley said, "However curiously deformed she is, I hope she's got big 'uns."

The showground was now a shanty town of wooden booths, wagons, tents and mechanical rides. Joseph saw Sam's wagon approach along the central thoroughfare.

Sam drew the reins and eased his horses, Sandy and Belter, to a halt. Harry petted the horses' snouts and gave them each an apple. Sam gestured for Joseph and the others to give him some room and opened the door of the wagon. A woman of normal shape and size backed onto the steps. Her yellowy, baggy dress looked like a cast-off, as did her light brown shawl and muffler. Despite the unflattering cut of her clothes, it was apparent that this young woman possessed a shapely physique. Joseph wondered if Sam had hired a beautiful, normal woman and intended to dress her up under a tenuous curiosity premise.

The woman made an extra effort to hold the shawl tightly around her face, yet she slipped as she stepped to the ground, her hand came free and Joseph caught a glimpse of her dark, luxuriant beard. The woman loitered by the side of the booth whilst Sam gathered the men in the tent, like a sergeant major addressing an unruly platoon.

"Her name is Alice or 'Miss Powell' to you. Rule number one, no touching. Rule number two, no funny business. Rule number three ..."

Scaley announced, "A shilling for the first man up!" and flipped a coin, but before Scaley caught his shilling Sam slapped him hard across the face.

"... Rule number three, no teasing. And watch your mouth because Alice will give you worse."

Joseph prepared behind his curtain. He liked to imagine the crowd in front of him and rehearse at least one run-through of his act as it helped him to deal with his nerves and anxieties. Joseph noticed Alice watching him through a gap in the curtain and beckoned her inside. She entered cautiously, keeping the shawl tight around her face, just beneath her sparkling blue eyes. Joseph could not read her expression, but assumed she would be less horrified than the average normal, being attuned to the oddity of her own condition.

"Hello. I am Joseph Merrick," he said, as if they had just met at a tea party. "How do you do?"

Alice did not reply.

"You are the bearded lady?"

Alice nodded.

Joseph was at a loss for how to continue the conversation and blurted out the first words that came to mind.

"Let the dog see the rabbit?"

Alice took great offence and left immediately. Joseph limped after her, forgetting his stick.

He found her by the wagons and horses, stroking Belter's snout. When she had finished petting the horses, Alice sat down by the wheel of the wagon and folded up her knees to her chest, like the lonely girl no one would play with. Away from his safe den of the performance tent, Joseph was suddenly lost for words. Apart from his mother, sister and a few words with Mavis, he had hardly conversed with a woman in his life.

Alice placed the index finger of each hand under her shawl and pulled it down. Her beard was as black as ebony, two inches in length. It was neat and tidy, but Joseph dare not ask if she trimmed it. Despite the beard, it was possible to determine the contours of her face. By the standards of normality she was both a beauty and a freak. Joseph estimated she was twenty-three or twenty-four, a couple of years older than he.

"I apologise for my flippant remark," said Joseph. "It is not an easy task. I remember my first night here ..."

"How can you subject yourself to this?" Alice gestured around her. "Parading yourself before others for the purpose of amusement?"

It was a tough question. Joseph replied, "I believe I contain two people, the man and the actor. The actor performs, the man observes from within."

"You are a man who has accepted life as a fool."

Despite her remark, Joseph sensed it would be allowable to sit near Alice. He leant his shoulder to the wagon and slid to the ground.

"This is my work. Without it I am destitute. I'll wager you are no stranger to hardship?"

"What do you presume to know of me?"

"That you are here to work. We are colleagues."

Alice laughed and shook her head. Joseph quickly countered, "I presume you know what it is to be shut away?"

Alice's demeanour changed in an instant. She seemed to be lost in a memory of pain.

"I endured a form of confinement, at the workhouse," said Joseph. "I was not quite a prisoner, I was free to leave. I thought I could escape my condition, by escaping from the world outside. But there was no escape. They say that the only place of tranquillity is the 'eye of the storm'. Here we are at the centre, hidden among everyone."

Alice looked deep into Joseph's eyes. She looked beyond his body. It was a strange experience, enchanting, unsettling.

Joseph heard shouts from expectant thrillseekers. The punters were here. It was time to show. Joseph clambered to his feet, somewhat unsteadily. Alice got to her feet and supported his forearm. She was obviously a good sort, helping a cripple. Joseph felt the soothing warmth of her hand, like the warmth of freshly baked bread, melting through his shirt.

Joseph directed Alice back into the tent, "ladies first". Alice stepped inside without retying her shawl. Sam, Charlie, Harry, Hunchie and Scaley were waiting in line and greeted her arrival with polite nods of the head. Joseph respected her courage, as unveiling her beard was the equivalent of a normal standing naked in public. Sam tipped his hat, then left the tent with Harry. Scaley and Hunchie got behind their curtains.

Charlie outstretched his hand and introduced himself. Alice shook his hand weakly, taken aback by the strangeness of events. Charlie directed Alice to her space and Joseph followed. There was a sturdy wooden stool, Mavis's hairbrush and mirror. Joseph had not seen the props since the big woman's demise.

Charlie said, "You have these rudimentary materials, but soon you will have a silken ball gown." Joseph reckoned Sam would not provide an expensive dress until he was certain Alice would not do a bunk.

"What shall I say?" asked Alice, nervously.

"Nothing for now," replied Charlie. "Just sit, relax and smile. Joseph, what would you advise?"

Joseph was flattered that Charlie sought his counsel and felt like a mature veteran.

"Imagine you are preparing for an outing to the park. Make your final preparations in the mirror. Make this image clear in your mind and lose yourself in your own reflection."

Charlie added, "If any ruffians misbehave, you are protected here by knights of the road." Charlie's verbosity made Alice smile, revealing pearly teeth and full red lips beneath her dark facial hair. Whatever ordeal she previously had endured, it had not diminished her health.

Alice bunched the dress around her lower back and retied the cotton belt cord so it was a tighter fit, showing the arc of her ample breasts and the slimness of her waist. Her collarbones were already exposed, although Alice gestured to the top of the dress and teased the buttons in her fingers.

"Should I, the buttons?" she asked.

"Oh no, no, no, no, no," stammered Charlie, but then reconsidered. "One button at most."

Alice opened one button to reveal an inch of cleavage. Joseph felt like a man looking over the edge of a tower, consumed by the urge to fall.

Sam's preliminary patter attracted a decent crowd to the front of the booth. Charlie's second effort brought more. Charlie entered the tent with ten to fifteen punters, an even mix of women and men and some children, a typical crowd. Hunchie's display lasted a little longer than usual because of an impromptu question from a child, "How are your shirts made?" Charlie closed the curtain on Hunchie's section to end his segment.

Joseph watched Alice's curtain through a gap in his own. It was yet to be embroidered with her name and had been turned back to front, concealing the 'Bride For Goliath' legend.

"And now," ad-libbed Charlie, "something very special. A remarkable young lady. A very beautiful young lady. She was perfect as a Goddess of Greece, almost too beautiful. God gave her a test, an affliction. A terrible, dreadful affliction. He cursed her face, sullied her rose. Even her own mother didn't know her. Will beauty shine through the darkest shadow? Behold, Alice, The Bearded Lady!"

Charlie unveiled the debutante. There was a sharp intake of breath. Joseph watched Alice. She fluffed her ebony curls with the brush and smiled into the mirror. She entered the trancelike state where performer and act become one. Her distant gaze and self-assurance surpassed the absurdity of the gimmick.

Charlie addressed the crowd. “Tell me, my friends, in all your years, has anyone seen such a beard on so rare a beauty?”

The crowd entered a trance. Joseph entered a trance of his own. He had entirely forgotten to change into his toga.

Alice stayed one week, then two. She took to performing, but kept her own company. She had a silent intensity, a fire behind the eyes and no one dare approach her. Alice took Mavis’s place on coach journeys, sitting beside Joseph and their bodies collided on every bump in the road. Alice kept looking at him. She must have been curious about his deformities. Joseph could find no other explanation for her lingering gaze. Nevertheless, the proximity of Alice’s beauty to Joseph’s deformity had an effect on him not unlike Scaley Boy’s staged reaction to music.

An unseasonal summer downpour washed out an afternoon in Aylesbury. The others stayed in the tent drinking, whilst Joseph sheltered in the living wagon, grateful for a few moments solitude. Joseph reread his copy of *Frankenstein*. He was uncomfortable reading near the others and embarrassed when asking Charlie to buy books on his behalf. For men, real men, any knowledge gleaned from beyond the bar room was treated with suspicion.

Alice climbed into the wagon and sat beside Joseph in her normal travelling position. Her thin dress was soaking wet, virtually transparent, and clung to her every curve. Water droplets formed on the curls of her long black hair and the whiskers of her beard. She asked a question.

“The story of your life. Is it fiction, or is it fact?”

“You have not said a word with regards to your life. Why should I venture details of mine?”

“You venture details night and day, Elephant Man.”

“I am flattered you have paid such attention to my act.”

Joseph saw a flush of crimson under Alice’s magnificent beard.

"Constructing an act is like constructing a building," said Joseph. "The foundations are my life, my experience, my character. Strong foundations are paramount, only then can the act stand firm and support the performer regardless of the fabrication on top."

Joseph wondered if his rambling response confused Alice. He felt like a deformed Jesus delivering a morally deficient parable.

"I understand," said Alice, "and that book, will you read with me? I have seldom read beyond the *Yorkshire Ladies Journal.*"

From that day on, no matter how late it was or how tired they were, Joseph and Alice found time to read, in the living wagon when the others were drinking, or a quiet corner of the tent. They read out loud to each other from the three books Joseph possessed, *Journey To The Centre of The Earth*, a collection of romantic poetry and Alice's favourite, *Frankenstein.*

Joseph did not hear any gossip regarding their time alone. His deformities put him above suspicion of any funny business, even by the anything goes standards of the freak show. Only Charlie made a few good-natured jibes about the amount of time Joseph and Alice spent together. To counter, Joseph invited Charlie to read with them. On the rare occasions he sat with Joseph, Alice and their books, Charlie fell asleep after no more than a couple of pages.

Joseph watched Alice grow in confidence as a performer. A rowdy young tough acted up in Oxford, but Alice shushed him with a finger to the lips and said, "Do you mind, I am trying to dress." The man apologised. Alice gave him a wink and he stared at his shoes, like an embarrassed youth before the most beautiful girl on the street.

The next day, in between showings, Charlie rushed behind Joseph's curtain as if he had discovered gold. Charlie said, "The girl has cracked it, she has found her catch line. 'Every daughter is her mother's rose'. Couldn't have come up with better myself!"

Sam invested in a black pencil dress for Alice, with purple lace. It complemented her body and accentuated her dark, mysterious beard. Charlie said women slapping their husbands out of an 'Alice-induced trance' was now a regular feature of the show.

Before long it seemed like Alice had always been part of the show, always been Joseph's friend and they had always read together. Joseph lived for nightfall and their time alone. They huddled together in the living wagon with a single, solitary candle, illuminating the text of *Frankenstein*.

Alice turned the page. She pressed her body against Joseph's body for warmth. It was dark, the showground was quiet and Joseph had no idea of the day, the date or his whereabouts in England. He had never been happier.

An Indian summer stretched into early October which meant the Nottingham Goose Fair was exceptionally busy. Thousands of punters swarmed into the showground by the forest. Joseph showed at least forty times on the first day, but now, near midnight, things were winding down. Sam roamed the showground in search of straggling punters. Joseph snacked on an apple, cutting away pieces with an old, blunt knife. Joseph heard Charlie commence his patter with a fresh crowd, hopefully the last of the night. Charlie's storytelling was drowned out by drunken abuse and raucous laughter. He appealed for calm, but was shouted down.

Joseph peered through the curtain. Six burly young hooligans in sharp suits were taunting Alice. Their rat-faced ringleader pestered her for a kiss, but Alice covered her beard with her shawl. Charlie tried to step in between Alice and her tormentor, but the man pushed him aside and snatched at the shawl. Alice raked his hand with her nails.

Charlie waded in, punches flew. Hunchie joined the mill but was knocked out immediately. Scaley Boy stayed behind his curtain. Harry ran in from outside and floored two of the gang, but he was set upon by the others. The rodent-faced tough bore down on Alice. Joseph removed his shirt, took the apple knife in hand and hobbled out from behind his curtain in his toga. He gave a fearful roar.

The hooligans were as horrified as if Joseph had been a real stampeding elephant and they ran from the tent. Only their ringleader remained. As he turned to face The Elephant Man, Alice smashed her vanity mirror across the back of his head. The hooligan staggered into Harry, who punched him in the face and threw him out. Charlie splashed water in Hunchie's face and he regained consciousness. Scaley emerged from behind his curtain and shouted after the hooligans, enquiring if they'd had enough. Alice flinched at the sight of the blade and hurried out through the rear of the tent.

Joseph changed into his normal clothes and set off in search of Alice. She had not gone far and was standing behind the living wagon to the rear of the showground. Joseph approached her cautiously from behind. Her fingers were ready for attack and clawed like talons, though when she saw Joseph, she released them. They had a good view of Nottingham, the silhouettes of houses, factories and twinkling gas lights. Alice spoke first.

"I will visit their town with a flaming torch. Burn their homes, burn their faces, make them like us. Let them live a day in our world, for they would surely die."

"Do you believe they are so different? They look in a mirror and die with shame. They come here to forget their fear."

"What do you care for normal people?"

"Not much. But your anger surpasses my own. I did not think that was possible."

"My anger can strip flesh from bone." Alice uttered the words with chilling certainty. Joseph had no reason to doubt her. "Next you will tell me you have 'forgiven them'. I will never forgive them."

Joseph answered, "All my life I prayed to God and not once did he answer. One night in the workhouse, thinking death was near, I offered my soul to Satan. I asked him for revenge, for life as man and a normal body. No one came. Nothing happened. I expected nothing from life, or any other person. I was completely alone. But look at me now, with this work and these friends. I believe I treasure you most."

Joseph's confession prompted a further confession. For the first time Alice spoke of her previous life, her youth in Leeds, the emergence of her beard and the loss of her beauty, the violent cruelty of her father and brothers, the lunatic asylum. Joseph was ashamed for his own self-pity, the assumption he was alone in suffering. He so deeply admired Alice's courage and her strength and wanted to tell her everything. But before he could speak, Alice reached out her left hand and held Joseph's right, his bloated claw.

It was the first time anyone had touched his deformities with any sort of affection.

As Alice held his hand Joseph remembered the other part of his bargain with Satan, his soul in return for a woman.

On the last night in Nottingham, Charlie suggested a 'drinking excursion' to the woods behind the showground. Sam and Harry declined and Scaley was already in a stupor from whiskey, so Joseph, Charlie, Alice and Hunchie ventured into the undergrowth. They entered the wood like giggling children. Hunchie made owl noises. Alice helped Joseph over a fallen tree trunk. His elbow accidently nudged the soft cushion of her breast. They arrived at a clearing and Charlie picked the spot for a fire.

"We shall split into pairs and gather firewood," said Charlie. He moved towards Alice subtly, trying to partition her away, but Alice took a step towards Joseph and linked her arm around his. Alice pressed her breast against him. If it was another accidental collision, it was an extremely pleasant one.

Charlie set off with Hunchie, leaving Joseph and Alice alone. They gathered twigs and pieces of wood. Joseph did the talking, babbling about inconsequential matters. Alice placed her bundle on the floor and gestured for Joseph to do the same.

"Men have always struggled to converse with me. Sometimes they can hardly utter a word. You, on the other hand?"

"You do not look at me with like other women, with fear or with pity. But something else."

"What else?"

"That you may have for me another purpose, a destiny?"

Alice moved towards Joseph and stood in front of him. She wrapped her arms around his shoulders and directed Joseph's hands to her waist. Their lips were practically touching. Alice closed her eyes, Joseph closed his. Joseph leaned towards her, mimicking real people in love, the courting couples, the ones who inhabited a different world. Joseph anticipated her soft, warm lips, the bristles of her beard and a sensation close to heaven. Instead, Joseph felt Alice's forehead against his shoulder. They held each other, swaying gently. Her tears dripped sporadically against his overcoat.

"I wish I had your strength," said Alice.

Joseph gently stroked her cheek with his good fingers. Alice's beard was far smoother than expected, as though the hairs had a special, feminine quality.

Alice caught Joseph's fingers with the speed of a reptile and Joseph was convinced that his careless gesture had destroyed their friendship. But her eyes grew wide and soft. She stroked the back of Joseph's hand with her fingers. Alice exerted gentle pressure onto his hand and guided it downwards, then slowly forwards, onto the tender, yielding flesh of her breast. She closed his thumb and forefinger around her nipple.

Alice reached for Joseph's right hand, his hugely deformed claw, and performed the same movement on her other breast. Joseph felt unworthy, that his abnormal hand should defile such beauty, but her blissful moans and his own arousal dispensed with shame.

"Do not move," said Alice. She reached down to his trousers, unbuckled his belt and put her hand inside. She took hold of him and caressed him. It was ecstasy.

Joseph heard Charlie and Hunchie approaching. Alice helped Joseph fasten his trousers, passed him his firewood and collected her own. She was just in time. Charlie and Hunchie arrived, arms laden with bundles of wood.

They lit the fire and passed a bottle. Hunchie played his whistle and told absurd, folkish ghost stories. Joseph feigned interest, but could not avert his eyes from Alice. Charlie took a small, dark bottle from his top pocket.

Charlie read from the brown paper label. "Behold, Dr Longsatff's 'Cretan Bull', 'tis the nectar of Hercules. Contains essence of ox, sinew of stag ..." Charlie uncorked the bottle and put it to his nose ... "and much booze."

"You'll go blind," protested Hunchie.

Charlie took a nip. He scrunched up his face to stop his eyes from watering. He delivered his verdict in a wheeze. "Potent."

Alice drank from the bottle and wiped her beard with her sleeve. Hunchie declined the bottle. Joseph took a sip. The Cretan Bull was more potent than ethanol. Charlie took only one more drink and Joseph declined; he was high enough already. Alice continued on the bottle, ignoring Hunchie's warnings. The banter continued. Alice stroked Joseph's hand when no one was looking.

Alice could hold her drink, but the Cretan Bull defeated her. Charlie and Hunchie carried her back to the tent. They lowered Alice into her sack, then climbed into the living wagon. Joseph tucked Alice under her blanket. She whispered, "Stay here with me," then sleep overtook her. Joseph pulled the blanket up to her chin and bade her goodnight.

Joseph awoke with a pounding, industrial headache. It was early and dull. The others were sleeping. Joseph clambered out of the living wagon. He was desperate for water and drank from the wash bucket. Alice was not in her tent. Joseph entered the novelty booth and tentatively opened her curtain.

Alice sat on the wooden stool with her back to him in her alluring black pencil dress, already in position for the show. She stared into the new hand mirror which Sam had bought for her. Joseph whispered her name. Alice turned to Joseph with a new face, which bore not a single hair, but a number of faint, pink razor scars.

Joseph always assumed the cure would liberate the afflicted. The opposite applied to Alice. She retreated into herself, resuming her solitary ways, keeping the shawl tight around her face. A parading role was out of the question, partly because Sam did not rate parading, but also because Alice was bewildered by her 'normal' appearance. She still performed, courtesy of a beard Sam purchased from a booth selling joke items, but it was not the same. Alice was effectively a passenger.

Late October was bitterly cold and autumnal. The Freaks of Nature decamped to Ilkeston for the street fair. It was early morning, the town was yet to rise and the cobbles of Market Square were covered in frost. Sam, Harry, Hunchie, Charlie and Scaley rose early to see Alice off. Joseph stayed in his own section of the tent to avoid the necessity of saying goodbye, but he secretly hoped to see Alice one final time. Sure enough, Joseph recognised the approach of her feet on the cobbles and she pulled the curtain aside. Alice wore no shawl, or muffler, revealing her strong feminine jaw, her full red lips and her high cheekbones. She wore the same plain yellow dress from the first day and had fashioned her sleeping blanket into a cape coat. Despite the makeshift ensemble, Alice ticked every box of conventional feminine beauty.

"Sam wanted his costume back." Alice smiled.

Though he was physically unable to smile, Joseph thought he should pretend to be happy.

"It is close to the end of the season, a good time to retire. At the height of your career."

"All I did was fluff my beard."

"You did it with a certain panache." Joseph saw Alice blush for the first time without her beard. "Where will you go?"

"London."

Joseph reached into his canvas bag.

"I would have brought Dick Whittington. But under the circumstances ..." Joseph held his copy of *Frankenstein* out to Alice. She took Joseph's hands instead.

"On the first night you told me, 'the eye of the storm'. I must follow your teaching again. I must go to the city and the crowds and throw myself in the midst of them. It is the only way I can think of returning to the world."

"You will survive and excel."

They teetered near to each other. A tear ran down Alice's smooth, white cheek, merging with a scar. Joseph raised his good left hand and tenderly dabbed the tear with his fingers. Alice pulled him close and embraced him. They held each other for a long time and released each other slowly. Alice gestured to her face.

"Sam said if it returns, so can I."

"Then I hope I never see you again."

Joseph turned his back and unfolded his costume, ready for for his act. Alice stayed for a few more seconds. He heard her wipe her nose and dry her tears and then she was gone. A sudden urge came to him, a rush of energy, a voice, "Run to her, do something!" Instead, he did nothing. Joseph waited for five minutes, ten minutes. It felt like his insides had been stolen.

Joseph uncorked a bottle of port and drank in solitude. Instead of helping him escape, the booze had a reverse effect, sharpening his awareness of the present, the leery punters, the steam horse carousel, the report of Charlie's firecracker outside the novelty booth. When Charlie pulled the curtain, Joseph was ready in his toga and displayed his body, the worst in the Empire, the worst in the world. He told his story, delivering his act to the highest standard, even though there was so little inside him he felt like a ghost. Medieval in vulgarity, tasteless in spectacle, sophisticated in fraud, Joseph's world was the freak show. It was everything that he had.

Chapter 7 – The Music Hall

The saloon bar of the public house provided the Briton with ad hoc novelty entertainment, a singer, a comic, perhaps an innuendo-laden play. But as sure as the addict expands his palette for a more potent drug, the masses demanded a new fix of entertainment. The fair came to town but once or twice a year. Theatre was dull and worthy with no drinking permitted in the main auditorium. In response, a new form of entertainment provided the thrill of the fairground in a theatrical setting, with gallons of booze aplenty. The masses were soon hooked on their new opiate, Music Hall.

Gaieties and Hippodromes provided a mind-boggling array of speciality turns: mentalists, singers, single cyclists, comedians, clog dancers and negro minstrels. There was Jenny Hill, 'The Vital Spark', The Moore & Burgess Minstrel Show, Alfred Vance, 'The Jokey Gentleman'. Songsmith Arthur Lloyd was king of the music hall, with his maritime masterwork, *Married to a Mermaid.*

There was always a place on the bill for human oddity, especially in the provinces. Turns like Zampi: the One-Legged Gymnast earned a working man's weekly wage for a single night's performance. Such opportunity did not escape the attention of Sam Thomas. At the end of the travelling season, Harry returned to winter quarters in Margate, where Sam had other minor business concerns. Scaley and Hunchie were loaned out to another promoter who exhibited freaks in backstreet emporiums. Sam accompanied Joseph and Charlie on an exhausting tour of provincial music halls.

As their tour necessitated a great deal of train travel, Sam commissioned a tailor to make Joseph a disguise for his deformities. The finished article was a kind of grey pillow case, stitched onto the base of a black peaked cap. It resembled a legionnaire's hat, except that the flap covered Joseph's entire face and head. A small circular hole, the circumference of a half-crown, provided sight for one eye. Joseph's sinister headgear attracted attention, although there was no way he could have gone out in public without a hood. The presence of Sam and Charlie also kept intrusive types at bay. Sam treated himself to a sober new suit and bowler hat. With his hard-lived face, he looked like a boxing bank manager.

Joseph was booked for runs lasting up to a week. In a major city, such as Birmingham, it was possible to transport Joseph between several venues, including The Gaiety, The Holte and Ladywood Place, on the same night and therefore increase his earnings. On a freezing cold Wednesday in early February, Joseph appeared at the The Holte. Sam and Charlie escorted Joseph from the carriage around the back of the building to a cramped and dingy dressing room. Charlie sat with Joseph as the other turns dressed and tried not to stare at the strange, hooded man. Joseph's stomach churned with nerves, not aided by the pervading reek of the deposit left by Felix: Juggling Jack the Acrobat's Very Clever Dog. Sam was elsewhere, buttering up the owner over a drink, so Charlie escorted Joseph away from the dressing room, backstage, behind the curtain. They watched the other acts in progress.

Every punter was a veritable Caesar of the games with their fickle thumb of judgement determining a performer's fate. If any turn failed to impress or induced apathy, the crowd condemned them to death by derision. Professor Portent: Mindreader was mercilessly harangued and driven from the stage. By contrast, the Jew Impersonator who followed him, brought the house down and was begged for an encore.

Each act required a wow of an opening to immediately command the attention of the crowd, such as Miss Jessica Crimson and her salacious 'Kiss Me' dance or Oswald the Levitator with a leap that defied gravity. Pratfalls or the suggestion of sex were very effective, although the most successful performers engaged the crowd on a sentimental level. Joseph was due on immediately after Mr Leslie Costello: Vocal Phenomenon. Costello's closing number was the story of a devoted son pawning his personal possessions to cover family funeral expenses, *The Angels Are Waiting For Mother*. His shameless vibrato singing style reduced two hundred and fifty hardbitten factory workers to tears.

The compère, also known as the Chairman, took the stage and announced the forthcoming appearance of the Elephant Man. Joseph was affected by a sweating fever and stomach pains, the familiar symptoms of stage fright. At these moments he pondered the absurdity of his career. Couldn't hold a job as a factory hand, couldn't hold a job as a hawker, paid now to reveal his unemployable body for the amusement of workers.

The seven-piece band improvised a brief introduction, an unsettling, dissonant drone. Joseph linked his right arm around Charlie's left and hobbled on, through a fog of tobacco smoke, to the centre of the proscenium stage. Charlie announced, "The year is 1862. The town is Leicester. Just an ordinary place, with ordinary people ..."

Charlie extended his usual patter to heighten the tension, but would not string out his introduction too long, wary of displeasing the audience. When the time came, Charlie whipped off Joseph's hood to predictable gasps and helped him out of his jacket, overshirt, and the glove on his right hand. Joseph wore his normal trousers. This drew more attention to his upper body, his most pronounced areas of deformity. Besides, it would have been impractical to keep changing in and out of his toga. The crowd in the stalls and the balconies shuffled forward for a closer look at the freak.

"He has been before the foremost physicians, the greatest minds of Vienna. Mr Merrick has baffled them all. There is no known cure for his remarkable condition. But please do not judge his brain by his body. Mr Merrick can read and write. His mind is as sharp as a tack!"

Joseph quietly performed three half-naked rotations. He had only attempted the verbal part of his act on one disastrous occasion, in Manchester, and the awful howls of laughter still echoed in his ears. It was the story of his musical hall career. Despite Charlie's attempts to keep the audience in maximum suspense and present Joseph with some degree of dignity, one wag always made an 'amusing' remark, inciting others.

"Imagine what his mother looks like!"

"Imagine what his missus looks like!"

"Like yours!"

"Where's the elephant?"

"Go on then. Drop your trousers!"

After the final show of the evening Sam, Charlie and Joseph took a carriage to the hotel by Snow Hill Station. Joseph roomed with Charlie. They removed their shoes, sat side by side on the bed and passed a bottle of whiskey between them. It was their usual end to the day, sharing a bottle, talking long into the night, stringing out the thinnest conversational thread for hours, like two old vagrants on a park bench. Joseph and Charlie discussed the merits of moving up to laudanum, opium and cocaine. It was all every tempting. But for Joseph, the thought of drugs brought back memories of the futile cure pills his mother forced him to take.

They finished the bottle and Charlie lay down to sleep. Joseph stayed in his sitting-sleeping position, hoping for dreams of Alice. He dreamed of her frequently, sometimes in mundane scenarios: they were back at the fair and it was 'business as usual'. In other dreams they were making love. He could hardly discuss this with Charlie, although when he woke the next morning, Charlie shared a dream of his own.

"You know what we should do, Joseph? Set up in London, an emporium. All the money's there."

"It is a tempting proposition. Although, if I were to stay in one location, would not my novelty diminish?"

"London is one enormous thoroughfare. New blood pours through all the time. If you stand still long enough, the city moves under your feet. You know what they say, 'When a man is tired of London, he is tired of life.' They'd never get tired of you, pal, not in a million years."

"We should go there, Charlie, as soon as possible."

"What would Sam say, us breaking our engagements?"

"Nothing. If we up and leave."

Charlie looked into Joseph's eyes. The birth of conspiracy passed between them.

"Forget I said anything," replied Charlie, but he could not hide his interest in the idea.

"These days Sam is entirely aloof," said Joseph.

"You've not known him long. Do not judge him harshly."

"You do not deny it, though?"

"No, Joseph, I do not. But what do I know of business?"

"You know barking like no other."

"It was Sam who taught me."

"And now you have surpassed him. Are you always to exist in his shadow?"

Charlie got out of bed and walked to the window. Joseph continued, "He has reduced you to a chaperone, the animal's handler. I am the bear, Charlie, no question of that. So yes, we reside in hotels, in relative comfort, but has not our manhood diminished?"

"You go then."

Charlie reminded Joseph of a beaten wife who was still fiercely loyal to her husband.

"My friend, it humiliates me to confess, but I cannot do anything on my own; my condition does not allow it. Besides, are we not a double act?"

Charlie continued to stare out of the window. He said, "I wish Alice was here."

Instead of prompting warm reminiscence, Charlie evoked the memory of loss. They would never see her again, so the conversation died. Charlie opened another bottle of whiskey, even though it was morning. Joseph drank with him in silence.

After Birmingham, Sam casually announced that Joseph was to begin a week's run in Leicester. Joseph nodded mutely as if it were just another town. Charlie and Joseph travelled second class, Sam travelled first. They disembarked at Campbell Street Station and Charlie hired a brougham which transported them to the Bell Hotel on Humberstone Gate. Sam made the necessary arrangements with reception whilst Charlie ushered Joseph upstairs.

Charlie and Joseph shared Room 12 on the second floor, whilst Sam occupied a superior suite above. Joseph removed his headgear and drew the curtains half closed for privacy. Humberstone Gate was just as he remembered it, bustling with horse-drawn carriages and pedestrians. It was a dim, grey, winter afternoon. The streetlights were warming up. Wharf Street was a short walk in the distance, home of Leicester's Gaiety Theatre.

"Another good room," said Charlie.

"Let us hope a good crowd."

"Do they get a good crowd, here at the Gaiety?"

"Never in my life have I been to the Gaiety." Joseph took a bottle of whiskey out of his suitcase and popped the cork. "It is no place for a God-fearing boy."

Charlie asked Joseph if he wanted him to look up any relatives. Joseph mentioned an Uncle Charles, but changed his mind. They drank through the afternoon, passing the bottle back and forth. Joseph took most of it; Charlie drank sparingly. Joseph turned the conversation to last summer at the fair, more at ease with the past than the present. It was like drinking with a condemned man.

Sam called for them at seven, and they left the Bell Hotel. Charlie and Sam kept close to Joseph, flanking him either side. As they approached the Gaiety, Joseph heard merry music and a loud, raucous cheer from inside the theatre, signalling the start of the show.

Sam, Charlie and Joseph entered the Gaiety via the back. A dogsbody showed them into a windowless dressing room already occupied by two fair-haired men, who were changing into garish yellow and orange stage suits, and a short, sleazy man who introduced himself as Mr Travis. Travis said that if Sam had exaggerated Joseph's condition there would be a 'sizeable reduction in fee'. Sam lifted the flap of Joseph's headgear. The fair-haired entertainers were agog.

Travis said that he was going to promote Joseph up the bill and invited Sam for a private drink. When they left, Joseph produced his own drink, a fresh bottle of whiskey. The two other men introduced themselves as Ebony and Cole, the main act 'Negro' entertainers. They blacked-up, using a piece of broken glass for a mirror, and rehearsed their comic dialogue in deep American accents. Charlie drank with Joseph, if only to prevent him from necking the lot.

When the time came Charlie led Joseph through a cramped corridor, past a troupe of scantily clad women in black and scarlet corsets. They were burlesque dancers, The Abandon Girls. Joseph accidently elbowed one of the dancer's breasts. She giggled, until she saw his sinister headgear.

There was booing and whistling from the main auditorium. The Vanguard Sisters' Tyrolean singing had soured the crowd. Three women dressed in rural Germanic dresses pushed past Joseph and Charlie in tears. Joseph stumbled and Charlie caught him under the arm. His headgear slipped down and he could hardly see, but Joseph heard the piercing voice of the Chairman.

"... A greater human freak there has never been, not since big Daniel Lambert. This fellow is deformed. He's hideous. He's a monster! Ladies and gentleman, they call him The Elephant Man!"

Joseph staggered to the front of the stage with Charlie. The crowd stamped their feet on the floor, drowning out the ditty from the house band. The Chairman was a tall, smarmy man in a novelty waistcoat. He wound his arm like a windmill to egg them on. Charlie, uncharacteristically nervous, was too intimidated to speak. The noise built. The tension built. The Chairman, despairing of Charlie's indecision, pulled Joseph's mask away.

After the initial shock, the crowd fell silent and the moment acquired a frozen-in-time quality. Charlie snatched the mask back from the Chairman and helped Joseph wriggle out of his shirt. Joseph hoped to conclude his act before the crowd became restless. He turned, revealing his back. Individual shouts greeted his freakish pirouette.

"For God's sake, put his hat back on!"

"And keep it on."

"I know him. He's the hawker!"

Everybody laughed.

"He couldn't sell me a pail of water if my house was ablaze!"

"He couldn't sell the dying a prayer."

"He's a hawker, I'm telling you!"

"Hawker! Hawker!"

A good many attempted to imitate Joseph, twisting their mouths and swinging their arms as if he were a primate. Joseph looked across the sea of faces. They had been tormented by their jobs and belittled by their masters, diseased by the grind of life. They had come here to purge themselves and had infinite reserves of bile. The Chairman took a timid step backwards.

Joseph stood before the mob, resigned to their abuse, remembering his remark to Alice about meeting contempt in 'the eye of the storm'. Back then, in performance, Joseph had the illusion of control and in Alice the illusion of love, therefore the illusion of hope. Now he was a reluctant factotum, hawking without his shirt. In place of books of matches, sewing kits and bits of thread, Joseph now sold the ridicule of his body. He wished he could whip through the crowd with a wheel-mounted Gatling, but the only bullets at his disposal were poetic.

"Let me regale you of a Great British travesty, the murder of a son of Leicester. They killed him each day, then raised him the next, in a gibbet by the Clock Tower."

The mob took great offence when the victim resisted, as Joseph knew from experience, and his retort met with an ugly roar.

"My name is Joseph Merrick and you are the murderers."

The first bottle whizzed past Joseph's cheekbone. Charlie ducked under the second. Brown glass exploded around them. Charlie curled a protective arm around Joseph's shoulder, forcing his head down. The Chairman dragged the Abandon Girls forward and the band played a risqué popular song. The girls combined their raunchy dance moves with an improvised Irish jig in order to avoid the broken glass. The bottles stopped immediately. The crowd were mesmerized by the girls. Joseph and Charlie slipped behind the curtain. The dogsbody swept the stage and ogled the girls from behind. Though the air was charged with violence, the Chairman had the instinct of an animal trainer.

It did not matter if an act was dreadful, provided it was sensational. Hate sold as many tickets as love. In the case of The Elephant Man, everyone who threw a bottle purchased another, which meant Travis made a big profit on alcohol. After the show, he took Sam to a nearby hostelry for a good drink.

Meanwhile, Charlie helped Joseph back to their hotel room. It took him an age to manoeuvre Joseph into his upright sleeping position because his cumbersome head was like a bag of coal. Charlie finally managed to wedge a plump pillow between Joseph's skull and the headboard. Joseph mumbled tired, drunken words. Charlie sat in the chair and watched the Elephant Man fall asleep.

Instinct told Charlie that his career had changed direction tonight. He reached for the bottle at the bedside, the remnants of the whiskey, and remembered how it all began.

Charlie's brother, Jack, was twelve years older, a young man when Charlie was a boy. Jack was the eldest son, the champion of the family, an ace swimmer and fine boxer, idolised by his brothers and sisters. Above all, Charlie was in awe of Jack's talking ability. Even when mother was furious with her children, one of Jack's cheeky quips always brightened her mood. Jack was highly paid as a waiter at Margate's upmarket Clifftonville Hotel and earned more than Charlie's father, a caretaker at the Zoological Gardens, affectionately known as Paddy.

Despite Jack's earnings, Charlie noticed his brother regularly asking their mother for loans. She would always concede, with the proviso that payment must be 'Friday, not a day late,' and to 'Never ask your father for money.' One night, when he was nine years of age, Charlie heard shouting. He crept downstairs and watched through the kitchen door. Paddy bellowed at Jack, who for once was silent and Mother was on the brink of tears. Paddy accused Jack of stealing from the hotel. Jack tried to deny it. Paddy produced an exhibit of evidence, the silver necklace Mother had found in his things. Jack confessed all. He had fallen in with a 'bad lot' who introduced him to 'ruinous vice'. Jack was gambling. Jack had awful luck. He owed a fortune to a gang of violent toughs. Paddy asked, "How much?" "Forty pounds," admitted Jack, a sum close to Paddy's annual salary at the time.

Mother wept properly now. Paddy disappeared elsewhere. Jack opened his arms to embrace his mother, but she refused to hug him. Paddy came back with an iron safe box and removed the largest bundle of paper money Charlie had ever seen, his father's life savings. Jack thanked Father profusely and said he had learned his lesson, gambling was 'a fool's game'. Jack vowed to "Pay back every penny and make a man of myself."

Jack left for London the next morning, taking the family silver with him.

For the next three months, the atmosphere at the McCallion household was one of mourning. Charlie spent as much time away from home as possible and took to bunking off school with his friends. They combed the beaches for loose change which had fallen from the pockets of trippers. When Mother asked about the money, Charlie lied about finding part-time work as a shoe-shine.

Just as the atmosphere at home started to lift, news came back from London. Jack was dead. His parents aged a decade overnight. They never revealed any specific details about Jack's murder. All Paddy said was, "Never a borrower nor a lender be."

Charlie never knew his parents attend church, yet suddenly God and Jesus were so frequently mentioned, Charlie wondered if they had moved in as lodgers. 'Sin', 'Immorality', 'Vice'; these were the new catchwords of his parents. They also acquired new friends from Margate's small but vocal tea and temperance brigade. Together, they protested against the town's debauched entertainment culture.

Mother and Paddy dragged Charlie along to their protests, so their youngest son would not stray from the path of righteousness. They canvassed on the Parade and Marine Drive and demanded the closure of Margate's entertainment 'Gomorrah', The Hall By The Sea. Singing hymns and distributing handbills was not enough for his parents. Mother threw eggs and Paddy threw punches. They went too far; they were ostracised by the tea and temperance brigade and despised throughout the town for spoiling harmless fun and, most importantly, business.

Then an act came to town that was too vulgar and controversial for The Hall By The Sea, a freak named Boneman: The Living Skelton, exhibited by Mr Samuel Thomas, Esquire. The show took residence in an emporium on Love Lane. One Kent newspaper referred to Thomas as 'The King of Sin'. Paddy resolved to 'see to it' and set off for the emporium, but returned with welts on his face. He said there was a young hardcase on the door. Paddy handed Charlie a box of matches as they would not suspect a child. Paddy implored him to "Burn it for your brother."

Paddy walked Charlie to the top of Love Lane and pushed him in the direction of the emporium. It was late in the evening, but still light. Three courting couples left the emporium laughing and whooping. The young hardcase guarded the door and stared at Charlie. Charlie fingered the book of matches in the pocket of his short trousers, having no intention to burn anything, but needing to make a show for his father. Another man in a jaunty suit arrived at the door. He had the air of authority. Clearly this was 'The King of Sin', although his palace was not much more than a hovel. Sam Thomas beckoned Charlie inside.

The interior of the building was cavernous and cold. Sam led the way down a dark corridor as the hardcase carried a lamp. Charlie was certain they were leading him to his death, but curiosity compelled him to follow. Sam stopped at a curtain and Charlie became aware of a monstrous presence behind it. Sam told Charlie a terrible tale about an explorer in India, who stole a sacred urn. "The curse ate the flesh from his body, but he did not die! Behold Boneman, The Living Skelton."

Sam pulled the curtain and Charlie was confronted by the most astonishing man on the planet: The Boneman, a human stick insect with not a single muscle and the flesh of a chicken wing stretched over his transparent body. Suddenly Boneman sprung into life, contorting his body into a series of impossible positions. Boneman's eyes bulged out of their emaciated sockets like apples. His knee joints were bigger than his head.

"If you look closely," said Sam, "You can see the very beat of his heart."

In time, Boneman revealed his exercise was oriental yoga, and his name as Albert Tupshaw, a big-hearted Yorkshireman and more hopeless gambler than Jack McCallion. The hardcase on the door was Harry and as for Sam, Charlie always thought that when Sam pulled back the curtain, he revealed more than a freak of nature – he revealed a different world.

When Charlie was sure Joseph was sleeping comfortably, he ascended the stairs to Sam's superior suite. Sam was expecting Charlie and had placed a bottle of chilled white wine in a silver cooler on the coffee table. Sam poured the drinks into crystal glasses. Charlie, excited at his first taste of proper wine, temporarily forgot the horrors of the night and took a big gulp.

"Don't bolt it, son. Savour the taste."

"Sorry, boss."

Sam placed his glass down on the table, next to a fat, unlit cigar.

"You hear of actors making the demands of emperors. The bigger the crowd, the bigger the monster. Young Joseph has no cause for complaint."

"Joseph does have a point, to a point. These music halls, he's a dancing bear. I feel terrible standing up there with him and ..."

"A crowd is easily led. Young Joseph's inner disposition incites them. We must find a way to restore his spirits."

Charlie was not sure and was keen to change the subject. "It'll soon be spring and all the fun of the fair."

"Not a chance. We have made the profit of years in weeks at the music hall. Joseph is gold and so are you. You are to be his road manager."

Despite Sam's direction to sip his wine, Charlie swallowed the lot. Sam poured him another one.

"I remember this boy, bent on trouble. Showed him The Boneman to scare him off, only he tells all the little children and brings them to my parlour with their pennies. Even though his father gave him a right royal hiding, he kept coming back for more."

Charlie could not help but smile at the memory.

"I'll raise you twenty pounds a year. Put you both in fine hotels. You will drink wine every night if you wish. The music halls of England shall be your personal emporium and I'm giving you the key."

Sam's pull of persuasion was the draw of the moon. Charlie told himself Joseph would get used to the stage, it was just a matter of time. He would come to enjoy himself as much as those halcyon days of the fair, with the old troupe and the lovely Alice.

Sam held out his hand. Charlie shook it. Charlie expected a backslapping celebration, Harry to emerge from the cupboard with champagne. But Sam flopped back against the settee, like an old, worn overcoat and let out a colossal sigh. "I'm tired, son."

Charlie did not know if it was a casual statement or a cue to go to bed. Charlie took it as the latter, shook Sam's hand again and said goodnight.

The next morning Sam fixed a bleary eye on the grandfather clock. The hour was ten! It was the longest he had slept in his life. Sam rose at once and chastised himself for being a lazy slugabed, but accepted that fatigue supported his decision to make Charlie a full partner.

Sam opened the top drawer of his bedside cabinet and reached for the management contract he should have made Charlie sign last night. It was poor salesmanship, unforgivable, but there was something about Charlie. Sam wanted to put his arm around him, advise him, teach him more of the world. Charlie would always be more than an employee, or a business partner and he would no sooner rush Charlie to sign a contract than harass his son.

In fact, not one of Sam's current associates knew that he had been married, or fathered a son; he had never told them.

Sam's son was born in the time of his youth when he was still performing his comedy act in any saloon bar that would have him on. His humour was dry as befitting his general demeanour, but Sam was not averse to a smile and a wink, or closing his act with a popular song, for he was a competent singer. When Elizabeth gave birth to Jeremy, no matter where his travels would take him, Sam felt the contentment of a life with roots and permanence. Unfortunately for Sam he felt it only fleetingly. Jeremy was born a 'different one' and lived for but a year. Sam's marriage died along with his son because Elizabeth blamed herself. She would not heed Sam's heartfelt plea, that there was nothing to forgive.

For Sam, Jeremy's affliction had not been a source of shame, but the inherent imperfection in all nature and his immense love for his son would never be dependent upon form. Nevertheless, Jeremy's death was the death of his youth and no matter where he went, or what he did, some part of his life would always be shrouded in darkness. Sam knew that he could no longer tell jokes, but he could tell stories. He resolved to search out the different ones so that they might perform and prosper together.

Sam decided to treat Charlie to a king's breakfast in the hotel restaurant, reasoning that Charlie could take a sandwich back for Joseph, if he was not sick from the drink.

He washed, dressed and went downstairs to Joseph and Charlie's room. He listened through the door for sounds of snoring or conversation, but heard nothing. Sam pulled the handle and stepped inside. The furniture was arranged in a neat, symmetrical fashion and the bed made with fresh linen. Sam checked the room number just in case, Room 12.

He ran down to reception, but the desk manager was engaged with the interminable questions of a dithering elderly couple. Sam burst through the hotel doors onto the pavement, stumbling, searching for direction, reminiscent of a punter made dizzy by steam horses. He looked both ways down the long urban valley of Humberstone Gate, pushed past pedestrians, and blundered into the road, into the path of a horsedrawn carriage which narrowly missed him. Sam zig-zagged to the other side of the road and back, oblivious to other carriages and the curses from drivers.

Joseph and Charlie must have gone to the station, but Sam couldn't remember the way. He tried to ask pedestrians for directions, but they all ignored him, because of his rough voice, strange accent and desperate manner. Sam followed a crowd down a wide street towards a solitary cock ower and circled around the structure, searching for direction. He was nearly mown down by another carriage. Sam rested his back against the Clock Tower, sank to the floor and sat on his backside.

A billboard boy stood over him, in a red and blue double-sided placard for The Gaiety Theatre, and passed Sam a printed handbill. The Elephant Man was the most prominent name, above even Knockabout Negroes Ebony & Cole and their world-famous Plantation Dance. Sam rolled the handbill into a paper cigar and flicked it away. He remained sitting against the ClockTower and watched the never-ending stream of people teeming into the square from all directions. Sam felt groggy, but also tearful and empty, like an abject mug punter, taken for every penny of his pay.

Reginald Dunham held his weekly audience with Gilbert Greystone at the former's elegant mansion near Hampstead Heath. The neoclassical residence resembled a more humble version of nearby Kenwood House, although the architect incorporated enough of the Palladian style for Dunham House to truly stand alone. Dunham commissioned the property after he made his first million.

Dunham occupied the mansion with his stern, glaring wife, a garrison of servants and the only one of his four daughters not yet to be married, Jemima. Gilbert estimated that Jemima was at least twenty-five years of age. She was a plain, awkward giggler with long, fair hair and a high-pitched, girlish voice. As such, any half-presentable man of good breeding represented prey. Mercifully Gilbert had been briefly introduced to Jemima just once. He imagined her as a giggling spinster of sixty.

A butler led Gilbert to a vast, roomy study with tall arched windows. There was a library of books for show, weighty tomes Dunham had not read and never would. Dunham welcomed Gilbert with a pumping handshake. Gilbert wore a dark grey day suit with a white pinstripe, emulating Dunham. Dunham went through the charade of offering him cognac, before dispatching the butler for Gilbert's milk. Elaborate card models of architectural works in progress were proudly displayed on three trestle tables. Gilbert feigned wonder as Dunham boasted about the buildings, a town hall, a museum and a concert hall. However, when Gilbert asked a simple question about Byzantine architecture, Dunham struggled for an answer.

The butler returned, placed refreshments on a coffee table and excused himself. Dunham took his seat, savoured the aroma of his cognac and stroked his side whiskers. The beam of light from the window settled on Dunham's head and highlighted the scalp beneath his combed-over hair. Gilbert produced a set of papers from his attaché case and began his report.

"Kingsway Lunatic Asylum, 28th February. Assisted by Dr Vale. Subject, male, 30 years. Apelike build, excessive body hair. Often found among criminals and the insane. Body covered with scars. Prominent cyst on sternum. Oversized reproductive glands, common among lunatics. An Englishman, who knows? I made the first incision ..."

Since Dunham became his patron, Gilbert had operated on six men and six women, at three workhouses and two lunatic asylums. The vasoligations were hit and miss, but Gilbert continued to employ the metaphor of replumbing a labyrinth of pipes. There was no telling whether the new system would work smoothly and efficiently, leak and require ongoing maintenance, or completely implode. Gilbert encountered all facets of success and failure. Dunham assured him that he had time and resources.

Dunham's minions took care of clandestine payments, leaving Gilbert free to concentrate on surgeries. The subjects were well selected, mental defectives and lunatics with befuddled minds and problems 'down below'. Very few awkward questions were asked. Nevertheless, the keynote was caution. After each meeting, Gilbert burnt his written notes in the hearth of Dunham's study, neglecting to inform Dunham of the secret carbons he kept at home.

Dunham understood eugenics like he understood architecture. He was ignorant of the finer points, but appreciated the overall project; he also had a gift for efficiency. As the female operation was relatively straightforward, Dunham encouraged Gilbert to speed up the procedure. Despite a couple of regrettable mishaps, Gilbert was soon able to perform the full operation in two-thirds of the time, without compromising the recovery process.

The Taygetus Eugenics Society also gathered momentum. Dunham attracted a new crowd of his business associates, cut from the same materialistic, anti-intellectual cloth. Membership of the society increased to fifty, with an influx of prosperous merchants, notable captains of industry, and even two members of the House. They were second-rate minds but first-rate allies. Together they would soon begin the long march towards eugenics legislation.

Dunham also invested in a state of the art projection machine, a Viewgraph, capable of magnifying photographic images upon the wall. Dunham said his associates were particularly interested in the physical anthropology of primitive peoples. In response, Dr Vale amassed a library of slides depicting savage young sirens with swaying breasts and flimsy grass skirts about their navel, sometimes without skirts at all. Gilbert gave lectures as the men ogled the Viewgraph. It seemed a bizarre compromise, sacrificing his integrity for the sake of purity.

Gilbert concluded his report for Dunham, placed the notes in the hearth of the study and set them alight. Dunham asked, "You seemed somewhat absent today, Greystone. Are you having second thoughts?"

"Not at all, sir. It is just ..."

"Yes?"

"I wish I could move out of the shadows, sir."

"You want recognition for your work. Of course you do. Great men often toil for years in obscurity and endure scorn. Look at Stephenson. Everyone laughed at his Rocket locomotive. And now? Stephenson is revered as a genius, his Rocket a masterwork. Fifty years hence, your surgery will be hailed as the new vehicle of human progress. This era's genius is Greystone."

Gilbert felt his chest rise at the compliment.

"I seek only to advance the race, sir."

"There is another way to go about it."

Dunham left his seat and walked over to the card model of the concert hall. A minute figurine depicting a courting couple stood in front of the building for perspective. Dunham stroked the female with the tip of his finger. Gilbert predicted the question Dunham was about to ask and had already rehearsed his answer.

"You should take tea with Jemima?"

"I cannot, sir."

"You refuse my hospitality?" blustered Dunham.

"Sir, if I may explain. Jemima is a charming, enchanting young woman, a shining beacon of femininity. Following our first encounter, I described your daughter's radiant disposition to my younger brother in the language of awe. Simon has asked me to humbly convey a request, to take tea with your daughter, at this magnificent homestead. Thus sir, in terms of an audience with Jemima, I must regretfully wait in line."

Dunham positively glowed at the news and addressed Gilbert as if already speaking to a much loved son-in-law. "Of course you must. You Greystones are men of honour."

Chapter 8 – Her Return To The World

Alice purchased a one-way rail ticket to London, disembarked at King's Cross Station and looked for rooms. A classified newspaper advertisement directed her to a boarding house for unmarried ladies in Highbury. The rent was extortionate, but Alice assumed that her regained 'beauty' and experience of retail would secure an appointment at a good boutique. She tried the bazaars of Soho and Islington, the arcades of Burlington and Lowther and countless emporiums along the length of Oxford Street without a single offer of work. Alice attributed her lack of success to her accent and intense demeanour.

She scaled down her aspirations and found work as a waitress in a bohemian cafe on Camden High Street. Alice served customers, washed dishes and also prepared food when the cook was drunk, for fourteen hours a day, six days a week. She suspected the proprietor, Douglas, a failed writer from a wealthy family, gave her the job because he could not take his eyes off her body. A different man propositioned her every hour.

Alice thought she was settling back into normal life, smiling at customers, holding light conversations, pretending to be impressed by the poetry the patrons wrote for her, until a fat Italian artist groped her backside in full view of everyone. Alice poured a pitcher of iced water over his head. Douglas sacked her immediately. Alice slapped Douglas and he called her a whore. She grabbed a bread knife, but was restrained by the other patrons. They threw her onto the street like a bucket of dishwater.

Later, in the small hours of the morning, Alice returned to Douglas's cafe with an arson kit consisting of a box of matches, a bottle of paraffin and a newspaper. She poured the paraffin at strategic points on the wooden door and stuffed the newspaper in the posting box. But when Alice tried to strike a light, she discovered that the matches were duds. Alice heard Douglas shout, "Who's there?" from inside. She hurled the paraffin bottle through the proprietor's beloved misted glass window and sprinted back to her rooms. She packed her bags and left before the others woke, leaving two weeks rent in arrears.

Alice spent the next morning lingering at Liverpool Street Station, wondering which train would transport her to Joseph Merrick. In a moment of clarity she asked herself how she would find him and where would he be? Christmas had been and gone, it was winter season and Joseph would be billeted in a backstreet emporium. Would he even want to see her? It was ridiculous folly.

An aimless walk took Alice onto Whitechapel Road, which must have been the busiest high street in London. Hundreds of pedestrians swarmed in every direction and a seemingly never-ending cavalcade of trams and carriages sped up and down the highway. The sheer density of people and vehicles, the noise and violence of their movements, made Alice want to scream. But fortunately, there were many narrow side streets and Alice escaped into a passage of slum dwellings not much wider than an alleyway. She stood on horse manure and potato peelings and fought her way through raggedy, billowing washing which had been hung across the walkway to dry. Alice pulled an old shirt away from her face and saw that an angry mongrel dog was blocking the passage in front of her.

The dog was achingly thin, tethered to a rail and its coat was crawling with lice. It was both vicious and pathetic, a scrawny anatomy chart of neglect, with protruding ribs and fragile quivering shoulders. The dog closed its feral mouth and its original growl diminished to a faint, pained whimper. Alice checked she was alone, cautiously approached the dog and very carefully reached for the string around its neck. The dog winced in anticipation of a beating, as if it knew only cruelty and it shivered as Alice released the tether. Alice expected the dog to run, but its release seemed only to aggravate its suffering. The dog retreated with its tail between its legs and returned to its familiar slum and the hearth of its abusive masters.

Alice re-entered Whitechapel Road, clear in purpose. She was not yet ready for freedom, but if fear and anger had poisoned and imprisoned her, it was time to boil the venom from her veins. The work she sought was not assisting in a boutique or serving in a café, but labouring in a pit of fire.

McReedy's jute factory in Stratford produced more than four thousand tonnes of cloth and hessian per annum. Seven hundred women were employed as machinists in a room the size of a concert hall. A further two hundred men were employed in the storehouse and engine rooms. Not even the loudest shout could be heard above the spinning mules and linen looms and Alice had to communicate with her co-workers using sign language.

A vast spider's web of wheel belts whirled above her head. Down below, the mules and looms reminded Alice of gigantic washing mangles with incessant metal teeth. Alice had her share of cut hands and near misses with her fingers, although the worst eye-witness account of a recent injury concerned a silly young woman who neglected to tie back her hair and was all but scalped by a take-in scroll.

Hilda worked to the left of Alice, Sue to her right. On the whistle Alice walked out with Sue and Hilda, the three of them linking arms, laughing, talking loudly, the machines still ringing in their ears. Most evenings they stopped off for a few, or perhaps many, beers and gins at the Bombay Grab. Sue and Hilda lived with their respective families by the Gas Light & Coke Company Works. Alice lived in a squalid lodging house near Old Ford Station, made bearable by its proximity to Victoria Park.

Sue and Hilda were decent companions, even if the conversation was as predictable as the next shift, complaints about the job, trivial gossip, anecdotes in the form of "I says to her - she says to me," and the most dominant conversational topic, men.

Hilda had heavy hips and a weighty backside, held at bay by the gravity of youth. "A whale in waiting," remarked Sue. Hilda fretted about her marriage prospects, but had already refused an offer of engagement, based on the paltry seventeen and six weekly earnings of the 'poor little Tanners boy'.

Sue confessed to having full experience of men, having been twice engaged. She lamented her childish error, letting Basil and Henry have relations, because then they broke it off. Sue said she wasn't falling for that trick again and next time there'd be none of that before there was a gold ring on her finger. It was a familiar anecdote and, if questioned by Hilda, Sue provided graphic accounts of what relations were like.

They called Alice 'Yorkie' and grilled her for details of her love life. Alice admitted to being serious about one suitor, but that he was working away and would never return. Sue asked Alice if her paramour was a sailor and Alice played along. Hilda said Alice should have married him before he went to sea, so he could have sent money home.

Alice was the target of many wandering eyes, but no man made a conversational approach, other than Thomas, a cabinet maker, tall with muscular arms and a pleasant smile. Thomas, according to Sue, was 'the handsomest bloke in the boozer, by a long chalk'. Thomas said 'Hello' to Alice and exchanged rudimentary pleasantries, but the conversation stopped there, with Thomas lost for words. Sue implored Alice to progress things with Thomas on the grounds that if you don't, hundreds will, as did Hilda, without even a mention of money. Alice said her heart was still with the sailor.

"Your loss is our gain," said Sue. "Half the blokes in here belong in the freak show!"

Three hours into her next morning shift, Alice realised she'd had enough. She deserved more. Perhaps she would see out the month to save extra money, perhaps she would not. It was done. Alice immediately experienced the light-headed freedom of the worker approaching the conclusion of loathed employment. Perhaps she would work on her accent, endeavour to smile more and try again in some boutique? Perhaps she would train as a nurse, or sign up as a waitress on board an ocean liner? Alice knew that this line of thought derived from an acceptance of loss and sent up telepathic words of farewell to Joseph Merrick.

There was an awful grinding sound from the loom. Sue shrieked and withdrew her hand and cradled it in her apron. A large circle of blood appeared. The foreman was fast on the scene and other workers gathered around. Sue would not give up her hand to reveal the injury so Alice bound Sue's forearm, using her work apron as an improvised tourniquet.

Alice and Hilda supported Sue either side and walked her up the High Street. Hilda said they should head west for the Mile End Infirmary and if they would not treat Sue, The London Hospital. Alice and Hilda attempted to commandeer a wagon or hail a hansom, but none would take her. "Oh, the bastards!" wailed Sue. "They've cut off me bleeding hand!"

On Bow Road, Alice noticed a silver name plaque outside a two-storey commercial building for Dr S A Greystone. Alice presumed the doctor plied his trade amongst the better-off residents of Bow, the middle classes of the Coborn and Lichfield Road area. Alice and Hilda entered the building and followed a well-upholstered corridor to its end. They held Sue steady and the tourniquet tight, so that she did not drip too much blood on the carpet. Three leather-backed chairs comprised a waiting area by the door of the physician's office. A beetroot-faced man with bushy side wiskers and ear hair occupied one of them. He lowered his newspaper, growled at the women and pointed to a sign on the wall that read, 'Respectfully, by appointment only'.

A prim middle-aged woman came out of the consulting room. She noticed the factory girls and hurried past them, as if they were disease carriers. A young, cleanly shaven gentleman stepped into the waiting lobby. He seemed more like a sandy-haired chorister than a doctor and wore a myrtle green tweed day suit.

"Please can you help, Dr Greystone?" said Alice, hoping that addressing the physician by his correct title would win favour.

"Take her inside, please," replied Dr Greystone, as the beetroot-faced man turned an angrier shade of purple.

Inside the consulting room, Dr Greystone removed his jacket and directed the women to an examination bed. Dr Greystone laid Sue down, drew liquid from a bottle into a large syringe, uncovered Sue's upper arm and inserted the needle into her skin. His movements were smooth and quick and Sue had no time to protest. Her eyes closed immediately.

"Please prepare a bowl of water and fetch swabs, by the window."

Alice and Hilda did as instructed. In the meantime, Dr Greystone unfurled the makeshift bandage and tourniquet from Sue's arm. Sue's index finger and middle finger were sheared off beneath the knuckle and the bleeding had been stemmed by ugly black blood clots. Dr Greystone poured a solution into the water and carefully cleaned the wounds.

"Who applied the tourniquet?" he asked. Alice worried that she had harmed Sue, but the doctor praised her. "Well done."

Dr Greystone gestured for Alice and Hilda to sit at his desk. Alice took the doctor's well-upholstered chair and Hilda took the patient's chair in front of it. They positioned themselves to watch Dr Greystone at work. Alice was entranced by his skilful movements, his impeccable manners and composure, her first glimpse of the British officer class in action. Yet Dr Greystone was no military man; he had a graceful university physique, hewn from rowing.

Hilda whispered, "Now she's in good hands ..." Hilda was keen to return to work, as the emergency dash from the factory would constitute unpaid leave. Alice nodded and Hilda left the room. Dr Greystone wound the bandages.

"She will regain good use of the hand. What is her name?"

"Sue, sir."

"I am Simon. And you are?"

"Alice."

"Would you stay with Sue, whilst I attend to Mr Wainman?"

Alice held Sue's other hand which was cold and clammy from the ordeal. Simon attended to the man in the waiting area and after five minutes returned. He positioned the chairs by the examining table and invited Alice to sit with him.

"My receptionist is away and I have not a patient for two hours. We will wait with Sue until she wakes."

"We cannot thank you enough, Dr ... Simon. How much do we owe you?"

Simon shook his head. Alice thanked him for his generosity and added, "I do not know how we will pass the time. In two hours we could read half of *Frankenstein*."

"You have read Mary Shelley?" asked Simon with great surprise.

"Well, yes."

Simon stammered an apology for presuming Alice knew nothing of literature. In fairness to him, her knowledge extended not much further than the few books she had read with Joseph. They talked. Simon was extremely well read. Every so often he offered another embarrassed apology for his original faux pas. There was something appealing about a man so masterful in his chosen profession, yet also so socially awkward. It was also unusual for Alice to be close to a man with no obvious agenda of seduction.

"You must instruct Sue to rest and keep the bandages clean. I will give her something for the pain. She will see me one week hence. And thank you for your theatre assistance. I do hope I wasn't too high-handed?"

Alice wondered if Simon had temporarily escaped the clutches of a domineering wife, which would explain his uncommon sensitivity. He wore no wedding band, but may have removed it for his work. The detail was unimportant.

Over the next few days, Sue recovered well, but fretted about her job, and more pressingly, how three fingers on one hand would affect her marriage prospects. Alice volunteered to accompany Sue back to Dr Simon Greystone and found herself counting the hours and days.

Chapter 9 – The Emporium of Exhibition

The East London district of Whitechapel was a moral frontier. Hard-working Londoners and European immigrants lived alongside criminals, vagabonds and prostitutes. Decent housing was difficult to find. There were terrible slums of grinding poverty, overcrowded tenements and rookeries. Families living eight or ten to a room, with medieval sanitation, were not uncommon. Thousands of children went without shoes on their feet. Some men were fortunate to find work on the docks, while many others went hungry in the overcrowded casual labour market. The workhouse in Charles Street had been enlarged in the 1860s to cope with demand.

Social reformers saw the poor of Whitechapel as victims of the rapacious free market and evangelists were drawn to the area. Ironically, they meant to deprive the lower classes of their one source of parity with the high, the social equality of sin. It seemed like every other woman was a prostitute. More than a thousand whores worked an area encompassing two square miles and there were no shortage of pubs and ale houses in which to solicit. Soldiers and sailors rubbed shoulders with the well-to-do who journeyed east in search of pleasure.

It was a dull, humid spring morning. Outside the Grave Maurice pub, on Whitechapel Road, a gaggle of drinkers waited impatiently for Frank, the landlord, to open. The group comprised of a meat porter, a soldier and three young couples made up of workmen and hard-drinking factory girls. The solider was about to hammer on the door with his fist, when he was distracted by the alluring call of a fairground barker.

"Libations, entertainments and a remarkable freak of nature, my friends, I have all you could possibly desire!"

Charlie wore a black bowler hat, tan brown shoes and a new chequered suit in purple, black and white. He would not have looked out of place as a comic vocalist in music hall. Charlie immediately commanded the attention of the group and proceeded to spin an implausible but amusing yarn about a fellow who was half a man, half an elephant.

"You could not encompass his head in both your arms and his mouth is replete with a trunk. His hand has the appearance of an elephant's foot, with five fingers as one!"

The meat porter jabbed Charlie in the chest with his finger. "Prove it!"

Charlie winked at his audience and extended his right arm with a flourish. "The Emporium of Exhibition is a stone's throw hence." Charlie was keen for the punters to follow him away from the pub as quickly as possible, Frank had already threatened him with violence for stealing custom. Fortunately for Charlie, they did.

Whitechapel Road was a fast-moving estuary of traffic, four vehicles wide. Two- and three-storey commercial buildings flanked both sides of the street, shielding dense enclaves of slums. The air was not good, as the tannery smelt rank today. Trams, carriages, and heavy goods wagons rumbled up and down the road. Charlie led his crowd less than fifty yards, past a tobacconist and a pawnbroker's to a nondescript row of shops, directly across the road from the London Hospital. The Emporium of Exhibition was a murky two-storey terrace, twelve feet in width with a flat roof, in between an Irish grocer's and a boarded-up building. There was no signage and the curtains were drawn. Charlie produced an old iron key and held it up for show. A curious workman tagged along at the rear of the group and Charlie waved him in before shutting the door. The punters jostled for room in the darkness and voiced their displeasure. Charlie illuminated an oil lamp.

There were four paintings on each of the two long walls, eight in total, revealing different views of the same monstrous humanoid, a man, a sort of man, a crumbling landslide of deformity. One could only assume the artist was out of his mind. Charlie lit another lamp. There was a rectangular ox-blood rug in the centre of the room and a curtain of the same hue above a door to the rear of the shop, which was emblazoned with the goldenrod motif, 'The Elephant Man'.

Charlie encouraged all to partake in a belt of Elephant Gin, 'for intestinal fortitude'. The punters each handed over a ha'penny and downed their gin in one. Charlie informed them that it cost an additional three pennies to see The Elephant Man. There were grumbles of protest.

"My friends, you are intrepid souls, driven by excitement and adventure. You seek the wonders of the world. Proceed and you will behold the most remarkable human being on the planet. Your pathway to destiny is thruppence."

The ground floor of the shop was narrow, but deceptively long and the front reception parlour extended fifteen feet to the rear. Charlie led the crowd through the ox-blood curtain. There was another curtain on a screen by the back wall. Nobody wanted to get too close, except Charlie. Floorboards creaked behind the screen. All were silent. 'It' was here.

"A pretty young wifey walks home from the fair. She's expecting a youngling, her head is full of dreams. Little did she reckon upon a nightmare. An elephant breaks free, stampeding straight for her, hooves of thunder, tusks of ivory, teeth of a giant devil. 'Watch out, missus, for the love of God!' Only just escapes with her life. As for the youngling? He was born, and he grew and he grew and he grew. Treasured by his mother, but tarnished by the beast. I give you, The Elephant Man!"

The conman's exaggerated patter was not far from the truth. There was a man, a sort of man, dressed in a toga. It was as if all the demented artwork had been pieced together to create one super freak. Yet he spoke! He gave his name as Joseph Merrick! He told of his family and his faith, his beloved mother's demise, his years in the workhouse and his final redemption. None would forget the grotesque deformity of Joseph Merrick or the sentimental beauty of his soul, or the way he recited his mother's poem, lisping like an eager child.

Since arriving in London Charlie and Joseph had enjoyed many good days of profit and the cheap gin seemed to make punters more generous with the nobbings. However, the flow of punters had been inconsistent, with too many quiet days. Charlie spent most of his time in or outside pubs, attempting to drum up trade from Whitechapel revellers.

Joseph took care of the accounts, storing the takings in a metal safe box beneath a loose floorboard. There was always money in the box, which satisfied Charlie, as he cared nothing for the details of bookkeeping. However, Joseph had been papering over the lack of money in the till with his own savings, which had now depleted to the last few pounds.

Mr McMeeken came by for the rent every Friday. McMeeken was a very short man, who compensated for his diminutive stature by employing hulking toughs to settle his debts. He was a man of few words, other than the odd reminder that, if Charlie was slow to hand over the rent, missed payments would 'incur consequences'.

It was a rough locale.

On Saturday afternoon, Charlie and Joseph were in the parlour waiting for custom, when a man wielding an eight-inch fish filleting knife burst in. He was whippet-thin, with a mop of red hair beneath his bowler, and dark copper stubble on his gaunt, pugilistic face. His hands bore fresh prison tattoos, a transfixed heart, a religious cross and initials J.B.

"Is you him?" the man spat at Joseph.

Charlie intervened and addressed the man calmly. "Sir, relax a while. You are in the home of The Elephant Man."

"Then I's in the right place."

"Sir," said Charlie, "we wish to help you."

The man turned his head to Charlie, still pointing the blade at Joseph.

"Is it true about his mum, frightened by an elephant?" The man was getting more upset, tears in his eyes. "Because my missus come in here the other week and was frightened by him. Now she's in the family way."

"Congratulations, sir," replied Charlie.

The man shouted at Joseph, "You've ruined her!"

Joseph held his chest and heaved for breath. "My m-medicine."

The man hesitated and Charlie took advantage of Joseph's distraction, reaching for the cosh inside his jacket and braining the intruder over the back of the head. The man dropped the knife and crashed into the wall, bringing down a piece of Joseph's self-portraiture. Charlie flailed about his head with the cosh, as if attempting to swat an errant bluebottle.

The man staggered out through the front door with blood running from the divots in his skull and fell onto the pavement on all fours. Charlie kicked him in the meat of his stomach. The man collapsed onto his face and curled up in a ball. Charlie leant over him, still brandishing the cosh.

"How dare you bring trouble here!"

Joseph watched through a crack in the door and saw the approval of locals. It was Whitechapel and the application of swift, merciless violence was the equivalent of exchanging cards in polite society. Afterwards, a giant plainclothes detective named DI Blake and two uniformed officers paid Charlie a friendly visit. Charlie was fined eighteen shillings by magistrates for a breach of the peace.

Another week passed with average business. On the Friday, Joseph showed for a group of merchants on a lunchtime jolly and a cohort of upper-class medical students from the London Hospital. However, the rest of the afternoon dragged without a single visitor. Joseph welcomed a day of relative quiet despite the financial implications. He and Charlie opened a bottle of port in the parlour.

There was a tentative knock on the door. Joseph limped into the display area and had only just changed into his toga, when Charlie ducked behind the curtain and said "Butcher's!" It was Charlie's code for a punter who simply desired a butcher's hook - look and that no theatricality was required. Charlie ascertained this either by the mood of the punter or by specific request.

Charlie led the man inside and pulled back the curtain without ceremony. Joseph beheld his one-man audience. The well-dressed gentleman wore an expensive black frock coat and the corners of his thick moustache drooped down past his top lip, giving his face a sullen expression. He had removed his hat, indicating good breeding by adhering to the correct etiquette for arriving indoors. His short, no-nonsense hair looked like a military cut.

The gentleman stared at Joseph with wide-eyed fascination, but none of the colour drained from his face. He had the silent gravitas of high office and great intellect. Joseph thought he was probably a man of science or medicine, given his earnest interest and lack of queasiness. The gentleman turned to Charlie, waiting for something to happen.

"Stand up, please," prompted Charlie and Joseph complied.

The gentleman's eyes probed different points of Joseph's body as if checking the walls of a house for underlying structural defects. Joseph turned full circle, slowly, two rotations. The gentleman indicated he had seen enough. Charlie politely gestured to the door. The gentleman nodded goodbye to Joseph with an unsure tip of the head. It was a curious encounter.

Joseph dressed and heard muffled conversation. He assumed Charlie was pitching for an additional contribution to the nobbings. Charlie closed up the shop and returned to the display area.

"Christ knows what they teach them across the road. He was after a private exhibition. Or not so private, with his chums. I said, 'Bring them here, sir, group discount.' 'That would be inappropriate,' says he, the cheeky bastard."

"And?"

"He was offering good money. A guinea."

Joseph could feel them rising from the mire of debt.

"When do I show?"

Charlie shook his head. "He wants to see it all, Joseph, naked as the day you were born."

"You did not even take his card?"

Charlie was surprised and a little hurt by the way Joseph snapped at him. He reached in his pocket for the card. Joseph snatched it from Charlie with his good hand. The doctor's name was Frederick Treves.

Charlie negotiated an extra eleven shillings on the fee Treves originally offered and agreed on the venue of the London Hospital. Treves sent an underling to the shop with the money and instructions for when Joseph was expected to arrive. On the afternoon in question, Charlie closed up the shop. Joseph changed into his long black overcoat, his legionnaire's cap and a sleeve to disguise his colossal right hand. The hardest part would be transporting Joseph the perilous thirty yards across Whitechapel Road without being hit by a carriage. Charlie stood at Joseph's elbow and linked his right arm through Joseph's left. Charlie had purchased a cheap navy blue suit and low top hat for the occasion. When Charlie waved his arms in an authoritative fashion, drivers slowed to his command, mistaking him for a policeman. They were more than half way across the road before any driver realised this was not an altruistic bobby helping an invalid, but something incredibly bizarre.

The London Hospital was the most aesthetically pleasing building in Whitechapel. It had been constructed when the district was all fields and still resembled a rural manor house. The main entrance beneath integrated pillars and a clockface seemed to welcome the sick inside. The ordinary patient could trust the well-bred doctors within and submit to their educated decrees, like rural peasants with their benevolent lord.

Once inside, Joseph and Charlie were escorted straight up to Treves's office. There were no pleasantries and Joseph was out of his clothes faster than an on-call prostitute running behind the clock. Joseph did not speak and wordlessly complied with Treves's simple, 'Raise your arm, please' instructions. Ten of Treves's colleagues squeezed into the office. In terms of medical curiosity, Joseph's body represented the discovery of a diamond.

One doctor stood out, a younger physician, who did not fit the profile of the average hospital man. He dressed more informally, in a green tweed. The doctor kindly asked Joseph if he felt unwell. Joseph said he was in good health, considering. The other doctors were astonished, as if a man of his physical appearance should not possess the power of speech. Joseph was invited back several times, with Charlie negotiating incremental raises to the fee.

Charlie shrewdly invested the money in promotions. Performers from the Paragon Music Hall drank at the pubs Charlie frequented. With a bit of charm and a few shillings, he managed to persuade many of the acts to perform in front of the shop, the urban equivalent of parading and dooring. The likes of Titch Tabern: Clog Dance Sensation gathered considerable crowds, enabling Charlie to lure punters inside.

The Elephant Man entertained all classes, from working men and factory girls to gentlemen in dinner coats. Word of mouth had a snowball effect, bringing more punters. Joseph and Charlie discussed a number of ideas to increase revenue by introducing more sellings, such as trinkets or keepsakes, before deciding on an autobiographical pamphlet. Joseph drafted a part-fact, part-fiction account of his life, staying true to his sideshow persona. *An Elephant's Tale* was cheap to print, popular with punters and highly profitable.

Joseph kept quiet about how close they had come to financial ruin. Charlie had secrets of his own. Every Monday Charlie requested a pound from the safe box for 'protection money' and disappeared to pay the mystery party. Charlie did not divulge details, hoping ignorance would exonerate Joseph if the police ever put him to the question.

Joseph and Charlie shared a quick drink each night after closing, before Charlie went his own way. Charlie's extra earnings allowed him to keep a single room on Buck's Row, behind the shop. When Charlie left, Joseph read alone by candlelight, or watched the street from his first-floor living quarters. Whenever Joseph looked across the road to the London Hospital he always wondered if Treves was still working, or had departed for home. Joseph imagined three or four immaculate children lining up for the return of Pater.

There were always prostitutes walking about, carefree young whores in garish dresses, derelict old ones in the uniform of scrubwomen. Joseph appreciated Charlie's sensitivity. Charlie kept his distance with his women so as not to torment Joseph with the sex he would never experience.

Exactly one week after the accident, Alice accompanied Sue to the surgery of Dr Simon Greystone. Simon examined Sue's fingers and confirmed that she was making a good recovery. Alice passed Simon a scrap of paper with the address of her lodgings. Simon called at dusk the next evening. They found a secluded spot in Victoria Park and laid out a blanket. Simon produced a bottle of good red wine from his medical bag and apologised for not bringing any glasses. Alice initiated the first kiss.

On the third occasion they went to the park, Alice plucked up the courage to ask Simon about his wife. Simon launched into an anguished and guilt-ridden monologue, emphasising a loveless marriage of convenience. The union had been arranged by his elder brother, Gilbert, for social advantage. Simon added that he and Mrs Greystone maintained separate chambers, which suggested the union was unconsummated. Alice was as inexperienced as Simon when it came to making love, but what they lacked in proficiency, they made up for with passion.

Simon suggested renting a small apartment, so Alice would not have to live in squalor or work in that dreadful place. She did not need a second invitation. The small apartment was actually a mid-terrace on Crowland Terrace, Islington, modest by the standards of affluence, but a palace to an ordinary worker. Simon stayed over on at least two nights a week, often three and they saw each other every day, if only for an hour at lunch. Alice spent her days exploring London, reading in coffee houses, enjoying a pleasant, semi-bohemian existence. She wore a dummy wedding ring to deter unwanted advances, although men approached her regardless.

Alice drifted out of friendship with Hilda, but kept in touch with Sue. After recovering from her injuries, Sue had found domestic work in the service of the Winchesters, a family of wealthy exporters who lived in Marylebone. Sue enjoyed her new employ and referred to the family as 'we' rather than 'they'. As the Winchesters were visiting the Downs that weekend, Sue had a rare day off and was free to meet Alice on Saturday afternoon at the Rose Tavern.

When Alice revealed her relationship with Simon, Sue implored her to pressure him into a divorce, then marriage, as soon as possible. She also asked Alice to pass on her thanks to him for the work on her finger stumps, which 'Healed fantastic!' Sue guzzled five double whiskey and sodas to Alice's three. She suggested a trip to the Winchesters' for a butcher's, as the other staff were away on the drink.

Sue led Alice to a square of magnificent mansions, with an oval water feature in the centre. The Winchesters' residence was a three-storey town house with mock Roman pillars by the front entrance. The drawing room led through to a dining room with a long mahogany table large enough to accommodate a dozen guests. Sue fussed with obvious pride, rubbing her sleeve against barely perceptible blemishes. The dining area opened into a room with a grand piano. Alice moved her finger along the black and white ivory keys. Sue said, “Don’t touch nothing!”

Alice looked at the array of framed photographs on the marble mantelpiece. Sue introduced the subjects as if the family were her own. Father Winchester, the stern patriarch, had a thick black beard and barrel chest. Mother Winchester was prim and unflinching. The well-drilled Winchester children posed with perfect stillness and obedience, sailor suits for the young boys, tweed hunting jackets for the older lads. The straight-laced girls wore white cotton dresses, trainee matriarchs for the next generation.

Alice imagined Simon growing up with his own Winchester family, receiving orders and obeying commands, sitting rigidly at the piano, petrified of a stray finger, a discordant note, the shame of disharmony, before being packed off to boarding school. Alice did not know what boys like Simon were taught exactly, but understood that some magic combination of Greek myth and relentless sport equipped the British upper classes to rule the world.

Simon belonged to the humanitarian wing of his class. They ruled, but were jolly nice about it, with genuine concern for the lower orders. When Alice and Hilda had brought Sue to his practice, bleeding and injured, Sue probably reminded Simon of one of the staff, a nice common lady, who nursed his cuts as a boy. Alice wondered what she was to Simon. Probably danger. The only risk for Alice was the one Simon minimised through modern contraceptive methods.

Sue continued to prattle on about the photographic portraits. It was a curious, half-drunk afternoon in an empty house, but Alice knew Simon a little better.

Simon had an afternoon off and Alice suggested a picnic. She packed a pork pie, sandwiches, a fruit cake, a bottle of white wine and two glasses. They carried the wicker hamper to the park in Highbury.

It was a beautiful summer afternoon. Alice watched Simon eat. Despite his demanding work and the drudgery of his home life, Simon exuded good health. She tickled his ribcage.

"May I eat it properly, dear? I fear indigestion."

"Ever so sensible, Simon!"

"I just don't believe merriment and mastication are easy bedfellows." Simon kept a straight face for a second more, then launched his own tickling assault on Alice. Highbury Park was far enough from Simon's practice and his marital home in Belgravia to allow them to relax. They kissed. Alice sat upright and reached into the hamper for the cake. Simon swallowed a mouthful of sandwich and patted the crumbs with a napkin. Alice's smile waned.

"Is everything all right, my dear?"

"I am sorry," said Alice. "Moments like these contrast with lives less fortunate."

"As part of my medical research I recently saw a man, hideously deformed." Simon gestured to the food. "Probably not the best subject."

"No. Go on."

"Well, the poor fellow. He was part of a freak show."

"A travelling freak show?"

"I think not. Some grotty little parlour in Whitechapel," said Frederick. "I have seen their like before, Alice. Dwarves and bearded ladies, paraded like cattle. What do you think possesses these people to display themselves?"

"Desperation," said Alice.

Simon nodded approvingly at her insight.

"At least the poor man has won a temporary reprieve. He is to appear before the Pathological Society, a day away from servitude as the magnificent Elephant."

"You mean the Elephant Man?"

"I think so."

"What is he called?"

"Maybrick? Meyrick?"

"My God."

"You know this fellow?"

"I have heard tell. How did he look?"

"Indescribable."

"I mean to say, was he well? Was he happy?"

Simon looked admiringly at Alice, interpreting her interest as compassion for a cripple.

"Happy in his own way. Why, when I enquired about his health he replied it was 'Good, considering.' Many invalids use happiness as a mask. They smile to hide the pain of affliction. But this man could not smile, owing to his facial deformities."

Alice held the knife above the cake as if suspended in time.

"You have a beautiful smile," said Simon. "In fact, you are the most beautiful woman in the world."

Alice did not hear him. He told her again. She apologised and pretended to listen, but registered not one word he said, because her mind was consumed with other thoughts, of human oddities, long-lost friends and enigmatic former lovers.

On his last visit to the London Hospital, Treves had asked Charlie if Joseph was available for a special exhibition for the fee of two pounds. Charlie said three. Treves offered an additional ten shillings. Charlie said, "Twelve and I'll shake your hand, sir." Treves agreed, but did not shake Charlie's hand when he offered it.

The brougham arrived at the Emporium of Exhibition at 6.30 p.m. Charlie helped Joseph ascend the steps of the carriage. The driver came down to lend a hand, but hesitated when he saw Joseph's hood. Charlie confirmed the destination as the Pathological Society in Bloomsbury and the driver nodded as if it all made sense. He must have assumed the strange man from Whitechapel was about to participate in some form of ungodly entertainment for the rich.

Charlie drew the curtains inside the carriage, leaving a crack for peeking outside, and Joseph removed his headgear. They each took a stiffening belt of whiskey from Charlie's new stainless steel hip flask and settled in to enjoy the view. The coach rolled west, through the City of London, past The Royal Exchange, St Paul's Cathedral and the University of Arts before reaching Bloomsbury. Never before had Joseph seen such affluence. Bloomsbury was a district of townhouses for the rich, university buildings, parks and garden squares. He was amazed that such wealth existed a mere three miles from the poverty of Whitechapel. The Pathological Society of London was how Joseph imagined an opera house.

Once inside, a porter directed Joseph and Charlie to a white, sterile room with two concrete slabs, presumably a butcher's shop for the dead. "Nice dressing room," said Charlie. Frederick Treves entered. He seemed hugely disappointed by Charlie's tartan chequered suit, as if his gaudy outfit besmirched the prestige of the institute.

"I trust the journey was amenable?" said Treves with a grimace.

"Absolutely, sir," said Charlie. "It is always a pleasure. Such a lovely place. Almost makes me wish I was ill."

"Indeed?"

"How many of your colleagues will attend today, sir?"

"Up to one hundred." Treves addressed Joseph. "But there is no need to be nervous."

"Are they aware his mother was frightened by an elephant, sir?" said Charlie.

"This is a school of rational science, McCallion."

"I can regale them of this tale at no extra cost."

"No extra cost? That would be a novelty."

Treves accompanied Joseph and Charlie to a grand lecture theatre. It was four steps up to the raised stage. There was a canvas dressing screen with a wooden chair behind it. Next to the chair was a table with a tape measure, callipers and other medical instruments laid out for the examiner. The examiner was a fellow of advanced age, bald on the top of his head, with round glasses and the air of a wise professor. He was accompanied by a young, peach-faced assistant. Joseph disrobed with Charlie's help. The assistant looked about ready to scream.

Charlie bundled up Joseph's clothes. Treves gestured for Charlie to move out of sight. The assistant directed Joseph to the chair behind the screen. Joseph rested on the back of the chair with his good hand to support his weight. Treves left the stage. Joseph waited behind the curtain. The medical men filtered in and found their seats, conversing in murmurs, as if settling down for a concerto.

The professor stepped to the front of the stage and the audience quietened in anticipation of his opening remarks. Joseph felt a lightning bolt of pain in his chest. His knees buckled and he gripped the chair, determined not to fall. He was about to cry out, but the pain eased slowly. Joseph told himself this pain was just another freak occurrence of his freakish body.

The assistant removed the screen. Joseph noticed alarm in the eyes of many, although the well-mannered, eminent audience kept their professional repose. If only, thought Joseph, it had been this easy at The Leicester Gaiety. The professor stood by Joseph, taking measurements of his body with the tape, positioning the callipers over his head, making announcements. One hundred men could see his private parts, but like an artist's model, Joseph was growing accustomed to nudity.

When the exhibition concluded, Charlie helped Joseph dress and they were led back into the morgue by a porter. Treves followed. The porter handed Charlie the money as it would have been grubby and low for a surgeon to handle cash. Charlie asked Treves for another crown. "You'd be amazed at how fast Joseph's walking slippers wear out, sir."

Treves ignored Charlie, produced his card and passed it to Joseph. Treves nodded goodbye with an air of finality and left the room along with the porter.

Charlie handed Joseph the hip flask, whilst muttering a complaint about Treves. Joseph took a drink and passed it back to Charlie. Suddenly another man swept into the room, obviously some sort of doctor, and positioned himself in front of Joseph for an impromptu examination. The doctor had light-brown hair, piercing eyes and a slight but strong physique beneath his immaculately tailored evening suit. Joseph took him for a disciple of modern muscular training. The man tapped his right foot. He seemed in a hurry, like a punter eager to stake his wager before the start of a horse race. The way he stared at Joseph's body without blinking was truly unnerving.

"Disrobe him again," ordered the doctor, without taking his eyes from Joseph.

"The exhibition is finished, sir," replied Charlie.

"What are you? His keeper? His manager?"

"His associate in business."

"To be a fly on the wall at your board meetings. Now look here, I have a proposition. I intend to buy him."

Joseph detected anger in Charlie's reply. "He is not for sale, sir."

"Of course he is. You people trade, do you not? That is how you procured him in the first place. Name your price."

When no offer came the doctor continued, "I represent a scientific community with a great interest in this form of handicap. The study of your man will help us understand and eradicate such impediments. Create a vaccine for others, as it were. I assure you no harm will come to him. He will spend his days in a clean, comfortable asylum with good food and humane treatment. Two hundred pounds."

Charlie shook his head.

"Three hundred pounds. I'll have my man run a cheque to your emporium. Or perhaps you'd prefer cash?"

"You can't, sir."

"There really is no need to haggle. Name your price."

Charlie put his arm around Joseph. The doctor blocked their way to the door and called Charlie a 'ghastly little man'.

Charlie put his hands in the front pockets of his trousers and in doing so opened his jacket to reveal the cosh. The doctor stepped backwards and to the side. Charlie closed his jacket. The porter entered, assumed the doctor was concluding matters and announced the arrival of the carriage. As they left the room, Joseph heard the doctor mutter, "I know you. You're the one from Leicester."

Charlie and Joseph boarded the carriage and passed the flask between them. Charlie launched into a long diatribe about Treves, the medical profession, the rude doctor and how he would regret not teaching him a lesson. Joseph brooded on the doctor's parting comment. There was no mention of Leicester during the examination, so how could the doctor know the location of his hometown? After more whiskey their good humour returned and the disquieting exchange was forgotten. When the coach arrived back on Whitechapel Road, Joseph and Charlie were singing the *Wild Rover*.

It was late, past eleven o'clock. Aside from sporadic drunken revellers and a smattering of prostitutes, the street was relatively quiet. Charlie helped Joseph disembark from the coach. The driver, having been paid in advance, set off immediately. Joseph dropped his keys on the floor and Charlie bent down to locate them. Joseph kept watch, although he could hardly see a thing through his legionnaire's cap. The street was dark but his hearing attuned to danger and he detected faint, cautious footsteps behind him. Joseph whispered Charlie's name as a warning and Charlie spun around, cosh at the ready. But when Alice Powell emerged from the darkness, Charlie dropped the weapon on the floor.

Joseph, Charlie and Alice went upstairs to the living quarters and Joseph broke open the brandy he was saving for a special occasion. Joseph and Alice occupied the two wooden chairs, sitting opposite each other by the crackling fire of the hearth. There was nowhere for Charlie to sit, but he was happy to stand, acting out stories from their tenure at the Whitechapel emporium. Charlie's monologues provided Joseph with the opportunity to quietly observe Alice.

Alice wore a chestnut-coloured pencil dress with a high neck, displaying her stunning physique, and a fedora hat. Her eyes were sparkling blue, and despite the soot and bad air of London, her skin was completely unblemished. There was something more relaxed in her mannerisms. Her feral defensiveness had gone.

"Twenty-five guineas we have earned tonight for a single, private exhibition!"

Alice was astounded by the sum. Joseph winked to denote 'embellishment'.

"Doctors, they were, Alice. Upper-crust dimbers. There was one fellow, offered cash for our Joseph here. Imagine a man like him poking around your insides? Terrible business."

Alice smiled weakly and shuffled in her chair.

"What of you, Alice?" asked Joseph. "Come, tell all."

Alice described her arrival in London and her former employ at the McReedy jute factory in great detail, painstaking detail, far too much detail for a woman who rarely said a commonplace thing. Alice was talking for the sake of it, skirting around more personal subjects. She had not removed her velvet gloves and caught Joseph looking at her left hand, searching for the tell-tale bulge on the fourth finger. Alice dispensed with her small talk and removed the glove.

Charlie whistled at her gold wedding band and Joseph raised his glass in the salute of a toast, so the quiver in his voice would not betray him. Charlie pressed Alice for details of her husband and her new life. She was now Mrs Bryson; he was an architect.

"I'll bet he had grand designs on you from the start," said Charlie. "How long have you been wed?"

"Oh, three months."

"How did you meet, a dance?"

"Yes."

"Where do you live?"

"Highbury."

"Describe the residence."

"Large, roomy."

"You must have servants: how many?"

"Enough."

Alice sounded like a shy girl unsure of her first romantic infatuation, rather than an architect's wife. Surely, thought Joseph, a woman who performed as a human curiosity and displayed her beard would not squirm before questions of mundane banality? Joseph thought that Alice was like Charlie with his women; she did not want to overplay the joy of her exciting new life.

"I'm still looking for one special little lady," said Charlie.

"You are looking prolifically," added Joseph.

"I am not."

"You have taken rooms one street yonder, to attend to your myriad matters of the heart."

Alice smiled at Joseph's teasing.

Charlie said to Alice, "Don't be a stranger." He babbled to correct himself. "For visits I mean. Friendly visits. Here or there. It's been too long."

Joseph asked Alice when she was expected home. Alice replied that her husband was away on business. They drank until first light. Charlie insisted on walking Alice to an omnibus. Alice declined his offer; she could handle herself. Many confident young women made similar statements, but for Alice this was certainly true. Besides, most of Whitechapel's criminal element operated behind closed doors in daylight, which meant for Joseph and Charlie it was nearly opening.

Joseph floated through the day and Charlie was also in high spirits, garnishing his patter with greater exaggerations than usual. In their spare moments they speculated about Mr Bryson. Charlie reckoned he was a posh type, a genius or a human Hercules. He also offered an alternative theory, that Alice could have married an old man resembling a walnut, for his money.

Joseph imagined Mr Bryson befitting the former description, a statue of handsome granite, with a chiselled physique of rugby and rowing the sculls. He pictured them together at their mansion, naked, in a four-poster bed, Alice nestling her head against Bryson, with her curls of ebony cascading across his chest. Bryson had everything: the love of a beautiful woman, a mastery of life. Joseph wondered if he ever kissed her small pink razor scars? Yet there was something puzzling Joseph. Alice was bohemian in appearance, relaxed in her manners and untamed in spirit; she did not cut the figure of a society wife.

Such thoughts were redundant. Joseph vowed to hide his true feelings. Alice would stay and remain his friend. He would not force her to reject him.

Unbeknown to Charlie, late after closing, Alice began to visit Joseph at the shop on at least two nights a week. It was Alice's suggestion not to bother Charlie with their arrangement. Joseph felt guilty favouring Alice, but knew that Charlie's nocturnal activities would keep him happy.

Alice lamented Joseph's inadequate diet and his bachelor's ignorance of cooking. To compensate, she brought homemade food or ingredients to cook over the hearth. They ate delicious stews, sausages, bacon, buttered potatoes and all varieties of fish. Alice brought smooth, rich red wines and chocolates from upmarket emporiums.

When Alice visited Joseph they always read to each other after supper. Sometimes they spoke all night, and Alice slipped through the back door moments before Charlie turned his key in the front. Joseph asked Charlie to arrange the purchase of a settee, under the pretext that he wanted to sleep by the fire. The settee enabled Joseph and Alice to read by the fire. Alice always kicked off her shoes after a few pages, placed her feet on one end and snuggled into Joseph's shoulder.

The wonderful evenings of friendship were reminiscent of their time at the fair, but the added benefit was the privacy and the homeliness of the room, even if it was a rather dingy room above a freak show parlour. For Joseph it was an insight into the precious home life of a young married couple, nourishing each other with food, warmth and affection after the trials of the work day.

Alice provided only brief details of her married life, making Joseph suspicious. One night, as she opened a second bottle of red wine, he plucked up the courage to confront her.

"I must mark the card of your husband, letting you walk these streets alone. Is he aware of your nocturnal adventures?"

"Yes, Joseph, my husband approves of my sojourns to the seediest parlours of Whitechapel."

But Joseph would not be deterred.

"I must ask. Are you even married?"

Alice played with the wedding band on her finger. "Sin is the heart of the matter. There is a man and we are engaged. But alas, he is married."

Alice unburdened herself of the 'Mrs Bryson' charade. She described her chance encounter with Doctor Simon Greystone through her friend's industrial accident and the events that followed. Alice explained that she shared a rented terrace with Simon and they spent at least three nights a week in each other's company. Joseph tried not to think about their love-making.

"His marriage is a charade of high society. There is no love. Once divorced, we will marry. That is my sordid tale."

"I hope you are not one of his many?"

"Hardly! Are you ashamed of me?"

"Hardly," replied Joseph.

"Please do not tell Charlie. I am not afraid he would judge me, but I wish to avoid complication."

Joseph felt for his wine glass on the floor. Alice reached down and handed it to him. She would have made a fine wife, thought Joseph, for a congenital cripple.

"When will you marry?"

"To divorce his wife and marry me is to disgrace himself and shame his family. He also has his professional reputation to consider. Moral constipation is the disease of his class."

Joseph said, "When I was a boy there was a girl on our street, sweet girl, attended chapel. At sixteen, she found herself in trouble. My father denounced her as a harlot. Yet when Mother died, I discovered the true date of my parents' wedding. I was almost born a bastard by a scant few weeks. The disease you describe afflicts all classes."

"Then you understand my predicament."

Alice kicked off her shoes, raised her feet to the arm of the settee and snuggled into Joseph's shoulder. Joseph reached for the pile of books on the table and picked up a Beeton's Annual. He opened the pages at random and selected a penny dreadful detective mystery, yet Joseph would have read from a textbook on long division to prolong the moment.

Chapter 10 – Duty

Gilbert Greystone lived in Bayswater on Thurrock Terrace, a quiet residential street which was lined with beech trees. His own home was situated in an exclusive terrace of three-storey white stucco properties. Thurrock Terrace reminded Gilbert of a row of pristine white teeth, but what was his life, he asked himself, if not the pursuit of purity? Gilbert's abode was an extremely well-appointed residence for a professional bachelor, but small in comparison to the majestic Belgravia townhouse that Dunham had purchased for Simon and Jemima.

Gilbert employed two staff, a housekeeper and cook Rosa, and a manservant, Andrews. Rosa was a Spanish spinster of twenty-eight years. She was an extremely diligent and conscientious worker, a skilled chef with a noble hidalgo face. Andrews was a bachelor aged forty-five years who lived in North Paddington. He had been an admiral's servant until the death of his master and was servile and racially sound. Gilbert approved Rosa's request to employ a part-time washerwoman. She was a low type with terrible grammar and Gilbert did not know her name, but she was clean and free from infection. The house and the upkeep of it consumed almost every penny of his salary. Yet Gilbert would never signpost his pitiful inheritance by residing in an inferior domicile.

Simon and Jemima accepted his invitation to dinner on Wednesday evening and Gilbert received his guests in the drawing room. The men dressed in dining jackets and black bow ties. Jemima wore a salmon pink bustle dress and her fair hair in plaits. She blithered on about his furnishings, the French table with the legs of a bandy bulldog, the various leather chesterfields, the paintings at eye level depicting the same sort of pastoral scene. Gilbert chose his home interior with an eye to conformity so that other people would lazily assume he was like them. Such complacent persons would be pliant to his will.

At seven-thirty sharp, Andrews announced dinner was ready and the Greystones adjourned to the dining room. Gilbert sat at the head of the table, confirming his status, and Simon and Jemima sat facing each other. Andrews frittered to and fro fetching food and charging drinks. Entrée: Smoked Salmon; Plat Principal: Beef Wellington; Dessert: Crème Brûlée. Jemima had a childlike disregard for conversational protocol and spoke without being spoken to.

"I notice your fine peony paper, brother Gilbert. I am a devotee of Bonaparte, but I am afraid my husband is almost tonally blind. On the one occasion I sought his counsel, he picked out the most dreary Maddox. Our drawing room would have resembled the wretched tunnel of a mine!"

Jemima laughed at her own remark and blew a small piece of new potato out of her nose. It ricocheted off the brass candelabra and landed by Gilbert's milk. Simon ignored the comment and polished off another glass of claret. Gilbert distracted himself with thoughts of his recent surgeries.

After many months of frustration, Gilbert believed he had finally hit upon the most reliable technique for vasoligation. Dunham was delighted with progress and Gilbert felt the elation of an artist producing his career-best work. The mishaps were no longer medical but administrative, a governor of a lunatic asylum who was in their pay, threatening blackmail. Dunham had the man silenced by arranging his beating.

Gilbert thanked Dunham for his continued support. "What are families for?" replied Dunham, but he stressed they were also for another purpose. Dunham was desperate to extend his clan with yet another grandson and kept dropping hints. Gilbert shared Dunham's anxiety. He needed Simon to sire a son for the sake of his own line, as the Greystones possessed no racial heir. Gilbert felt like a despairing dog breeder watching his apathetic hound circle the bitch. Meanwhile, Jemima was in full flow.

"I observed a creature from the upper floor, rummaging at the bottom of the garden. I said, 'There is a thing in the garden!' Simon replied, 'What thing?' He went to the window. What did you say it was, my love?"

"I cannot remember," sighed Simon.

"How could I possibly forget? 'A rabbit!' Why, brother Gilbert, this creature would have been a whale in the rabbit kingdom. It was in fact a fox. A fox of all things! Dear Simon, how you are the source of much merriment."

Simon held his glass up to Andrews for a refill.

Jemima added, "We have so little time to enjoy our home. My husband, your brother, works incredibly hard. His practice takes him away from our home overnight, on at least three evenings per week."

Simon twitched his glass away a moment too soon and a stream of claret poured onto the tablecloth. Andrews, like a good servant, insisted on taking the blame, even though it was Simon's fault for raising the glass and forgetting his table manners.

Under any other circumstance Gilbert would have taken Jemima's word as evidence of an affair. Yet Gilbert could not imagine his brother as a lover of women. He considered the possibilities. Was Simon a dreadful little sexual invert with a predilection for catamites? Did he maintain a room of carpet railway toys? Perhaps Simon checked himself into a guest house to escape from Jemima? Gilbert was not entirely unsympathetic. If Jemima were his wife Gilbert would have occupied his time with locum work on the moon.

Jemima finally observed protocol after dinner and retired to the drawing room. Gilbert sent Rosa to keep her company so she did not have to witter at the walls. He invited Simon into the living room to discuss family matters. The living room was Gilbert's one concession to the cult of wallpaper. Sensuous burgundy floral motifs reminded him of the female organ and many happy hours in theatre at the London Hospital.

The centrepiece was a four feet by three feet mirror above an imitation white marble fireplace, surrounded by serpentlike ornamental gilding. In front of the mirror, between two silver bookends, stood *The Problem Of and Solution To Negro Overbreeding* by his father, St John Greystone. Gilbert recently had the book rebound in dark red leather, owing to prolific study. Simon shuddered at the sight of it.

Simon sat on the chaise longue, nursing a glass of cognac. Gilbert paced the room, inspecting the ornaments, drawing out the tension in his brother's gut.

"You hardly said a word at dinner, Simon."

"Jemima tends to monopolise the conversation."

"Quite a raconteur, your wife."

"I am truly blessed."

"Imagine how you will be blessed with a son."

"If it is God's will."

"Indeed. Only the almighty can beget a virgin birth."

Simon's eye twitched, but he held his composure. He replied, "There are times I think you should have tied the knot with Dunham."

Gilbert wished he could tell Simon everything. Every sterilisation and vasoligation, on every mental defective, if only to amuse himself at Simon's humanitarian gibbering.

"I brokered this union to help you, because you alone were incapable. It is our duty to further the race. The Dunhams are fine people."

"You mean incredibly wealthy people?"

Gilbert knew Simon's life consisted of small verbal victories, not unlike the niggardly remarks of a disobedient wife. They consoled Simon for a few moments and he could pretend he was his own man, strong and defiant, before he crumbled beneath Gilbert's will.

"Would you rather the courtship of the working class, a joust with broken beer glasses? Lacerate the face of the next fellow and win the calloused hand of a factory girl?"

"I am led to believe they marry for love."

"Oh God!" spat Gilbert. "Out with it!"

"I do not love her, brother. It is a farce, a sham. I should never have gone through with it. She'd be happier with some twit from the tennis club."

"You will do your duty. By God you will."

Simon shook his head. Gilbert added, "You understand the concept of duty, as your nocturnal doctoring suggests. Have you extended your practice to the treatment of night owls?"

Simon tightened his grip on the glass and Gilbert thought he might have finally ignited something in his brother. But Simon relaxed his grip and replied with resignation, "It is possible to recite a vow and lie, but one cannot fabricate desire. That is all."

Gilbert left Simon to wallow in cognac and self-pity and joined Jemima in the drawing room. He dismissed Rosa, positioned two French chairs directly facing each other and requested Jemima to sit with him. Jemima obeyed. Gilbert moved his chair closer and their knees were almost touching. She reminded Gilbert of an overgrown girl, lost in her voluminous dress.

"Jemima, you are my dearest sister, a wonderful young woman."

"My dearest brother, you are a wonderful man!"

"I must broach with you a subject of extreme delicacy. Your marriage, is it all it could be?"

"We have happiness unbound."

"Have you engaged with your husband on a biblical level?"

"Well, I ..."

"My dear sister, there is no need to blush. It is a simple medical question, requiring a simple honest answer."

"Yes."

Gilbert forced himself to reply calmly, so as not to shout in her face.

"Dishonesty is a sin. I represent your father on this issue. To lie before your father is to lie before God. I ask again, have you engaged with your husband on a biblical level?"

A long silence passed. Jemima admitted meekly, "No."

"Why not, Jemima?"

"I fear he does not love me, I fear he does not want me. On our wedding night he lay beside me cold and motionless. He sleeps each night in a separate chamber. Some days I am overcome by tremendous weeping ..."

Gilbert gripped the base of his chair wishing it was Jemima's throat. Never had the urge to kill been stronger. But there she was, a million pounds or more, a piece of inane porcelain. To break her would shatter eugenics, wreck the dream and retard humanity. Gilbert knew that Dunham's patronage was vital and that all patrons must be indulged and by proxy, their families.

"The early days of marriage are plagued by awkward moments and beset by little fears. It is the same for every young love. Worry not, Jemima, my brother yearns for you."

"Then why does he not touch me?"

"Simon is as gallant as a knight of old. He will not proceed without your command. Signal you are ready from the turret of your love castle. Light a fire, lower the drawbridge and Simon will gallop across the divide. Together, your love will be legend. Tonight, you will be my guests."

Jemima stopped snivelling and nodded in agreement. Gilbert was elated. She had presumably read much romantic fiction and was receptive to cotton wool metaphor.

Gilbert excused himself for bed, but instead of entering his chamber, locked himself in the spare room adjoining the guest bedroom. The room was essentially a store room for his surplus books and medical periodicals. The street lamp outside provided enough light for reading and Gilbert occupied himself with a paper on urinary fistula. Minutes later Gilbert heard footsteps and his guests entering their room. Gilbert cautiously removed the pastoral landscape from the wall. The picture covered a narrow bore hole, half the circumference of a man's index finger, but enough for a view. Andrews had lighted candles in the guest room as per Gilbert's instruction. Jemima and Simon stood but five feet in front of him.

Jemima pounced on Simon, thrusting her face for a kiss. Their teeth collided. Simon winced but Jemima ate into his mouth. She reminded Gilbert of a stout yeoman attacking a chicken carcass. Jemima broke the kiss and tried to help Simon undress, but fumbled incompetently. Simon stepped back, removed his bow tie and unbuttoned his collar, as if he was preparing to place his neck in a noose. Jemima fidgeted out of her evening dress, standing all over it. Their shadows danced like erratic spiders. Finally, they were naked.

Jemima's ribs jutted from her bony torso and her breasts were not much bigger than a man's, though her nipples were erect and prominent. She was young and healthy, an adequate broodmare. It amused Gilbert to observe that the lower part of Simon's body had overcome the higher principles of his mind.

Jemima slid beneath the bedsheets. Simon followed and their inept kissing resumed. Simon rolled on top of her. She gasped at the first incision. Simon began the heavy work and the bed creaked like a fat man in a rocking chair. Jemima's wheezing brought to Gilbert's mind a terminal consumptive labouring up a flight of stairs. Simon made a sound like a man clearing his throat in a library. The bed stopped creaking. The deed was done.

Moments later Jemima's began her trite 'It was wonderful' pillow talk. Gilbert hoped she would now prompt Simon to proceed regularly, vigorously and efficiently towards the desired conclusion. If it was a boy, Gilbert foresaw a power struggle with Dunham for influence. If it was a girl, no matter. Either way, in a few years time, Dunham would no longer have the whip hand and the Greystones would have an heir. Gilbert quietly left the room and tiptoed towards his own bed chamber with a glowing sense of peace and contentment. The dawn of eugenics was approaching.

Chapter 11 – The Redeemers

On the Mile End Road a small congregational church came under the influence of a man named Reverend Robertson. Robertson, a well-bred man of fifty, had prospered in commerce, until the demon of drink and women of the night brought him close to oblivion. Penniless and without work, Robertson considered shooting himself with his father's old hunting rifle, when Jesus saved him. It was unclear if Robertson had been ordained in any formal sense, although he was a powerful hellfire orator and physically resembled Rembrandt's Moses in a dog collar. Robertson claimed that Jesus specifically instructed him to save lives and souls in the East End of London. His congregation of forty were equally inspired and joined Robertson on his evangelical missions, manning soup kitchens and preaching on street corners, imploring street-trading prostitutes to pray with them. Robertson called his congregation 'The Redeemers'. Charlie called them a pain in the arse.

One Saturday lunchtime, a crowd stopped outside the emporium to watch an impromptu performance by the celebrated Music Hall snake act, Salasie and his Boa Constrictor. At the end of Salasie's act, Charlie flung open the front door and invited all assembled to behold a freak of nature who was 'Half a man – half an elephant'. Robertson, who had been canvassing with The Redeemers outside The Grave Maurice pub, rushed over to the emporium and demanded an end to this unspeakable blasphemy. Robertson was shoved aside by eager punters and jostled by the crowd. From that day on The Redeemers added a vigil by the shop to their weekly itinerary.

The protest group usually positioned themselves outside the empty building next door to the emporium. Robertson would make a long hectoring speech, whilst his followers distributed handbills and bothered potential punters. Once a week had been acceptable and sometimes attracted trade, but the Redeemers were now a daily fixture. As the police held Charlie responsible for any commotion outside the shop, he clocked up a litany of fines.

Joseph watched The Redeemers from the upstairs window during an afternoon lull. Charlie joined him. Joseph hoped Charlie would not notice the crystal drinking glasses Alice had left on the table, but he was too busy observing the street. Today's gathering of Redeemers were solid types, married women or retired men, as the day was a work day. They were all in thrall of Robertson, their belligerent prophet of purity. Joseph could just about hear his address.

"For a few the streets are paved with gold, for the many they are paved with tears. Avarice, despair, immorality, the foundations of this tower of Babel. An open sewer known as the Thames divides our city. To the West Sodom, to the East Gomorrah ..."

"These do-gooders are killing the business," said Charlie.

"They will be gone before long, to the next attraction."

"That is wishful thinking, friend." Charlie took a nip from his hip flask and passed it to Joseph. "They will not listen to reason because they have only faith. We cannot hurt them, because they live to suffer. I know this mob, Joseph, they evangelise from pain. They would not save the world anymore than they would save themselves."

Charlie's unusually philosophical and perceptive comment astonished Joseph, but they were no closer to a solution. That night someone threw a brick through the front window. Charlie blamed The Redeemers. He boarded up the window. The shop was a fortress. Charlie suggested relinquishing his room on Buck's Row and sleeping nights at the shop as a precaution. Joseph said Charlie needed his leisure to release the tensions of the work day. Luckily for Joseph, Charlie agreed.

By now, Alice was coming to see Joseph as many as five nights a week. The time they spent in each other's company, their simple routines of supper, reading and pleasant conversation, were the perfect tonic for his nerves. Joseph gave Alice brief accounts of the recent troubles and attempted to gloss over the worst of it, but she was not easily fooled.

It was summer, though the room was always cold. As Alice prepared the fire, padding old newspaper and advertising handbills around the kindling, something caught her attention, a hellfire tract from the Redeemers. In case any sinners missed the point, the pamphlet came with a mimeograph of a man screaming in agony as fire consumed him. The man, with a chequered suit and disreputable bootlace moustache, was the exact likeness of Charlie.

"What will you do," asked Alice, "if they force you out?"

Joseph let out an involuntary sigh. "Charlie has a vision for legitimate investment. McCallion's Novelty Emporium. An Aladdin's Cave of amusements, gifts and joke items and the world's most curious cashier, half a man, half an elephant."

Joseph attempted to mimic Charlie's voice, but the words sounded dead to him.

"If I understand correctly, Charlie believes that if you reside behind a till rather than a curtain, the police and evangelists will leave you alone?"

"What am I to do, Alice? They would deny me work as a man and now it seems as a freak."

After lighting the fire Alice poured two glasses of white wine and sat next to Joseph on the settee. Joseph watched the charred remains of the damnation tract float up the chimney.

"What of you, Alice? How is your doctor?"

"I have had many free nights as of late. It will not have escaped your attention."

"It has not."

"Simon is neglecting his house calls. I know him less and less."

"Absence makes the heart grow fonder." Joseph regretted using the cliché, but could not think of anything else to say, as he had virtually no experience of these matters.

Alice repeated the word 'absence' and reached for her beard like an amputee for a missing leg. When she realised what she was doing, she lowered her hand.

"I am told I am beautiful. I am meant to be beautiful."

"You are beautiful."

Alice brushed aside the compliment. "The normal person seeks to possess beauty. Not as a bearer but as master; that is why they cage birds and collect dead butterflies. At the same time they torment the afflicted, anyone deemed uglier than them. So they loved me, they hated me and now they covet me once again. This face has borne desire and disdain, the hypocrisy of the normal world."

"I cannot begin to tell you how much I respect you. How you have built a life. Disfigurement is all I have known."

Alice held Joseph's hand. Her touch released a torrent of words, all the pain he had previously held back from her.

"I hate these people. I hate them because of their lives, their freedom. I cannot walk the streets without a chaperone and a cowl! When I was a hawker and a crowd gathered to taunt me, I wished I could infect them with my condition. In my mind's eye they transformed, men and women, deformed like me. As they begged on their knees for a cure, I laughed at their lamentations."

"Everyone wishes their affliction on another. I wished my beard on a hundred women."

"A cripple educates the normal by bringing to consciousness his suffering. To gain fair treatment. If the cripple were strong he could win power through fear. When you said we should burn their world, you were right."

"Remember what you said to me in response: not all of them have malignant hearts?"

"No, I said I treasure you as my friend."

There was frustration in his voice. Joseph added, "I think you should leave."

Alice appeared hurt and confused and remained in her seat, in hope of an explanation. Joseph said, "Ever since you returned, you have put my life in turmoil, because you were almost my lover. I can no longer endure the pain of your friendship or the agony your beauty, because you are already lost."

"Nothing has changed, I tell you."

Alice rose to her feet, keeping hold of Joseph's hand so he would join her. They stood in front of the fire.

"Remember the woods? We are back there again. But this time there is no Hunchback, no Charlie. It is you and I. There is nothing to disturb us."

Joseph thought Alice was playing a joke, until she placed his good hand onto her breast. Joseph withdrew his hand immediately, as if he had touched the outer surface of a scalding cooking pot.

"Is this a game?" he asked her.

Alice smiled and placed Joseph's hand back onto her breast. She was a magnet and would not release him. Joseph was a grateful captive to her power. Every nerve in his body crackled like electrical cable and an immense yearning welled within his chest, his longing for this woman, his dream of holding her and loving her and bestowing her with tender ecstasies. Alice took Joseph's right hand, his hugely deformed claw and placed it on her other breast. She seemed to beckon him for the kiss. Joseph hesitated.

"I fear you pity me," he said.

"When you would have kissed my bearded face, was that through pity?"

"No, desire."

"Then you know why I am here."

Alice guided his hands around her hips and wrapped her arms around his shoulders. She closed her eyes. He leaned in for the kiss. Joseph summoned every ounce of his muscle power to his thick, fleshy lips. The floor melted beneath him. This sinful human pleasure was heaven on earth.

Chapter 12 – The Bleeding Blade

The Redeemers became more confrontational in their approach, positioning themselves in two groups either side of the emporium, watching for punters and cutting them off in a pincer movement. If the Redeemers missed anyone on the way in, they badgered them on the way out. Charlie was now attending to complaints from Donohoe, the grocer next door, who was concerned about losing custom. Charlie placated Donohoe by purchasing a barrow-load of old fruit and vegetables. The produce was never intended for consumption.

Charlie transferred the fruit and vegetables into tin buckets, handed a tough little urchin two pennies, and told him to assemble a gang of chums. The Redeemers arrived outside the shop after lunch and Robertson launched into his afternoon sermon. The urchin and chums approached them from behind and pelted fruit at the righteous evangelists. Onlookers and passersby, many amenable to trouble, joined the affray. Stray fruit and vegetables hit innocent bystanders. Fistfights broke out. One of the Redeemers, a timid retired clerk, was knocked unconscious. Robertson implored the Lord to strike down the sinners, before he himself was struck between the eyes by a putrid apple.

Within minutes there was a fearful hammering on the door and shouts of "Police!" Joseph watched through the curtain of the display area as DI Blake, a plain-clothes subordinate and two burly constables barged inside. Blake shoved Charlie against the wall and held him there. Blake was a bear of a man, over six feet tall, with a brown bushy moustache. He towered over Charlie and summoned his most intimidating voice of the law. "You've done it this time, McCallion. Incitement to riot!"

"I am innocent of all charges, sir!"

"Your little gang of ruffians assaulted good citizens!"

"Please, sir. It was self-defence. Those do-gooders brought trouble to us."

"You bring trouble to this whole bloomin' district! You admit it then?"

The plain-clothes subordinate held up a bottle of Elephant Gin. "Selling liquor without a licence, sir."

"Those are for our own consumption, officer."

Blake jabbed his finger in Charlie's face. "Don't try my patience, son."

Joseph crept back behind his curtain and waited for the inevitable intrusion.

"Oh yes," added Blake, "we shall also interview the poor bugger you put on parade. Might be grounds for charging you with kidnap?"

"Joseph performs of his own free will, sir. We are legitimate entertainers."

"In my book you're a bloody hooligan!"

Blake pushed Charlie up the stairs, towards the living quarters. His plain-clothes subordinate continued the search downstairs and entered the display room. He reacted to The Elephant Man with minimal shock and Joseph realised the detective had already visited the premises, posing as a punter. He looked like a thousand other men from the East End, pinch-cheeked and under-nourished.

"Detective Sergeant Mann. You are?"

"Joseph Merrick, sir."

"Occupation?"

"Professional Curiosity."

"And how long have you been a 'professional curiosity'?"

"Two years, sir."

"Previous employ?"

"Factory worker, hawker. I have an autobiographical pamphlet, sir ..."

"Does McCallion beat you?"

"No, sir."

"Stand up and remove your clothes."

"But sir?"

"I intend to inspect you for evidence of assault. You will undress, or should my constables assist you?"

Joseph stood and unbuttoned his shirt.

"Violence is the currency of common criminals," added Mann sanctimoniously. His conceit was short-lived as sounds reverberated from upstairs, a body hitting the wall, muffled blows, pleas for mercy. Joseph felt Charlie's pain in the roots of his teeth.

Upstairs in Joseph's living quarters, Charlie flung himself against the wall with a cushion against his midriff ensuring plenty of sound, but soft contact. Blake punched the padded seat of the settee. Charlie threw himself on the floor, cushion first, for a crash landing. He writhed and kicked his legs. Blake punched the settee again. Charlie cried, "No more, please!" Blake pulled Charlie to his feet by his lapels, as if lifting a light suitcase. Charlie poured whiskey from his flask into two tin cups. He noticed Joseph had somehow acquired fancy glassware along with a library of new books, but this was no time to worry about such details. Charlie handed Blake his drink.

"Can't you do something about these do-gooders, Mr Blake?"

"Like what?"

"Some of the girls I know, know of, in a certain profession, consider the reverend a valued, regular customer. He's a bloody fraud!"

"If religious hypocrisy was a crime I might well arrest most men in Britain."

"Nib him for nicking off the collection plate? They're all at it!"

Blake chuckled and shook his head. "You know what this lot are like, Charlie, outraged citizens. They're whiter than white and you're a cockroach, in the eyes of many people. As time goes on, things get softer, weaker, watered down, even around here. One hundred years ago public entertainment was rat-fighting and bear-baiting, hanging a treason case and chopping his member off. That's all gone; it's indecent now."

"I guarantee you, Mr Blake, in one hundred years, punters will still be paying for freaks of nature."

"They're still paying for rat fights, but that doesn't mean it's proper, or legal, or that I have to tolerate it on my manor."

"We can go down the road, can't we, Mr Blake?"

"Yes, Charlie. Head east. Barking, Dagenham, Persia. Don't stop until China."

"Please, Mr Blake, you've been a good friend to this business. A stay of execution? Three months?"

"Three months! Three hours more like. I'm being asked questions about how you've managed to stay open. I'm supposed to nib you."

Blake slammed the flat of his hand against the wall with fearsome force.

"I'd have to give you a proper seeing to. You'd wind up in chokey and all."

Charlie opened his wallet and produced a princely white fiver. The money made Blake salivate more than the booze, but he did not take it.

"One week to settle up, Charlie."

Charlie nodded in resignation. Blake handed Charlie his empty cup, then speared two quick jabs into his face, a left and a right beneath the eyes. Charlie fell backwards and smacked his head on the floor. Blake used his foot to roll Charlie to one side, to prevent him from swallowing his tongue.

"Sorry, old son," said Blake regretfully. "They'd think I was losing my touch."

Charlie's eyes were swelling shut and he could not stand without losing his balance, but despite Joseph's protestations, Charlie set off for his lodgings, weaving like a drunkard after a heavy session. It was unwise for a 'businessman' to be seen in a vulnerable condition, given the number of violent thieves who stalked the area. When Alice arrived at nightfall, Joseph told her the whereabouts of Charlie's rooms and she hurried off to check on him. Alice came back an hour later and said that Charlie was still groggy and disoriented, but was now comfortable in bed. Alice said he could not be badly injured because he attempted to kiss her and proposed marriage, presumably mistaking her for one of his sweethearts.

Satisfied Charlie was safely in bed, Joseph and Alice retired to theirs.

Joseph awoke in the small hours of the morning and remained in his sitting-sleeping position. Alice slept by his side, so peacefully and serenely that she could have concealed the moon beneath a single, delicate eyelid. Her ebony curls cascaded onto his abdomen.

In the fortnight since they had made love, water tasted like champagne and stale bread like the finest steak. The mundane filled Joseph with childlike wonder and he laughed at commonplace things without knowing why. When it came to the physical part Alice showed Joseph what to do and he did what he was able. To his surprise it was more than enough. Joseph still struggled with kissing, as his rubbery lips had the dexterity of a sponge. He kept apologising for getting it wrong. Alice laughed and praised his manful effort. Joseph asked Alice if he was succeeding with the main activity. She stared at him as if the answer was obvious.

Joseph lived his life under a cloud of ever-present calamity. Success, contentment and love all brought great anxiety, as if a moment of happiness would intensify the pain of the next disaster. Joseph wished his back was strong enough to complete a day's labour and his hands possessed a manly trade. He wished he could wield a hammer, shift a plane, construct something more than a lie, because then he could support the woman beside him. This woman held his destiny. This woman held the night. Joseph watched Alice sleep until morning.

Alice ventured out and returned with breakfast foods. Joseph dressed and joined her in the living quarters. Alice laid out bread, cheese and cooked meats on the table and mashed a pot of tea on the fire. Despite the appealing fare on offer, both Alice and Joseph picked at morsels.

"I would like to thank you," said Joseph, "for tolerating my table habits."

"You apologise for kissing, for eating, always apologising. You could not be mistaken for anything other than an Englishman."

"I was offered work on the continent, you know."

"Finish up your breakfast. We will tidy the shop."

"No," said Joseph. "If you and I were to venture to another place, my affliction could sustain us. What of it, Alice? Would you go with me elsewhere?"

"What of Charlie?"

"That is not the question. Would you go with me?"

Alice would not answer him.

"You would go with your doctor alone," said Joseph. "I will work ten times harder than any man has worked. Love you ten times more than any man on earth."

The room suddenly appeared cheap and sordid, as if the spell of their intimate moments had been broken. Two ill-matched lovers were exposed in the harsh light of day, one beautiful woman with spectacular marriage prospects, one hideous freak in search of a sideshow. Joseph cursed himself for the folly of delusion. How could he hope to support a woman, when his own body could not support itself?

A terrible chasm opened within him, worse than any contemplation of unemployment or penury. If Joseph was on terms with the Lord, he would have dropped to his knees and asked Alice the most important question of all.

Charlie awoke in his room oblivious to the time. He tried to sit, but any movement only aggravated the searing pain of his headache. Charlie surmised it was day due to the shaft of light creeping in through the curtain, an old shirt Alice had kindly tacked to the window when she checked on him. She had also removed his jacket and his shoes.

Charlie occupied the upstairs room of a decrepit tenement, furnished by a bed and a single wooden chair. The bare slats of the floor were covered with indeterminate stains from previous occupants, most likely the discoloured liquid of overflowing chamber pots. The ceiling was sagging and black with mould. It was a grim hole, but it was Charlie's first room of his own, and for that it was a special place. The girls he brought back here often lived in worse.

Paying for women represented personal defeat, but it was the only way Charlie could guarantee company. He would not employ the girl unless he was her first of the night and for this he paid ridiculous sums, as much as ten men, so the girl would not leave until dawn. Charlie kept bottles of booze under his bed, port wine, whiskey and gin as a further incentive to stay. Although Charlie would not employ the same girl on more than two or three occasions, in case she became his beloved. Charlie could not bear the thought of another man touching his beloved.

He questioned the women about their lives. Katie was a real good-hearted girl, but the gin deranged her. After a few drinks she threw a bottle at his head for no good reason. 'German' Annie was remarkably pretty and lithe for a woman of forty. Charlie could not believe she had borne ten children. Natasha was a gorgeous Russian, who lived with her family in an overcrowded tenement in Spitalfields. Remarkably, she did not drink, saved her money and hoped to open a florist's shop. Sweet young Jane had a wonderful singing voice. Her voice was so pleasant and tender that Charlie did not object when she brazenly attempted to pick his pocket.

Even a hardened prostitute has compassion for a lonely man. They all asked Charlie why a nice fellow like him could not find a proper sweetheart. Charlie always replied there was a very beautiful girl, but they had been separated by fate and she was now betrothed to another. When they asked Charlie her name he gave another, Annabelle or Abigail. He would not have them repeat her name, the name of his beloved on lips that would kiss a thousand men, or worse.

For the first time in his career, Charlie had to concede he was sick of the business. He was sick of barking meaningless words and telling silly stories, of sacrificing his life to the cause of low entertainment, when his own existence was devoid of substance and love. He was sick of being hounded for the sake of a show; perhaps, finally, he was done. But he would not forsake Joseph and would support his friend. Charlie decided to tell Joseph about his brother Jack and hoped Joseph would understand why he had told him. Like most men, Charlie found it nearly impossible to communicate his deeper emotions to another man, even his best friend, relying on a hearty backslap to express anything from joviality to sentiments close to love. Indeed, love was foremost in his mind.

When Alice tucked him in bed after his beating, Charlie beheld her beautiful face, hovering above him like an angel. She placed a cold wet towel on his forehead and held his hand. Charlie could not remember precisely what he said, but hoped his mouth of showy patter had expressed his genuine feelings. It did not matter that she was married; he would no longer hold his tongue. When Charlie left home to join Sam, his mother said he was going to hell. Perhaps through the love of a beautiful woman, he would redeem himself and escape this squalor, the poverty of his lonely life.

There was a dainty little knock on the door. It must be fate, thought Charlie, it must be her! Charlie staggered out of bed, a carousel wheeling in his head. He used the wall to support himself and opened the door. Charlie was confronted by a whippet-thin man with a mop of red hair beneath his bowler and dark copper stubble on his sunken, pugilistic face. His hands bore prison tattoos, a transfixed heart, a religious cross and initials J.B. It was someone he recognised.

"Do I know you, sir?" asked Charlie, to distract the man. Charlie felt for his cosh, but his jacket was hanging on the chair, the cosh was in his jacket and Charlie was confused and concussed. The assailant lunged forward and stabbed Charlie with a quick lateral thrust, retracting the blade as if it were the stubborn cork on a bottle of blood. Charlie's legs gave way immediately and he fell to the floor. The assailant ran from the room. Charlie lay on his left side and cupped the wound beneath his sternum. Blood rushed through his fingers. He could not feel his legs, his body was warm and heavy and his brain was instructing him to sleep.

It was a dreadful way to die, on the stained wooden floorboards of a filthy slum. But Charlie was already somewhere else, on an unspoilt beach of white, golden sand.

The sea stretched out like an infinite turquoise carpet in front of him. The cyan blue sky was populated by playful, cotton-wool clouds and a pleasant sun warmed his back. There was a mild sea breeze and the air was fresh with salt. This was not Margate, but some exotic island. It was paradise, because Alice was with him. The breeze positioned a single ebony curl across her beautiful face, like the mooring rope of a wandering vessel. She picked up a handful of dry, powdery sand. Charlie brushed the hair away from her face and cupped her cheeks. Alice closed her eyes in expectation of the kiss and offered her full red lips like the petals of a hibiscus on the shoreline. She placed her arms around him and released the sand. It ran through her fingers and dispersed into nothing, like the final measure of his lifeblood.

Gilbert Greystone's day had not gone well. After morning surgery at the London Hospital he had taken the afternoon off for research purposes, travelling to a workhouse near Holborn. The master, a detestable but compliant man, had promised Gilbert a male imbecile. But when Gilbert arrived at the workhouse, a new man occupied the master's parlour – Timkins, a temperance Christian, who explained that his predecessor had been dismissed for gross incompetence. Fingers in the till or a resident scrubwoman, thought Gilbert.

"What is your business at this establishment?" asked Timkins suspiciously. Gilbert said he periodically offered his services as a locum, by way of charitable endeavour. Timkins was delighted and Gilbert spent all afternoon supporting his lie, with his stethoscope pressed up against hundreds of rheumy paupers.

Hours later Gilbert could still smell the stink of them, despite a thorough wash with carbolic at home, and he arrived at the Taygetus Eugenics Society in Mayfair somewhat underprepared. The function room at the club was full of new members, Chamber of Commerce types, who despite their wealth, remained small-minded little shopkeepers at heart. Gilbert noted the prevalence of pitiful physiques amongst these so called captains of industry. Almost every man possessed a barrelled or a distended paunch, the direct result of gluttonous meals and alcoholic over-indulgence. Bald heads and double chins predominated, as did cigar-brown teeth. Tubercular coughing and wheezing were an unwelcome staccato accompaniment to Vale's slideshows of buck naked savages.

Only one of the new recruits was a masculine exemplar. Whiting was a man of thirty-five years, average height, but magnificent proportions, with strong shoulders, a broad chest and a flat stomach. His hair was light, Nordic blond, yet his keen, healthy face and near perfect posture were indicative of the British officer class. Gilbert was appalled to discover that Whiting was lost to the profession of advertising, marrying catchpenny doggerel with inane imagery to purvey tawdry products, such as tinned chicken soup. Nevertheless, he was a fine physical specimen.

Gilbert approached the front table as Vale buffed the skeleton of an ape with his handkerchief. Vale had recently extended his kinship theory away from the skull, to other parts of the anatomy, burglars with the arms of orang-utans and so on. Dunham stood next to Vale. Gilbert bowed his head in deference to his father-in-law, but Dunham glared at Gilbert. The room fell silent, aside from the obligatory cough and wheeze.

Dunham said, "When Jemima was a little girl I bought her a pony. I cannot tell you how much she loved that horse. At just one year of age, in winter, it contracted a fever and died. I thought Jemima would never recover, but that grief is nothing, nothing, compared to her present devastation. Your brother demands a divorce!"

"There is clearly a mistake, sir. Simon is insanely in love with Jemima."

" 'Unfortunate marriage of convenience', says he, 'should never have gone through with it' says he. Then he adds another detail. There's a harlot to boot."

Dunham gripped the sides of the table until his knuckles went white.

"Let me describe a day in your brother's life. He sees his patients, fornicates with a prostitute, then crawls back home to my daughter, my beautiful daughter, and defiles her with his dirty devil. He's had his fill of Jemima. Cast her aside for a whore!"

Simon's infidelity explained his supposed nocturnal surgeries and proved to Gilbert that his brother was not a dreadful sexual invert. Then his relief turned to anger, anger at Simon's selfishness.

"Sir, when I observe my brother and your daughter, their harmony is the metre of Shakespearean sonnets. I assure you his devotion his absolute. I can scarcely imagine the agony of Simon's remorse. The guilt must be a knife in him."

"If I ever see your brother again, that would be the least of his problems." Dunham calmed a little and released his grip on the table. He must have detected the embarrassment of his peers, being a captive audience to decidedly un-British behaviour.

"Remember what I said about Stephenson's Rocket? Their annulment shall be faster."

Gilbert took a step forward and bent his knees. He would have got down on them if necessary.

"Sir, whatever you think of my brother, please do not forsake eugenics. From your acorn of initiative a mighty oak grows."

"Mighty oak!" screamed Dunham. "You have diseased my family tree. I will cut you out! Cut you out!"

Dunham picked up the viewgraph and hurled it at Gilbert. Gilbert ducked. The viewgraph whistled past his head and exploded on the floor. Men restrained Dunham as he thrashed like a rabid dog. Every member of the society stared at Gilbert with the nerve to imply it was his fault, apart from Whiting, who could not disguise a smirk of mischief.

"Greystone!" said the pipsqueak Vale. "You're not welcome here!"

The following morning, after a sleepless night, Gilbert employed a locksmith and gained entry to Simon's practice in Bow. The locksmith did not ask Gilbert for verification of identity, there was no need. Gilbert's bearing was the master key to any door in the country. A brief search of Simon's desk yielded papers for a rented property in Islington and a spare key.

Simon's rented terrace was an ode to bohemian decadence and was strewn with books. Various soft furnishings betrayed a woman's touch. Upstairs, the bedroom to the rear of the property performed the function of love nest. A tall cupboard contained three of Simon's suits and eight pencil dresses, three bustle dresses, along with a selection of predictably sluttish undergarments. Gilbert deduced that Simon's harlot was at least a high-class prostitute and more likely to be free from disease. Even so, Gilbert wore his medical gloves to inspect the bed. He detected the woman's scent on the duvet and found her long black hairs on the pillow, though was surprised to discover no evidence of recent carnal secretion.

Gilbert took the undergarments and spread them on the kitchen table. He read one of Simon's penny dreadful murder mysteries, *The Bleeding Blade*, wondering if the text could provide an insight into his brother's mental and ethical decay. Half an hour later, Gilbert heard a key in the front door. On discovering the door was already unlocked, Simon rushed in jubilantly calling, "Alice!"

Simon registered Gilbert's presence with the expression of a patient in receipt of an unexpected suppository. Gilbert gestured to a chair of interrogation he had positioned in front of the table. Simon flopped into it, like a criminal resigned to his punishment. His hangdog expression was a stark contrast to the mound of gaudy underwear in front of him.

"Her name is Alice."

"Yes, I gathered."

"Her name is Alice and I love her."

"You are romanticising the act of fornication. Love is for old maids, brother."

"And what would you know?"

"That love has little to do with betraying your wife and subjecting her to a complete mental breakdown."

Simon averted his eyes in guilt and shame. Gilbert rose to his feet.

"You have ruined Jemima, destroyed her life and in the process, your career. No man will tolerate his physician as a filthy philanderer. Who'd trust a beast with his wife, for God's sake? You're a disgrace to your profession, a disgrace to your family. You're even a disgrace yourself. You have broken the seventh commandment. You will burn for eternity in hell. Look at you crying. You're a bloody shower."

Simon rubbed his streaming eyes on his sleeve for he had no handkerchief.

"Where is she?" demanded Gilbert.

Simon shook his head and mouthed, "I don't know."

Gilbert did not expect to break Simon so quickly and completely. Instinct told him to deliver a brotherly pep talk, the sort of tripe a weakling would want to hear.

"Look here, old boy, here's what to do. Clean yourself up and make haste home, bouquet in hand and apologise. Sexology states that wife is secretly proud and surprisingly forgiving. The liaison is proof of husband's manhood, if you will. Come now and purchase your garland of atonement. Fifty red roses to delight her heart."

Simon nodded his head and wiped tearful mucus from his nose. Gilbert helped Simon to his feet and patted him on the back for good measure.

"One last thing. This whore of yours, I trust you employed the correct sanitary precautions?"

Simon swung a powerful punch from the hip, like an athlete hurling a discus. His fist connected with the bridge of Gilbert's nose, sounding a loud crack of cartilage. Gilbert skidded across the top of the table and landed on the floor, taking most of the underwear with him. Gilbert gripped his nose to stem the bleeding, but the hot, salty blood poured back into his throat.

Simon removed his belt and folded it in two, exposing the bulbous steel buckle. He flogged Gilbert's shoulder blades, his spine and his kidneys. Gilbert balled up like a cowering spider, disoriented by pain, reduced to the level of a tormented animal. After twenty lashes Simon dispensed with the belt, picked Gilbert up by his lapels, marched him to the front door and shoved him out onto the pavement. Gilbert landed painfully on his hands and knees.

"If love is for old maids, brother, there is hope for you yet!"

Simon slammed the door. Passers-by whispered and pointed. Gilbert tried to regain his feet but could not stand. A middle-aged woman stepped forward to help. She was accompanied by her son, a pudgy youth of twenty, who appeared to be a congenital imbecile. Gilbert waved them away, but they would not leave him; they must have been infernal Christians. The woman placed her arm around Gilbert and the youth offered him a boiled sweet from his paper punnet. Gilbert blew a blood clot from his nose onto his suit. The woman offered him a frilly handkerchief and said, "There, there," as if his own wretched condition made him a brother to her defective son. Gilbert was crying and he could not stop himself. Moreover, he would never forgive himself.

Joseph spent the morning sitting quietly in the entrance parlour, waiting for the devastating news, so shocking and raw, to become a tangible reality. Joseph needed proof of Charlie's demise, some sort of cathartic mortuary attendance. He wanted to see the body. But then a grieving freak could hardly be afforded a special audience with a corpse.

The worst part was breaking the news to Alice when she arrived at the shop and sharing her tearful desolation. Eventually they composed themselves and ascended the stairs to the living quarters. They opened the last remaining bottle of wine and remembered their friend.

Charlie's body was now the property of the London Hospital, a plaything of the medical profession, a dead mouse to a cat's curiosity. A well-bred medical pupil would practise his skill upon Charlie's corpse. Would he remember Charlie from the emporium? His fantastic yarn about a young woman and a marauding elephant? Would he remember how Charlie whipped away the display curtain with the flourish of a matador?

Joseph loved their friendship because Charlie was devoid of conventional morality. Charlie did not see deformity as a blessing or a curse, a measure of human goodness or a misshapen incubator for the soul. To him, it was strictly business and the worse the deformity, the better for profit. As a result, Charlie was entirely incapable of pity. Therefore, in many ways, his friendship liberated Joseph from the moral obligations of affliction: being a nice cripple for Jesus, being a good boy.

Alice suggested a ceremonial gesture to send off their friend, by way of a cremation in the fire. The only paper to hand was a copy of Joseph's sellings pamphlet. Alice and Joseph stood by the fire and said goodbye as Joseph fed the pamphlet to the flames. Another sordid life had been mercifully erased and would be quietly forgotten. Nobody would remember the Yorick to a freak.

Alice removed her gloves. The gold band of her make-believe marriage had been replaced by a genuine silver engagement ring.

When Alice had returned to her lodgings, she told herself that if Simon was not there, he never would be. She had found him in the kitchenette by a pile of her underclothes, nursing bruised knuckles. Simon said, "My brother besmirched you. I should not have struck him, but my love for you is immense." He dropped to his knees and offered the ring. Alice accepted on condition of a provision of support for a friend. Simon would have agreed to anything. No man can negotiate with his love for a beautiful woman.

Joseph sat back on the settee. He raised a toast with the remnants of his wine.

"I want to help you," said Alice.

Joseph shook his head.

"Why not?"

"It is obvious."

"Not to me."

"Because I am a freak and you are a normal person!"

Alice reached for her purse and pulled out all her available monies. She removed all her jewellery except for the engagement ring and placed them in Joseph's lap.

"Joseph Merrick, this is the deposit on lodgings and I will bring you more. You are staying here, in London and I will support you. If you utter one word of disagreement I will roast your head in the fire."

They made all sorts of elaborate plans. Alice intended to find comfortable rooms for Joseph and visit him daily. There would be ample time for him to rest and consider his options. Joseph asked if she had approved such measures with her fiancé. Alice said the matter was in hand. Joseph said he had means, but she warned him not to touch a penny of his savings. Alice suggested buying Charlie a funeral and a headstone, but they both knew it was a futile idea.

Joseph imagined his life as a cosseted shut-in, in a vast suburban home, large enough to accommodate a secret in the attic. A housemaid of robust constitution would bring him books and food and the daily newspapers and also remove his chamber pot. Alice would converse with him infrequently and rarely once her children were born. The little ones would be forbidden entry to his room and warned that a sick relative, Alice's 'cousin', was very unwell. His demise would be commemorated by a discreet funeral at the local church attended by Alice and the good Dr Greystone. A vicar who never knew him would deliver a eulogy as if he knew him and Alice would lay a flower by his headstone in a quiet corner of the grounds. Agnostic mothers pray through fear. Therefore Alice would pray for her husband, for her children and finally herself, to be spared the return of affliction, so that God might spare them all.

It was time for Alice to leave the shop for home. In lieu of a hug, she awkwardly adjusted Joseph's collar and told him, "All will be right." She vowed to return the next morning in a carriage, and made Joseph repeat the rendezvous time of 8 a.m. to ensure he would be ready and waiting. When Alice left, Joseph packed his savings box, a change of clothing and a single book in a haversack. He arranged the money and Alice's jewellery on the table and added a few shillings from his own savings box to compensate for her carriage, a wasted journey and the necessity of another lie.

Chapter 13 – Soaring Sensations

Gilbert Greystone's childhood home was 'Valhalla', a Georgian country mansion on five acres, six miles from the Oxfordshire market town of Thame. In the Easter of 1862, when he was fifteen years of age, Gilbert returned home from boarding school, excited about spending the vacation with his father. St John Greystone had recently retired as a practising surgeon in order to devote his time exclusively to racial research. Not that retirement slowed the old man, who at the age of fifty exhibited the trim physique and keen reflexes of a fencing champion, along with seemingly unlimited vigour.

On the first day of the holidays his father set off on his white thoroughbred stallion, Pegasus, for a morning gallop in the shadow of the Chilterns. On his return, St John had promised to employ Gilbert as his understudy, annotating papers on primitive savages and their hereditary mental defects. When Father was not home by luncheon, Gilbert set out on his own steed in search of him.

A half hour later, Gilbert found Pegasus casually drinking from a stream. One hundred yards further on Gilbert discovered his father in long grass by a beech tree. St John Greystone was lying flat on his back, eyes still open, face etched in a smile. Gilbert hoped it was one of Father's jokes and he would spring to life at any moment. He felt his father's body for a pulse, every main artery, as Father had taught him, but detected not a murmur of life force. Gilbert lay beside St John's body in the grass for quite some time, perhaps four or five hours, wondering if it was possible by proximity to his father to merge with his spirit and accompany him as he left the world, so that they might conquer death together. When Gilbert was still alive at dusk, he set off on his horse for Valhalla.

In the days that followed, Gilbert pestered his mother to be placed in charge of the funeral arrangements and she yielded to his superior will. Gilbert oversaw the conveyance of the body to the private crematorium, as per his father's wishes and returned the ashes to the family estate. He also arranged for Pegasus to be sent to the knacker on principle.

Gilbert invited Simon and their mother into the garden to scatter the ashes. Magnificent red kites soared above, forming a predatory guard of honour. Little Simon's bottom lip quivered. Mother was haggard at forty. Gilbert assumed Father had married her for purely genetic reasons. She was once reckoned to be beautiful. Gilbert read aloud from *The Problem of and Solution to Negro Overbreeding*, concluding with his father's final, poignant dedication.

Farewell my friends of the foremost race.

Gilbert felt his father's power coursing through his veins. St John Greystone had set him free, with unstoppable momentum, towards a heroic destiny. Gilbert knew God was near, but not a specific god, or a weak, Christian conception of the divine. To Gilbert 'God' was an abstract term for all that was powerful and just. The death of his father was his birth as a man.

Recent events had besmirched the purity of the memory.

Gilbert had been a stranger to fighting. The only beating he saw his father administer to his mother was controlled, ethical and justified. Gilbert saw little violence at school, using other boys as instruments of his will where necessary. He had stopped punching, twisting, and kicking Simon by the age of nine. Fraternal dominance was entrenched by then. All of which made Simon's assault in Islington even more shocking and injurious, the physical manifestation of Mother's financial betrayal.

He had set his broken nose and treated his belt buckle lesions in a bath infused with iodine. Gilbert's superiors at the London Hospital believed his account of a 'riding accident' and afforded him two weeks leave. He was, on paper, an exemplary employee. Fortunately, his nose healed in a more or less a symmetrical fashion and the scarring from the belt buckle was minimal. But when he returned to work, Gilbert could not shake the lethargy of his convalescence.

The normal joy of surgery became a chore of drudgery. Gilbert delegated most of his caseload to subordinates under the pretext of developing their professional skill. The only operations he performed were minor procedures, requiring minimum effort. Not even the worst examples of defective delinquency, the feeble-minded, idiots or imbeciles of the East End, with their self created maladies, could fire Gilbert's blood. His apathy at the degeneration of race was indicative of his own decline. Gilbert cocooned himself in his office and indulged the folly of horology, tinkering with the inner workings of pocket watches to fill his days.

Gilbert felt sufficiently forgiving to pen Simon a short letter, suggesting a meeting to resolve their differences, careful to avoid any hint of contrition on his part. He believed that the weak are prone to guilt, especially when they have acted boldly. Consequently, Gilbert expected a prompt reconciliation on favourable terms. He sent the letter care of Simon's medical practice in Bow. When he received no reply, Gilbert travelled to Bow, to find that Simon's plaque had been removed from the building. There was also a new resident of the property in Islington. Gilbert engaged a private investigator named Stevens, a ghastly former police detective, on three guineas a day. Stevens presented a dossier within the week.

Dulwich Village was a mere four miles south of London Bridge, a short train journey from the city. Gilbert disembarked at the new Dulwich station, with Steven's directions in hand. He followed the twee village High Street, flanked by old mansion houses to a vast public picture gallery where art was wasted on plebeian elements. He continued along meandering country lanes, passing cottages, more country houses and the admittedly impressive Dulwich College grounds. The townsfolk were the moneyed middle classes, peasants or servants. Every so often a cul de sac of bijou contemporary houses appeared. Dulwich was technically a village and still within the county of Surrey, but Gilbert recognised the creeping mediocrity of suburbanisation. Fields and pastures would become public parks and Dulwich London. Little clerks would dream about living here. According to Stevens, Simon lived here.

Gilbert followed Stevens's directions to a lane on the outskirts of the village, consisting of three country houses. Two properties faced each other across the lane, twenty feet apart. The remaining property occupied a more secluded plot at the end of the lane. Gilbert approached the secluded house which had no perimeter wall or gate and was surrounded by a dense thicket of hawthorn and wild rose bushes. It was a magnificent Georgian country house, ever so slightly gothic. Roman pillars supported a balcony above the door. Gilbert was reminded of Valhalla and felt an ache of nostalgic homesickness.

Gilbert cautiously entered the courtyard. He saw no signs of life at the front of the property, but heard the whistle of a workman at the rear. Gilbert entered the thicket of trees and used them for cover as he advanced behind the house. The thorny branches of the hawthorn and wild rose stabbed Gilbert repeatedly through his day suit. Sweat oozed from his skin. Progress was painstaking, but Gilbert's safari rewarded him with a concealed vantage point.

The rear of the property appeared to have been designed by a demented glazier, with an enormous glass house of plants and a moronically huge conservatory. Gilbert did not like the garden either, regarding it as effeminate and over-elaborate with too many non-native species. The unnecessarily large lawn was the size of a cricket square. The garden served no purpose, other than to create work for the white-shirted old man with a floppy hat and sun-leathered forearms.

This country house was way beyond Gilbert's and therefore Simon's means. Gilbert cursed the investigator Stevens for supplying false information, but at that exact moment Simon stepped onto the patio with a glass of lemonade. The intervening months had been kind. Simon was trim and tanned in a white polo shirt and loose fitting flannels, resembling a decadent tennis professional at rest. Simon gave instructions to the old gardener in his customary, non-domineering way, taking extra care not to offend the lower orders.

Gilbert wondered if Simon embezzled money from Jemima before the annulment. But if this were true, and Gilbert informed Dunham, such news would hardly broker a joyful reconciliation. Gilbert's nose itched and his eyes streamed. He tried to convince himself it was hay fever, rather than the legacy of his beating.

The harlot emerged from the conservatory in a light blue summer dress with her black curls tied in an informal ponytail. Gilbert knew this jezebel was highly gifted in the aesthetic sense, with bountiful breasts and a suggestively pouting face, thus appealing to the lowest male instinct. The investigator had failed to inform Gilbert of the most critical development, because the harlot went back inside and brought out a pram. Simon joined her, they kissed. They doted on the child within. She picked up the boy, clad in dark blue swaddling clothes, and held him to her breast, his nephew, the racial heir!

For three days, Gilbert did not rise from his bed at all.

When he eventually dragged himself back to work, Gilbert made no effort to hide his horology. The guts of watches were spread across his desk, along with unread medical journals. Even the black tea display case of his treasured bladder stone collection acquired a thin layer of dust. However, an unopened letter caught Gilbert's attention, being addressed in a hand he did not recognise. It contained a dinner invitation from Whiting, the well-proportioned man of the Taygetus Eugenics Society.

Gilbert took a carriage to Whiting's Kensington abode for the appointed time of 6.45 p.m. The residence was a tasteful semi-detached in white stucco, the stylistic cousin of a Tuscan villa. Whiting himself answered the door clad, like Gilbert, in a black bow tie and dinner suit. Gilbert was immediately impressed by Whiting's pale blue eyes of Nordic purity. It was a bittersweet observation as the blue reminded Gilbert of the insincere and seductive blue eyes of the harlot. Whiting showed Gilbert into the drawing room.

Gilbert expected the interior of a bohemian bazaar, given the semi-artistic nature of Whiting's profession, but Whiting's French tables, leather chesterfields and patterned wallpaper were much like his own. The walls, however, were covered with glossy framed advertising posters, shamelessly hawking pipe tobacco, corsets, bicycles, bath soap and a host of other products. These travesties were obviously Whiting's creation and their prominent display spoke of his vanity. An oil painting depicting a heroic British cavalry charge was the lone piece of conventional artwork.

Whiting had the body of an overgrown jockey, but he was strong and handsome enough to portray an officer in a tacky operetta. Had it not been for his evident cunning, he could have played the best friend of the gallant protagonist. Whiting offered Gilbert a drink and teased him by asking if he took soda and ice with his milk. Gilbert almost laughed at his own expense. For a man he barely knew and did not trust, it unnerved him how at ease he felt with Whiting. It also appeared that Whiting had given his staff the evening off and the two of them were alone.

They dined in a small room, intimately lit by two silver candelabra. Whiting served dinner, a solitary Beef Wellington with steamed new potatoes and gravy. The beef had the consistency of velvet, being not quite rare, but not overdone. The pastry was golden and butter-crisp and the gravy contained the deepest flavours of the meat. It was highly irregular for a man to cook for another man, but the food was delicious. Gilbert offered an understated "Very good" as his verdict. They ate in silence. Whiting drank claret. It would have been a shame to ruin the meal with small talk.

A portrait of a British Officer occupied the wall facing the table. His blood-red tunic was adorned with medals. The officer had Whiting's countenance with a florid complexion. The inscription read 'T.P.T. Whiting 1819-1868'. The cavalry barracks on Kensington Road were less than a mile away. Gilbert concluded that Whiting had inherited well and presumably enjoyed a private income.

After dinner, Whiting invited Gilbert to the drawing room and recharged their drinks. Whiting offered Gilbert a cigarette from a silver case. When he saw Gilbert's distaste for tobacco, Whiting chose not to smoke. Gilbert took a closer look at the framed advertising poster for Briley's Midnight Flake Tobacco. A cartoon depicted a kindly-faced father in a white nightgown and cap, cradling a wailing infant in each arm, his twins. All the while he chuffed on his pipe. The man had a placid, idiotic smile. The slogan read, 'Never alone at midnight'.

"Please, do not be shy," said Whiting, inviting an appraisal.

"This sort of thing is designed to venerate mediocrity. The implicit message is, 'Here you are, friend, muddling through life in your jolly nice ho-hum way, trying to be a good egg and make the best of things. Even though your existence is full of drudgery, it is enriched with love. This tobacco will provide a crutch as you muddle along."

Gilbert addressed his remarks to the picture like an art critic deconstructing a pretentious work.

"Why is husband nursing the children and not one of the staff? Why is wife absent? Am I to understand that Briley's Midnight Flake is a pipe tobacco for weaklings employed in the work of women?"

Whilst Gilbert would vehemently defend his position on advertising, he did not wish to imply cooking was effeminate and thus offend Whiting for an excellent dinner. Whiting smirked and clapped his hands in light applause.

"This particular advertisement increased consumption sevenfold," stated Whiting with great self-assurance. He gestured to the other portraits in the room: a woman playing tennis in a comfortable corset, a soap advertisement with a black boy scrubbed white and finally an advertisement picturing a courting couple riding their bicycles in the clouds, with the promise of 'Soaring Sensations!'

"This tenfold, this twelvefold, this twentyfold. Tell me, Greystone, for all your efforts with the Taygetus Eugenics Society, how many people did you actually convince?"

"Our membership was one of quality, not quantity. Opening our doors to all and sundry would have defeated the very purpose of eugenics. An elite."

The word 'elite' dribbled incongruously from Gilbert's tongue.

"Fifty flaccid rheumy old men. Ignorant lecherous drunkards. What an elite they are, Greystone! You are a surgeon, accustomed to delivering bad news. You must now receive it. You singlehandedly failed to elicit any genuine interest in eugenics."

"I have observed you, Whiting, and this charming abode. I think you fancied yourself as a master tactician, a strategist, a general. But you were too much of a coward to take up a commission. So you devoted yourself to advertising, commanding a second-rate army of the needy and greedy. A man like me cannot be held accountable to a man like you. What the hell are you doing with eugenics?"

"I wanted to sell something I believed in for a change."

The sincerity of Whiting's answer shocked Gilbert and he felt strangely compelled to apologise. But before he could reply Whiting produced a set of silver keys and added, "I want to show you something."

Gilbert followed Whiting along the downstairs corridor to the rear of the property. Whiting stopped at a door with security bolts at the top and bottom, clicked open the padlocks and ratcheted the bolts to one side. Gilbert smelt old, musty objects but could not see a single thing. Whiting illuminated a lamp, revealing a military enthusiast's dream of wall-mounted flags, sabres, swords, rifles and bayonets. Gilbert was hugely disappointed. To him, military collectors were second only to model train enthusiasts in their intellectual cretinism.

Two mannequins modelled the red British uniform and the light green tunic of the Russian infantry. As the lamp warmed up and the light improved Gilbert saw that the midriff of the red coat was ripped and raggedy from shrapnel and stained with dark intestinal blood. The right sleeve of the Russian had been sheared off at the elbow by artillery. The white trousers were soiled by the viscera of a grievous abdominal wound.

Whiting lit another lamp to illuminate a gigantic cabinet in the corner of the room. It was seven feet high and five feet wide with a depth of four. The cabinet was the same dark, mysterious hue as Gilbert's bladder stone display case. Its doors were fastened by a central padlock and two security bolts. Whiting fluently unlocked the mechanism and flung open both doors simultaneously.

A hide of human flesh hung on the back of each door. The subjects were presumably selected because of their elaborate tattoos. One hide was covered with vicious blue ink serpents, the other was emblazoned with a proud lion's head and the legend beneath: God save the Queen. There were four levels of shelves inside the cabinet packed with glass containers, an abattoir of human body parts pickled in formaldehyde. The bottom shelf contained hands and feet. The top shelf contained a variety of ears, noses, and penises of indeterminate race.

Yet the two middle shelves provided the *pièce de resistance*. Each of the shelves held six severed human heads in glass display jars, divided into rows of three by two. Gilbert reckoned the majority of the exhibits were Slavic, trophies from the Crimean War, although British heads were also amongst the display. The most prominent Briton had the large nose and angular cheeks of a lower-class city dweller, no doubt a common infantry man. A jagged horizontal gash ran from the soldier's temple to his destroyed left eye and his mouth remained fixed in an anguished pout, capturing the moment of death. The centrepiece was the head of an Indian Kaffir, with the macabre symmetry of a bullet hole square between the eyes. Whiting's father had been a superb curator of the battlefield and the collection was immaculately maintained by his son. Gilbert sent a silent apology to Whiting and his father for underestimating their intellectual culture and aesthetic taste.

Whiting picked out the glass jar with the head of the slaughtered British soldier, put it under his arm and stepped away from the cabinet. Gilbert followed him like an engrossed museum visitor on the heels of a visiting professor.

"The officer is the superior warrior. In tactical awareness, leadership and pure fighting ability the soldier is not even close. Yet what is the officer without the soldier? What is an army? It is nothing. What is it that unites them, Britons high and low? Inspires them to fight and die?"

Whiting stood by a wall-mounted Union Jack. It was the size of a large tablecloth, grubby and frayed, a retired battle standard, yet Whiting stroked the flag with the affection of an infant's hair.

"You want eugenics, I want eugenics and so would millions of other Britons, but nobody will fight for the Taygetus Eugenics Society. But they'll fight for this, they'll die for this. If we can only make clear that eugenics is the national defence, we will raise an army and conquer the scourge of our race."

Gilbert felt himself in the presence of a great speechwriter, a colossus of propaganda breaking free of his chains. The exhilarating sense of liberation rekindled his fire for eugenics and, for the first time since his beating, Gilbert was able to evoke the memory of his father without feeling shame. Even the severed head in the glass jar seemed to nod approvingly.

"Are you with me?" asked Whiting.

The question was entirely redundant. Gilbert would have followed Whiting to hell in that moment.

Chapter 14 – Drowning

Joseph Merrick sailed to Belgium on a third-class steamer passage, with the hope of resurrecting his sideshow career. His new manager, Monsieur Baptiste, met him on the gangway at Ostend. Baptiste was a red-headed, moustachioed showman with a solid European paunch below his sternum. He wore a navy blue suit with a white waistcoat and physically resembled a rotund Napoleon. Baptiste spoke good English. On the train to Brussels he described Joseph's new home in glowing terms. Joseph, he said, would perform in 'A theatre like the Royal Albert Hall, of wonder and wine, where our pockets overflow with gold.'

In the carriage from the station Joseph took the opportunity to observe Brussels, which he thought a picturesque city. Many of the buildings looked like ornamental music boxes, with decorous eaves and turrets, bringing to mind an illustrated picture book of the brother Grimms' fairytales. Joseph was intoxicated with hope until the carriage entered Brussels' equivalent of Whitechapel, a dense, impoverished district where prostitutes openly solicited.

The theatre of wonder and wine was an old tavern on a seedy side street. The ground floor was partitioned into two rooms, one for the freak show and the other for an illegal drinking club. A man named Vogels held the rank of Baptiste's loyal lieutenant and performed the function of doorman and money-taker. Vogels was tall and thin with close-set eyes and towered over people to intimidate them, like a human viper. Vogels was also a former prizefighter and it took little provocation for him to dust off his old skills. His favourite targets were drunks, who were less able to defend themselves.

Every so often, Baptiste rounded up a crowd of punters from the bar and brought them through to the freaks' display area. Joseph appeared alongside:

Wolfman, a native of the South Pacific, four feet in height with handfuls of wiry black body hair and a savage, animalistic face.

Lobster Boy, a young Belgian aged twenty at most, with strawberry-blond hair, the face of a cherubic pickpocket and an unusual pair of deformed, pincerlike hands.

Lucienne, a middle-aged woman with the body of an aging, exotic dancer, who dressed entirely in black. Her act appeared to be little more than acting out a spooky story. As if to compensate for the nothing gimmick, Lucienne displayed a Himalayan cleavage. Lucienne was also Baptiste's woman. Joseph often heard her screaming abuse at him late at night.

Finally there was Strongman, a hulking boulder of muscle with a crew cut and handlebar moustache. Strongman wore cotton gym trousers and performed bare-chested in order to display his muscular upper body. He bent iron bars behind his neck, invited men to punch him in the gut and concluded his act by raising a huge blacksmith's anvil effortlessly above his head. Strongman also wrestled 'catch as catch can' any punter who was fool enough to take him on.

Baptiste had little appreciation of suspense and every curiosity, except for Joseph, was on open display. Joseph remained hidden from view behind a decrepit ladies' dressing screen, adorned with tacky trees and flowers, which would not have looked out of place in a brothel. He still wore the same toga and it had not been washed since London. The once white cloth was now a dingy shade of grey and reminiscent of Big Mavis's wedding dress.

When the punters had their fill of the other attractions, Baptiste introduced Joseph as 'The Son of the Elephant Mother' and exclaimed "Ici!", Joseph's cue to hobble from behind the screen into sight. The average crowd consisted of workers, prostitutes, servicemen, or lowlifes, with faces of simultaneously French and Germanic character. Baptiste forbade Joseph from speaking to the audience and he did not care, as acting the part demanded energy, concentration and some degree of spirit. The punters were affected by Joseph's lethargy and the exhibitions petered out in silence.

As soon as he was back behind the screen Joseph huddled in his thick black overcoat to keep out the cold. It always seemed to be raining in Brussels and the walls of the old tavern were constantly damp. His life's savings were secreted in the lining of his coat, his precious fifty pounds in white fivers. Since his arrival in Belgium, Joseph had only received a few francs of his agreed money, with Baptiste promising the full amount at the unspecified season end.

Joseph was too inert to question anything or worry about his health. He kept the frequent stabbing pains in his chest a secret, assigning them to the reduced circumstances of his life. He lost his appetite, ate infrequently and, other than watery coffee, the only available beverages were foul-tasting liquor and strong amber beer. Joseph's extensive deformities made it virtually impossible to notice a decline in his body. The only outward sign of inward neglect were his ribs protruding through the flesh more than ever.

The only person who regularly spoke to Joseph was Strongman. Once or twice a week they shared a bottle of the terrible liquor, conversing in the Strongman's sixty words of English and Joseph's twenty of French. The Strongman showed Joseph the tattoos of eagles and daggers on his forearms and attempted to explain their significance. Joseph guessed they were marks of military service. Joseph showed Strongman a sketch of Alice and tried to explain that she had been his love. Strongman nodded along respectfully, despite barely understanding a word, punctuating Joseph's monologue with pleasant remarks: "Beautiful ... Special ... Very nice."

Lobster Boy and Wolfman were drinking partners. Their nightly sessions began with toasts of friendship and ended with acts of violence. At the climax of one lengthy session, Lobster Boy bent his bottom forward to imply the Wolfman was a homosexual. Wolfman responded by taking a bite out of it. Lobster Boy drew a pocket knife and swished it around in his pincer. Vogels was forced to separate them.

The season came to an abrupt end when Strongman left without notice and Lobster Boy and Wolfman argued with Baptiste over money. Vogels knocked both freaks unconscious and threw them onto the street. Lucienne and Joseph put on a piecemeal show for diminishing crowds. At night when Lucienne went to bed with Baptiste, Joseph had the room to himself. He wrapped himself in the extra sleeping blankets, the ones that Lobster Boy and

Wolfman left behind, for warmth. He knew he was in danger, but he had not the energy to move a muscle.

One morning Joseph awoke to find Baptiste and Vogels in front of him. Joseph clambered to his feet in honour of their status, but kept the thick woollen blankets around him. They felt like an extra layer of protection on top of the money in his overcoat. Baptiste inspected the contents of room, the few discarded props of Lobster Boy and Wolfman, the macabre 'Child of The Bat'. He seemed to regard it all with considerable disgust and regret, even though it was his show.

"Monsieur Merrick," asked Baptiste, "have you heard of Le Pétomane?"

Joseph had read of the Frenchman in a London newspaper. He knew that Le Pétomane's anal dexterity stage act was breaking box office records at theatres throughout Europe. Joseph shook his immense head to the negative, because he did not want to say anything to provoke his employers.

"That man is, how we say, a 'freak of nature'. He can sing with his behind! Play the trombone! How many people pay to see Monsieur Le Pétomane? How many pay to see you? In England you make a big noise, here you are ..."

Baptiste blew a raspberry. Vogels smiled and revealed his chipped, predatory teeth.

"Monsieur Merrick, why do you fail here?"

Baptiste had a habit of asking rhetorical questions, although Joseph sensed he wanted an answer.

"Monsieur Baptiste, when I show, I do not speak."

"And?"

"If I do not speak, they believe I am in pain."

"We are all in pain," replied Baptiste. Vogels balled his fists.

"It is the season *fini*, Monsieur. Time to receive what you are owed."

Baptiste nodded to Vogels, who in one fluid motion stepped back, opened his coat, pulled a revolver from his belt and aimed between Joseph's eyes. Joseph stared down the dark tunnel of the barrel and saw Alice at the end of it. Vogels cocked the firing hammer. Joseph said goodbye to his beautiful lover and braced himself for the explosion of his brains. But instead of pulling the trigger, Vogels teased the three prominent bulges of Joseph's forehead with the barrel, stringing out the tension of his imminent demise. Baptiste jabbed Joseph's chest with his finger and tugged at the lapel of his overcoat.

"You think you can take the shirt from my back? No, no, mon ami. I take the shirt from yours!"

The third-class quarters of the steamer were located deep within the hull and were similar to an army barracks in their no-frills, functional asceticism. There were no windows and passengers slept on the bare wooden floor. One hundred passengers occupied the hold, which would have provided cramped accommodation for fifty. One rancid latrine served the whole third class and the oppressive aroma of sweat, urine, excrement and tobacco was getting worse by the hour.

Joseph was fortunate to secure a warm and relatively comfortable spot by the wall next to the engine room. The sinister disguise of his headgear worked in his favour, as it had on the passage to Belgium, as no one would venture near. He had extra room to move his arms and stretch his legs, but was careful with his movements. His overcoat was hanging by a thread after Baptiste and Vogels had ripped through the lining and relieved him of his life savings. At one stage of the robbery Joseph feared they were going to relieve him of his life. However when Baptiste and Vogels got their hands on the cash, they lost all interest in hurting him. In fact, they were so entranced with avarice that they neglected to search the soles of Joseph's walking slippers, in which he had concealed a single white fiver of English money along with the small amount Baptiste had already paid him. The steamer ticket to England consumed most of these funds and Joseph was virtually destitute.

In spite of his dire circumstances, Joseph was taken by a desire to see the sea. He had stayed below deck for the entirety of his initial crossing and was determined to salvage at least one memorable experience from the disaster of his European adventure. At least one more memorable experience before he died.

Joseph navigated his way around the passengers lying on the floor. If anyone saw Joseph approaching they moved aside for him, quickly and anxiously, as if his touch was the hand of leprosy. He left the hold and ascended the narrow, twisting iron stairs, rising above the confinement of third class and the chug of the engine room. A heart pain disabled him and he paused to draw breath. He thought about giving up and going back to third class, but the smell of sea air spurred him on. Joseph ascended the final flight of steps and emerged onto the deck into daylight.

A cold sea wind cut through his overcoat and chilled his face through his mask, though the overall effect was invigorating. The wind was strong, but not a gale and a child could have flown a kite without losing their grip. Joseph saw a crowd of well-dressed passengers through the narrow hole in his visor. They parted for him as he veered to the port side of the deck and then to starboard. He did not know if he was allowed on deck, but did not care. He headed for the horizontal picket of white barrier rails, leant against the steel and pulled off his headgear.

The sky was a mountain range of white clouds tinted by metallic grey. The sea was a blue-green Chinese dragon, undulating with hidden power, giving only a subtle hint of its infinite might, surrounding the boat for hundreds of nautical miles on all sides and falling to immeasurable fathoms beneath. Aside from Alice, it was the most beautiful sight he had ever seen.

Joseph inhaled a deep breath of sea air, which cleansed his lungs, refreshed his mind and made way for new thinking. Joseph finally accepted that his career was over. It was over because the world had changed. The good, normal, modern citizen would no longer tolerate the old-fashioned freak show in their society. The new modern freak must have ability, not disability, and appear in theatres, like Le Pétomane, because then the normal could convince themselves they were being entertained by a talent rather than a curse. Every modern man and woman was a Russian doll beneath layers of civilisation. At the core was a small person with a tiny mind, a simple peasant still fascinated by deformity. They had evolved from cruel children into repressed adults, who would not admit they were cruel children at heart. Their moral sensibilities made Joseph redundant.

Joseph looked down at the hull of the steamer cutting through the water like a gigantic sabre and felt the urge to throw himself into the sea. What a magnificent way to die, he thought, to reside in the sea for eternity, untouched by man, oblivious to life on the surface. If he leant his body over the steel barrier the momentum of his oversized skull would flip him over the edge in a front somersault. Joseph placed one foot on the bottom rail and the palm of his good hand on top, positioning himself for a decisive push forward. But just as he saw Alice's face in the barrel of the gun, Joseph saw her eyes in every sapphire of the sea. The chances of holding her in his arms again were a million to one, but as long as she was part of this world, he could not bear to leave it.

Joseph compared himself to a drowning man struggling and sinking and sinking the more he struggles. In conventional employment the sum of his labours had been a rapid descent to oblivion. The man who makes no effort floats, therefore Joseph considered an interesting possibility; if he stopped struggling to survive, would other forces conspire to support him? Normal society owed him a debt that might be replayed though emotional exploitation. Their hypocrisy led them to condemn the freak, but would it also compel them to care for the cripple?

Joseph thought out some interesting possibilities. He could pretend to be blind, epileptic or moderately insane and gain admission into one of the more salubrious homes for incurables. He could present himself at a church, pretend to 'see the light' and become a beloved pet invalid to a vicar. His career as a freak was finally over but, through the cunning exploitation of his bodily condition, his life as a cripple could continue.

A high wave rose like an emerging whale and hit the side of the ship. The salt water spray refreshed Joseph's face, his lopsided mouth, his bulging lips, the strange lumps on top of his forehead. He felt the corner of an object against his ribs. Baptiste and Vogels had overlooked a seemingly inconsequential item in the lining of his coat. He reached into the split and produced a card. The wind nearly blew it from his hand. It was the card of Dr Frederick Treves.

Chapter 15 – The League of Decency

Whiting thought that the best way to gather a crowd for their social purity initiative was to pimp Gilbert as a whore, offering free medical checks for children. They both agreed the venue should be near Whitechapel, but not within the district. Whiting proposed Bow, surmising that decent families from the higher echelon of the working class would be concerned by the number of feckless vagabonds and by proxy mental defectives bordering their locale. Many middle-class families also lived around the perimeter of Victoria Park. Their hand-wringing moral conscience and worried outlook on life made them receptive to the gospel of social purity. Gilbert agreed and added that Simon's old patients from his general practice might lazily assume their beloved Greystone had returned to the area.

Whiting took a few days' leave from his employ and set about sourcing a venue. A religious organisation known as The Redeemers owned a large meeting hall on the Bow Road. Their leader, Reverend Robertson, had evidently persuaded his congregation to invest in the building. Robertson must have been sure of attracting vast crowds of new followers and filling his coffers, but was now desperate for funds and, to this end, to hire out the hall.

The building had started life as a warehouse, before a short tenure as an early primitive music hall. Its high walls were wood-panelled with outstanding acoustics. The ceiling windows reminded Gilbert of the operating theatre at the London Hospital and there was electric lighting if needed.

On first evening of the initiative, one hundred mothers brought their children and formed an orderly queue for good Doctor Greystone, who was seated behind a makeshift partition. The children wore shoes, indicative of the high-grade working class. Gilbert also examined at least two dozen children from the lower middle classes. Whiting stayed in the background, gathering intelligence.

Gilbert was grateful to Whiting for carefully targeting decent people with handbills. There were hardly any trainee consumptives or apprentice bladder stone candidates. Only one semi-imbecile, a lowly woman, arrived in the queue with three idiotic children in tow. Whiting politely told her that she had been misinformed and there was a one guinea fee for examination. Bravo Whiting!

Gilbert administered a pill here, an injection there and implored those mothers to dispense with the can in favour of fresh produce. Gilbert examined one runt of a boy, Thomas or 'Little Tommy' as his mother insisted on calling him, who had nothing much medically wrong with him, nothing short of mollycoddling by the mother. Gilbert told the boy his puny physique was the result of poor posture. He showed the lad how to stand with his stomach in and chest out and instructed him on a few simple exercises, the knee bend, the press-up and the burpee.

Word spread at the London Hospital and other medical establishments. Creeping Jesus physicians and surgeons volunteered their services, assuming that Gilbert was a good egg like them. Gilbert took the least evangelistic man, Dr Carter, along with him to the second meeting and he was glad he did. More than two hundred mothers brought their children to the hall. Whiting told Gilbert to leave the majority of the doctoring to Carter and handed Gilbert the script of a trite, sloganistic speech. The front stage was the size of a boating jetty, elevated to the height of three feet with a wooden lectern. Gilbert ascended the steps, took the stage and addressed all present.

"My dearest friends, my name is Dr Gilbert Greystone and I am delighted you have joined us here. Medical care is a great expense for hard-working families. Indeed, after settling our weekly accounts and feeding our children, there is hardly a penny left in our pockets. I hereby pledge to continue these free checks for children. The children of hard-working folk!"

And so it went on, the text lobotomising Gilbert with its banal Jack and Jill metre. He received a rousing ovation nonetheless. Afterwards, Gilbert asked Whiting why he insisted on employing the term 'doctor' and not 'surgeon'. Whiting replied, "A surgeon hacks at bloodied stumps. A doctor cures you with a smile and a lollipop." Gilbert could not deny Whiting's genius in exploiting the inane sentimentality of the patient.

They needed a name for their initiative. 'The Greystone quest for health, hygiene and social purity' was Gilbert's choice. Whiting preferred 'The League of Decency'. Gilbert spun a coin, Whiting called heads: The League of Decency was born.

Whiting prepared Gilbert a longer speech for the next meeting, with the keynote of 'Healthy Children for a Healthy Empire'. Afterwards, a gaggle of mothers asked if Dr Greystone sold health tonics. In response Gilbert prepared a placebo of syrupy water, priced at three pennies per bottle. Whiting did brisk trade on the medicine table, providing the League of Decency with ongoing funds and donations to Robertson's church. The zealot was a good ally and an enthusiastic recruitment sergeant.

Gilbert was concerned that The League of Decency had little appeal for men and Whiting agreed. Sport was the new national obsession amongst men of all classes and potentially a powerful recruitment tool. Whiting hired Trinity Rovers' professional Billy Briggton for a string of personal appearances. His fee was twelve golden sovereigns, two hundred packets of Three Castles cigarettes and ad hoc treatment for his sexual diseases. Gilbert felt like a clown tick-tacking a football on stage with Briggton, before toeing the orb into a miniature goal signed 'Good Health', yet husbands now attended with their wives.

Briggton wore his full Trinity Rovers' uniform, a white jersey with red vertical stripes and a pair of knee-length white shorts. He stood before his gawping acolytes, arms folded, foot on the ball, as if it were the chest of a smitten opponent. Gilbert and Briggton delivered Whiting's script to the letter.

"Tell us, Briggton, how many cigars do you smoke on average to relax you for the game?"

"None, Dr Greystone. Nor cigarettes. Or a pipe even. Smoking is heavy on the chest. If the opposing fellow smells of tobacco, I round him to the goal."

"A wonderful message, especially for youngsters. If you want to be fit for the game of life, be like Briggton."

"I imbibed the doctor's health tonic before we played Etonians," added Briggton. "If you recall, I scored the hat trick!"

Within minutes the medicine table was empty and men shook Gilbert's hand, vowing to renounce tobacco. Gilbert could not help but admire Whiting's skilful manipulation of the masses and their barnyard instinct to follow the herd.

It was eerie how much he and Whiting had in common, their approach to physical exercise as but one example. If not for the pressing business in hand, they could have spent hours discussing calisthenics and the Indian clubs. Gilbert's streaming nose and running eyes, the legacy of his beating, streamed and ran no more. And when Gilbert took to the stage, the fatigue of his workday was replaced by energy.

The only major difference of opinion was Gilbert's growing frustration with the cloak-and- dagger approach. Gilbert stressed the imperative of introducing eugenics, if not in name, in principle. Whiting finally agreed and prepared Gilbert a speech for the next meeting. He encouraged Gilbert to learn the text by heart so that he could look his followers in the eye when addressing them. Whiting also expanded the bill of speakers. Edifying speeches enchanted a crowd of three hundred. Dr Carter on 'Marital Hygiene', Reverend Robertson, on combining children's bible study with corporal punishment, Miss Emily Harrington on 'Chastity and Womanhood' and of course 'Briggton's Ball Skills'.

Moments before Gilbert was expected on the stage for his address, Whiting presented him with a tailor's package wrapped in brown paper. Inside was a waistcoat emblazoned with a Union Jack. Gilbert was furious at Whiting for purchasing such a ridiculous item of clothing, but he did not have time to protest. He dressed in the garment with the reticence of an older boy changing into a loathed school uniform. Whiting helped him back on with his top coat, but as he did, he expertly massaged Gilbert's shoulders. The tension left Gilbert's body and he tingled with electricity. He bounded onto the stage, inciting a burst of applause from of the crowd.

Once on stage, he lost all sense of inhibition and removed his top coat in a flourish. His waistcoat inspired spontaneous patriotic 'Huzzas!' Gilbert improvised, rolling up his sleeves to reveal his strong surgeon's forearms. His movements were far from clinical and brought to mind a strong, honest artisan preparing for a job of manly work. Whiting stood on the front row at the head of the crowd. His excellent posture mirrored Gilbert's comportment of masculine strength. Together, they would test their manhood.

Gilbert summoned Little Tommy on to the stage.

"Three months ago, this fellow, Little Tommy, was brought to me by his mother. Tommy was a weak, sickly child. His posture was feeble and defective. I set him about immediate exercise. I instructed Mother to double his intake of milk. I also prescribed liberal libations of my health tonic. Look at him now, a bruiser to be sure! Squeeze, boy!"

The boy squeezed Gilbert's hand and he winced theatrically. "Little Tommy is as strong as an ox!"

There were ripples of good-natured laughter. A wooden table had been placed on the stage, with a mysterious object, the size of a child's toybox, under the cover of a tablecloth. A volunteer handed Gilbert a glass of milk. He raised the glass to the crowd.

"To sustain his health, this boy needs nourishment."

Gilbert extended the milk to Tommy, then took it away.

"He shall not receive it."

There was a collective intake of breath, murmurs of uncertainty. Gilbert stepped a couple of paces to his side, leaving Little Tommy marooned centre stage. Gilbert approached the table and whipped away the cloth, revealing a crude card model of an institutional building.

"The Workhouse!" exclaimed Gilbert. "For some their committal is a matter of misfortune. For others, it is destiny. Did you know, every single workhouse is ram-packed with mental defectives? They say they are unable to work. But does ever manual labour preclude such persons?"

There were nods to the affirmative, grumblings of agreement. Gilbert raised his voice and jabbed his finger through the air.

"They treat the workhouse as a holiday, a rest-up from gin. They receive free board, free lodging, free medicine and we foot the bill! They beget defective offspring, tens of thousands of children, these feckless souls, bequeathing their impairments to the next generation. Their children take food from the mouths of your children. They weaken the race and weaken the Empire."

Gilbert poured the milk onto the workhouse model. Little Tommy was on the brink of tears.

"Do not blame the children, blame the parents. If they will not work, they should not breed. Medical science can stop them. Humanely. Painlessly. Together we can stop them."

There was passionate applause, shouts of 'Hear, hear!' Gilbert felt light-footed. Whiting's text was a magic carpet beneath him.

"We will not waste charity on defective idlers. We will ensure that good food goes to good children, like Little Tommy. For the strong not the weak, our good, good children who are the future of the British Empire!"

The crowd roared as if Briggton had smashed in a wonder goal. Gilbert wrapped his arm around the boy. Tommy sunk his face into Gilbert's Union Jack waistcoat, overawed by the intensity of the crowd.

Gilbert thought public speaking was a necessary evil. But now it seemed this rather vulgar form of address was a gilded chariot for the crusade of eugenics. Whiting set the wheels in motion, Whiting the Merlin of mass motivation, with his mesmeric strategies and masterful speechwriting. Whiting applauded with the rest of them, smiled a cunning smile and transfixed Gilbert with his pale blue eyes of Nordic purity.

Gilbert was grateful to Whiting for teaching him the full value of stagecraft. By masquerading as a doctor he had rediscovered his purpose as a surgeon.

Chapter 16 – You Are Britain

Gilbert was not due at The London Hospital on Saturday, but had instructed Andrews to wake him early regardless. After breakfast Gilbert completed a routine of stretching exercises, press-ups and an energetic half hour with the Indian clubs, before a thorough scrub and vigorous application of a coarse towel. He dressed in a grey tweed day suit and spread the transcript of the latest Whiting-authored speech over his bed. He wanted to perform the script in front of his dressing mirror and practise his hand gestures, in order to deliver an absolute optimum performance at the next League of Decency rally.

Deciding upon a full dress rehearsal, Gilbert changed into his Union Jack waistcoat. The fabric had been sullied by the grasping hands of his followers and was due to be cleaned. The slightly grubby flag reminded Gilbert of the retired battle standard in Whiting's collection. Indeed, whilst Gilbert and Whiting spent many joyful hours in each other's company, the Beef Wellington dinner was the one and only time Gilbert had visited Whiting's abode. His intense longing to revisit the display cupboard was such that he had to physically bite his lip, so as not to blurt out his request and ruin himself in the eyes of Whiting.

Andrews entered the room, holding a telegram. Gilbert was about to berate his manservant for not knocking, but his servile face spoke of tragic news. Gilbert snatched the telegram. His immediate concern was for the health of his nephew and the news was indeed grave, of illness, but mercifully the boy was not affected. Gilbert prepared a serum, packed his medical case and made haste to Dulwich.

A worried old housewoman answered the door of Simon's magnificent country house. She showed Gilbert into the drawing room and asked him to wait. Her manners were polite, but her breeding was coarse and common. Gilbert observed how Simon and his harlot had transferred the bohemian decadence of their Islington love nest into their Dulwich home. Infernal houseplants predominated and the wall mounted-picture portraits were depraved modern impressionism. Japanese-style vases and ornaments however, were indicative of good taste.

There was a prominent photographic portrait on the mantelpiece depicting Simon, the harlot and Edward. Edward was still an infant, yet Gilbert saw the reflection of himself as a boy, eyes alert with superior intelligence and the makings of a noble jawline. Gilbert, engrossed in the photograph, did not notice the harlot behind him.

"Good day, brother," she said.

Her face was pale with hollows of sleep deprivation beneath her eyes and her lank curly hair was tied back in a ponytail. She wore a light green dress, exhibiting the form of a buxom Venus fly trap.

"Mrs Greystone," replied Gilbert. "Sister."

"Thank you for your presence in our hour of need." Gilbert detected the trace of a northern accent. Could this comely temptress really be the progeny of toothless millworkers?

"He is in good hands, I take it, his physician?"

"Simon trusts Dr Carrington with his life."

Her voice tapered off on 'life'. Gilbert observed with his professional eye a stoic woman on the brink of collapse.

"Edward is elsewhere? The risk of infection ..."

She nodded to the affirmative.

"Did Simon ever speak of my work?"

She shook her head and Gilbert wondered what possessed him to ask such a silly question. This woman would be too preoccupied with her own beauty to comprehend the racial imperative of an Empire.

"Alice, if I may call you Alice? I was a fool. It is my eternal shame to confess, during your courtship, I attempted to come between you. I did this because I thought it was best for Simon, best for you both. I said wicked things and was rightly punished.

I prayed to God for forgiveness. Would you find it in your heart to forgive me?"

"There is nothing to forgive," said Alice. "It is trivial in the scheme of things."

"I tried to contact him, to build bridges and be permitted time with your wonderful family. May I see him, sister?"

Alice stepped forward and held Gilbert's hands. "He needs you at this time, more than any other."

Her blue eyes clouded with genuine feminine compassion. Gilbert thought she must have accidentally fallen in love with Simon, whilst luring him in and extracting his marrow.

The old physician Carrington briefed Gilbert upstairs. Carrington gave a dry professional-to-professional prognosis of Simon's typhoid, before remembering his bedside manner and adding, "Though we may fear the worst, we must hope for the best."

"He is a Greystone!" asserted Gilbert. "A fighter!"

Carrington shook Gilbert's hand, firmly approving of his pluck, and took his leave. Gilbert opened his attaché case, put on his tan leather medical gloves and entered the sickroom.

Simon was asleep on the four-poster bed. His bedshirt was soaked with fevered sweat and the sheets were gathered around him in a state of disorder. His brown-blond hair was lank with perspiration and the room was thick with the miasma of a sick man's breath. There was a blue and white water pitcher on a dresser cabinet along with bottles of medicine and a small pile of unused towels. The bedroom was devoid of femininity or ornament. Simon must have been quarantined to a guest room. The curtains were half drawn and the windows closed. Gilbert lamented Carrington's neglect of good air and prised both windows ajar. Simon awoke, muttering in delirium. His face was a ghastly yellow.

"Simon," whispered Gilbert, "brother ..."

Simon smiled pleasantly, as if the fight had never occurred and Gilbert had arrived on a happy, social visit this Saturday afternoon. Gilbert rested on his knees by the side of the bed and held Simon's right hand in an overhand way, as if the brothers were preparing to arm wrestle. Simon gripped Gilbert's hand with the strength of fraternal love and also the strength of a patient desperately clinging to life. The reunion granted Simon a moment of lucidity.

"I have been asking for you, brother."

"Well," replied Gilbert, "here I am."

"Have you met my wife? She is wonderful, is she not?"

"She is, I must humbly concede, a better match by far."

For Gilbert, this admission was no bedside flattery. In spite of her whorish morality, helotic social origin and her present state of immense fatigue, Gilbert saw this 'Alice' as a fine physical specimen. The non-English curls of her jet black hair alerted Gilbert to possible miscegenation with a low race. But at close quarters, the trained eugenicist recognised a desirable strain of Mycenaean Greece, a complement to her shimmering Anglo-Saxon.

"You must meet my son, your nephew," said Simon.

"I have seen his likeness; a magnificent young man!"

Simon started coughing. Gilbert extricated himself from Simon's grip and hunted around in his medical bag, from which he removed a small glass bottle, no larger than a jar of ladies' perfume, containing a clear solution. Gilbert crouched over Simon and held the bottle to his brother's parched lips.

"Come on," said Gilbert, "there's a good fellow."

Simon took two deep sips and swallowed. The liquid eased his throat. He took another sip and was thirsty for more. Gilbert withdrew the bottle and used the bedsheet to dry his brother's mouth. Simon mumbled contently, slipping back into the feebleness of his fever. Gilbert stayed on his feet and paced by the bed. Simon reopened his eyes. Gilbert spoke first.

"Your wife said I should not apologise. I believe I should."

Simon shook his head to signify 'no need'. Gilbert added, as if to clarify his previous remark, "I am sorry it has come to this."

Simon flinched at a sharp, incisive pain. Gilbert addressed Simon in a raised whisper.

"There's this chap Whiting, hell of a fellow. I initially dismissed the cup-and-ball deceit of his advertising, but he's shown me the way. Put simply, if you promise people everything they want, they will give you everything you desire. Stand beside the Union Jack and you're unstoppable. Winning the trust of the common man is akin to winning the trust of a dog, with a flag in place of a biscuit."

Simon moaned in pain and his skin poured with sweat. Gilbert continued, "On my first visit to Dulwich I noticed the proliferation of non-native species, the Indian Bean Tree for example, not just in your garden but throughout this village. Does purity mean nothing to you people? Britain's rise is a consequence of race. Our future, therefore, is the ascension of race. Defectives are an invasive species, damaging and destroying the organism. You presently symbolise the worst of this. You are Britain, they are strychnine."

Simon clawed at the bedsheets. He tried to cry out, but the invisible grip of poison tightened around his throat. Gilbert stepped nearer.

"You subjected me to barbaric violence. You said I was incapable of love."

Gilbert opened his jacket and displayed his Union Jack waistcoat like an artist's model brazenly presenting her breasts. Simon convulsed and gripped the wooden slats at the edge of the bed.

"Is this the love of which you spoke?"

Simon was fitting like an insane epileptic, shaking every timber in the room. He twitched a final convulsion and emitted a deathly, strangulated wheeze. His eyes rolled up twelve o'clock high. Gilbert contrasted Simon's vulgar demise with the clean, crisp fatality of his father.

Gilbert heard urgent footsteps. He dropped to his knees, held Simon's lifeless hand and summoned up tears by imagining ammonia had been poured into his eyes. He took a deep breath and cried, "Brother!"

The door burst open. Dr Carrington and the widow beheld the corpse. She buried herself in the arms of the family physician and began to wail. Gilbert thought the widow resembled a quayside tart on discovering her beloved Jack Tar had been lost at sea. He pounded the mattress with his fist, reprising the chaotic violence of Simon's last moments.

"Oh no!" cried Gilbert. "Oh God, no!"

It was his brother, his tragedy. There was no way that woman was going to upstage him.

Chapter 17 – The London Hospital

The London Hospital on Whitechapel Road was a fine-looking institution as if the architect had intended a cross between a stately home and a modern university. The hospital had a reputation for clinical excellence and was well served by a small army of diligent staff. Porters and scrubwomen ranked as privates, nurses – corporals, matrons – sergeant majors and surgeons – captains. Colonels of administration oversaw daily affairs and the chairman, Carr Gomm, was field marshal. The London Hospital treated seven hundred patients at any one time, poor and ordinary folk from London's East End, many of whom, as a result of injury and illness, were unable to work. The medical staff healed many wounds, saved many lives and consequently saved many grateful families from the misery of the poorhouse. They also found time to stitch glass-fighting drunks on the busy Accident Ward.

The patients' garden was situated in private grounds behind the hospital. The garden was lined with pretty shrubs and beech trees, bordering an immaculate grass lawn and it was almost impossible to believe this oasis of tranquillity was set within one of the poorest and most densely populated districts of London. A few minutes of convalescence here was medicine itself.

A secluded stone courtyard known as Bedstead Square was located in the south-east corner of the grounds. It was flanked by an old commercial building, which had been donated to the hospital in the old days and was now used mainly for storage. The building was also home to the most famous hospital patient in Britain, 'The Elephant Man', Joseph Merrick. Joseph occupied the basement flat, hidden away behind a wrought-iron gate fence, down a short flight of stairs. Joseph's quarters were the most private in the hospital complex, as one could not see in through the basement-level window from any part of the main institution, the grounds or Bedstead Square.

It was spring and the sun rose early. Nurse Duggan brought Joseph his breakfast tea and porridge. Duggan was Joseph's favourite nurse. She was a straight-talking, no-nonsense woman, with reddish-blonde hair and the build of a milkmaid. Duggan kept a flask of brandy and gave Joseph a crafty nip on occasions. Joseph was rarely allowed alcohol under normal circumstances and was careful not to ask for drink, for fear of displaying an interest in any sort of vice.

Joseph's rooms were furnished by gifts and donations. There was an oval dining table and rectangular coffee table with a silver tea set, along with a tartan pattern settee and three comfortable chesterfields. On the west wall, a sideboard of five feet in length was home to a collection of china ornaments and brass figurines. On the east wall, a tallboy style bookcase was well stocked with novels, magazines and journals. The mantelpiece above the fire place displayed his most recent cards and telegrams from well wishers. All in all, Joseph's rooms had the homely but incongruous decor of the best suite in a small family hotel.

Joseph spent a great deal of time at his writing desk, either sketching to pass the time or answering correspondence. He sat down, opened the desk drawer and ran his finger along the old newspapers the nurses had saved for him. The press had made much of his extraordinary story.

When Joseph returned from the continent, he had intended to present himself to Dr Frederick Treves at the London Hospital. However, he only got as far as Liverpool Street Station before he was surrounded by a crowd and taken into protective custody by police. Joseph handed Treves' card to the desk sergeant. Luckily, Treves answered the wire from the police station and Joseph was released into his care.

Joseph was optimistic about spending a few days at the hospital with, at best, Treves brokering his passage into some other institution. After several days on the isolation ward, Treves accompanied Joseph to an audience with the hospital board, at least one of whom remembered Joseph from his previous exhibition at the Pathological Society in Bloomsbury.

As the well-bred grandees asked him questions, Joseph sensed a desire to keep him at the establishment, so he tailored his answers accordingly in a bid to win admittance. Joseph embellished many details of his time as a curiosity, describing himself as an unwilling captive of sin rather than an active participant. To elicit extra sympathy, he also professed a deep religious faith. The plan worked and Joseph was allowed to stay at the hospital, although special funds would be required for his upkeep.

In December 1876 the hospital chairman, Francis Carr Gomm, wrote a letter to the *Times* newspaper, which was published in full. Carr Gomm's letter outlined details of Joseph's condition, described his gentle character in glowing terms and ultimately appealed for donations towards his permanent care. Even with the headlines before him Joseph was astonished by the phenomenal success of the appeal, which had returned enough money to sustain him in comfort for life.

After thousands of shows as a freak of nature, relentless travel and years of work, Joseph had not one penny to show for it. But with one concise letter Carr Gomm performed the most lucrative feat in the history of the business. Incredibly, the vast majority of people who sent money would never see Joseph in the flesh. Yet Carr Gomm had not intended to exploit a single punter; he was driven by genuine humanitarianism. Sam Thomas would have been driven to the madhouse!

Critically, Carr Gomm's letter emphasised Joseph's supposed childlike qualities. In doing so, he inadvertently transformed Joseph's body into a theatrical prop, absorbing the audience in the sentimental melodrama of his early life. Joseph was not a man trapped inside deformity, he was a child trapped inside deformity, the Oliver Twist of twisted limb, a hideously misshapen Tiny Tim. How much had the evocation of childhood always been Joseph's secret appeal?

Joseph had not seen much of Carr Gomm, who sat on the highest throne of administration, but the chairman was friendly when they were introduced. The surgeon Joseph saw most frequently was Frederick Treves, who called at his rooms several times per week. Treves asked Joseph many questions out of genuine curiosity, although Joseph suspected that Treves was gathering material for a yet-to-be written book.

Joseph asked Treves many questions in return. One of his questions, about Treves's home, resulted in a field trip to Treves's luxurious Wimpole Street residence. Treves fussed around Joseph like a maidservant, concerned for Mrs Treves's ornamental finery. It took all of Joseph's willpower to resist the self-destructive urge to steal a piece of silver or blunder into the china cabinet.

Joseph was quietly amused by the way Frederick Treves introduced him to the nurses, as if his body was more shocking than the viscera and gore they dealt with on a daily basis. Before long, even the most faint-hearted nurse became attuned to him, like a punter on the fifth viewing and his body represented nothing more disturbing than a pile of dirty laundry.

Treves had his share of upper-crust airs and graces and the prerequisite British facile optimism, that all is fair, even though it isn't, and all will end happily, even though it won't. But if Treves was Joseph's master, Joseph considered him a good master and a man of integrity to boot. There was little doubt Treves had profited from their association and bought himself a high-class meal ticket, but he had also earned Joseph a place at the table.

The notoriety of the appeal brought Joseph many visitors, at least two thirds of whom were female. Joseph was eager to receive his well bred benefactors. Given their generosity was the only thing standing between a life of comfort and death in the gutter, polite afternoon tea was hardly an onerous privation.

He requested guide books on modern social etiquette such as *How One Should* by Mrs Elizabeth Horncastle and *The Manners of English Gentlemen* by Mrs Jemima Dunham-Scott. Even so, Joseph was careful to make subtle, deliberate faux pas. For example, when Dame Constantine paid a visit, Joseph addressed her as 'my lady' rather than 'madam'. He also addressed a high-ranking clergyman as 'my lord' rather than 'your grace'. To display too much finesse would invite scrutiny. The disabled were supposed to try hard and come up short, especially loveable cripples.

Joseph's visitors delighted in his manners, his modified handshake, his command of parlour pleasantries such as "How do you do?", "I am delighted to make your acquaintance", "May I offer you a cup of tea?"

They loved the way he said grace before his opening bite of fairy cake, how he balanced his china teacup and saucer in the crook of his enormous right hand, how he stood whenever a lady entered the room, rising to his feet with great physical difficulty, proving that grotesque deformity could not impair English good manners. And the manners had to be English. Joseph could not imagine another Briton agonising about the moral ramifications of taking a second jam bun from the three-tiered cake stand.

Joseph realised his value in fulfilling an English fantasy, that the savage, monstrous and bizarre peoples of the world could be dressed in a suit, schooled in the bible and tamed. If it was possible for a creature like 'Merrick' then one day the Congolese savage, the cannibal of New Guinea and the sexually promiscuous tribes of the South Sea could partake in afternoon tea with a delicately raised cup, a lightly buttered scone and pleasant conversation pertaining to the weather. Like Joseph they would be permitted the occasional low level faux pas of a misplaced 'your grace' or 'my lady'; in fact it would be expected.

Joseph appreciated the difference between the 'cripple' and the 'freak' and was careful to present himself as a cripple. The cripple is the product of accident, whereas the freak is a creature of will and therefore is a suspicious character, for all good Christians know that disability should enrich the soul and not the pocket. Those who condemned the freak had endeavoured to save the cripple, as he rightly predicted. But then Joseph was aware that not all the British public were so generous in spirit.

Chapter 18 – Sin and Steel

The League of Decency rallies filled public meeting rooms and town halls throughout London, yet no matter how far from the East End they ventured, Gilbert Greystone always considered the Redeemers Hall in Bow their spiritual home. The League filled the hall to its 500 capacity at least once per month.

An immaculate white banner with black lettering announcing 'The League of Decency' formed a crossbar above the speaker's plinth. Union Jack flags bookended the stage at the sides. The speakers and important guests sat on a line of chairs on the front row, with the rest of the audience standing behind. A local choral society provided musical accompaniment and they hunkered down in a makeshift orchestra pit by the front of the stage. They were a small band, nine in number, but the gusto with which they played made them sound like ninety.

Whiting sat on the front row with the other speakers, whereas Gilbert waited in the wings at Whiting's suggestion. Whiting said Gilbert's absence from the main auditorium created a mystical aura. Gilbert was a god watching from afar, 'Knowing all, seeing all, preparing to swoop down and deliver the lesson, benevolence, or judgment'.

Whiting had given notice to his employers and committed himself full time to the League of Decency. Gilbert wished he could do the same, but Whiting advised him to stay at The London Hospital for a while longer, as his standing at the institution enhanced his status.

Gilbert's position, peering from the back curtain, allowed him to observe the crowd. The League were attracting an eclectic church of parishioners, half from the working classes, and half from the middle, with the balance of males and females split evenly. The working men would be good soldiers if conscription were ever necessary, whilst their wives were typically one or two births into their mothering careers, searching for reassurance that Britain would maintain dominance and thus ensure a bright future for their offspring. The women of the middle classes stood straighter, wore their collars higher and always appeared to be sucking on an imaginary lozenge. Their faces held an expression of permanent disapproval, which was the foundation for effective child discipline.

Whiting signalled to the band, the drummer sounded a long, tantalising roll, and all sang *God Save The Queen*. Gilbert had never seen such pride in the faces of ordinary people. They were bestowed with abundant racial riches, of Viking kings, Roman emperors and conquering Anglo-Saxons. They understood eugenics, implicitly, in their sense of racial right. If Gilbert's eyes did not mistake him, these working folk and middling professionals had acquired an almost noble bearing. Blood purity made a sovereign of every healthy Briton.

The anthem concluded with rapturous applause and Councillor Dukes, the Master of Ceremonies took the stage. A rotund and jolly man, father of eight, hard-working public servant and lay preacher, Dukes performed his task with the perfect blend of humour and humility.

He began by introducing Dr Carter. Carter was a solid opening turn, as stern as an undertaker's assistant and fixated with 'self-pollution'. He read from microscopic handwritten notes, without making eye contact with the audience. Most decent people suspected that solitary vice was ruinous to health, though were not certain why. Carter left them in no doubt whatsoever.

"The youth who partakes in the singular evil is analogous to the opium fiend. The power of the poison replaces the force of life. The fiend requires the vice to function, yet the vice destroys the fiend. A temporary life is preserved by the act of suicide. Symptoms of influenza afflict the victim, cold sweats, shivering hands, streaming eyes and coughing fits. The internal organs, the heart, kidneys and liver, collapse. Two to three weeks of agonised torment can be expected. When death arrives with screams and epileptic convulsions, it is in fact a mercy."

At this point in Carter's speech, the auditorium was utterly silent.

"Be aware of the danger signs: secretiveness, sitting on hands, unnecessarily long periods of time in the privy or water closet. Hands in pockets – boys, outspokenness – girls. In the tragic case of solitary vice, vigilance saves lives."

Carter left the stage to stilted applause. Not one man or boy dare place his hands in his pockets. Everybody was frozen with fear, watching for signs. Reverend Robertson took the stage and announced, "Vigilance saves lives from solitary vice, not to mention souls!" His vitriolic opening line immediately energised the crowd.

Robertson described his recent mission to Whitechapel whilst waving his arms in a frenzy, as if giant bats were attacking his head. He reminded Gilbert of an Italian with rabies.

"I walked among the destitute drunkards, imploring them to drink from the cup of the Saviour. I walked among prostitutes, begging them to embrace the Lord. I walked among their users, lustful paying men, beseeching them to seek not carnal pleasure, but delight in Jesus. I returned to my homestead at midnight and bathed for one hour, two hours, fearing I would never be clean. I took a length of cable to my back, twenty lashes, thirty, until the flesh was raw! I fell to my knees and prayed for their salvation, my salvation and yours, in the name of God, the Empire, and the League of Decency!"

Robertson could make an eternity in hell sound like a night of passion, as if the thirteenth apostle was de Sade. He once dislocated his shoulder during a speech by striking the lectern with tremendous force. Gilbert reset the joint in the back dressing room, with no anaesthetic at Robertson's insistence.

Next came Miss Hawk, a prim schoolmistress who favoured vicelike corsets and wore her long dark hair in a painfully tight bun. Gilbert was convinced that one sneeze would scalp her. Hawk presented a dozen boys and girls with an imitation white pearl pendant. All had taken the 'Pledge Of Purity', vowing to abstain from physical intimacy until such time as they married and all forms of vice, solitary or otherwise, for life. "Applaud our champions of chastity," ordered Hawk. The number of pledgers stood at two hundred and forty-eight.

Dukes introduced the midfield four of Trinity Rovers and their ball skills. It was better to associate with a team rather than a player in case there was scandal with the individual. Whiting learned this the hard way when Billy Briggton wandered drunkenly in front of a tram. The very first youngster to sign up for the Purity Pledge, John Montague, was presented with a football.

All sang *Rule Britannia*, before Dukes introduced Whiting. He wore a royal blue evening suit for tonight's appearance, which accentuated his pale healthy skin, light blond hair and fair military moustache. Whiting wore inexpensive suits, so his clothes would not betray his wealth. This attempt at tokenistic humility amused Gilbert, because of how it failed. Whiting's physical bearing and intellect would always make him superior to the audience.

"As a society we know vice," said Whiting. "We know prostitutes, pimps and peddlers. We know bawdy houses. We know where they congregate. Entire streets are designated dens of iniquity and decent folk fear to walk them. There is talk of a problem with no solution and much wringing of hands. Is it not a question, then, of wringing necks?"

Whiting's remark inspired sudden, passionate applause. Gilbert particularly enjoyed Whiting's emerging problem versus solution theme, evoking warm memories of his father's book.

"Our constabulary cannot win this battle alone. But what of our army? The finest in the world? We have warriors at the Wellington Barracks desperate to serve their country. Let them find glory at home! Squadron, advance on the pimps, the prostitutes and their punters. Fix bayonets. Turn the cannon on the bawdy house! Take back the streets and take no prisoners, so that decent folk can walk them, families, hand in hand. We must fight sin with steel!"

The crowd roared. A one-dimensional orator would have continued pumping them up. Instead, Whiting dotted a handkerchief under his eye and dried an imaginary tear.

"It gives me enormous pride to inform you, my father was a soldier."

Men and women cried along with him, particularly those who were themselves the children of Victoria's warriors. Gilbert could have watched Whiting all night.

Whiting introduced Gilbert, reading aloud from one the many adoring press cuttings about his work. Whiting had already cultivated many favourable newspaper connections through his former advertising profession and was responsible for authoring most of the news articles under pseudonyms such as Jonathan Priest and Brigard Mayfield. Tonight, Whiting quoted Brigard Mayfield: "He is a fine man, a doctor, a leader, with the healing hands of an angel, a heart of gold, and a burning passion for Britain. He is the leader and founder of a great moral movement, an evangelist of common sense, this writer for one is a convert ... Dr Gilbert Greystone!"

The crowd roared. Gilbert strode to the front of the stage and shook Whiting's hand. Whiting's pale blue eyes of Nordic purity were sulphur flames, emanating from the palms of the wizard Merlin, and the audience seemed to rotate around them. Gilbert had not felt this way since Whiting flung open the doors of his magnificent collection. This was the second consecration of their partnership, here before the hordes of their movement, destiny reaching out to them like the Lady of The Lake. Gilbert and Whiting finally released hands and Whiting returned to his seat, with the grace of a ripple upon sacred water.

Gilbert performed his now standard routine, whipping away his jacket to reveal his Union Jack waistcoat, freshly laundered this morning. The red was the hue of an infantry tunic bathed in a gourd of blood. The blue was the velvet of Victoria's crown and the brine of the seas she commanded. White were the clouds above her domains. Gilbert rolled up his sleeves to defend it all with his hands, England, Britain, The Empire, every rosy-cheeked youth cricketing on the village green.

"In art, in culture, in science, in sport, in medicine, in commerce, in battle, Britons are best, I'll tell you! Our achievements are unprecedented in the history of the world!"

The crowd roared like a golden lion on the Royal Arms. Gilbert wrote almost all of his own material now, but showed his transcripts to Whiting beforehand. Whiting always improved the text with his sharp sloganeering.

"I am proud, I am honoured. My friends, I am deeply afraid."

Gilbert paced to the left of the stage and bowed his head, as if preparing to give a patient a grave diagnosis.

"The Greek Empire was built in marble, yet crumbled in dust. When I look upon the derelict graveyards of Rome, the ruined brick of Hadrian's wall, I am reminded that every empire has fallen, every empire in history! They fell through decadence. Decadence leads to decay. The Roman with games and his orgies, the Greek with his wine and his boys. Live by every word you have heard this evening, every command of chastity and purity. Britain will not fall through filth!"

The crowd applauded. The drummer tapped out a military tattoo and an old bearded soldier marched onto the stage. He was seventy years old and his chest no longer filled out his faded red tunic, but three lines of medals announced a formidable warrior. Gilbert did not know the soldier's name, only that Whiting paid him ten shillings, a bottle of Navy Rum and two pounds of shag tobacco. The old solider greeted Gilbert with a crisp salute, faced the crowd and stamped his feet to attention.

Gilbert held up his palms to signal for calm. The applause eventually subsided. The old soldier passed Gilbert an ammunition clip from his belt.

"Behold here a charger of bullets, the steel of which Mr Whiting speaks. Now consider the legion of social failures who eat our bread and drink our milk. Who idle at our expense in 'shirk' houses and prisons of 'soft' labour."

Gilbert removed bullets and tossed them away one by one.

"So this bullet goes to imbeciles and this to idiots who cannot work and will not work, and will breed and breed, until we are left completely defenceless!"

Gilbert held up the empty ammunition clip.

"Our Empire has a new enemy, the enemy within. Defective delinquents!"

The crowd seethed and hissed as if a villain had taken the stage and was stalking Gilbert from behind with a dagger.

"We rejoiced when Parliament brought through The Idiots Act. Yet on closer inspection, we decried their cowardice. Not one word on compulsory sterilisation! The Act makes clear the difference between idiots and lunatics; the calf with two heads to one side, the calf with three legs to the other. To reduce defective stock we must cure the broodmare responsible. And when Parliament unshackles our hands, this doctor will administer the vaccine."

After the thunderous applause died down Gilbert added, "Once the herd has been neutered they will not graze idly. Oh no, they will be put to work, in new facilities. They will manufacture munitions!"

Little Tommy, clad in an imitation Gilbert Greystone waistcoat, took to the stage and handed a fresh charger of bullets to the soldier. Little Tommy saluted. The solider ruffled his hair. Gilbert began his closing address, in his best oratory voice, with the authority of God, compassion of Jesus and the warm paternal trust of a well-bred British doctor.

"To take up the sword we must take up the pen. Write to Parliament in support of sterilisation. Sign petitions, tell your friends, march forth as The League of Decency. I believe we can move mountains together. For I truly believe, with God as my witness, that you, yes you, are the best of The British Empire!"

Gilbert acknowledged the crowd's hysterical adulation with a humble bow and 'Thank you'. He waved the other speakers onto the stage. They were reluctant to join him, as if unworthy, but he beckoned them upwards. They stood behind Gilbert in a wedge formation. Gilbert waved Little Tommy forward and placed a fatherly arm on his shoulder. Whiting signalled to the orchestra. The drummer sounded a roll. When the trumpeter blew the introduction for *Onward Christian Soldiers*, the crowd erupted with fresh euphoria. They sang like a choir of heaven.

Gilbert and Whiting occupied their own private dressing room and slumped in opposite chairs like exhausted actors. The door was open with Brooks performing the role of sentry. Brooks was a former soldier and fearsome drunken brawler who had been picked out of the gutter by Robertson. He was a classic hardcase recidivist, a man of seething, submerged anger. Brooks' conversation tempered his violence and he was a disciplined, loyal bodyguard. He wore a plain white sailing jersey with a Union Jack sewn onto the left breast.

Outside, in the corridor, Robertson canvassed Carter, attempting to convince him that 'if a youth incites another youth to commit solitary vice, then his hand should be cut from his body with a scythe'. Carter could not entirely disagree. Whiting signalled for Brooks to close the door and leave them.

"He had best barricade the door if Miss Hawk comes this way," said Whiting jovially. "Her eyes did not leave your body all night."

Gilbert ignored the comment and asked Whiting, "What of your political strategy?"

"I have sounded out chaps from both sides of the divide. There is considerable admiration for your way with the masses. Should you not run yourself?"

The prospect of political power excited Gilbert, before his vision gave way to hours of political drudgery, turgid committee meetings and endless, pointless debate.

"Persuasion is your art, Whiting, and it was wasted on chicken soup. I suppose you've got it all mapped out?"

Whiting smiled and towelled sweat from his brow.

"I have identified a borough. The incumbent is a drunken fool. I will warn him of the lust of the imbecile, as a matter of public record. He will ignore me. Sadly and shockingly, one of his constituents will die, an innocent woman, defiled in unspeakable ways. Naturally, a member of our organisation will happen upon the crime, Brooks for example, and turn the knife upon the imbecile. There is public outrage and the inevitable question, why did we not employ the scalpel beforehand? I will stand against the fool who ignored the warnings. As I prepare for Parliament, you prepare for surgery."

"It is a bold, honourable plan, but we have no guarantee, Whiting. None at all. Those indolent fops! If Guy Fawkes entered Westminster today, they would still be debating his removal as he blew them to smithereens. We are not moving mountains on sterilisation, we are not moving anywhere. There must be a faster route to the summit."

"The most notable defective in the country resides at your hospital. They use him for their ends. Imagine if we could use him for ours?" Whiting delivered his comment in a flippant tone, not considering it worthy of proper attention, but even his throwaway remarks were brilliant. Gilbert was about to respond with a daring proposal, when Whiting produced a set of silver keys and twirled them in his fingers, the keys to his *special room*.

"Come on," said Whiting alluringly, "we have earned ourselves an hour's indulgence."

Chapter 19 – Demented Artwork

In his rooms, by the window, Joseph sat in a comfortable chesterfield, occupying his morning by flicking through the most recent edition of *Templar* magazine. Nothing caught his interest and he put the magazine down. Joseph hobbled to the book cabinet, which was stacked with alternatives: Dickens and Jules Verne. His eyes settled on the leather-bound spine of *Frankenstein*. There was one hour until the nurses arrived with his luncheon. He felt the urge to do something bold.

Joseph sat at his writing desk and unlocked the drawer where he kept his secret sketchpad hidden beneath old newspapers. He placed three already completed drawings of garden birds within the front cover, in case anyone entered, because he did not want to invite the appraisal of his other works, which were chiefly portraiture. One figure dominated his studies, a young woman, with cascading jet-black hair. Joseph romanticised her in various settings, indoor and outdoor, with many well-drawn nude studies of her gorgeous body.

Joseph used a black pencil to sketch the outline of his latest work. He pictured the woman sitting on a wooden chair with her legs together, her knees angled to the left-hand side and both her arms behind her head. Gradually, he added the finer details of her intelligent face, and the erotic sensuality of her body. If ever discovered, Joseph knew his demented artwork would offend all reasonable standards of taste and decency and raise questions about the most unusual feature of his body, his normal loins.

His genitals had been photographed on admission to The London Hospital and safely confined in a medical journal. His genitals were normal flesh, but superfluous flesh, wasted like the deformed. His manly penis and testicles were the accidental property of a child and entirely disconnected from desire. He was supposed to be oblivious to beastliness. Joseph's drawings of a beautiful, naked woman were evidence to the contrary and the moral equivalent of forging money in his rooms.

His mental fantasy of their bodies together was an exhilarating and revolting tableau, a beautiful Eve and demonic Adam. But Joseph would never draw them together. In Joseph's opinion, to be pictured with her would have disgustingly defiled her beauty. Indeed, he was grateful there was not a mirror in the room, lest he shatter the abomination of his own reflection with the butt of his walking cane.

Alice was unquestionably the most beautiful woman Joseph had ever seen and to him the most beautiful woman in the world and as such he questioned if she had ever existed. Literature and myth were full of stories about beautiful women falling in love with repulsive men, because of their perfect properties of soul. For Joseph, these tales were the most heinous lie fiction had ever created. Only the blind could avoid the truth that 'like attracts like' and beautiful women only gravitate to ugly men who are rich. The storybook protagonist is always handsome and noble before he is cursed and regains his princely bearing through redeeming love. Joseph would never be arrogant enough to presume he possessed a beautiful soul, yet all invalids, fictional or otherwise, were supposed to possess them.

Until recently three emotions guided Joseph's life: fear, resentment and despair. But since his admission to The London Hospital he had come to enjoy the contentment of total apathy. Joseph had given himself up to fate, lost his will and in doing so befuddled his mind. He was a fallen leaf in a river of consciousness. Forces he could barely comprehend determined his destiny and therefore his truth. Losing one's grip of reality and not caring was both the serenity of dementia and bliss of captivity. Perhaps by preserving the image of the woman he loved he was preserving the remnants of his manhood? Perhaps she was a story he created in despair, to delay the inevitable suicide?

The front door opened. Only medical staff entered without knocking. Joseph fumbled with his sketchpad and dropped it on the floor. He bent forward and retrieved the pad with his non-deformed hand as the Union Jack waistcoat of Dr Gilbert Greystone loomed into view.

"Please continue, Merrick. I would not dream of disturbing an artist at work."

Joseph added a few stokes of the pencil to the garden birds he had already drawn.

"I remember when you first came here with that ghastly little man, what was his name?"

"McCallion, sir."

"Wound up here on a slab, you know, gutted like a fish. But look at you now."

Joseph disguised the tremor in his hand with another pencil stroke.

"May I?"

Gilbert extended his hand like a schoolmaster preparing to inspect the work of a pupil. Joseph presented a loose leaf sketch of a sparrow. Gilbert refused it.

"What of the newest work?"

Joseph did not hand Gilbert the sketchbook, but reluctantly opened the cover. As the less risqué sketches of the beautiful woman were towards the front, Joseph hoped the first portrait would satisfy the doctor's curiosity.

"Good Lord!" said Gilbert. "She reminds me of someone."

"A sweetheart, sir?"

"More like a sourpuss."

Gilbert noticed an old newspaper Joseph had left on the desk.

"Our League of Decency cannot have escaped your attention?"

Joseph made no comment, hoping Gilbert would assume his ignorance of Social Purity, and its fulsome editorials.

"Put simply, if one of your charming visitors baked a cake with bad eggs, afternoon tea would be most unpleasant. In genetic terms, the current generation of Britons are the ingredients for the next. There are many bad eggs. We intend to break up the batch. I doubt you will see the day; your heart condition is common knowledge. You were born too soon, Merrick."

"Had it been later, sir, I might not have been born at all."

"Quite so! But now that you're here." Gilbert took a step back and instructed Joseph to stand. It was not unusual for a physician other than Treves to examine Joseph, but always with Treves in attendance. Joseph rose to his feet, steadying his enormous right hand on the back of the chair.

"Disrobe completely," ordered Gilbert.

Joseph did not want to undress, but the urge to follow a doctor's orders was almost irresistible. He was a common, deformed, failed hawker and former professional freak. The man in front of him was a surgeon, with a first-class body, first-class mind and total command of the lower orders. In terms of social station, Joseph was a fool before a king.

"But, Dr Treves, sir?"

"Dr Treves is away."

"Perhaps, then, we should wait until he returns?"

Gilbert became aware of his closeness to Joseph and rocked back on his heels, as if fearing the transfer of infection. But in stepping away from Joseph, Gilbert took the sketchbook from the table. He withdrew to the middle of the room and flicked through the pages. The loose-leaf studies of birds fell to the floor. Gilbert smirked at the nude drawings. Joseph felt more naked than if he had complied with the doctor and disrobed.

In Gilbert's opinion, Treves watched over Merrick like a flower vendor guarding his precious street pitch. When Treves departed the hospital for three days, to attend and deliver the keynote address at a general symposium, Gilbert knew it was time to stake his claim. After Gilbert visited Merrick's rooms he called an urgent meeting with Dr Wainwright for the following morning. In terms of seniority and power, Wainwright was just one rank below Carr Gomm. Gilbert wanted to secure Wainwright as an ally and use him to convince Carr Gomm that the Merrick problem required a bold solution.

Gilbert presented himself at Wainwright's office, 9 a.m. sharp. He did not wear his patriotic waistcoat, in deference to the solemnity of his concerns. Wainwright was a semi-retired surgeon. To compensate for being bald on his scalp he sported a closely trimmed neckbeard of white side whiskers. He also wore round reading glasses and removed his spectacles whenever matters displeased him. Wainwright appeared astute and logical, although Gilbert remembered his overblown reaction to a trivial budget deficit. Gilbert suspected Wainwright was a secret worrier. It was this weakness he sought to exploit.

Wainwright invited Gilbert to sit at the opposite side of his mahogany desk. After thanking Wainwright for the privilege of an audience, Gilbert began his report by stating that whilst Joseph Merrick was on the surface a God-fearing innocent, et cetera, et cetera and we should praise the outstanding work of our friend and colleague, Dr Treves, et cetera, et cetera, there were grave concerns about Merrick's mental state.

Gilbert produced the confiscated sketchbook from his attaché case. Wainwright took the sketchbook to the window, where there was better light, and slowly inspected each page in silence. Wainwright cleared his throat, took his seat and placed the sketchbook on the table between them.

"I have only conversed with Merrick on two separate occasions, yet he seemed a pleasant type of fellow. Unless I am very much mistaken?"

Wainwright phrased his question with great uncertainty. Gilbert replied, "Sir, in his life as a so called 'curiosity' Merrick broke bread with unscrupulous charlatans, the scum of the earth. His capacity for thought is limited, but I am certain he has absorbed their animal cunning. Merrick would have us believe he is innocent as a child. Yet these sketches reveal a different side of his character, hitherto unseen. In addition, whenever Merrick is pressed for information about his life, his replies are tremendously inconsistent. Dr Treves admits this freely. Can any consort of degenerates emerge unscathed? Can criminal activity produce a Christ?"

Gilbert's find of the sketches was an unintended bonus and lent credence to the accusation he had already prepared in advance.

"On my visit to his rooms I also closely examined Merrick's bedlinen, whereupon I discovered *secretions of sin*."

Wainwright pulled his glasses away from his nose and Gilbert felt a warm glow. He felt as if he were speaking at a League of Decency rally; the audience had relinquished their will and were utterly compliant to his.

"Since his case came to public attention Merrick has been visited by royalty and corresponds with nobility. What if one of his dirty, filthy sketches found its way to a lady of rank? What if one of his visitors discovered him in the practice of his habit? What if my dear widowed sister paid Merrick a call and he attempted to ravish her? Even if she survived, my God, what then the reputation of this hospital?"

Wainwright's face assumed the pallor of a weak-stomached civilian who had blundered into one of Gilbert's more visceral surgeries. Gilbert continued, "Is it not time for Merrick to be placed in a more appropriate facility for both his benefit and for ours? I know of an asylum, sir, a first rate institution ..."

Gilbert was distracted by a knock on the door. Wainwright called "Come!" and in walked Frederick Treves. Gilbert spontaneously rose to his feet, feeling like an observer in his own body as the discipline of social etiquette overrode his hatred for the man in front of him.

Wainwright explained, "When you informed me of your need to discuss Merrick's case, I immediately wired Dr Treves."

Treves shook Gilbert's hand, then Wainwright's. Gilbert and Wainwright sat back down; Treves politely declined Wainwright's offer of a chair.

"I must apologise for dragging you from the symposium, Dr Treves," said Wainwright.

"Let us come straight to the point, sir," replied Treves. "There are concerns over Joseph?"

Wainwright précised Gilbert's report and handed him the sketchpad. As Treves inspected the drawings his face remained impassive beneath his sullen horseshoe moustache.

"Why did you not come to me directly, Dr Greystone?" asked Treves.

"Had you not been required elsewhere, sir, I would have immediately sought your counsel."

Treves directed his next remark to Wainwright. "Sir, Dr Greystone was right to present these sketches, though I fear his concern is misplaced. Whilst these may not be to our taste, they are no barometer of degeneracy. The nude has been a study of art since ancient times. Do we condemn Michelangelo's David as the work of a raving lunatic?"

Wainwright went doe-eyed with admiration for Treves.

"What of his habit?" Gilbert asked them. "What about it?"

"You have the soiled article in your possession, Dr Greystone?" said Wainwright.

Gilbert searched his mind for an elaborate excuse, anything to avoid saying 'No'.

"In my opinion Merrick is of sound mind and good character," added Treves. "Only yesterday afternoon Joseph took tea with Lady Winston and her ladyship presented Joseph with the most generous gift of a card tower. I called in at his rooms, on the way to this meeting. Joseph has already started work and was as happy as my son on Christmas morn."

Treves' sentimental report caused Wainwright to smile like an idiot. Gilbert could only watch as his hard-formed iceberg of suspicion melted away.

"Perhaps we should visit Joseph's rooms?" said Treves. "To put Dr Greystone's mind at rest?"

"Sirs ..." offered Gilbert. "My mind is already at rest, thanks to Dr Treves."

A round of handshakes concluded the meeting, although Wainwright subtly gestured for Gilbert to stay behind. Treves left the office. Wainwright tapped his fingers on the desk.

"I find your intervention here somewhat irregular, Greystone. Merrick is under Dr Treves's supervision."

"I sought only to help, sir. My concern for Merrick's wellbeing led me to his rooms."

"I worry that your surgical duties, combined with your extracurricular activities, are leading to fatigue. Fatigue leads to errors. A surgeon cannot make mistakes."

"Dr Treves said I was right to raise my concerns."

Wainwright agreed and made some fawning closing remarks about how Treves was the best surgeon in Britain. Gilbert thought about his brother, because right now he felt like Simon must have felt, when Father praised Gilbert as the model Greystone, and chastised Simon for being weak and inferior. The favourite son can do no wrong. It was a terrible feeling.

Chapter 20 – A Brother in Christ

Alice knew Simon was held in high esteem by the local community. Even so, she was quite unprepared for the deluge of cards, flowers and tributes that followed his death. Over one hundred and fifty mourners arrived at St Peter's church for the funeral, including Simon's old patients from Bow, new patients from his general practice in Dulwich and the poor agricultural labourers he treated for free. Gilbert Greystone delivered a lengthy eulogy, praising 'An outstanding physician, brother and Briton'. In the following weeks, Alice shut herself away at home, with Edward and her two elderly staff, the Ronsons. Mr Herbert Ronson was a multi-skilled handyman, his wife Magdalene an experienced housekeeper.

Alice was so wrought with grief that she had not the slightest inclination to leave her bed, but her son gave her reason to rise each day. Edward's hair was sandy brown, but his young face was a kaleidoscope of different aspects, still settling upon a fixed identity. It was a shining face, good and kind, and his laughter was the music of birdsong. No beauty she could ever possess would compare with the beauty she had created and Alice hoped innocence had spared him the anguish of grief. Whenever Edward reached for something that was not there, Alice worried that his hand was exploring the void left by his father.

Gilbert unintentionally eased Alice out of her darkest depression by incensing her with his uncouth behaviour. He invited himself to Dulwich, at irregular hours, disturbing Edward's daily routines and making demands billed as 'suggestions' for Edward's upbringing and future schooling, going as far as to plan Edward's future entry into medical college. Alice made a polite but firm request for Gilbert to leave them to grieve. Gilbert was amenable and reduced his visits accordingly, although Alice would have preferred him to reduce them to nil.

As much as Alice wanted to remain a recluse, she knew that becoming a social leper would disadvantage Edward. He would one day step into the world and begin his journey to manhood, via the bearpit of the schoolyard. The thought of her son as an outcast, because his mother was an eccentric, was intolerable. One had to be part of one's local community, fit in, contribute, 'do one's bit'. Alice resumed her charitable work with local societies, raising monies for the Dulwich Almspeople and acting as a friend for the Dulwich Picture Gallery.

Her return to local life met with great approval and other widows offered all sorts of suggestions for hobbies in which she might find solace. Mrs Gascoigne, a widow of eight years, recommended the baking of cakes. Mrs Turner Brown, a widow of twelve years 'staved off insanity' by devoting herself to the local dramatic society. It appeared that wholesome British busyness was the cure for any wound of the soul. Alice already had a new hobby of sorts. She kept a secret scrapbook of newspaper cuttings and correspondence relating to Joseph Merrick, 'The Elephant Man'.

When the letter for Joseph's appeal was published by *The Times*, Alice immediately sent a cheque to the London Hospital for £50. It was a considerable donation, worthy of its own sub headline, but Alice stressed in her covering letter that she wished to remain anonymous. She received a thank you letter from the hospital, assuring her of discretion and also an open invitation to visit Joseph at any time. Alice declined, but continued to monitor his progress in the newspapers. Joseph was the subject of semi-regular stories, especially if he received a visitor of rank.

If her scrapbook was ever found Alice assumed she would be taken for a silly widow with a sentimental obsession, mothering a cripple to mourn a husband. There was so much she missed about Simon: his warmth, his kindness, his intelligence and humour. Simon rarely spoke of his childhood and Alice assumed that his upbringing had contained a great deal of emotional pain. For the same reason it was a great relief that Simon rarely asked Alice any questions about her past. If anyone enquired about her upbringing, Alice told them that her father was a prosperous northern cotton merchant, who moved the family south for reasons of trade, and that she had met Simon by chance at a tea dance. Simon had been happy to play along.

Sometimes Alice wanted to tell all of her well-bred friends that she was an imposter of social class, and was actually a factory girl, a freak, at best a boutique assistant. She wanted to draw a long sharp knife horizontally across her cheekbones, creating new scars to merge with the old, and acknowledge her father's scorn. She would have set about destroying all beauty, had it not been for the beauty of her son.

So Alice continued her life of charitable works and motherly routine, Edward's bathtime, Edward's bedtime, his meals, his naps and his stories. She did not lacerate her brother's face with a razor, attack her father with her teeth, perform as a freak or make love with The Elephant Man. A good wife understood the necessity of denial, a good mother even more so.

Alice invited Mrs Oliver, the wife of a prominent barrister, for afternoon tea. Mrs Oliver was also a friend of the Dulwich Picture Gallery and her son Joshua was the same age as Edward. As if tiring of grief, Alice threw her black muffler and charcoal veil to the back of the wardrobe and wore her favourite sky-blue summer dress. It was midsummer and the thought of wearing black was ridiculous. However, Alice worried that her dispensation of widow's weeds would somehow offend Mrs Oliver. Her new position in society plagued her with these dilemmas of etiquette. As a compromise Alice put on a comfortable dark blue dress that looked black in a certain light.

Alice and Mrs Oliver took afternoon tea in the garden, beneath the tall apple tree. Mr Ronson had constructed all the garden furniture himself. Joshua and Edward played on the lawn with a small football and a rainbow-coloured spinning top. Mrs Ronson supervised the children. It was a pleasant engagement.

Mrs Oliver, like so many wives of Dulwich, befitted the profile of the English rose. She had taut, clear skin, unstained teeth and wore her dark brown hair in a modest bun. She was achingly Christian, pragmatic and pleasant, with a rock-solid core of morality. Alice, like Mrs Oliver, also possessed an extremely agreeable character, yet her eyes betrayed a precocious maturity, a secret knowledge, a will. She still possessed the body of an exotic temptress and her beauty had not escaped the attention of local gentlemen, who pretended to remain ignorant of the matter. Alice felt, therefore, that Mrs Oliver held the feminine upper hand, even though she was greater in beauty. The perfect Englishwoman was a rose, not a hibiscus flower.

As Alice and Mrs Oliver sipped tea and nibbled on cucumber sandwiches, Alice sensed her guest was building up to an important announcement. Mrs Oliver put down her cup and saucer and took a breath. Alice braced herself for an account of family illness, financial difficulty or sexual impropriety. Instead, Mrs Oliver delivered a report of her visit to the room of Joseph Merrick, The Elephant Man.

Mrs Oliver described the initial shock of Joseph's dreadful appearance and said she nearly bolted from the room. Joseph, however, made his guests feel most welcome through his polite introductions, intelligent conversation and the impeccable manners of an English gentleman. Mrs Oliver said that Joseph naively believed his condition was caused by his mother being frightened by an elephant.

"It is the most remarkable act of God," enthused Mrs Oliver, "a man despoiled by deformity with a beautiful soul." Finally pausing for breath in her monologue, Mrs Oliver must have noticed Alice's faraway expression and assumed that something she said about gentlemanly behaviour or a beautiful soul brought back memories of Simon.

"I must apologise for chattering on, Mrs Greystone. Though once you have met Joseph Merrick you cannot fail to be captivated."

"He has that effect," replied Alice absentmindedly. "I mean to say, you are clearly captivated."

"His plight moves me. As does his appeal. I am told Mr Merrick is comfortable, although any charitable endeavour requires ongoing support. I hope you do not think me presumptuous, Mrs Greystone. I know you are a most generous benefactor of local causes ..."

"Will five pounds suffice?"

"Five pounds! Why Mrs Greystone! Joseph extended an open invitation to his rooms. Mrs Singleton has already agreed to accompany me. You must also attend. We would all be honoured by your presence."

"I fear that Joseph would not want to see me."

"'Joseph'. It is like you have met him already!"

Alice prepared to leap in and to refute Mrs Olivers theory, but stopped herself at once, realising the remark was probably a compliment concerning her compassionate nature rather than a probing question.

"Why would he not want to meet such a charming lady?"

Alice remembered the aftermath of Charlie's death, as Joseph fed his *Elephant's Tale* pamphlet to the fire, going about his task with stoic resignation, as if the cinders of the pamphlet were the ashes of his dreams and he had always expected them to burn. When Alice returned to the shop the next morning and Joseph had vanished, she was not entirely surprised, but also relieved, relieved to be spared the drawn-out amputation of another goodbye.

"Because," replied Alice, "he may believe that in spite of our best intentions, we will all fail him eventually."

"Then it is of added importance we do not. Can you imagine what it is like to be so physically afflicted that the mere sight of your face draws derision from crowds?"

Mrs Oliver's remark transported Alice to a world within a world. The glare of the sun on the spinning top was the gleaming edge of a straight razor. The innocent laughter of children was the cruel, vicious mockery of her beard. It was the memory of the world as it once was and would be again if affliction returned, the waking nightmare of the former defective, now supposedly cured.

"When I look into his eyes," said Mrs Oliver, "I can see the wound in his soul. It is the burden of his former life, his rejection, his suffering. Aside from material comforts, the greatest gift we can bestow upon Joseph is our warmth, our kindness ..."

"Our love ..."

"Yes, Mrs Greystone, for a brother in Christ."

Joshua laughed. Edward tried to trump him with a high-pitched scream. The world fell away from Alice and she cried. Everything around her was darkness.

Gradually, Alice became aware of the sounds of summer, tweeting birds, buzzing bees, the faint beating wings of a butterfly. She dried her eyes on her sleeve. Everyone was looking at her, Mrs Oliver with kindness, Mrs Ronson with parental concern. The children were no longer playing and Edward had a haunted expression, instinctively aware of his mother's pain. Alice was about to apologise for her outburst, rush forward and embrace her son, but Mrs Oliver placed her hand on Alice's thigh and held her down.

"My dear Mrs Greystone, he longs for the human touch."

Ever since Gilbert Greystone had confiscated his notebook, Joseph's nerves had been at their worst. It troubled his heart and turned his stomach that a man who hated him, and he hated in return, had stolen a deeply personal artefact. Joseph felt like the victim of a burglary. He also feared the repercussions of his artwork, expecting all kinds of embarrassing, difficult questions and perhaps the intervention of psychiatrists. But nothing more was mentioned. Gilbert Greystone did not revisit his rooms and Joseph was given a new sketchbook, although the original was never returned.

Joseph did not draw and diverted his energies to constructing his cathedral card tower. He also made an extra effort to impress his visitors. The most recent new face was a woman called Mrs Oliver who visited his rooms with her rather stiff husband, a barrister. At first Mrs Oliver beheld Joseph as if he were an ungodly apparition, the image of her future death and Joseph worried that the merest glimpse of his physiognomy had permanently traumatised her.

Fear had initially compelled Mrs Oliver to leave, but her feet were cemented in English duty. Mrs Oliver asked polite questions about his lovely room and how long his card tower would take to complete. Her wildly oscillating voice settled back down to a crisp, friendly modulation. By the end of the engagement they were conversing like affectionate cousins. Now Mrs Oliver was back for more.

It was a glorious summer afternoon and Mrs Oliver wore a white bustle dress embroidered with horizontal violet stripes. The dress was tighter on her bosom than the last occasion and Joseph noticed her prominent breasts. When she dressed in front of the mirror, Joseph imagined Mrs Oliver rehearsing her most friendly but neutral expression, her best face for cloaking revulsion. It would never have occurred to Mrs Oliver that a celibate cripple would notice her breasts, or that his misshapen mouth was capable of kissing her pinkish areola.

This time Mrs Oliver entered alone and Joseph shook her right hand with his left. She explained why she was unaccompanied.

"Mr Merrick, I am terribly presumptuous. Two charming ladies, friends, are outside in the square. Both are moved by your remarkable story and would consider it an honour to meet you. They fully understand it may not be possible and there is no pressure ..."

"The more the merrier, Mrs Oliver," replied Joseph and he gestured to the coffee table of treats. "We have sandwiches, cakes, fancies and a whole gallon of tea!"

Joseph intentionally inserted these little exaggerations to display the innocence of enthusiasm. If hospital patients were expected to partake in chirpy whimsy for the duration of their stay, incurables were expected to partake for life. Mrs Oliver enjoyed the remark.

She went outside to Bedstead Square to fetch her companions whilst Joseph readjusted his light blue and silver necktie and assumed his favoured position for receiving guests. He stood eight feet from the door, resting against the back of a French chair with his good hand for support. He rotated his left shoulder to put his body at a slight diagonal so the most normal profile of his face would be visible at first. Once his guests became inured to his hugely deformed head, the claw would be less of a horror. Joseph also favoured the left side of his body as he usually wore a white carnation in his button hole. He wore the flower to assure guests that he was not a monster.

Mrs Oliver stepped inside and called through her first friend, Mrs Singleton, a girlish woman of thirty, blonde-haired with suntanned skin. Her complexion and physique spoke of outdoor leisure, horse riding, afternoons at the tennis club. She was curious and wary, beholding Joseph with astonishment as if he were a giant mole burrowing up through the centre of the court. Joseph said, "How do you do, Mrs Singleton?"

Mrs Singleton stood in front of Joseph and nodded a silent greeting. Joseph did not offer his hand, because he did not want people to feel obliged to touch him. Guests usually found the courage to shake his hand eventually, especially the womenfolk. For them it was an act of compassionate daring, akin to mutual masturbation with a leper.

"May I introduce," said Mrs Oliver, "Mrs Greystone."

Joseph told himself this was a dirty trick of the doctor and expected one of his relatives to bluster in, a harsh unsympathetic woman, a spy, who he would have to treat with the utmost caution in a flawless display of gentility. However, it was Alice who entered instead.

Joseph felt the shock of a normal person confronted by The Elephant Man. His immobile face betrayed none of his shock, but his defective heart quickened pace. Alice wore a dark purple pencil dress, trimmed with black lace, reminiscent of the garment from her fairground days. She stepped forward and stood next to Mrs Singleton. Her eyes sparkled like diamonds, alive with secret knowledge.

Now Joseph realised why he no longer drew pictures of Alice. Only a great artist could capture the depths of her character. Next to Mrs Singleton, a beautiful woman in her own right, Alice was a magnum opus. Her outer beauty was enhanced by the inner qualities few normals acquire. Her torture and torment, her flirtation with madness and death, her pain, bestowed on her a profound aspect. The faintest of pink razor scars gleamed on her cheek. But there was something else about Alice, a new shade of beauty. It was the love of a real man, thought Joseph, the final stroke of the masterpiece.

Joseph ignored his self-imposed protocol and approached her, limping across the carpet, dragging his leg. He stood in front of Alice, realised he was too close and shuffled backwards. His gesture unintentionally broke the ice. Mrs Oliver smiled, Mrs Singleton relaxed. Joseph's body was utterly bizarre, but his actions were familiar. Beautiful women were accustomed to grown men behaving like bashful children around them.

Alice extended her right hand, which was encased in an ornate glove of white and purple lace. Joseph reached out with his left. Their skin touched through the gaps in the lacework. Joseph could hardly meet her eye. The magic of her touch activated his body, restoring his spirit and his mind. Now Joseph understood why he devoted his time to handicrafts. The hospital patient must enter a form of emotional stasis in order to preserve their sanity.

"I have waited a long time for this moment, Mr Merrick."

"What have I done to deserve the company of such a beautiful woman?"

Mrs Oliver said, "Bless him."

"Compliments pour from you, sir," said Alice. "You have a way with women."

"There was only ever one woman, Mrs Greystone ..."

Joseph's voice acquired a deep, manly tone and he uttered the words with the sincerity of a vow, transcending his lisp. Mrs Singleton fidgeted in discomfort and Mrs Oliver gripped her purse in front of her. His remark accidentally introduced the doomsday proposition of 'that'. Joseph added, "... that woman, my dearest mother."

Mrs Singleton said "Aww". Mrs Oliver said "Aww". The stink of sex was replaced by the scent of lavender. Alice shared a nod of conspiracy. Mrs Singleton, comforted by the remarks, offered her hand to Joseph.

After an interminable round of "No, after you," the guests helped themselves at the buffet table. Mrs Oliver insisted on plating Joseph's food for him and pouring the tea. The conversation puttered along. Mrs Singleton asked identical questions to those Mrs Oliver had asked on her previous visit. Mrs Oliver nodded along to Joseph's answers, as if she had not heard them before. Alice remained quiet and was content to watch Joseph with her beautiful eyes.

When Mrs Singleton asked about the card tower, Joseph invited the ladies for a closer look. Mrs Singleton and Mrs Oliver went to the model. Alice waited behind and approached Joseph.

"Thank you, Mrs Greystone, for attending my rooms."

"I deeply regret not seeing you sooner."

"We all have commitments, Mrs Greystone."

"That is precisely why I should have come."

"Have you a family, madam?"

"I have a son. Edward."

"You must be very proud, as must your husband."

"My husband is dead, sir."

Darkness entered the hollows of her eyes. Joseph thought he would rather lose her to one hundred men, than have her endure one moment of suffering.

"I am truly sorry, madam, my condolences for your loss, I ..."

Mrs Singleton and Mrs Oliver were examining Joseph's card tower with the reverence of their children's schoolwork. Alice reached for Joseph's lapels and drew him closer, as if shaping up for a kiss. Joseph inhaled the aromatic perfume of her flesh and remembered her naked body, the salt of her skin, the scent of her hair and her long, sweet kisses. Mrs Oliver and Mrs Singleton returned from the card tower. Alice pretended to brush crumbs from Joseph's jacket.

"You are getting along famously," observed Mrs Oliver.

"Yes," replied Alice, "like old friends."

Gilbert Greystone arrived at the widow's residence unannounced, brushed past the housewoman and found her in the drawing room with Edward. They were finishing breakfast. Dirty, empty plates and the remnants of poached egg were scattered across a table cloth. Toys were strewn everywhere. The widow sat on the floor, playing a game with her son. Gilbert recoiled at the scene of domestic disorder, more common to gypsies and savages. Yet even at two years of age Edward stood out as superior stock.

To Uncle Gilbert, the boy's gallant face and intelligent eyes were a testament to the Greystone strain. But the widow had dressed him in an imitation sailor's uniform, the lowly rank of able seaman! With his excellent posture and obvious martial deportment Edward could have commanded the fleet. However, Gilbert was adamant that his nephew would never debase himself to the level of service, commanding galleons of rugged sodomites or battalions of lawless cannon fodder. The boy had a higher purpose, as yet unknown.

Gilbert inspected the toys. Several unmanly stuffed animals lay beside a game with some educational merit. Single numbers from 1 to 10 were painted on small wooden blocks along with the symbols for addition, multiplication, subtraction and division. It was unknown if the boy or the widow had arranged the formation 3 + 3 = 6. The widow shamelessly addressed Gilbert from her position on the floor.

"Edward is a very clever young man, is he not, Uncle Gilbert?"

"We shall see."

The widow shrugged, a mother's vanity, indifferent to any remark that did not venerate the genius of her offspring. She handed Edward to the housewoman, who walked him from the room, cooing in her lowly syntax. The widow brushed crumbs from the front of her white summer dress. Gilbert looked away in embarrassment. She no longer wore the black of mourning, disgracefully disrespecting her husband. Gilbert wondered if she ever mourned Simon with a single, genuine tear.

"To what do I owe the pleasure of this visit?"

"A rather awkward matter, sister. I was informed by a colleague that you visited the rooms of one Joseph Merrick."

"Yes," she answered, as if visiting the lair of a deformed defective was the most natural thing in the world. Gilbert balled the fist of his scalpel hand then released the pressure.

"Dear sister. Many women of a certain disposition, with good intentions, make the acquaintance of Merrick, but I could not advise more strongly against it. Merrick's bacteria, tiny invisible crumbs of disease, cling to their garments, not unlike your breakfast. They return home and transmit the infection to their children."

"Dr Treves does not think so. When I extended an invitation for Joseph to visit my home, both he and Mr Merrick were eminently amenable."

"Dear God, woman! What about the boy?"

"Edward loves visitors, even you."

Gilbert swept the line of photographs from the sideboard with the palm of his hand. He gesticulated like a crazed orang-utan and bellowed, "How dare you disobey me! How dare you!"

The widow grinned like a haughty wife who deliberately incenses her husband to strike her and Gilbert felt like a hapless dupe. The lowly housewoman appeared at the door. Gilbert shouted, "What?" in his most commanding voice, designed to wither the lower orders. She held her ground. The widow had evidently cultivated a coven of wilful disobedience. She nodded to the housewoman to signify all was well and dismissed her.

Gilbert decided that now was the time to test his hypothesis regarding Simon's ill-gotten wealth. He immediately felt his advantage return, like a man engaged in a duel of swords about to produce a concealed pistol.

"It is time for some pertinent questions. How do you maintain this manner of living? How did a general practitioner afford a country mansion?"

"We manage."

"Your husband embezzled a great deal of money from his former wife, I think. Her father is blissfully unaware at present. One word from me and you'll be out on the street, Edward will be my ward and I will leave you to rot in the poorhouse, or worse."

"I thought money was a moot point after your mother donated your inheritance to deserving causes?"

"Deserving causes? She bankrolled a negro Babylon with money that was rightfully mine! You are in no position to gloat. She gave away Simon's inheritance also."

"She gave away your half alone and swore Simon to secrecy. Simon inherited a sizeable sum, a sum I inherited from Simon. My husband was no embezzler, he was an honourable man. Therefore every brick of this house and penny in the bank belongs entirely and legally to me."

Gilbert felt as if he were on stage before the League of Decency and the roof had fallen down on his head. Whilst trapped and immobile the cheering hordes of his followers melted away and in their place a colossal stage emerged, with Negro minstrels in garish top hats and tails, singing, dancing, caterwauling like alley cats. Gilbert's mother rode above them at the stern of an imitation pleasure boat. The widow rode on the bow in an emerald green mermaid costume, exposing her bountiful naked breasts. The conductor turned to Gilbert from the orchestra pit. It was Simon, directing the minstrels to laugh at him, with baritone, "Ho, ho, hos" and falsetto "Hee, hee, hees."

"I tolerated you for the sake of my son," she said. "But I find you have nothing to offer, not in wealth, not in character. Never return."

Gilbert returned home to Bayswater and threatened Andrews for not being fast enough to the door. He retreated to his study and brooded on the crisis of the widow.

Whenever Gilbert questioned her about personal matters she was extremely evasive, revealing only that her father made his fortune in cotton and sent her to finish schooling in London. Yet any decent establishment for young ladies would have seen to her crude provincial accent in days. Gilbert's hypothesis was thus: if not a formal prostitute, she was the nearest thing, a Gaiety Girl or an exotic dancer. She had travelled to London with the sole intention of snaring a gentleman via depraved seduction.

The only documentary evidence of her background had come to light at Simon's funeral. After the service, two dozen mourners went back to Simon's residence to guzzle tea, gorge sandwiches and wallow in grief. Gilbert had taken the opportunity to explore the property, surveying different rooms and investigating private papers. He found their marriage certificate from Coldstream, Scotland and the listing Alice Rose Powell as born Leeds, West Yorkshire, 6th October 1860, occupation listed as 'Spinster'. Father's occupation not listed. 'Orphan'. A pack of lies. They had obviously eloped to take advantage of lackadaisical Scottish law and cover up salacious details.

Gilbert could have travelled to Leeds and investigated her background at any time, but had taken no action. He knew why. It was the same reason a sick man avoids medical examination. Gilbert was afraid of what he might discover. At face value his nephew was as pure as snow, but what if some latent defect or dreadful impairment of her family lurked like a cesspool beneath? What if Edward was the product of the most frightful mixed breeding, the high with the low, a stallion with a donkey, a despised mongrel hybrid, a hinny? 'Blood purity,' wrote St John Greystone, 'is the wax of Icarus's wings, whereas miscegenation is the sun.'

The League of Decency, Britain, The Empire, the new dawn of sterilisation – if Gilbert fell, it would fall. He could not seek Whiting's counsel on this matter, even though he desperately wanted to. Gilbert ordered Andrews to pack an overnight suitcase, took a hansom to St Pancras Station and bought a first-class passage to Leeds.

Chapter 21 – Curious and Singular

The nurses fussed over Joseph's breakfast, his case of clothes and his bag of medicines. Joseph felt like a youth preparing for a year at boarding school, rather than three nights at the home of a generous benefactor. Although, when he considered the prospect of time alone with Alice, he felt as giddy as a schoolboy. Joseph was grateful for the sly nip of brandy Duggan gave him from her flask, which calmed his nerves and steadied him for the coach trip. The same driver who transported Joseph to Treves's residence handled the journey, presumably because he was inured to his deformities. The train was out of the question for obvious reasons.

Joseph spent the short journey south fastidiously checking his summer suit for creases and adjusting his necktie. When the air in the carriage smelt fresher and cleaner, Joseph peeled back the corner of the window curtain. The coach slowed to a sedate pace and entered a pretty village, which in spite of the newly constructed cottages and houses, retained its old world character. Joseph saw a massive cathedral-like building, which had to be Dulwich Picture Gallery. A languid young man, a student, sat on a white wooden bench, eating an apple. It seemed unlikely that a single defective had ever been born here.

The coach pulled into a quiet lane and Joseph closed the window curtain. He did not want to frighten any of the residents if they happened to be outside. The driver halted the horses, opened the carriage door and helped Joseph down onto a gravel courtyard. Joseph found himself within the grounds of a magnificent Georgian property with Roman pillars above the front door. If someone had asked Joseph to draw the ideal country house in his sketchbook, this house would have been his study. Alice's home was tucked away at the end of the lane, forming a natural cul-de-sac, a good twenty to thirty yards away from the two other properties. Joseph heard no other carriages or voices, only birdsong and the playful bark of a distant dog.

The driver unloaded Joseph's cases and two staff approached, an elderly man and woman who were seemingly husband and wife. The man had the squat, sturdy build of a retired manual worker, side-parted grey hair and a tough, but friendly face. The woman was about sixty years of age with a strong, lithe body. The lines on her face spoke of a lifetime worrying about the problems of others. Both said, "Hello, sir." Their minimal, contained shock suggested they had been thoroughly briefed about his physical appearance beforehand.

The woman invited Joseph inside and her husband carried his case. She directed him along an airy corridor, slowing her walk to compensate for his limp. Joseph caught glimpses of high-ceilinged rooms. There were many items of luxurious furniture, expensive ornaments and plants in elaborate vases. Joseph did not feel intimidated by the finery, as when he had visited Frederick Treves's residence, because everything here belonged to Alice.

The corridor was the full length of the house. It veered to the right then straightened again to a back door. The woman showed Joseph onto a stone patio with steps leading down to the garden. The garden stretched out from the south and east of the property in an L formation with a huge lawn, many plants, flowers, fruit bushes and a gigantic conservatory and plant house. Hawthorn trees and wild rose formed a perimeter which only the most determined intruder would attempt to penetrate. A low hedge at the rear of the garden offered a view of expansive farmland. The total privacy of the house and its garden put Joseph at ease. He was confident that every leaf of every tree would conspire to hide him from view.

Alice was playing with Edward on the lawn. She wore a long-sleeved white summer dress with a crimson ribbon around her waist. She smiled and waved at Joseph, as if recognising a friend across the boating lake of a public park. She hoisted Edward to her bosom and he rested his head on her shoulder. Alice's long dark curls cascaded across Edward's face and he kneaded them in his short chubby fingers. Her carefree demeanour contrasted with the desperation of the moment. What the hell is she doing, thought

Joseph, bringing a child close to me? Thankfully, by virtue of the angle Alice held Edward, he could not see Joseph. Joseph guessed that the child was between two and two and a half years of age.

Alice introduced the Ronsons. Both husband and wife greeted Joseph with a hearty handshake and insisted on calling Joseph 'Mr Merrick', as if he belonged to a higher social stratum. Joseph thanked Mr Ronson for carrying his suitcase. The Ronsons politely took their leave, Mr Ronson returning to the plant house and Mrs Ronson heading for a wooden picnic table by a large apple tree.

Alice rocked Edward and grimaced playfully, to signify 'Phew, he's heavy!' Her total lack of trepidation unnerved Joseph and he thought the boy would have been somewhere else for the duration of his stay. Alice put her face close to Edward's, ruffled his sandy hair and wiggled his fingers.

"Edward, we have a visitor."

Joseph had observed such adult meets child encounters on the streets of Leicester. He knew he was incapable of the standard ice-breaking routine, smiling ingratiatingly, making funny noises, bear hugs to display his manly strength, or bribes of sweets or money. The child stirred. Joseph was worried the boy would fear him. He also felt the instinct of self-defence, being afraid of the boy, any boy, the laughter of children.

Edward showed no sign of either fear or love. He was evaluating the strange humanoid and would in a few moments decide whether to laugh or cry, or bury his face in his mother's breast. Edward reached out to Joseph with his hand and opened his palm like a little starfish. Alice took a step nearer. Edward reached for Joseph's forehead. Joseph closed his eyes and bowed his head forward, with the dignity of a king approaching the executioner's block.

Edward stroked the middle bulge of Joseph's forehead, then the protrusions beside. Emboldened, Joseph raised his head and let Edward touch his face in the way of a blind man. Edward ran the palm of his hand along Joseph's cheek and groped his pudgy lips, squeezing them like a sponge. Joseph raised his right hand, the massive claw, to Edward's level. Edward looked upon the hand with great fascination and gripped the upper part of the claw. Whilst Edward was engrossed with his right hand Joseph tickled

Edward's ribs with his left. Edward laughed. Alice was delighted. Joseph had remembered the trick from Uncle Charles.

Mrs Ronson took Edward to play by a tartan picnic blanket. Alice linked arms with Joseph and led him to a table beneath the apple tree. They sat on wooden garden chairs with thick padded cushions. Two glasses and a bottle opener had been placed on the table. Alice reached into an ice chest, produced a bottle of beer and poured them each a drink.

"It is unusual for a lady of your station to drink beer," said Joseph.

"Do not worry," replied Alice, "Mrs Ronson is used to me by now. And she will not call you anything other than Mr Merrick, no matter how many times you ask her."

Alice held her glass up for a toast. "Absent friends."

Joseph saluted, took a drink and watched Edward play on the lawn. He toed a ball and ran after it, enjoying his game. Other than Edward's instinctive love for his mother, his world was without status or rank. He had not learned to subdivide into ugly, beautiful, normal, defective. When would he learn and who would teach him?

"I cannot believe you introduced your son to me."

"Why not? He lives here. Besides, you have made a friend of him."

"He is young, innocent, unaware of my obvious deficiencies."

"That is the sort of thing the boy's uncle would say."

"What I mean is, I am a freak of nature."

"Joseph, to keep him from freaks of nature would be to keep him from his mother."

Her candour left Joseph breathless. Alice took a long sip of beer. She said, "When I read of you at the London Hospital, I wanted to run to you. But I had to restrain myself. I thought, Would Joseph want to see me? Would he forgive me? When your life was in ruins, I deserted you."

"Do not be ridiculous. I left of my own accord."

"Those cured of affliction are aloof from their kind, joined in sympathy but not in pain. But you were always with me, like the dormant disease of my body. And unlike my affliction, I longed for your return. My home is your home, whenever you want, for as long as you want."

Joseph shook his head and whispered, "It is improper."

"Do you recall the most hurtful thing you ever said to me?"

"I believe so."

"Then say it again."

Joseph took a breath.

"I am a freak and you are a normal person."

Alice held his hand under the table. "A normal person is everyone else when you are alone in affliction. But you are not alone, you never have been and you never will be."

"There is something I must make clear," said Joseph. "I do not love you because there is only you, but because there could be no other."

Joseph felt serene with this beautiful woman, in this beautiful garden, on one of the best days of the English summer.

In the early evening the Ronsons returned to their cottage and Alice invited Joseph back inside the house. She sat Edward in his high wooden feeding chair in the dining room and announced she was going to prepare Edward's supper in the kitchen. Alice suggested that Joseph read Edward a story from an illustrated children's book to keep him occupied.

Joseph was struck by the strange sound of his own voice. His diction had definitely improved through conversing with visitors of high rank, though he still had the accent of a common man. He felt ill at ease reading stories about talking farm animals to a one-child audience, but Edward paid rapt attention. Joseph even felt confident enough to act the part of some of the animals.

After the meal Alice encouraged Edward to say goodnight and took him to bed. She promised to return and serve dinner. While she was gone, Joseph explored the dining room. With its many potted plants and oriental style ornaments, the decor bore the hallmarks of Alice's individuality. Indeed nothing about Alice was commonplace; relinquishing her widow's black, drinking ale, the invitation to Joseph in the first instance.

Joseph inspected a photographic portrait of Alice with her husband, Simon Greystone, a handsome man with none of the disdainful superiority of his brother. Joseph imagined Simon Greystone dining here after work, comforted by the same family activities, reading to a child, the aroma of a home-cooked meal. Alice had always given Joseph the illusion of manhood; she was now creating the semblance of marriage.

Alice served a delicious lamb shoulder with lightly buttered new potatoes. She had also concocted a summer fruit pudding. After dinner Alice showed Joseph through to the drawing room. They sat side by side on a cushioned chaise longue and slowly made their way through a bottle of chilled white wine. Joseph noticed a dog-eared copy of *An Elephant's Tale*, in amongst the ornamental keepsakes.

Alice asked Joseph to fill in the gaps between his departure from the shop and his admission to the London Hospital. In return, Joseph asked Alice about her life in Dulwich. Though their daily routines were markedly different, it was obvious their lives shared the same banality. Life for widows and incurables is a waiting room before death, but as long as Joseph and Alice were together there seemed the possibility of another existence. Two hours passed. Outside it was dusk. The distant half moon was a signal to Alice and she took Joseph's hand.

She led him up the creaking staircase to the upper floor, treading lightly so as not to wake Edward. Joseph leant heavily on the banister and the wall, having left his walking cane in the dining room. Alice stopped by Edward's room, checked on him, then took Joseph's hand and led him to a room across the hall. Joseph saw the outline of a woman's dressing table in the twilight. The bed was positioned to the right of them, a grand four-poster with rolled floral curtains at either side. Alice closed the door behind them and went ahead of Joseph. She stood with her back to the window, silhouetted by the moon and the faintest trace of daylight.

Alice slipped out of her summer dress one shoulder at a time and shook the garment to the floor. She pulled the tie on her bodice to release her breasts. Her body was pale and luminous, a study in marble. Alice helped Joseph remove his clothes. She removed his tie, his jacket, his trousers and his undershorts.

Joseph compared Alice with the women who visited him in his rooms. To the likes of Mrs Oliver and Mrs Singleton he represented a lame man to Jesus. Each and every visit to his rooms was a pilgrimage to the miracle of their own healing powers; their Christian, humanitarian, parlour pleasantries.

Yet here, with Alice, there were no pleasantries, no intricate manners, just two naked people who felt an equal amount of desire for each other. Their nudity seemed completely natural, as if their layers of formal clothing had been the only abnormality. Joseph placed hands on Alice's body and she shivered at his touch. He felt as if he were touching the outer surface of humanity and that it would at last receive him with warmth.

Joseph and Alice took to bed and embraced, each gaining strength from the other. They were freaks of nature, man and woman. Their respite from affliction was love.

Joseph sat with his back against the headboard, his head and shoulders propped by several pillows, whilst watching the tentative rise of dawn through the window. Alice held him tightly. In a couple of hours, before the Ronsons arrived, Joseph would need to make his way to the guest bedroom. Until then, he was happy to savour the moment.

"Long ago," said Joseph, "I held a distant hope. A primitive prophecy, that if a woman loved me in the fullest sense I would be cured."

"I am sorry it did not work. We must try again tomorrow."

Joseph stroked her cheek. Alice asked, "When I visited your rooms at the hospital I did not notice a mirror. Was that your idea?"

"To profess love for my own reflection would serve me well. It would be taken as evidence of love for the God who disfigured me."

Alice raised her head from his shoulder. "You should see yourself."

"No."

"How else will you straighten your necktie? It was crooked when you arrived yesterday."

Alice climbed out of bed. Joseph rose reluctantly, resolving to go through with the exercise if only to keep her happy, to stop her from asking again. He followed her to the half-length dressing mirror. Joseph looked above the line of the mirror at first, but natural curiosity drew his eyes to the glass.

His reflection confirmed beyond any doubt that he was a hideous monster. The creeping light of dawn made every rise of deformity a mountain, every fall a ravine. Joseph tried to correct his crooked Mr Punch smile, but his face disobeyed him like a boulder. His mind raced with imaginary schemes and bargains, what he could offer or sacrifice to make things better. Yet the only thing he possessed, his only currency, was his warped and contorted body.

Joseph saw Alice's reflection beside his and immediately forgot his woes. He told her, "You are beautiful."

"Why do you say that?"

"You are a curious, singular woman."

"You are a curious, singular man."

Alice took her bodice from the table top. She bound the material into a scarf and tied it around the bottom part of her face in a bandit's mask, covering her mouth, her nose and her cheekbones so that only her eyes were visible. Alice held Joseph's hand. Their fingers merged. The sun rose outside.

"It is easier to bear with you," said Joseph.

Alice replied from beneath her mask.

"It is easier to bear together."

Chapter 22 – Manners Versus Might

Gilbert Greystone arrived at the widow's residence in a brougham. He instructed the driver to wait and rapped on the door with the butt of his cane. "You again!" snapped the indignant housewoman. Gilbert elbowed her aside and strode into the drawing room. He flopped onto the chaise longue, reclined and placed his feet on a French table. The soles of Gilbert's shoes were caked with horse manure. He had neglected to scrape them on purpose.

The housewoman scurried away to locate her mistress. Gilbert noticed a pamphlet on the sideboard titled *An Elephant's Tale*. The pamphlet was neatly and symmetrically positioned between the ornaments and the photographs, as if this tawdry piece of filth was a great work of literature. Gilbert read the pamphlet. The widow arrived in a figure-hugging blue dress, sluttish and inappropriate for a mother of decent social station.

"What a yarn," said Gilbert without lowering the pamphlet. "He truly is the Dickens of doggerel."

"Did I not make myself clear, that your interest in this family, whilst duly noted, is entirely unappreciated? Mr Ronson will return from his errands presently. If you are still here, I will ask him to remove you by physical means."

Gilbert rose to his feet and rolled up the pamphlet, tapping it against his free hand like a paper truncheon.

"Let me tell you a story. The protagonist is a young girl, a provincial prole. The setting is grim West Yorkshire. Her tale is not unlike Rapunzel, albeit with a different type of hair."

Gilbert stroked an imaginary beard. For the first time he saw fear in her eyes, desperation.

"Confined to her rooms as a prisoner, she dreams of a daring escape. One day, she steals a razor and lacerates her brother's face.

Perhaps the fairy godmother intervenes? For she emerges in London, a princess of sorts, on the arm of a dashing young doctor."

Her bottom lip quivered and her eyes welled with tears. Finally, the widow was completely in his power. Gilbert felt like dancing a jig by the fireplace.

"The newspapers will love this story, when I supply the evidence."

"No."

"Yes, sister! Yes! The most sensational expose: Dulwich physician's widow is bearded freak razor woman! Your son will hate you. It will destroy his life."

"If you love him, you would spare him."

"I would rather remove him from the planet then have him spend one more day with you! So here is the next chapter in our tale. Wife cannot cope since the passing of husband. She's beset with grief. She's bloody hysterical. Her home is no place for a child. Edward goes to live with kindly Uncle Gilbert and sees mother once a year for the sake of appearances. If she remains quiet and obedient her reputation survives and thus, her son survives."

The widow dropped to her knees with a very pleasing clack on the hardwood floor, head bowed, utterly destroyed. Gilbert stood over her.

"I wonder if you met Merrick before, in the sideshow? I once read an account of a woman obsessed with felating barn animals. That's a night of candle-lit romance for you. Savour those memories, dear sister, for you will never see Merrick again."

The widow's tears dripped onto the floor. Gilbert felt like whacking her around the face with the pamphlet, but disdainfully flicked it into the fireplace instead.

"Ah yes, the denouement. 'They all lived happily ever after!'"

Gilbert returned to his residence, handed Edward to the housewoman Rosa and informed her that the boy would be a guest for the foreseeable future. Rosa was surprised and delighted, as women are when handed a random child and commenced the standard idiotic baby talk. Rosa's broken English had been unimportant until now, but Gilbert did not want Edward to acquire poor linguistic habits, and made a mental note to dismiss Rosa at a later date. For the present time he instructed her to make the boy comfortable whilst he attended to papers in his study.

Gilbert sat down at his desk and reviewed his successful mission to Leeds. The town was the worst of both worlds, pretentious and provincial. Delusions of grandeur were all too apparent in the ghastly Roman pillars of the ostentatious town hall. However, their Yorkshire pudding bureaucracy was amenable to bribery. An avaricious clerk had taken Gilbert's money and directed him to a rather quaint lunatic asylum. Gilbert opened his journal and wrote in longhand.

"The boy's mother is a psychically and mentally defective harlot with the morality of an imbecile. She is highly volatile and extremely violent, yet cunning enough to convince the authorities she was sane. At some point in her wretched life her affliction diminished, revealing a superficially pleasing countenance."

Gilbert heard the faint echo of Edward's laughter. He continued writing.

"Initial examination of Edward Greystone; pulse normal, reflexes normal, everything normal, if not superior. He is after all, a Greystone. His mother's facial beard was almost certainly a product of gynaecological malformation. But what of the condition of her mind? What of the unseen disease, the lingering germ plasm of heredity? A defective mother begets a defective son."

Gilbert ripped up the paper, screwed it into a ball and threw it away in frustration. The paper ball bounced off his padlocked drinks cabinet, which contained not one drop of alcohol, but several of Whiting's specimen jars, including the severed head of the British soldier. It was unclear if Whiting had given Gilbert the exhibits as gifts, or if they were on extended loan. He had also encouraged Gilbert to borrow a number of other body parts, including the skinned back of the patriotic infantryman. Thoughts of Whiting usually brought Gilbert joy; they now made him incredibly lonely.

In his advertising career Whiting had developed cunning means of manipulation, but never stayed true to an idea. Therefore, was Whiting faithful to eugenics or merely a whore? If he was not committed, he could not be trusted. He could not be trusted with a secret of this destructive magnitude.

Gilbert's fealty to eugenics was a shrine of gold, but could not offer him a definite answer as to whether the boy was doomed. In this sense science was inadequate and mathematics was the only truth. Then Gilbert remembered Edward with his number blocks, 3 + 3.

A test of mathematics would determine Edward's destiny!

Gilbert instructed Rosa to take the afternoon off. He also told Andrews to make himself scarce for a few hours. When the house was empty Gilbert carried Edward into the drawing room. He emptied the toy box the widow's housewoman had packed and found the wooden number blocks. Gilbert sat Edward amongst the other toys to occupy him.

He returned to his study and unlocked the drinks cabinet. The small jar of strychnine solution that saw to Simon was beside the Briton's head. Gilbert took a syringe from his medical bag and filled the barrel. He locked the cupboard, returned to the drawing room and placed the syringe on the mantelpiece next to *The Problem Of And Solution To Negro Overbreeding*. A Godlike voice said, "Father approves."

Edward attempted to draw Gilbert's attention to his game. He ignored his nephew and placed the wooden number blocks on the carpet. Gilbert gave little thought to the consequence of failure, other than he would sooner end himself at nightfall than swing like a common felon. He assured himself that with chief examiners such as Hippasus and Pythagoras, the test was beyond reproach and promised to be pitiless in delivering the verdict.

Gilbert set out the sum 3 + 3 = and jumbled the numbers, so that Edward would have to search out 6. Gilbert pointed to the sum and called his nephew. Edward crouched on his hands and knees and raked his small hands through the pile of wooden blocks. He picked out the number 5 and put it in his mouth, laughing inanely. Gilbert went to fetch the syringe, but as he turned away Edward threw the number 5 to the floor, picked up 6, and placed it down to complete the sum.

Gilbert was delighted and ready to call the trial a success. But then he asked himself, what if the boy simply remembered the sequence of numbers and lacked the wherewithal to calculate? Gilbert knew he had made the test too easy, too easy by far. The child was not yet three years of age and multiplication would be fiendishly difficult, a more fitting test of ability for the Greystone racial heir.

Gilbert rotated the symbol for addition forty-five degrees, so it was now the symbol for multiplication and the sum read 3 x 3 =. Edward was puzzled. He put his fingers in his mouth and gazed up to his uncle, unsure. Gilbert timed thirty seconds on his pocket watch. Edward lost interest all together, held up a stuffed toy dog and imitated a bark. Every second was agony. 10 seconds diminished to 5, 4, 3 ...

Edward looked once again at the numbers and rotated the number 6 so the sum read 3 x 3 = 9.

By jove, he did it!

But then, thought Gilbert, what if the boy has simply copied my action of rotating the object? As if reading his mind, Edward called out "Nine!" and held up nine tiny fingers, evidencing his working out.

Gilbert lifted Edward above his head and twirled him around the room. If the widow's blood was the oil of a ship's engine adulterating an unblemished bay, then Greystone blood was the ocean, restoring purity. Not one trace of dirt or defilement remained, obliterated by the tide of racial right. Gilbert kissed Edward's forehead. The boy laughed and smiled, high above the ground. He must get used to heights, thought Gilbert.

Together we will soar upon gilded wings, towards the pinnacle of purity.

When Joseph returned to the London Hospital he felt more like an imposter than ever. It had been a week since his visit to Dulwich and his affectations of innocence and piety, his normal behaviour, still lacked lustre. He dispensed with his handicrafts, stared out of the window and forgot to wear a necktie. Joseph's visiting benefactors and his nurses made peculiar little observations phrased as questions. Was he 'unwell', 'melancholy' or 'fatigued'? Treves asked if Joseph truly enjoyed his trip to the Greystone residence'? Joseph assured Treves it was the finest three days of his life.

Joseph had sent a note of thanks to Alice, wording a standard letter of gratitude, as he was sure the communiqué would be vetted before it was sent. He had not yet received a response from his beloved. It seemed ridiculous and irrational, but with each day that passed Joseph persuaded himself something terrible had happened. He was yet to be convinced that his life was more than the sum of humiliation, pain and disappointment, although nothing had gone horribly wrong for quite some time. Joseph chided himself for being overly suspicious and pessimistic, but it was now a full week since he had sent the letter.

Such fatalism led Joseph to a sleepless night. By evening time the following day, he was exhausted and retired to bed early. When a needle entered his left bicep Joseph woke very slowly, initially assigning the stinging pain to an awkward sleeping position. But when he tried to raise his arm in protest his body was no longer responsive to his mind. A tranquil wave of euphoria overwhelmed the last embers of consciousness and transported him to oblivion.

Joseph came to at his writing desk in a blaze of brilliant light. He was fully dressed and a half-finished cathedral card tower awaited work in front of him. Joseph tapped the knuckles of his good hand on the desk. He also heard the distant grind of heavy wagons on the Whitechapel Road. Everything in the room was in order. It was real. But as soon as Joseph thought of Alice, the card tower collapsed, the room dissolved and he was engulfed in darkness.

Joseph felt as if he had travelled to a different location. He was unable to open his eyes and his senses were still leaden with the sedative. He heard well-spoken voices, two men arguing. One voice sounded chillingly familiar.

"Listen to me ..."

"No, you listen to me. You are Ahab and he is your whale. You will drag us down with you. How dare you bring him here!"

"I can do as I want. I am not only founder, I am also leader. So says Brigard Mayfield! If it wasn't for me, you'd be selling chicken soup."

Joseph drifted in and out of consciousness. He heard applause and singing, the music of a band and the National Anthem. Joseph presumed this was reality and slowly opened his eyes. He was sitting on the floor of a cramped, makeshift dressing room with his back against a yellowish chaise longue. Across the room, a performer made his final preparations in front of him.

Gilbert Greystone stood before a half-length vanity mirror positioned on a rickety table, practising oratory poses, puffing out his chest, pleading with his hands, wagging his finger as if scolding a mischievous dog. He wore a Union Jack waistcoat with the sleeves of his pristine white shirt up rolled up to the elbows, exposing his muscular forearms. His sandy-brown hair was combed in a neat side parting. There was a wisp of grey in the root of his hair.

Gilbert jabbed his finger down, once, twice, three times, practising the climax of his speech. After basking in twenty seconds of imagined applause he examined his pocket watch and turned to Joseph.

"When I first I saw you at the workhouse, I knew our destinies were entwined. For you embody everything of which I would rid the world, the deformed, the defective, the weak, the worthless."

"I am stronger than you think."

"You are not strong, you're slippery. You put on an act because you wanted something for yourself."

"A skill you appear to have mastered, sir."

Gilbert chuckled. "You have made a career out of manipulating others through sentiment. You made a living, survived the gutter, subsist now in undeserved luxury. Imagine then the power of sentiment in my hands, as a tool of the empire, as the lubricant for my will."

A roar went up from the crowd; they must have been several hundred strong. Joseph's stomach lurched.

"You will behold before the night is through, Merrick. By God you will."

"You are aligning yourself with the Lord, Dr Greystone?" It was a bold question, but Joseph reasoned his only chance was to play for time and hope someone came to his rescue.

"Don't talk to me about religion. For too long defectives have hidden behind the church. We are told they have a purpose because they have soul. What poppycock! The British Empire is built on bullets and battleships, steam and steel. A man must produce, or he must perish. His soul has not the value of a can of tin."

Gilbert kicked Joseph directly in the solar plexus, exploding the air from his lungs. Joseph's heart pounded with the force of a sledgehammer and tempo of a woodpecker. The chaise longue slid backwards but luckily held him upright.

Gilbert returned to his dressing mirror, calm and sanguine.

"Believe it or not, I don't blame you. Your parents were clearly defectives. You are not responsible, but you will face the consequence. The procedure is relatively painless."

"My father was a coachman ... my mother was ..."

"An angel, I know. I have heard you before."

Joseph wheezed for breath. "You cannot ... Dr Treves will ..."

"But what can he say, Merrick? What can he do? A patient can discharge himself at any time. You have volunteered for my course of treatment, have you not?"

Joseph shook his head.

"I can be very persuasive. Take my brother's widow. After years of conniving and denial, she has entrusted Edward to my care. I wonder why?"

Gilbert stroked his chin. Joseph's heart was agony.

"The poor woman has been afflicted by a hysterical nervous disorder. She's taken to her bed. I fear for her health, Merrick, I really do. Perhaps the asylum would also be a mercy for her? We could stop off at a barbershop en route?"

Joseph tried to hold his composure, but could not resist the urge to beg. "Please, I'll ..."

Gilbert stepped in front of Joseph. He braced himself for another kick, but none came.

"I know you'll obey, Merrick. You're the most polite and compliant defective I have ever encountered. I suppose this encapsulates the essential difference between us. You live by manners, I live by might."

A burly man in a white sailing jersey hoisted Joseph to his feet. Gilbert called him Brooks. Brooks propped Joseph under his arm and walked him from the room. He was totally dispassionate, handling Joseph like a bale of hay. Gilbert led the way along a corridor.

Three of Gilbert's acolytes were conversing by the backstage curtain, two young men and a woman, wholesome lower-middle-class types, ambitious volunteers. One of the men exclaimed "Merciful God!" as Brooks passed by with Joseph. Brooks sat Joseph down on a wooden chair. A small crack in the curtain afforded Joseph a back view of the blond orator and a front view of the crowd, who numbered around five hundred. Two Union Jack flags flanked the stage. Joseph tried to stand, but Brooks pressed him down. There was nothing to be done, other than listen to the rather trite speech in progress.

"... They ignore our warnings about defective delinquents ... lecherous layabouts lying in wait, hunting like jackals, for normal girls ... I continue to lobby parliament, tirelessly, endlessly, with your vital support ... My father's regimental motto, 'Difficulties do not deter'... Nothing will deter our glorious charge of decency!"

The speaker received an impassioned ovation and shouts of 'Bravo, Mr Whiting'. As the applause died down Whiting signalled to the band and they sounded the opening of salvo of *Abide With Me*. The crowd drew a huge collective breath and sang in perfect unison.

Whether a man had faith of not, *Abide With Me* was a powerful exhortation and Joseph felt awe, dread and wonder reverberate in the pit of his stomach. Deformity had made him an alien to his countrymen and these singing Britons of the League of Decency would surely loathe him for his very appearance. Yet for the length of this song, Joseph felt strangely at one with them, because however much the populace hated deformity, or however much they hated him, Joseph could not bring himself to hate his country, because his country would never betray him. The hills and hedgerows were beyond human prejudice. His native soil was the womb to which he would one day return. Genuine decency, the purity of the true British spirit, the finer qualities of Alice and Charlie, Reverend Summers, Uncle Charles and even Samuel Thomas, would always endure.

Gilbert took a step nearer the curtain, preparing for his introduction. Whiting turned to face backstage, knowing that Gilbert was watching. But instead of introducing Gilbert, Whiting left the stage without a word. Gilbert simmered with rage and the crowd murmured during the lull in proceedings. The act of defiance from one of Gilbert's own comrades gave Joseph a glimmer of hope.

A rotund, balding fellow bumbled on stage. His rambling introduction for the 'Leader and Founder' was full of waffle, ums and ers and obviously ad-libbed. Nevertheless, the crowd immediately warmed to him as his lack of preparation was interpreted as tongue-tied reverence for 'The Leader'. His final words, "Dr Gilbert Greystone!", sounded a roar of approval.

The band struck up the refrain of *Abide With Me*. Gilbert regained his composure, stepped through the curtain and took the stage. Joseph saw proud men and stern women struggle to contain their straight-laced emotions.

Joseph recalled Reverend Summers's old Sunday services. A harsh critic would have considered the sermon predictable, the lesson bland and the congregation docile. But through it all there was an underlying kindness, a feather-light call to arms: moderate the worst of your own behaviour, give the next man a helping hand and actively support the unfortunate. By contrast, the message of social purity was crush under foot, stamp out the weak and kill your beastly urges. Gilbert raised his hands to quiet the crowd, but the volume of adulation increased. This was an electric church.

"You have afforded this doctor a hero's welcome."

The crowd erupted. Gilbert pulled his most sincere face and shook his head to imply 'I am no hero' and to shamelessly exploit a bigger ovation.

"When I think of heroes, I remember dear, departed Captain Webb and his swim of the English channel. Imagine how the captain felt after twenty-five gruelling miles, when the shore of Calais loomed into view, so near, yet so far. Webb was possessed by a second wind of patriotic power and he pumped his arms and kicked his legs until he reached terra firma, cried 'Land Ho!' and 'God save the Queen!'"

The crowd roared 'Huzzas!'

"Good people, the dream of compulsory sterilisation is within sight, but we are still at sea! Dig deep, donate, pawn jewellery if necessary. Write letters, sign petitions, tell your friends. I know I can depend upon each and every one of you, because I believe in heroes!"

The crowd cheered and applauded Gilbert as if he were a British sporting Hercules. Joseph reckoned the crowd were also paying homage to themselves.

There was an interlude of gentle fun when a young boy, clad in a white woollen bathing suit, was ushered on stage. His name, Tommy, was stitched across the back of the outfit in red and blue letters. Tommy pretended to breast stroke and crawl to the immense delight of the crowd. When the applause for his turn subsided Gilbert announced, "When we achieve our goal, I personally guarantee the first neutered defective will be The Elephant Man, Joseph Merrick!"

The audience did not know how to react. There were only a handful of cheers from the habitual cheerers and much talk amongst themselves. Joseph often wondered if word of his appeal had reached all strata of society. It was possible that many, if not all in attendance had never heard of him. Yet if the working or the lower middle classes knew of his daily routine, how would they react to his apparent life of leisure?

"Good people, let me explain. Joseph Merrick is the deformed incurable of London Hospital, afforded special treatment and rooms. Men and women, high and low, answered his public appeal. I myself donated one week's pay. I was hoodwinked. We all were. Joseph Merrick is a fraud!"

There were more voices of support now. Gilbert was their man, their Messiah, they so desperately wanted to believe him: all they needed was a little push.

"As you are aware, I am employed at the hospital. I have observed Merrick at close quarters. He has many visitors, remembers to be kind and gentle, to drink his tea and mind his manners. When they are gone he reverts to type. Merrick smokes tall cigars and drinks French brandy. He claims he is unable to work, but how would he know? He has applied for not one single vacancy. He refuses to volunteer in the hospital kitchens and help others, despite living on the charity of others. He is workshy, feckless and lazy."

A number of people started to boo.

"What is more, Merrick has no faith, yet endlessly quotes the bible to elicit sympathy, bearing false witness for personal gain. It is perhaps inaccurate to declare Merrick as entirely without faith. Oh no, he is disgustingly devoted to the way of Onan!"

A ripple of outrage went through the crowd. Joseph felt their hate in his bones. Brooks put his hands under Joseph's armpits and scooped him up from the chair.

"But rejoice, Merrick is in our care! He will be kept in a cell, safely under my supervision, until I am legally sanctioned to remove the risk. Good people of the League of Decency, Joseph Merrick is here!"

Gilbert signalled to Brooks. He frogmarched Joseph forward, through the curtains. The crowd made a low, rumbling noise like an army of brooding gorillas and Joseph's legs almost gave way. Brooks propped Joseph up against the lectern and stepped into the background. The crowd jostled forward for a closer look.

"Have you ever seen such a spectacle? His right hand is hugely deformed, but his left is untouched. We cannot know all of creation, but surely the parts of his body preserved by God have been commandeered by Satan. Stay close by Reverend Robertson!"

Gilbert gestured to the reverend on the front row of seats. A white Moses beard covered the reverend's florid face and Joseph remembered him from Whitechapel. Robertson moved a restraining arm around the small child in the next chair. It was Edward Greystone, in his Sunday-best shorts and blazer jacket.

Edward held a miniature wooden crucifix in each hand, both painted with a Union Jack. He had evidently been given the trinkets to play with to occupy his attention and he was currently improvising some sort of game. The sight of Edward filled Joseph with determination. Alice had given Edward life and Joseph his manhood. In the absence of a father he must set an example for the son.

"It can now be revealed that Merrick's father was an imbecile. His mother was an imbecile. His brothers and sisters, uncles and aunts! How many more? When will it end?"

"My family were no imbeciles!"

The acoustics of the hall were very good and Joseph's remark astonished the crowd. Gilbert whispered in Joseph's ear.

"If you do not desist, I will not use chloroform when I operate."

Joseph stepped away from him and announced, "They were less than perfect, but I loved them!"

Gilbert grabbed Joseph's arm and tried to pull him away from the lectern, but Joseph resisted. A League of Decency crowd expected all manner of stagecraft, but this unseemly behaviour was clearly unplanned. The act of restraint developed into a wrestling match. Some of the crowd shouted for Gilbert to unhand Joseph, others to strike him. Brooks lurked by the rear of the stage, awaiting an opportune moment to intervene. Whiting, however, leapt from his seat and strode onto the stage, holding up his hand to signal stop. Gilbert released Joseph and the crowd were still. All eyes were on Whiting. His hand was a judge's hammer and everyone awaited his verdict.

Whiting lowered his hand, opened both arms in a placatory gesture and said, "Let him bear witness."

The crowd politely applauded Whiting. Gilbert seethed. Whiting gestured to Joseph, inviting him to speak and stepped away to the side of the stage, leaving Gilbert and Joseph in the centre.

Joseph looked again to Edward and was oblivious to the crowd, just as Edward was oblivious to the restraining arm of his chaperone Robertson. Joseph strained his mouth to speak as clearly as possible, so his lisp was barely of consequence.

"My mother was no imbecile, my father was no imbecile. In body and mind they were just like you. They were honest, decent people, who hoped for a healthy son. The son they were given was me. My condition tore my family apart. I was an outcast, doomed to die, so I became a 'freak' and it saved me. I found another family, a family amongst friends ..."

Gilbert interrupted. "He speaks of family. Good people, ask yourselves, would you wish this curse upon your children?"

There were murmurs of approval. He was winning them back.

"We cannot pretend to tolerate these defects, we cannot lie to ourselves."

"When I am gone, who is next? Those with the slightest mental or physical impairment?"

Whiting moved forward, attempting to stop Gilbert replying to Joseph's question, but could not bridge the gap in time.

"Of course," answered Gilbert.

"Those with crossed eyes, those with buck teeth?"

"Of course!"

"A limp, a withered arm, a pot belly?"

"All defectives are kith and kin. Their removal from life is the purpose of eugenics."

There was a collective intake of breath from the horrified audience, faces etched with worry and betrayal. They were no longer strong and safe in their number. Gilbert had broken the whole into pieces. Every man and woman was an individual slide of bacterium beneath a microscope and the fear returned, the terrifying question of their daily lives: "Am I good enough?"

"You have shown your true colours, sir, and they are not the colours of your waistcoat." Joseph's remark was accompanied by cheers. Whiting backed away from Gilbert. Joseph continued. "Infirmity does not end with me. For who among us is perfect? The Lord teaches compassion."

"You do not believe!" interrupted Gilbert.

"I believe we must fight evil in all its forms."

Joseph's retort received shouts of support and applause, but Gilbert was not yet beaten. He suddenly became relaxed in his body and pulled a sly expression.

"You hate yourself, Merrick. You loathe your condition. All your life you have prayed to be normal, at times to God. At times I'll wager, to Satan."

The crowd hissed at the word Satan and Joseph felt as if he were falling down a hole. Gilbert was God, God knew his secrets. He would receive his judgement here.

"You would have sold your soul to be free of affliction and who would blame you? Imagine the life you could have led? You could have married, raised a family. Instead you were cursed. You want to be free. You want to be normal. You agree with everything I have said. Tell the truth, for once in your life. You owe it to these people."

Joseph thought he might crumble under the pressure of the doctor's ultimatum and the intense glare of a volatile, unpredictable crowd. He would have remained silent and accepted his fate, if not for the presence of Edward and his love for Alice. He sensed she was with him, holding his hand, reversing the roles of their first encounter, willing him to display himself, to stand with courage, to enter the eye of the storm. Joseph spoke directly to the crowd.

"There was a time I longed to be just like you. I hated my body. I would have given my soul. But in this respect my friends were my saviours. Especially my friends, like me. For as I felt love for these curious people, I felt something more for myself."

"I recently met a fine young boy. Not disabled, quite normal. You might even say he is perfect. He treated me as an equal. He became my friend. The doctor says we 'cannot know all of creation', which leads me to conclude, that boy could have been my son, as much I could have been yours."

"So in answer to the question, I have not overcome this impairment, but I have learned to live with myself. And I would like to continue this life. Would you let me?"

There was a long silence. Joseph wondered if he had lost them after all. But then the first person applauded, then the second and the third until there was a resounding, cacophony of applause. Women had tears in their eyes and so did men. It was a dignified response, tempered by British restraint, acknowledging the orator had brought them to their senses.

The child Tommy broke free of his mother and clambered onto the stage. He approached Joseph, fascinated by his unusual appearance. But as Tommy passed by Gilbert, he accidentally stepped on the leader's foot. Gilbert slapped Tommy around the head with the flat of his hand and the blow was seen and heard around the hall. Tommy's father had been following his son with the intention of restraining him, but he continued his stride and shoved Gilbert into the lectern. Brooks ran in and knocked Tommy's father unconscious with a single punch.

Angry men and women pushed forwards. Some broke through, others tripped over the front row of chairs. Gilbert hid behind Brooks. Punches flew. The band clambered over each other for safety. Robertson grabbed Edward's hand, but Edward resisted. Joseph tried to get forward to Edward, but a dozen men and women rushed onto the stage and formed a protective cordon around him. It was impossible to get through the crowd.

Edward lay down and made his body heavy. Robertson picked up Edward's ankles and dragged him, like a human wheelbarrow, towards a side exit. Suddenly, Robertson's head exploded in a vapour cloud, his eyes rolled up and he collapsed, face down, on the floor. His assailant wore widow's clothing and a black veil over her face. She dropped the remaining shards of the bottle and brushed the glass off Edward, careful not to cut him. Alice removed the veil and hugged Edward. Joseph felt weightless in the arms of the crowd.

Chapter 23 – Towards Valhalla

"A sorcerer falls, a hero rises" by Brigard Mayfield, East London Herald, June 24th 1889.

Today, a former champion of public morality, surgeon Gilbert Greystone, languishes in disgrace, struck off and shamed. Let us remind ourselves of the details. Police acting on anonymous intelligence conducted a search of Greystone's residence. Thereupon they discovered his treasured 'collection', the bodily remains of British servicemen positioned in vile displays of anthropomorphic taxidermy. Brave patriots were procured by Greystone for his own ungodly amusement, denied a Christian burial, defiled for the national defence. It is an insult, a blasphemy, an outrage. But let us not dwell on Greystone's disgusting, degrading perversion at length in a family publication.

Those of us who knew Greystone are soiled by association, his patients, his colleagues, and his followers. Those children, those parents, those idealistic young persons who rallied to his war cry of simple purity. Should we have seen through him? It is impossible to say. Greystone was a skilled sorcerer, a man of two lives. The cracks in his veneer, rumours of medical malpractice, only briefly emerged before his entire facade collapsed.

As a sorcerer falls, a hero rises, festooned with the Union Jack.

Mr Whiting knew the League of Decency would be forever tainted because of the involvement of Greystone. Therefore Whiting, the son of a soldier, proposed to disband the League and divert its substantial funds to the charitable relief of wounded servicemen. His masterplan met with deafening 'Ayes'. Whiting, a brave, principled man, published an open letter in this very newspaper publicly challenging Greystone to a boxing benefit under the Queensbury Rules. Greystone has declined by silence. He has shunned atonement as we shun him, for all traitors are cowards. In Britain men of action are men of honour. Men like Whiting. Huzzas!

Gilbert Greystone was awoken by a shaft of sunlight streaming in through his bedroom curtains, settling across his eyes and reflecting on the empty brandy bottles cluttering the floor, like ornaments in a second-hand bric-a-brac shop. Gilbert buried his head under the covers. They smelt abominable, but he had no intention of changing them. Not one item of clothing or linen had been laundered since his staff deserted him. Gilbert did not know what time it was, how long he had slept, or even the day.

Gilbert reached out of bed and found a bottle. He tested the contents with his nose to ensure it was brandy and not the bottle he passed water into during the night. After a lifetime of total abstinence Gilbert had taken to strong drink like the proverbial duck to water. He had also dabbled with cocaine, laudanum and morphine, but alcohol was the only vice that had stuck.

The bedside table was piled up with old newspapers. Gilbert did not know why he kept the reports relating to his downfall; perhaps it was his last ember of vanity? Not one word of the ruckus at the rally made the news. 'Dr Decency and his private mausoleum' was the keynote of a lurid press feeding frenzy. High-priced legal chicanery saved Gilbert from prison, though his fine and suspended sentence, his disgrace in the eyes of decent society, were the equivalent of the death penalty.

The day Brigard Mayfield's editorial went to press, a neighbour from three doors hence, retired Colonel Rackham, drunk after dinner, staggered up Thurrock Terrace. Rackham shouted for Gilbert to meet him in single combat, before discharging his old service revolver through the front window. Gilbert cowered on the floor for cover. Rackham's gunshots were cheered with hip hoorays by the neighbours.

Mrs Taylor, the widow in an adjoining property, posted regular letters through Gilbert's front door. Her remarks ranged from 'Tidy your gardens or have a man tidy your gardens, they are awful overgrown,' to 'Have your front windows reglazed at once, wooden boards are frightfully vulgar,' to 'Do the decent thing. There are a number of methods at your disposal. Please consider other residents. Do not put them at risk, by gas, for example. A length of electrical cable makes a sturdy noose.' How he had underestimated women!

Gilbert had placed a daily order with a delivery boy, bread and cheese and a bottle of brandy, and took to his bed. He slapped his face for weakness and pulled his hair. He admonished himself in his father's voice. He even had to remove the photograph of Edward from his bedroom as he could not look upon his nephew's face without bursting into tears. His accumulated debts were more than twice the value of his house. He expected the bailiffs to arrive at any moment.

Enough was enough!

Gilbert dragged his naked body out of bed and retrieved his Indian clubs from the cupboard. He stood in front of the mirror and began a routine of exercise. Gilbert's body was soft, his arms were weak and the clubs felt like they had been filled with lead in his absence from activity. Ten minutes of gentle exercise made him feel like vomiting, but he pushed on for ten minutes more.

After exercise, Gilbert washed and shaved for the first time in weeks, then poured his brandy down the sink in the scullery. He retired to his study, wrote a letter and entrusted the delivery boy with the post. The reply to Gilbert's letter arrived via telegram, the very next day. Whiting had agreed to the meet him on Friday afternoon.

It was mid-September, though summer showed no signs of abating. The heat from the sun was searing and the city air was thick with humidity. On the Friday afternoon, Gilbert caught an omnibus at Paddington Station, disembarked at the Thames and lingered by the south end of Westminster Bridge. Gilbert beheld the architectural wonders across the water, the magnificent Houses of Parliament and monolithic Big Ben. In the afternoon sun, Westminster shimmered like a cathedral of gold. Even in darkness, a corona of yellowish light appeared to surround the towers of sandy limestone. Suicide cases were drawn here like moths. On a clear night, thought Gilbert, it must be like swimming to the moon.

Gilbert had chosen the venue for a number of reasons. The south end of Westminster Bridge was close to St Thomas Hospital and medicine was still a source of strength, even though Gilbert would never practise again. Gilbert also believed that Whiting would be more inclined to meet him in public. If Whiting feared a revenge attack it was not without good cause. Gilbert had spent the morning sharpening his scalpel. He had placed the blade in the sheath of a small hunting knife and the sheath inside the breast pocket of his park suit. Gilbert knew that a park suit was a ridiculous choice for the city, but it was the cleanest suit in his possession. The material hung from his body, owing to lost muscle tone.

Gilbert tried to compensate for his clothing by purchasing a haircut. The barber bungled a short back and sides, giving Gilbert a lopsided crew cut, accentuating the pronounced grey in the roots of his hair. Gilbert felt like a man emerging after a long illness. He drew suspicious looks from the clerks, merchants and solicitors who passed by him on the bridge. He was a reduced figure, in a silly suit, loitering at a working hour. They probably took him for a gentleman gambler in terminal decline. Two men in top hats and tail suits approached along Westminster Bridge, and Gilbert recognised Brooks and Whiting.

Whiting had dispensed with his moustache and was cleanly shaven, a fresh-faced Pitt the Younger. He had gained strength and vitality and seemed a foot taller than before. Despite his treachery, Whiting was a credit to his class, confirming that Britain was the azure main of eugenics. Brooks's broad shoulders tugged at the seams of his suit. He had the decency to avert his gaze in guilt.

Whiting rested against the stone wall beside Gilbert and looked over to Parliament, sharing the angle of Gilbert's eyeline. Brooks kept a respectful distance out of earshot, but remained close enough to intervene if necessary.

"Magnificent, is it not?" said Whiting.

"You could almost forget what it stood for," replied Gilbert.

Whiting chuckled at Gilbert's remark. A westerly wind brought up a whiff of sewage from the Thames. Whiting winced and turned to face Gilbert. Gilbert knew not what to say or do and had not rehearsed any sort of speech, so he spoke from the heart. He said, "I should kill you."

"You'd better crack on, old boy. House convenes at three."

"Your boxing challenge was a laughable charade."

"That was extremely foolish of me. I remember the way you dispatched with Little Tommy."

"I overestimated that boy, those people. By God, they were weak! There I was before them with the world on the plate, offering the elixir of eternal strength. In the final analysis they preferred apathy, sympathy, a defective. Perhaps I should have sobbed about my father falling from a horse? Then they would have pitied me."

"You were a gifted orator, a match for any man in there," Whiting said sincerely.

Gilbert ignored Whiting's compliment, taking it as a tactic to disarm him. Gilbert replied, "I can understand their betrayal, as much as it sickens me. As for yours ..."

"I betrayed nothing."

It was Gilbert's turn to laugh. Whiting adopted a firm tone as if explaining an obvious truth to an ignorant constituent.

"It was not about what you believed, but what they wanted to hear. Family and country, school and church. Hard work, hymns, assertions of 'well played'. Boot on leather, cork on willow, but you brought it back to eugenics. You, dear Greystone, betrayed everything we created."

"But what was the purpose if not eugenics?"

"Come on, Greystone, use your head. There are no countries left to conquer, only people to exploit. I want them to be weak and defective, because then they'll need me. A second-rate army of the needy and greedy, marching on tinned chicken soup!"

At that instant Gilbert knew Britain was doomed and envisioned a conquering army marching across Westminster Bridge, column after column of invaders in Prussian blue uniforms. Would they preserve Westminster or lay it to waste? Designate the area as zoo apparatus for mental defectives and orang-utans? The image did not disturb Gilbert so much as the thought of Whiting's magnificent collection gathering dust in a neglected police locker.

"But what of our ...? What about ...?"

Gilbert could not finish the sentence. Whiting looked sorrowful. A couple of well-suited but servile men passed by them, officers of the secretariat.

"Now look here, they probably think you're tapping me for a loan." Whiting opened his wallet which was stuffed with five pound notes, enough to buy a thoroughbred. Whiting proffered the wedge of cash, but Gilbert stared into the water. He had forgotten about the scalpel for a moment, but was now aware of the pouch pressing against his ribs. Whiting closed his wallet, tipped his hat and walked away. Brooks followed by his side.

Gilbert drew the blade and, in a single motion, grabbed Whiting's face from behind with his left hand and sliced his throat with the right. A horizontal ravine opened across the centre of Whiting's neck, cherry red and pouting like the mouth of a whore. Blood gushed forward in search of Westminster as if the incision had breached the wall of a powerful crimson dam.

Yet Gilbert's blade remained in his jacket unsheathed. He had taken hold of Whiting's overcoat, but all he possessed was a wagging finger. Brooks positioned his fist to punch Gilbert, but seeing there was no danger, lowered his arm. People were looking. Whiting gently pulled Gilbert's fingers from his lapel and readjusted his overcoat. He stepped forward and whispered in Gilbert's ear, "Greystone. You're an imbecile."

Gilbert walked home in an aimless arc, dawdling around Regent Park and Primrose Hill until his feet blistered. He arrived back in Paddington at dark. Using a small dressing table to barricade the front door from the inside, he entered the drawing room, crouched by the fireplace and lit a fire, using an old medical journal for kindling. When the flame caught, Gilbert smashed a French chair against the floor and fed it to the blaze. He picked up his father's book from the centre of the mantelpiece, *The Problem Of And Solution To Negro Overbreeding*. The leather-bound cover had been grazed by a bullet when Colonel Rackham shot through the window. Despite the blemish, the book was a touchstone to happy times.

Gilbert recalled the wondrous Christmas of 1857 when he was a boy of eight. Mother's family, Quakers all, were not given to Yule.

Nor was Dr Greystone, for that matter. But something was different this year. Father instructed the staff to prepare for Christmas in the modern fashion. The house was furnished with a tree and festooned with the trimmings. Father even allowed Mother to invite her family for the festive meal.

The prospect of a free meal and after-dinner evangelism brought them in numbers. Uncle John, Uncle Thomas, Aunt Elizabeth, Aunt Phoebe and a bevy of cousins. After making a fuss of Gilbert's semi-incontinent infant brother, father invited everyone to the drawing room. They assembled around the gigantic Christmas tree, nine feet high with twinkling decorations. Identical Christmas presents in green wrapping paper surrounded the tree. Father invited the Quakers to each take a gift. Mother's face curled up in horror.

Uncle John, Uncle Thomas, Aunt Elizabeth, Aunt Phoebe and all the children were each the recipient of a leather-bound first edition, *The Problem Of And Solution To Negro Overbreeding*. Aunt Elizabeth burst into tears. Uncle John bleated on about emancipation, like an indignant lamb, a high-pitched woolly Wilberforce.

The guests left in carriages. Thereafter Father invited Gilbert, just Gilbert, to his study. It was the first time Father had permitted Gilbert to enter and he marvelled at the many leather- bound books, the magnificent marble fireplace and the panoramic view across the family estate, which was deep in virgin snow. Father invited Gilbert to sit next to him on the chaise longue and they read Father's book together. Though not fully understanding the work, Gilbert understood his father's greatness. The fire blazed, snow fell outside. They read fifty pages, one hundred pages. Father helped Gilbert to pronounce unfamiliar words: 'vasoligation', 'sterilisation', 'miscegenation' and explained their meaning.

For the lesson on miscegenation his father invited Gilbert to the window. He explained that the snow was pure. If Gilbert was to play in the snow, leave footprints, besmirch purity, the snow could never return to its original form. There was no reversal to contamination. Father placed his arm around Gilbert's shoulder.

"Purity," said Father, "must be made anew."

Gilbert contrasted the past idyll with his squalid present reality. His broken furniture and boarded-up windows. His estrangement from Edward, his thwarted dream of eugenics. His public disgrace, his flaccid body, his cowardly scalpel, Merrick, the widow, Simon berating him, "If love is for old maids, there is hope for you yet," and Whiting.

And Whiting ...

Gilbert rummaged through the store cupboard in the servants' quarters. He was relieved to find a glass jug of paraffin, one gallon in capacity, virtually full to the top. To hell with the bitch Mrs Taylor, and her neighbourly consideration, Gilbert had chosen the vessel for his final voyage, a Viking longboat aflame.

He went back to drawing room, uncorked the paraffin jug and splashed it over the furniture, the walls and the rug, careful to avoid the fire for now. Gilbert ran the jug down to three pints, fed another chair into the fire for good measure and placed the jug directly in front of the hearth. Gilbert knelt by the fire and held Father's book across his chest. The glass of the paraffin jug began to discolour.

A spark popped from the fire and landed on the rug. Gilbert flinched and gripped Father's book. A long crack snapped down the length of the jug towards the paraffin. Gilbert kissed Father's book, placed it down in front of him, removed the scalpel from his pocket and unsheathed the blade. He placed the base of the handle on the palm of his hand and rested the point of the blade just below his eye on the cheekbone.

Towards Valhalla!

The jug popped and shattered, the room filled with flame. Gilbert Greystone pushed up.

Chapter 24 – Signs Of Life

On Saturday morning, after the nurses brought him breakfast, Joseph dressed and washed. He laid his suitcase on the bed, packed his shaving soap, wash kit, a day suit, an evening suit and a selection of undergarments. Although Joseph already had enough clothes and toiletries at Alice's home, he was careful to keep up appearances.

Treves entered the room, exchanged salutations and gestured for Joseph to continue his packing, like a benevolent army officer instructing a private to 'Carry on'. Joseph struggled to secure his suitcase with his one good hand. Treves stepped in without a word, secured the fastener and hoisted the suitcase to the floor. He resembled a father helping his son pack for boarding school, or a coachman assisting an important client.

"Mrs Greystone is undoubtedly your most generous benefactor. You are her most prolific guest."

"You do not object, sir?"

"On the contrary, Joseph. Fresh air and home comforts are the best medicine you could possibly receive. How are you this morning?"

"I feel I could run a mile, sir."

Apart from receiving visitors in his rooms, Joseph slept almost constantly. He rationed every waking hour in order to preserve his strength and energy for the Dulwich visits, preferring to save his pain and fatigue for the hospital. Even then he attempted to downplay his symptoms. He did not want to be denied access to his love.

"You may wonder why we do not make public our gratitude?" said Treves. "It is a question of modesty. Mrs Greystone and a number of your other benefactors do not wish their gift to be known. It is their right to privacy and we must respect that right. Do you understand?"

"Of course, Dr Treves. You could not comprehend the kindness Mrs Greystone has shown me. I must also thank you, sir. I owe you a debt I cannot repay."

"Please pass my regards to Mrs Greystone," Treves replied.

It was 9.55 a.m., five minutes to the arrival of the coach. Treves lingered, incubating a question.

"Months ago there was discussion about a number of your sketches. Your studies of a female subject, to be precise. I believe the figure bore an uncanny resemblance to Mrs Greystone. However, you produced these sketches before you had been introduced. Perhaps this was providence? Perhaps coincidence? Would you care to explain?"

"Have you read *Frankenstein*, Dr Treves?"

Treves nodded. Joseph continued. "You will recall that the monster is so terribly lonely and longs for the company of a woman. He demands his creator construct him a bride. Frankenstein takes the heart of one woman, the limbs of another and pieces together a patchwork companion for his monster. My muse is a patchwork woman from the women I have seen up close. The eyes of one woman, the mouth of another, until I was left with the woman I would wish to marry."

Joseph saw the colour drain from Treves's face.

"Do you think it strange, sir, that a man would yearn for a mate, a man with the outer appearance of a monster?"

Treves thought about the question for a long time, before replying. "No, Joseph, I do not. It is a shame, a terrible shame, that there was not a woman on this earth like you."

A porter arrived at the room and collected Joseph's case. Joseph picked up his walking stick in his good hand. Treves said, "May I ask if she had a name?"

"Yes, sir, Alice."

The colour drained from Treves's face once again.

"Coincidence, sir," assured Joseph. "Pure coincidence."

The fine spring weather allowed Joseph, Alice and Edward to spend all day out of doors in the garden. Mr Ronson did a fantastic job of preparing for Easter, particularly his mosaics of different daffodil varieties. The garden was aglow with yellow, orange and gold. Bees meandered between blossoming flowers. The blackthorn and wild rose trees were frosted with blossom and Edward was fascinated by the frogs in the pond.

Edward loved to play football. Alice did the majority of the legwork, which allowed Joseph to participate as a semi-mobile goalpost, balancing his walking stick in his stronger left hand and gently toeing the ball with his right. Edward nearly knocked Joseph to the floor with an act of innocent roughhousing by rugby tackling his leg. He was a robust young lad, three years of age, and would be four by Christmas. Alice warned Edward to be careful. Joseph teased Alice for regarding him as a piece of porcelain. She kissed Joseph on the cheek when Edward wasn't looking.

Edward kicked the ball towards the undergrowth, by the trees. He ran after the ball, but stopped to inspect something on the ground in front of him. Alice joined Edward and Joseph caught up with them. A hedgehog lay face down on the edge of the lawn, midway between cover and open ground. The normally skittish animal was oblivious to the three humans and its ribcage rose and fell with rapid, shallow breaths. Edward tugged at Alice's dress for clarification. She explained that the hedgehog was unwell. Alice fetched the dark green picnic blanket and positioned it over the disabled creature, leaving enough space for it to breathe. Her actions reminded Edward of bedtime and seemed to satisfy him that the hedgehog would make a full recovery.

The next morning, Joseph, Alice and Edward returned to the garden. The hedgehog was in exactly the same place, dead. Joseph wondered how the boy would react to his first encounter with mortality, having been too young to remember the passing of his father. Edward concentrated on the corpse of the animal, wondering what to make of it all and held his mother's hand.

Alice told Edward to select a spot in the undergrowth for the burial. Joseph had already procured a trowel from Mr Ronson and proceeded to dig the grave with his one good hand. The ground was harder than expected but he was determined to fulfil the masculine role. Alice used the blanket as a hammock and carried the hedgehog to the grave. Edward wanted to help, so Joseph let him shovel the earth back into the hole and they patted it down together.

The three of them stepped back from the grave. Alice stood in the centre, with Joseph to her left and Edward to her right. She held their hands. Edward asked, "Is the hedgehog in heaven?"

Joseph thought the reply was best left to the mother, but Alice squeezed his claw as a prompt.

"Yes, Edward, the hedgehog is in heaven."

Alice squeezed again, encouraging a more detailed explanation.

"He is with many other hedgehogs. He is very happy. And he thanks us for our kindness on earth."

Soon after, Edward resumed his game, kicking and running after his ball. Alice played alongside him and Joseph resumed his position as semi-participating goalpost. The pond was a mass of mating frogs. Daffodils were luminous in the sun. Bees meandered between flowers. Joseph looked back to the small mound of earth in the undergrowth and thought about the hedgehog, dead amongst the signs of life.

Alice rose once during the night to check on Edward, then settled into a deep sleep. Joseph savoured the touch of her skin and the scent of her hair, prolonging the sensation of each exquisite moment. Even the low rumble of her intermittent snoring was the subtle music of the night. At twenty minutes to six Joseph placed a moist kiss on the two foremost fingers of his good hand and touched them to Alice's cheek.

Joseph extracted himself from Alice's arms and removed himself from bed. His cumbersome movements awoke her. He whispered, "Go to sleep," and Alice closed her eyes at once. She must have assumed Joseph was going to the guestroom before the Ronsons arrived, but he was actually preparing to depart. When the driver Wilson conveyed Joseph to Dulwich, Joseph had slipped him a few shillings and had asked to be collected at 6 a.m., rather than nine on the day of departure.

He dressed adequately without help, shuffled across to Edward's room and slowly opened the door. Edward slept in the foetal position, cuddling his stuffed toy dog. Joseph remembered their first encounter, when Edward gripped his deformed right hand and Joseph tickled him with his left. Joseph wanted to kiss Edward on the cheek, but feared that his lumpen footsteps of approach would wake the boy. Joseph raised his deformed right hand once again, this time to wave goodbye.

Joseph crept downstairs and waited by the front door for the coach. But before the coach arrived Alice came down the stairs in her nightgown, bleary-eyed with sleep. Joseph confessed that he had arranged the coach for an earlier time. Alice told him off for not packing, went upstairs for his suitcase and brought it down. Her return coincided with arrival of the coach.

Alice kissed Joseph on the lips and hugged him. She said, "Take care, my love," as she always did when he went back to the hospital. She released her grip and opened the door. Wilson took Joseph's case, politely averting his eyes from the beautiful and well-to-do woman in her bedclothes. Alice's long dark hair cascaded over her shoulders and her chestnut-brown nipples teased the thin fabric of the nightdress. Alice was not an early riser, but her beautiful pale blue eyes were slowly coming to life. Joseph said, "Goodbye, madam," and followed Wilson to the coach. He did not look back, because Alice always stayed by the door to wave him away. His expressionless face would reveal nothing but deformity, but he did not want to risk the onset of tears.

Nurse Duggan helped Joseph unpack and gave him a brief examination. She took his pulse, listened to his heart and attempted to disguise her concern. Joseph's remark, "Will I live to a hundred?" brought nervous laughter. A porter delivered a telegram. Mrs Dwyer and Mrs Rogerson, the wives of wealthy merchants, were unable to attend their scheduled visit at two, due to a Rogerson family illness.

Joseph put the rest of the morning to good use. He went through every drawer and cubbyhole in his rooms, all of his possessions, his personal correspondence and his drawings. There was no trace of incriminating evidence, no evidence of his secret life.

Duggan brought his lunch, beef stew. Joseph said he was tired and intended to take a nap in the afternoon. He asked Duggan for a nip on her flask to help him sleep.

"Just the one," said Duggan and she poured a generous measure of brandy into a china teacup.

"Thank you for all you have done for me," said Joseph.

"See you tonight, Mr Merrick."

The last nurse of his life sashayed from his rooms, with her plump, pleasing buttocks, the sight of which had given comfort to many an ailing, dying man.

Joseph finished his drink and perused the bookshelf. He had a wide selection of magazines and literary journals, mainly *Cornhill* and *Temple Bar* and many books. Pride of place was his Holy Bible, bound in leather, like the flesh of an aging black grape. Joseph could not touch a bible without remembering chapel with his mother, Sunday school, Reverend Summers and four years in Leicester Union Workhouse.

The bible instructed Joseph to hope, but the hope of the cripple belonged to the dead. They were not worldly people, but angels in waiting. When they died, they would ascend to heaven, softly and elegantly on butterfly wings. Life until then was a mire of misery. Should they take their own life to accelerate their ascension, the destination was Hell. For the incurable, the relief of suffering is not the relief of pain, but convincing oneself that the suffering is bearable, even willed, a gift from God. "It made me a better person. I would not change it for the world ..." The incurable does not move out of pain, but confers harmony on the impotent healer.

Joseph could never reconcile the contradictions, nor in his opinion could Reverend Summers. But then, Summers had more to lose from an abnegation of faith. Joseph was grateful to Summers for his help and counsel and wished there had been a way to thank him. Perhaps it was best they had parted ways. The evangelical Christian is very much like the showman. Every encounter is an opportunity. Every outsider is a potential convert, a punter. The hidden agenda always intrudes. Yet if moral vanity is the indulgence of believers, intellectual vanity is the extravagance of the atheist.

It was time for action.

Joseph removed his jacket, his favourite blue and silver tie and his cufflinks. He hung the jacket and tie neatly on the back of a French chair, then positioned his thinnest, smallest pillow in the conventional sleeping position. Joseph sat on the side of the bed and untied his shoes. There was something subversive about sleeping during the day, whilst others worked. That was also why it was good to make love during the day. The soft white pillow was a woman's breast and the distant rumble of commercial vehicles on Whitechapel Road were a soothing lullaby. They would lull him to sleep for eternity.

Joseph attempted to lower himself carefully onto his back. He took the bible in his good hand and used his claw to support himself. When he was lying down, Joseph intended to place the bible on his chest, between his hands, where they would expect to find it. But as soon as Joseph lowered his head to the line of his shoulders, his colossal skull pulled him backwards. He completely missed the pillow and banged his head on the wall.

He came to rest on his back, diagonally across the bed. His mighty head sank into the mattress like an anchor on a line of silk. The sea supported the anchor and held the thread, for how much time he knew not. He had dropped his bible and felt around the bed, but it was not there. His odd resting position was not his design for death, but then his existence had hardly been a template for life. Why did Alice find delight in a body where he found only shame and disgust? Why had he, a deformed defective, been blessed with the happy miracle of her love?

He was glad that Simon had left Alice money and she would see out her life in comfort without needing to work. Joseph knew Alice was not destined for a life serving others, because life serves beauty. The afflicted exploit pity as the beautiful exploit desire. Alice had no wish to exploit anyone, therefore Joseph came to the conclusion that, in addition to a beautiful body, she also possessed a beautiful soul.

If Joseph possessed a soul, it was elevated by a single loving woman. Work, church, the Empire, the human morass known as society, when compared with her love, all was nothing. Their tender days together had been something close to heaven. Therefore, in the delirium of death Joseph did not feel himself ascending to the sky, but moving back to earth, to the garden with Alice and her son. Alice wore her beard in his dying vision. Joseph always thought it suited her.

A man who goes to his deathbed unfulfilled does not fight against the end of his life, but the end of his dream, his unrealised potential, prolonging the inevitable by minutes or hours or even days. By contrast, the man who has lived fully approaches the grave lightly; he has no reason to fight death because he has exhausted his life.

Joseph Merrick breathed his last with ease.

Chapter 25 – The Sun

The hospital Chairman, Carr Gomm was considerate enough to write Alice a personal letter informing her of Joseph's demise. The announcement of his death made the newspapers a few days later. It was the second time she had lost a love, although Joseph's death affected Alice in a different way to Simon's. There was no funeral, no mourning period and no one enquiring after her health, because superficially nothing had changed. A charming well-to-do lady and benefactor of many good causes had supported a good cause to its inevitable conclusion. There was always the next good cause.

Alice did all she could to distract her mind and delay the inevitable onset of grief. She volunteered as Mr Ronson's gardening assistant and busied herself with hard physical labour. When the apple tree did not flower this year and necessitated removal, Alice set about the task single-handed, despite Mr Ronson's fears she would 'do herself a mischief'. Alice felled the ten-foot tree with the axe and saw, dug through the roots, and levered up the stump with an iron bar, working to complete muscular exhaustion.

The Ronsons were pragmatic, stoic people. They had lost two sons in infancy and buried three of their eight grandchildren. Aside from expressing their genuine sorrow when Alice informed them of Joseph's passing, there was nothing more to say. Mrs Oliver was a different matter. Alice managed to put her off for two weeks, claiming to have a heavy cold, before finally agreeing to meet for afternoon tea.

Mr Ronson had moved the garden furniture away from the apple tree crater to the patio. Alice stared at the hole the ground as Mrs Oliver prattled on about the tragic life and death of Joseph Merrick. How he was so polite and kind, and well-mannered and well-dressed and remarkably clean. How he was intelligent, well-spoken and so adept at handicrafts. Mrs Oliver lamented, "A gentle soul, who transcended his terrible affliction, with piety and humility."

Eventually Mrs Oliver came to the question.

"Why do you think poor Joseph lay down on his bed in the regular fashion, when he knew full well that his head, as large as it was, would surely ...?"

Alice replied, "Because he wanted to die."

"But his life was full of love."

"Did you love him, Mrs Oliver? Did you really?"

Mrs Oliver was lost for words and her bottom lip quivered. Alice remembered, "*For a brother in Christ*".

"What of his mortal remains?" asked Mrs Oliver. "The hospital must surely afford him a Christian burial?"

"It does not matter what they do with his bones, if they make a hat stand of his bones, his remains are irrelevant."

Alice's remark killed the conversation and Mrs Oliver left soon after. Throughout the rest of that day Alice worried about having permanently offended her friend. Alice knew about the gossip in the village, speculation about her dark curled hair, rumours of tempestuous gypsy blood in the recesses of her ancestry. She did not want to make life difficult in Dulwich, especially for Edward when he was older. Later that evening, Alice called unannounced at the Oliver residence and was received by Mrs Oliver in the drawing room.

"I must apologise for my outburst," said Alice.

"Please do not. It is not ..."

"You were a guest at my house and I ..."

"There is no need to apologise. It is I who should have ..."

Mrs Oliver was frightfully English, apologising when something was not her fault and both she and Alice had acquired the middle-class disease of being unable to finish their sentences. Polite society would always forgive Mrs Greystone for the occasional act of savagery, provided she was jolly nice for the most part. English sensibilities had saved the relationship.

Following the rendezvous, Alice felt a little better and finally plucked up the courage to sort through the few possessions Joseph kept in the small wardrobe of the guest bedroom. There were two day suits, two night suits, and a selection of smaller items. Alice pressed the tweed jacket of his day suit to her face. It was three weeks since the day of his death, Friday 11th April 1890, yet the scent of Joseph's body had been replaced by the stale, dusty odour of the cupboard. When Simon died Alice hoarded his clothes for more than a year, leaving them available for his naked, wandering spirit, as if one day he would step out of the cupboard, fully dressed and restored to life.

Alice removed Joseph's suits from the cupboard and placed them on the bed, deciding on a donation to the church collection. At least one working man would benefit from a good, if misshapen suit. Alice noticed an ornamental wooden box on the ledge of the wardrobe. She opened the lid and immediately recognised her own hand on a bundle of letters, the formal correspondence she had sent Joseph at the London Hospital. There was an unopened envelope at the bottom of the box marked for 'Alice'. Joseph's final note! It was written on a single sheet of paper with a floral motif, the type he used for thank you letters.

"My dearest Alice, knowing me as you do, you will understand my decision ..."

Alice's tears fell onto the letter, merging with the ink and running to the bottom of the page in long purple rivers. There was also a pencil drawing marked for Edward. Joseph had pictured Alice and Edward holding hands in the garden. Up above in the sky, next to the sun, Joseph and a hedgehog waved from a cloud.

The following morning was overcast, but the sun broke the clouds around noon. Alice took Edward into the garden and laid out a blanket on the lawn. It was warm enough for her to wear a short-sleeved white summer dress. She had dressed Edward in navy blue short trousers and a long-sleeved red polo shirt. Mr and Mrs Ronson prepared lunch and joined them in the garden. After lunch, the Ronsons returned to the house. Alice had not yet told Edward about the death and would now address his persistent question, "When is Uncle Joseph coming?" with a final, definitive answer. Alice walked Edward to the spot where they had buried the hedgehog and knelt down in front of him. She unfolded Joseph's drawing and used the picture as a prop to explain. Edward pointed to the burial ground and said, "In there?"

"Yes, son," confirmed Alice, "in there."

Tears rolled down Edward's cheeks and onto his polo shirt. He did not cry histrionically, like a child who has fallen and is not badly injured, but cries because they believe they should. Edward did not bawl or wail, he simply wiped his tears with his sleeve in an understated fashion, as if on some deeper level he understood. Edward waved goodbye to the ground, then the sky and hugged his mother. She held him for a long time to conceal her own tears.

They sat back on the blanket. Alice read to Edward and taught him arithmetic from a children's textbook. Every mother champions the abilities of her son, but Alice thought that Edward might have a special talent for numbers. After the informal study period they played football. It was a beautiful afternoon. The hawthorns, and wild roses were in full blossom, as were the two cherry trees Alice had assisted Mr Ronson in planting last spring. Mr Ronson had landscaped the crater of the dead apple tree into a raised bed and planted dahlias for later in the year. The daffodils had all but gone, but many bluebells had taken their place.

Alice said it was time for refreshments. She poured Edward a glass of lemonade, asked him to sit down and please drink it slowly. It was a safe, motherly command in a quiet, ordered village – Dulwich, a comfortable, semi-rural, soon-to-be suburb of London. Passion was reserved for bee keeping, country dancing and the local historical society. Romantic love was for book clubs, amateur dramatics and daydreams.

Alice shielded her eyes from the sun. The sun shone on country houses, churches, village greens and English cricket grounds. The sun shone on mill towns, cities, factories and slums. The sun shone on prisons, workhouses and lunatic asylums. The sun shone on Scotland, Wales, Ireland, India, Australasia and all of Her Majesty's dominions. The sun, they said, would never set on the British Empire. Everyone knew their place and everything was determined by the likes of Gilbert Greystone and Simon Greystone, regardless of whether they possessed the moral authority. But by this unwritten law and the way of things, Edward had a future. He would one day attend college, then Oxford or Cambridge, take his place in society, marry well, dine with an Old Boys' Society or reject it all if he chose to.

At this moment in time and for as long as she lived, Alice accepted that she must uphold her societal position for the sake of her son. It was a lesson she learned in the asylum long ago. It was possible to be a lunatic, provided one did not act like a lunatic. It was possible to be a freak, provided one was cured. Whilst she hated her beard, she could not deny that a life of affliction was more authentic than a life of beauty. Gone were grown men dancing and prancing around her, like clumsy bees attempting to gain access to her flower. In their place the Elephant Man, Joseph Merrick.

Alice fell in love with Joseph like a young woman with an older man, attracted to his worldliness and experience. Though she was two years his senior in age, Joseph was seasoned in deformity. To Alice, he was never more attractive than when he threatened to reject the world, because only a man who shared her hatred of normality could join her fully in love. Loving a man who was doomed to die was like loving a garden in autumn, where decay is tinged with golden beauty. Alice thought Joseph should have died in the autumn and not the spring. Autumn is the season of the beautiful death.

Edward presented a bluebell to his mother as a gift. Alice took the flower, kissed him on the cheek and ruffled his sandy hair with her fingers. She rose to her feet, picked him up and held him to her breast. He was heavy, but she held him high. Alice turned to the sun. If the meaning of life was to find a cause for which one would die, her son gave her grounds for survival. But what part of Joseph Merrick would last in time?

Alice knew that when Treves wrote the story, the world would encounter Joseph as a child. They would assume he so desperately wanted to be like others in sleeping on his back, it was an infantile experiment, a mishap. They would deny him the manhood of will. Joseph was presumed to have died grasping for normalcy and so was considered a model defective, a defective who annihilated himself. Yet his life was singular and his death unique.

Courage is forced on the afflicted. They are denied a life of quiet cowardice. Joseph did not think of himself as brave, only that he did not want to die a pauper, so chose a career of bold immorality to live. But in saving himself from the workhouse and embarking on life as a freak, Joseph may have saved others. The power of his sideshow persona was felt throughout British society. Because they took him to their hearts, they would not put him to the sword. They would now think twice before turning the blade on other defectives.

So Alice held her son to her breast and remembered Joseph Merrick, his life, his legacy and their love.

One day the sun would set on the Empire, but the flame of their love would burn. It would outlast the Empire, it would outlast the sun. The flame of their love would burn through the ages. Of that she was sure.

29851924R00177

Printed in Great
Britain
by Amazon